Journey to the Crimson Sea

TREASURES OF
3
THE CARIBBEAN

Journey Crimson

to the

Sea

JIM & TERRI
KRAUS

Tyndale House Publishers, Inc. WHEATON, ILLINOIS

Designed by Timothy R. Botts
Edited by Rick Blanchette

Scripture quotations are taken from the *Holy Bible,* King James Version.

Library of Congress Cataloging-in-Publication Data

Kraus, Jim.
  Journey to the Crimson Sea / Jim & Terri Kraus.
    p.   cm. — (Treasures of the Caribbean : 3)
    ISBN 0-8423-0383-9
    1. Pirates—Caribbean Area—History—17th century—Fiction.   2. Historical fiction. gsafd.
3. Christian fiction. lcsh.   I. Kraus, Terri, [date] .   II. Title.   III. Series: Kraus, Jim.
Treasures of the Caribbean ; 3.
PS3561.R2876J68   1997
813′.54—DC21   97-23016

Printed in the United States of America

02   01   00   99   98   97

7   6   5   4   3   2   1

Journey to the Crimson Sea

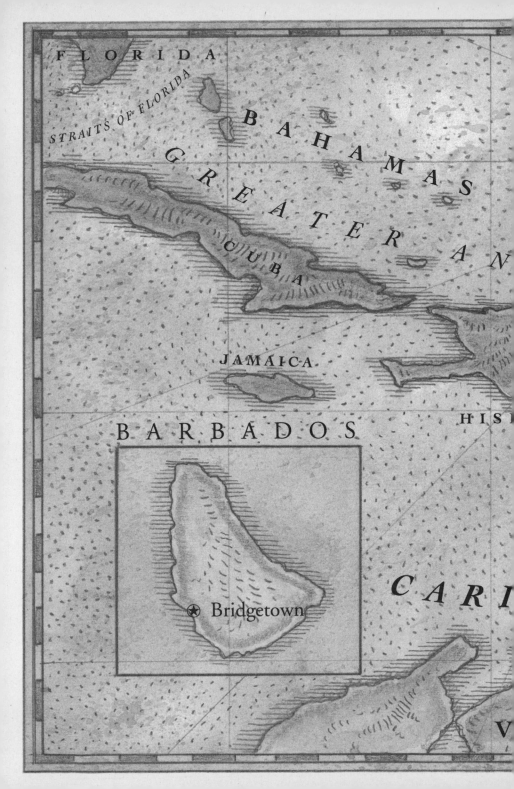

CHAPTER

I

Caribbean Sea
25 March 1644

The *Dorset Lady*, a small rakish galleon of English design, headed south at last to Barbados, tacking into gusts of blood-warm westerly winds over crystalline Caribbean waters. The bleached canvas of her sails billowed out, her mast groaned, and the ropes squealed against the oak yardarms as if in an eager response to the journey. To every sailor on deck, the ship's sounds were most comforting; they were the sounds of a vessel heading home.

The ship turned again to tack against the wind, the sea swells breaking clean against her stubby bow. In the salty mist, a rainbow appeared, spanning the rigging, dancing above the ship, sharp and clear in the dappled afternoon sun. As if prodded by its beauty, the *Dorset Lady* charged ahead into that hovering light and elbowed into the waves, catching the wind full and firm, slicing through the light chop. Gulls coasted behind her, cawing loudly and searching for the small fish sluiced up in the vessel's wake.

"Set her course to Bridgetown, straight and true," shouted out Captain Malcolm Trent.

At the sound of his barked command, the entire ship jostled into action. The crew scurried about, shouting back and forth to each other, yet at least one passenger was oblivious to their hawking and climbing, ignoring them as they set the sails and rigging for the voyage home.

Vicar Thomas Mayhew lowered his battered frame onto the thick wooden steps, bleached bone white from the sea and sun, that led from the main deck to the quarterdeck of the ship. He could not stop the groan from escaping his lips, and he winced as he sat, his knees popping loudly, his arms trembling from such a simple task. He looked toward the bow and could do nothing but smile and offer God his praises. Thomas closed his eyes for a moment and let the reality of being rescued sink into his bruised and aching body. He was *free*. The mere sound of that word brought prayers of thanksgiving to his lips.

Upon the forward deck lay William Hawkes, on his back, nestled on a thick bed of canvas. His head rested on the most precious of pillows— the lap of his wife, Kathryne. She stared down at his face, tenderly brushing at his hair, which was matted with salt and blood, and bent to him, nuzzling her lips on his reddened forehead. Barely able to marshal his strength, he reached up and stroked her cheek. Then his arm fell loosely to the canvas.

She must have whispered that she loved him, the vicar thought, *for I can see his smile from here.*

Then the vicar looked up, his face raised to the afternoon sun.

"Dear God," he whispered, his words catching in the wind, "I can offer no greater words to thee this day than to echo their joy to thee, O merciful Father. I thank thee for thy most gracious provision and protection."

As the vicar offered his prayers to God, Will felt Kathryne bend toward him and gently kiss his forehead.

She whispered, "Dearest William, you once rescued me . . . and now I have rescued you. I daresay that settles our score, my sweet." And she laughed softly.

Will used his full strength to touch her cheek, wishing he could embrace his beloved, but his arm soon fell to his side. Her laugh was the magical sound of angels, he would say later, and it colored the very air about him with love.

■ ■ ■

The vicar and William, as well as three other sailors from the *Villa Terra Nova*, had cheated death by the narrowest of margins. They had been tossed into the sea following Radcliffe Spenser's horrible death at the end of a jagged, savage spike of lightning. Within heartbeats, their ship was ground to planks and splinters on the shallow coral and the angry black reef and shoals. As if guided by a divine hand, Thomas and William had clung together in the wild and turbulent surf and were nearly dashed against a small bit of decking and sail, which ultimately offered their salvation.

For days they clung to that piece of wreckage, the five of them, capturing rainwater and dew in the canvas, catching a few fish in a crude net. All would have ceased to draw breath in no more than a dozen hours had not Kathryne and the *Dorset Lady* suddenly materialized from the waters to the east.

The hand of Providence moves in a most mysterious way, the vicar thought. *No man can deny that almighty God provided for our protection and rescue.*

Thomas again looked to Will and Kathryne. Will, his head still resting in Kathryne's lap, appeared to be in a deep slumber—and with good reason. It was he who had stayed the watch for those days while clinging to the wreckage. It was he who had rigged the canvas to collect the rain. It was he who had prayed aloud and petitioned God to see them through.

Thomas stood from the steps, his muscles and joints in pain, yet he felt as free as a great seabird with its wings outstretched and gliding toward home. The ship had been underway for no more than the passage of an hour, and Thomas had not moved, save to take water and greedily devour a plate of biscuits and dried fish. Grabbing at the ship's rail, he began to shuffle toward William and Kathryne.

Captain Trent at the helm lurched to offer his assistance after observing the vicar's shambling along the slippery deck. Thomas held up his palm, bidding him stop.

"Good Captain, I ask you to return us home in haste. Do not leave your post for me. I will be fine . . . just a reoccurring bit of trouble developing my sea legs is all."

"I'll be sailing as fast as the winds allow, . . . Father . . . Vicar . . . sir."

Thomas smiled. "Please call me by my Christian name, and that is Thomas. With these rags I am sure I look as far from a man of the cloth as the dawn is from the dusk."

"Indeed, . . . Thomas," Trent said, a degree uncomfortable over addressing a holy man by his given name. "Well then, I suppose it be me task to catch the better winds. If the trades stay as firm as they are from the west and at our bow, then I shall have us home within no more than a few days."

The captain looked into the skies, the winds blowing strong, tousling his hair. "Travelin' to the south against the wind be always a tryin' journey, what's with fightin' the breeze every league of the way." He sniffed the air again as if testing the power of the wind. "No more than a few days, Thomas. A week at most."

The vicar nodded and continued his shuffle toward Will and Kathryne. Only moments earlier, the crew, silent and quick, had erected a small canvas awning over the pair to keep the sun from them and provide a protection from the winds. Kathryne insisted that Will remain on deck and not be placed in cramped quarters below, quarters effused with the fetid smell of sweat, rum, and foul bilge water.

Thomas bent as he approached them, peering under the canvas. Kathryne looked up at his arrival, a beatific smile on her lips, her green eyes sparkling, a match for the most dazzling jewel or the deepest sea the vicar had ever seen.

"My lady," Thomas spoke, "we have not been formally introduced, but I am Thomas Mayhew. William and I were . . . companions in Hadenthorne."

"Vicar Mayhew," Kathryne replied, her voice a whisper so as not to waken her husband, "'companion' does not begin to describe what you are to William. I feel as if I have known you all my life, for William has seldom let a day pass without mentioning your name to me. Your words and teachings—your life—simply echo through him, good Vicar."

Her voice is indeed the voice of an angel, Thomas thought. *I am beginning to understand why William would not let us die at sea.*

"Lady Kathryne, I would be pleased if you would call me Thomas."

"Please, Thomas, will you sit? It is most uncivil of me not to offer comfort. You have suffered a great deal."

Thomas sat at the edge of the canvas mat. He could hear William's rhythmic breathing. Kathryne had yet to move, cradling her husband's head in her arms. Thomas looked at Kathryne as she gazed down at William again. *She is indeed a most beautiful woman.*

"This is a curious time, my lady—"

"Kathryne. Please call me Kathryne," she whispered.

"This is a most curious time, Kathryne. We have been thrown together in a most extraordinary manner. Neither you nor I have had such pleasure of even a single meeting. Yet I believe we both know each other well."

Kathryne nodded, and Will moaned softly and rolled to his side. Thomas lowered his voice.

"Kathryne," Thomas began, "I do not know the words to use to express my thankfulness. We all would have perished if not for your intervention. We owe you our lives."

Kathryne held up her palm, bidding him stop. "Thomas, it was not my intervention that saved you. It was God's. I had come to present these waters with a memorial for my husband, whom I was sure had been taken from me. Our Lord offered you protection, not me."

Thomas lowered his head. "But he used you as an instrument, good lady, and I am ever so grateful."

The canvas flapped above them, waving and snapping in the breeze.

Thomas leaned closer to her and whispered, "How is William? It was he who stayed awake nearly our whole time at sea. He would not let any of us slide from our perches in the night. From that I can understand his need for sleep."

Kathryne pulled a blanket closer around William, patting it smooth and snug.

"I am not trained in things such as this—medical matters and all—but it appears that there are no deep or festering wounds. The wound in his calf appears to be healing. His breathing is solid and clear. And while his face is flushed from the sun, I detect no hint of fever."

Nodding, Thomas replied, "Then Providence did watch over him."

Will moaned again and turned as he slept, and Thomas arose, holding his finger against his lips, indicating that silence is what Will needed.

Kathryne nodded, then added in a whisper, her lilting voice sweet and clear, "But, Thomas, may I ask one favor?"

How could a man say no to that voice? Thomas thought. *Or give displeasure to that angelic face by denying a request?*

"Any favor I am able to do, I will."

"Could you return in a while and pray with me?" she asked. "I think such a day as this calls for our thanksgiving."

Thomas nodded again. "I would be honored, Kathryne."

And as he stepped away, she called out after him, her voice just a note above a whisper, "And perhaps they could bring some dinner for us as well. . . . There is something about . . . the sea air that has made me quite peckish."

Kathryne blushed in the golden light of the afternoon and hoped the vicar had not seen it. For it was not the sea air that triggered her ravenous appetite; it was her impending motherhood. She was perhaps six weeks into nature's wonderful spiral, and that shift in her body brought upon her all manner of new cravings and appetites. She blamed the growling of her stomach on the newness of her condition. But to call out such a fact—that she was with child and ravenous—in the company of rough sailors did not seem quite proper. She hoped Thomas had not heard the growling, even though William, from where he lay, stirred in his slumber as if in response.

■ ■ ■ ■ ■

That night the moon rose over the black sea, a golden radiance flickering over the colorless waters. The *Dorset Lady* sailed forward,

her sails full of strong night winds. A few sailors gathered at the vessel's
stern, keeping watch, speaking in low, quiet tones. One sailor pulled
out his fiddle and played a series of haunting ballads and ancient songs
learned from his father, who had learned them from his father, each
playing to the night sky on the cold and desolate moors of northern
England.

Thomas brought Kathryne a meal of biscuits, cheese, and a delicate
smoked fish. The vicar had helped himself to seconds, thirds, and even
fourths. Kathryne was too polite to eat her true fill and stopped after
consuming just one large platter heaped with food. She roused William
for only a moment. He consumed a great tankard of weak wine, a small
biscuit, and then slumped to the canvas mat again, sound asleep. He
had complained only of thirst in the few words he mumbled. Yet he did
manage to present his wife with a wide smile just before his eyes closed.

Kathryne and Thomas had sat together those few golden hours, as
the fading sun dipped from the sky. They prayed for many moments,
but Kathryne saw how tired the vicar was and allowed him to be brief
in his petitions and praises. She knew that God well understood the
frailties of man but knew the fullness of their hearts. *Duration does not
indicate holiness,* she remembered Rev. Parsons once remarking.

As the sun set in a crimson blaze and the moon rose, she had reached
up and folded back a section of the canvas awning. Looking up into the
sky, its darkness now brimming with a million points of starlight, she
leaned first to the right, then the left. In a moment she saw the familiar
constellation, then looked to the north and found her star—the North
Star—glimmering against the blackness. Her hand rested on Will's
shoulder as he slept, peaceful and calm.

"Thomas, do you believe the Almighty has a plan for each one of
us?"

Thomas blinked several times and looked into the vast array of stars
over his head. "I do, Kathryne."

"Do you think that his plan remains out there for us to discover, or
does he plot out our lives so that the discovery is a simple matter and
we have little say in the final outcome?"

Thomas elbowed his body up to a sitting position. He was fighting
sleep as well.

"I believe he has placed each of us where we are to fulfill his great
purpose. I think we do what God wants by our daily worship and
service and obedience to him. That is his plan. I would venture to say
that the rest of what goes on is often just . . . our lives," he answered,
holding back a yawn.

Kathryne sat there in the dark and, a moment later, watched as the vicar slowly slumped to the canvas. He began to snore softly. She slipped a pillow under Will's head and tucked his blanket in about him. She rose carefully and placed her blanket over the vicar and made her way, silent, to the bow of the ship.

The darkness was full and complete then as a thin scudding of clouds slipped across the sky and obscured the moon and the stars. She felt her way along the sea-smoothed railing to the vessel's point and stood there, the breeze spilling about her face and lifting her hair from her shoulders. She closed her eyes to the dark and listened as the ship cut through the waves with a splashing hiss.

As she thought about the child that was now within her, her hand moved instinctively to her belly. She lovingly patted the area, though no hint of her condition yet showed. "The rest of it may be just our lives," she spoke into the darkness with a certainty. "Yet I so look forward to seeing this life that God has granted."

She breathed in deeply, letting the sea air fill her lungs, and lowered her hand again to her belly. She spoke in a whisper to the skies. "Thank thee, God, for this child. Show us the path thou wouldst have us walk. Give us the strength to overcome the obstacles in our way and the perseverance to continue."

She breathed in again and felt the life inside of her body tug and nudge gently at her soul and heart. She knew that it would be some months until she would feel the child truly move in her womb, yet she knew as certain as drawing her next breath that her body was being readied. Her hand smoothed over the area, and she lowered her head, then spoke in a voice that only mothers possess. "Are you telling me that you will love the sea as does your father?"

Her soft question was answered with another small nudge of her heart, and Kathryne looked up into the blackness before her. She watched as the clouds parted, pushed by the winds. She turned, and just over her shoulder glimmered the North Star. It flickered alive and bright, as if a beacon for her heart.

"Show us the way, dear Father. Show us the way on thy seas."

26 March 1644

The following dawn, William stirred and groaned and began to blink his eyes in the early morning light. Kathryne was at his side and reached out and touched his shoulder with her open palm. She leaned over and looked into his eyes.

He blinked again, and his tongue felt his lips, chapped and burnt by the sun. He lifted his head slightly, peering intently at her face.

"I had a dream of heaven," he croaked, his voice hoarse and weak, "and now that I am awake, I see that it has come true, for your face is before me."

Kathryne smiled and bent down, and with the weight of a butterfly, kissed his lips. "No, dear husband," she whispered, "it is my dream that has come true—that your eyes be opened this day."

The winds grew slight, and the journey required a second full day of long, slow tacks into a weak southwesterly wind. At times when running into the wind, the vessel seemed to perch upon one spot and wait, deciding if she truly wanted to advance or not. During that second day Will drifted in and out of sleep, and when his eyes were not closed in slumber, he desired water, food, and Kathryne's presence nearby.

Kathryne's original assessment of Will's condition was, for the greater part, accurate. None of his wounds or bruises were so severe as to be life threatening, yet the path that the musket ball had torn through his calf continued to ooze a thin stream of blood and clear liquid and caused much discomfort. At least that is all Will admitted to feeling.

Yet when he first tried to stand upon that leg, he tumbled to the deck, clutching at the wound in pain, upset that his body was betraying him.

Kathryne had no medicinal herbs or potions, but she dressed the wound as best she could, washing it first with a mixture of rainwater and brandy, causing Will to tense and stiffen in response.

"Was the wound this distressing at first?" she asked Will as she tied the bandage tight to his calf, trying to keep the worry from her voice.

"It did not seem to be. The night of the attack and the days afterward . . . well, to be true, I scarce noticed it. There was an ache, but not this type of knifing pain."

Kathryne tucked in the loose ends of the gauze, then smoothed it flat against his leg.

"I am sure Luke will have a remedy or potion that will provide quick healing."

William merely nodded and tried to smile. He knew, as did Kathryne, that in the public houses and docks of Bridgetown, as well as any port in the world, there resided a number of sailors who spent their final days on land, hobbling about, missing a limb, making do on peg legs and crutches. Sailing was dangerous, armed conflict even more so, and the end of such activities often measured in broken and torn bodies.

"I am sure the salt water has done it some good," Kathryne added, attempting to convince not only Will but herself. "I am sure that the pain will cease and it will mend itself."

Will awoke that dark night and blinked in the faint, silvery moonlight into the vastness of the black, undulating sea. He looked then to the stern, where Malcolm Trent stood silent at the helm, guiding the ship ever southward, ever closer to home. The bow sliced through the warm waters with a comforting spray hissing back.

Kathryne lay next to Will, clutching at a small corner of the blanket that was bunched about Will's shoulders. He smiled and slowly sat up, slipping the blanket back over her huddled form. No more than a few feet away lay Thomas, a blanket plus a section of canvas draped over his frame. Will breathed in deep the clean air of the night and edged his way to the rail. He pulled himself up and knew that his wound was a serious matter, for unless he supported himself with his arms, he would not be able to stand.

Perhaps it is as Kathryne said, he thought, *a simple matter of a temporary nature that Luke will be able to treat when we return. Perhaps it is just the freshness of the wound and the exhausting time spent in the sea that hobbles me so.* He lurched about until he was half sitting, half standing by the ship's rail.

Malcolm, peering into the dark, saw Will jostle about and took three steps toward him to offer assistance. Will's right leg protruded out from the rail, stiff and ungainly. He waved Malcolm off with a silent palm held up to bid the captain stop. Will had no desire to wake Kathryne and no desire to discuss his condition just yet. Malcolm nodded and returned to his post.

Will reached down and massaged his knee for a moment, then straightened up and stared into the darkness before them. Sailing on a near moonless night as this, one felt enveloped—almost over-whelmed—by the blackness of the sea. A small lantern mounted at the forecastle, and one to the stern, did little to penetrate that blackness. So absolute was the absence of light that Will felt as if he could reach out before him and part the dark with a wave of his hand and it would adhere to his skin.

This was what sailors called the deathwatch—the darkest, latest watch, hours after the moon slipped into the waves and hours before the sun would reappear. It was the heart—or the very soul—of the night, the time when the weak and sick most often found their final rest. On most naval vessels, from the confining hammocks in sick bay, Will recalled, sailors could be heard moaning, crying out. During the death-watch, their shrieking was oft replaced with a gentle moan moments before they slipped from their mortal coil. *It seems the same in any sick bay on any ship. If a man was to meet his end, it was on this watch that he so often entered that final portal,* Will mused.

He breathed in again. He knew that he was in no mortal danger—at least not yet—for he knew that men survived injuries as severe as his and much worse. But would he be tested by God one more time—tested with a crippling, dismembering wound?

I seek to do thy will, dear Lord, Will prayed, *and I seek to live for thee with a healthy body. If it is in thy divine plan, Lord, I ask that I remain whole—for Kathryne's sake as well as the child that is to come.*

A child.

As he prayed that word, his heart swelled inside his chest.

Dear God—a child. How much more perfect can a gift be?

He looked back at Kathryne, whose face was lit with gold by the gentle flicker of the forecastle lantern. Will knew that there was no other sight in all the world that was as beautiful as she, her features softened, somehow softly sculpted with a gentler hand now that her womb was nurturing a new life.

He lifted his face into the warm breeze and remembered, his thoughts streaming into his awareness, a parade of recollections. He thought of his mother, Elizabeth, now many years gone, whose joy and love of God colored his every boyhood moment.

How much she would have been pained to know for how long a time I had turned my back on God.

He thought of his father, Samuel, lying beside his mother in the rustic quiet of the cemetery, amidst the scent of roses, nestled by the walls of St. Jerome's Church in Hadenthorne, Devon, England.

How proud he would have been to see his son—now a landowner, married to such a wonderful noblewoman as Kathryne.

He thought of Thomas Mayhew, the saintly vicar who became his guardian and raised him to adulthood and who now slept no more than three steps away. He thought of the years they lived together in the vicarage of St. Jerome's Church in Hadenthorne and the struggle it was at first to blend their lives together in that tiny cottage.

How good it is for my soul to have this man in my life again.

Will continued to remember. He thought of his buying and selling goods through the Antilles, of terrifying storms at sea, of his descent into piracy, of battles and cannon fire, of the clatter of musket shots and the clanging of swords in the midst of angry smoke . . . and of his long climb back to God. He thought of Kathryne again, and how they met—he discovering her hidden in the closet of the captain's cabin on the *Plymouth Spirit*. He recalled with a heady rush his feelings for her during the time he held her as his captive . . . her imploring face by a bejeweled waterfall on his secret island, speaking of faith and love and . . .

Without her I would still be lost in my own sin and anger, he thought.

He closed his eyes, letting the winds wash over his face, and prayed.

Lord, thou hast brought me a great distance to this place. My life is to me but a miracle of thy grace, for it is not because of my searching, but only because of thy relentless, loving pursuit that my soul rests in you this day. If it be thy will to present with me a handicap for the rest of my time on this earth, then it be thy will, and may it be done. Help me face life with faith and joy. Help me be the proper husband to Kathryne and the proper father to our child. Regardless of what becomes of this body, I will serve thee. Always.

He opened his eyes and turned to the east. At the edge of the horizon there began the faintest of glows as the sun prepared to rise again, a faint smudge of light diffusing the blackness. It was at least an hour before dawn.

Will smiled, his soul more at rest now than he had ever known. He knew that the light would come and the day would arrive and fill the world with brightness.

Island of Barbados

Herbert Gleeson took a threadbare square of linen, mottled red from dust and sweat, and pulled it across his forehead, leaving thin ochre streaks across his brow. He looked up into the fading sun, his forehead looking like a native's wearing ceremonial paint.

He stood in the midst of the slave quarters, a small circle of mud-and-wattle buildings patched together by darkies laboring into the night after their regular work was complete. A handful of small fires burned, the fermenting smells of the cane and the sugar mill mixed with the roasted smells of corn, beans, and yams. Despite the fact that most slaves died within the passing of their second year on the island, some lived long enough to anticipate a growing season and were industrious enough to plant their own little gardens, even to raise a chicken or two. It was better for Master Carruthers, the plantation owner, Gleeson knew, for every plant that they grew themselves meant one less item of food he needed to provide. And if slaves wanted more than the single issue of rough cloth each year, they were expected to earn it themselves.

Gleeson spit on the ground and took a swig of muddy rum to kill the taste of the sugar in his mouth. He looked about, his sneer now a constant expression. He kicked at a thin draping of stained cloth that marked a doorway into one hut. A black woman reached out with a gasp and drew the cloth closed.

"Blimy," Gleeson muttered, his anger rising. "If they thinks I might be interested in more than a peek now and again—well, they be wrong. I gots me standards, and bein' with a slave woman ain't on me list." He snorted again and took a long draw on his ladle of rum.

The slaves had formed rudimentary family groups, Gleeson observed, and a few even participated in some sort of marriage ceremony. What they did after the fieldwork was completed was their own business. Master Carruthers did not care, and neither did Gleeson.

A tall dark man slipped out of a narrow opening in a nearby hut and peered forward, as a bird arches its head looking for a tasty worm.

"Massa Glees'," he whispered, "you be wantin' somethin'?"

Gleeson spun around, his rum splashing in a potent semicircle in the dust at his feet.

"You stupid lout!" he shouted. "See what you made me do?" He threw the empty ladle at the black man's head. The slave ducked, and the ladle rattled off in the distance. The small village went very quiet and still. Each slave knew that a drunk overseer was dangerous, and Gleeson was one of the most dangerous. He could—and had on more than one occasion—rain down fists, pistol butts, and heavy cudgels on anyone who might cross him. Only the week before two slaves had died at his hand as he beat at them with a pick handle for working too slowly.

"Where be the darkie named Matuma?" Gleeson shouted. "I done heard 'e be thinkin' of manumission."

The slave cringed and stepped back further into the darkness. Gleeson jumped forward and grabbed at the black man's shoulders, striking him with the full weight and power of the back of his hand across his face. As the slave tumbled to the ground holding his jaw, Gleeson kicked out, catching the man's ribs with the toe of his boot. The overseer's face twisted into a smile as he heard, and felt, a rib splinter at the end of his kick.

"You black savages!" he screamed out, and kicked again, aiming at his stomach. "You tell 'im that he won't be buyin' his freedom afore Gleeson be gettin' 'is. You tell 'im that I won't be lettin' 'im leave with 'is handful o' gold."

He kicked again, his foot halfheartedly making contact with the black man's spine. Gleeson turned and stumbled away, heading back into the darkness of his squalid hut no more than a hundred yards to the east.

In a few moments Gleeson was back at the small shack permeated with fetid smells. He fell across his soiled bed, the liquid in his stomach roiling and bitter. He gulped hard, trying to hold it all down.

"Two more years," he cried, a mix of bitterness and rancor. "Me freedom dues ain't due for another two years."

Lord Peter Carruthers had informed him in no uncertain terms that very afternoon that each dead slave would cost him six more months of servitude. The slaves who died at his hand had thus far cost him an additional year of servitude. His expected freedom dues—the few pounds and a few acres of land to be rewarded to him at the end of his contract—now would not be his until he turned forty.

"And how many turn forty on this forsaken island?" Gleeson whined. "How many?"

31 March 1644

The *Dorset Lady* returned home to Bridgetown late in the afternoon, nearly a week after Kathryne had virtually commandeered the vessel. All hammering and sawing and bartering on the piers ceased as its sails appeared in the northwest. A slow parade of citizens filed toward the docks, expecting to receive a grieving widow and ready to convey their heartfelt condolences.

But there were no condolences needed as the ship bumped against the pier and was tied off. Will stood at the bow, his arm encircling Kathryne's waist, in this instance more for support than affection.

The faces of the small crowd assembled were blank, and their voices mute. It was as if they had collectively viewed an apparition, a ghost returned from the beyond. They greeted the passengers of the *Dorset Lady* with silence, deafening and roaring.

Then from the rear of the few dozen witnesses on the pier came a cry, "It be Cap'n Hawkes!"

"Egads! It be a miracle, pure and simple!" another man cried.

"He ain't dead!" another man shouted, ever alert to the obvious.

"Run off an' fetch the gov'ner!" another shouted. "He wanted t' be informed as soon as she returned."

Then, as if the floodgates had been opened after a spring downpour, the crowd swamped the small *Dorset Lady* and clamored aboard, surrounding William and Kathryne, shaking his hand, hugging her. A few began to weep as well, a gesture William found to be most curious, yet touching.

"You be safe!" a woman cried.

"It be a miracle!" another feminine voice cawed out.

William held up his hands, calling for quiet.

"Good citizens," he called out, his voice still raspy and thin, "I thank God for bringing me home. It is his doing that brought me back."

Heads nodded and bowed, and a murmur of *amen*s whispered through the gathering. Will stopped and scanned the crowd, now growing larger and more anxious for news. To his left he saw the familiar face of Abraham Hunt, who had sailed with him on the *Artemisia*.

"Abraham!" he called out. "Might I be asking you a favor, if you would?"

Abraham scurried to him and nodded vigorously. "Anything you ask, Cap'n Will, I be most happy to see done."

Will bent to the man's ear. The crowd was growing in size and volume. "Could you run and find Luke?" he whispered loudly.

Abraham leaned back, staring at Will. "You be sick, Cap'n? You not look it, if you ask me. Most fit indeed." Will nodded, then winced, biting at his bottom lip to keep from crying out. "And tell him to bring a stretcher from the fort."

Abraham stared hard at Will, a most confused look on his face. He looked at Kathryne, whose face was a blank mask.

"I can't walk," Will said softly.

■ ■ ■ ■

Within moments, Luke loped down the pier, his wide, bare feet slapping at the wooden decking with a hollow and clapping thump. Behind Luke, running in a bunched pack, followed the entire company of blackamoors Will employed at the fort, all eighteen of them. To a man, they saw Will not as a mere mortal, but one who was a half step from heaven. It was he who rescued them, providing them work and shelter. It was he who told them about God. Between them a stretcher seemed to float, as each man attempted to possess at least a part of it in his hands.

"Massa Will!" Luke cried out. Luke was viewed as the island's best healer, and a trusted physician. But he also knew that to elbow his way through a crowd would be an invitation to trouble. Most white settlers would never deign to let a black man come close to them, let alone touch them as they passed. It might be well for Luke to provide ministrations in private, but to be touched by him in public would be a clear rending of the accepted social fabric.

Those assembled quickly spread, and Luke jumped to the rail of the *Dorset Lady* and clamored to Will's side. The crowd had surrounded the rest of the crew, buttonholing them for a detailed reporting of William's rescue. Within another heartbeat, Luke was at Will's side, his face beaming in thankfulness.

"Luke be welcomin' Massa home."

William smiled and held out his hand. Luke grinned wider and shook it heartily. Will had always been a notable exception to the divisions that existed between black and white skin.

"Thank you, Luke."

Luke stood back at arm's length and peered down. He pointed at Will's right leg. "Massa Will feel hot in de leg?"

Will shook his head no. "This day it is neither hot nor cold, Luke. It is as if I can feel nothing at all."

Luke grimaced, then knelt before Will and gingerly touched at the bandage with the merest tip of his gaunt finger. "Lady Kat' be doin' de bandage?"

She nodded.

"It be done fine." He poked at it with a sharp jab. "Dat hurt?"

William shook his head no.

Luke stood up and waved to the blackamoors with the stretcher. They spilled over the rail, four and five men to each side of the thick canvas carrier.

"Massa Will, we be carryin' you. Walkin' be bad right now."

Kathryne placed her hand on Luke's forearm. He turned suddenly and stared down at her thin, delicate fingers. It was the first time a white woman had ever placed her hand upon his black flesh.

"Luke, you can make this better, can you not?" Her voice was edgy and tense. "It is no worse than other wounds you have healed, is it not?"

Luke looked at her long and hard. "Luke seen dis before. Don' look good, but Luke try to help."

He turned away for a moment and was about to bark out an order to the men carrying the stretcher, when he spun on his heel and peered deep into Kathryne's face. He cocked his head a bit and turned it half sideways. He stood back and leaned away from the pair, then leaned in again close and intimate.

"Lady Kat' be wit' child?" he asked, his voice soft as velvet, and hushed, for he wanted no other person to hear his words. "Luke see dat kind of look in Lady's face."

Kathryne did not answer, but a flush reddened her, and she looked down at the deck in a most perplexed manner.

"Luke kin tell, Lady Kat', but he not tell no others," he said firmly.

"Well den," he continued, stating even more firmly, "I knows Massa Will best be healed den. If he be a fadder to dat child, he best be." He paused for a moment, nodded to himself, then added, "We be gettin' him to his bed."

Luke turned to the blackamoors and waved them to his side, calling out to them in their chirpy, birdlike African language. He reached down and took Will by the waist and helped him bend into the stretcher.

The crowd, now silent and hushed again, all peering in intently, parted as Will was hoisted off the ship and passed over the vessel's railing, hand over hand, to the blackamoors waiting on the pier.

"God bless you, Cap'n Will," one of the crowd called out. His cry was echoed by a dozen more voices.

Kathryne kept pace with her husband as they wove through the oncoming townspeople, who began arriving in a steady stream. She stopped at the end of the rickety dock, just on the dusty street that rimmed the harbor.

"Luke," she called out, "we best arrange a carriage to Shelworthy. It would be much too far for Will to be carried by these men."

At the head of the small phalanx of blackamoors, Luke turned, his face confused. "Lady Kat', we not be goin' to dat house," he said, pointing north to Shelworthy. "We be goin' to *your* house," he said, pointing in the direction of the cottage, which had been built overlooking the sea no more than a league from where they stood.

"But Luke, our home was destroyed by the attackers. William cannot stay in such a confusion. There is no roof nor bedding. We must go to Shelworthy."

Luke stopped, oblivious to the stares of the crowd that still swirled about them. "Lady Kat', dat house," he said, pointing in the direction of their cottage, "dat house be fixed. We done fixed it."

Will raised himself up from the stretcher, the canvas and wood groaning as he elbowed about. "Fixed it?" he asked, his voice incredulous. "But, Luke, how did you do that? Who did that? Why?"

Luke chattered for a moment to the blackamoors. Will struggled to catch the import of even a single word, but they spoke too fast.

"Massa Will," Luke said as he knelt down next to Will and explained, "Lady Kat' left and God say to me she be back, and dat you be back. And God say dat house needs fixin'. He don' say why, he just say do. And we do what God say."

Luke indicated with a sweep of his hand that he meant the entire group of blackamoors had accomplished the repairs. Will looked about at their beaming faces, their smiles wide and toothy. Luke stood up and leaned to Kathryne.

"God don' say nuthin' of de child. But Luke know de reason now. We fix dat house for de baby. God want de baby be born in dat house."

Kathryne looked to Will's face, then to Luke's. Both were marked with a grin.

"Thank you, Luke. Thank you all." She nodded to the entire group and smiled. "Then let us make haste to our home."

In town to arrange a delivery of hoes and machetes with John Delacroix, Herbert Gleeson watched the parade of well-wishers clamoring about William and Kathryne. At the edge of the dock, he saw the face of Matuma, grinning and waving to William. Gleeson knew that the slave had just acquired his freedom through the shrewd trading and selling of crops, chickens, and voodoo charms to other slaves.

A slave earning his freedom was not frequent, to be sure, but it did occur. One must be very clever, very shrewd, or both, as Matuma had been, and add a copper or two to his pocket every day until his coffers reached the purchase price that his master had paid for him. Once that happened, the slave could ask to purchase himself back—manumission, it was called—and if granted, then could set out on his own.

The lot of the indentured servant was much the same as the slave, but for a more defined period. Young men and some young women, many of them from Ireland or Scotland, posted themselves as a living bond, offering their lives in exchange for a better life. At the end of the prescribed time, which was most often three to four years, the servant would be issued a few pounds and a few acres of often rough and unclaimed land. It was enough of a draw to attract thousands of willing workers. Even though the conditions were horrible, and most died before coming into their freedom dues, it was alluring for the destitute and hopeless of the British countryside.

"A free darkie," Gleeson muttered. "That be a laugh. A free darkie before I gets me freedom . . . why, it ain't natural nor right."

Matuma followed the other blackamoors to the Spenser cottage as Gleeson trooped off to the chandlery, looking for his supplies. He kept looking over his shoulder, thinking he saw that smiling black face every time he turned.

"This island be needin' a bit o' change," Gleeson muttered as he made his way along the uneven planks of the pier. "And perhaps I be the man to be doin' somethin' 'bout all this that's gone wrong."

Gleeson stopped, turned to face the fort, and smiled.

"Now with Mr. Hawkes bein' wounded and all," he whispered to himself, "it be a most perfect time to do some considerin' and some changin'." He wiped at his forehead with the tattered sleeve of his shirt, leaving a whiter swipe of skin where the dirt was cleared.

"And Gleeson be the man to do it," he said, happy to convince himself.

■ ■ ■ ■ ■

William and Kathryne's small cottage had indeed been repaired in a most admirable fashion by the blackamoors. New rafters, fashioned out of a stand of native wood and a thick thatching of palm leaves, now browning in the sun, formed the roof. Not as durable as slate or straw, it would last only a year or two—more than enough time to seek out a more permanent replacement. A great pile of charred wood, bits of burnt furniture, and other debris was at the rear of the house, remnants from the attack. Inside, the cottage walls were scrubbed clean and freshly whitewashed. Three new windows sat in place, all borrowed from the fort's damaged buildings. Furnishings inside were still sparse—a large, rope-tied bed, a rickety table salvaged from the Goose, and a clutch of mismatched, three-legged stools garnered from a dozen different sources.

Above the windows and doors and by the roofline, the outside of the cottage bore the signs of charring and smoke, but the home was solid and secure again. As Kathryne walked up to the newly painted front door, she sniffed the air. It smelled of a mixture of smoke, paint, palm leaves, and newly hewn wood. She filled her lungs with air and felt her stomach lurch a bit. It was not unpleasant, but it was a lurch, nonetheless.

Seems as though you have a most definite set of opinions, little one, she thought to herself. *The sea, this house . . . what will you tell me next?*

Once inside the house, Luke immediately began his ministrations to William's wound. He stripped away the bandages, all the while clucking his tongue softly. Kathryne sat by Will's shoulder, holding his hand in one of hers while balling a lace handkerchief in her other.

Luke washed the wound in water laced with rum. Will tried not to flinch, biting his lip to prevent him from crying out as the alcohol found its way to the center of the wound. On either side of Will's calf, nearer his knee than his foot, was a small, puckered circle, the entrance and exit marks of the pirate's musket shot. The skin about those small circles was purpling and edged in black. Luke bent down and peered at both sides, grimacing all the while.

He bent to his canvas satchel, which was filled with several small leather bags of herbs, leaves, and dusty powders. He shuffled things about and extracted a small daggerlike blade. Kathryne's eyes widened in panic.

Luke spoke quickly. "De skin be black here. De flesh be spoilt," he said as he pointed with the blade of the knife. "Dat blackness travel up de leg . . . make a man most sick. Make a man die. Luke be cuttin' dat blackness first. It be powerful hurtin', but it mus' be cut. Luke mus' be cuttin' now, for de black climbs de leg if it not cut out."

William propped himself up on the bed. He, too, had seen other doctors slice off portions of greening and blackened skin from the leg or arm of an injured sailor. He recalled how he had covered his ears as he lay in his hammock on the naval ship he first served upon, trying to drown out the screams as a physician's blade sliced through a man's sensitive flesh.

What troubled him more than the pain, which he was sure would not be inconsequential, was that this was most often the first step in removing the entire limb. So seldom did the physician's procedure work, sailors often joked it was a simple way for the doctor to double his fees, since the need for a second surgery was never in doubt.

Will looked up at Kathryne, her face gone white and frightened, her hands tensed and clasped together in a tight knot.

"Kathryne, you must leave now," he rasped. "This is no place for a woman."

She shook her head no. "My place is beside you, William," she insisted, her voice at the close edge of trembling. "We promised that we would stand by each other in sickness and in health, did we not? I will not abandon my vow. I will remain with you."

Luke looked at her tight lips and focused eyes. "Lady Kat' kin stay, Massa Will. It don' be wrong. She be prayin' while Luke be cuttin'."

Will knew that he could not win this argument with the both of them in agreement. He nodded weakly and lay his head back down on the bed.

Luke called out through the open window to the blackamoors, who were watching, their faces a sea of concern. In a moment, four of them shuffled to Will's bedside and, with a most deferential touch, placed their hands on Will's shoulders and legs, wrapping their long, sinewy fingers about his limbs.

"Luke don' want no wigglin' when de hurt gets most powerful."

Luke rinsed the tip of the blade in rum, then placed its sharp tip at the edge of the wound. Kathryne clamped her eyes shut and squeezed Will's hand in hers as tightly as she could. Will clenched his teeth together and nodded.

Luke closed his eyes for a brief moment, his lips barely moving, then opened them and began to cut.

CHAPTER

4

31 May 1644

A full two months had passed since that first tumultuous day that marked the return of William to Barbados. The joyous island exulted in the fact that his life had been spared, yet their joy was dulled and muted by the severity of his injury. As visitors exited the Hawkeses' home, most attempted to mask their deep concern for Will's health with expressions of optimism and of God's provision and great protection.

Kathryne's father, Aidan Spenser, governor of Barbados and all the Lesser Antilles, had left Will's side that first day, remarking how well William appeared "considering his great ordeal and all." Aidan was so thankful to God that Will had returned alive, for he knew it was because of his urging that Will had agreed to undertake the attempt to recover the stolen English treasure. Yet as Aidan had returned to Shelworthy, the thick blanket of guilt that covered his heart would not leave, for he began to blame himself anew. While he was gladdened at the outcome of Will's voyage, Aidan cursed his own actions that culminated in his daughter's husband possibly being sentenced to live as a cripple for the rest of his days.

Missy and John Delacroix came and went often those first days, entering with plates of food and treats, bringing with them smiles of encouragement. They left more subdued than when arriving, for Will took precious little nourishment as he lay in his bed, sweating with fever or shaking with chills. He could consume only the smallest portions.

John, in an attempt to provide assistance, brought with him one day a set of crutches, hand carved from the thick branches of a native tamarind tree. They were strong and sturdy and would bear Will's weight with ease.

When Will saw them and spied on John's face the barest hint of pity and shame, he barked out, angry and terse, that they should be thrown into the fire. "I will not hobble about as a beggar on crutches!" he shouted, then collapsed back onto the bed in a fit of coughing that racked him to the core. "I am not a cripple!" he coughed. John, embarrassed and hurt, slunk out of the room, carrying his well-intentioned gift with him.

Yet despite his anger, William had yet to stand unaided since his return.

Both Vicar Coates and Vicar Petley from St. Michael's visited regularly. Vicar Petley seemed to have softened since Will's return, and his heartfelt supplication to God for healing often brought Kathryne to the verge of tears.

Even with all the prayers of the island, Will remained little changed.

Luke, Kathryne, and Thomas Mayhew developed an informal rotation by Will's bedside. Luke would add his powders and poultices to Will's leg, assuring all that this latest combination would prove more effective than the previous concoction.

Thomas would sit and read to William—from the Scriptures mostly, but chapters from other books as well, books they had shared at the vicarage in Hadenthorne when Will was a boy. This seemed to comfort William greatly. If Will dozed while he read, Thomas would fold a satin bookmark between the pages, then pray, his lips moving softly, until Will awoke again.

Kathryne's day began at Will's side and ended there as well. For only a few hours would she leave him, for there was much more repair work that needed to be accomplished to the cottage before the child was due to be born. Will could not perform such management, so the burden of supervising the tasks fell upon Kathryne's delicate shoulders.

A proper nursery was needed. The cottage had to be enlarged for quarters where Mrs. Cole and other servants would be housed. Storerooms were required, and a summer kitchen was needed due to the island's heat, which at times became intolerable. A flurry of orders, letters, and material requests were issued from the dining table of the cottage to Weymouth, England, and to Jamaica, the Dutch ports, and ports of the Mediterranean. Furnishing a household took a great deal of careful planning, as the materials had to be gathered from dozens of different locations since little was available locally, and as she needed the services of a small army of tradesmen.

During these weeks, as Will lay still, through the long hours of thinking and waiting, as she sat alone and watched her husband's sleeping face, she never envisioned any outcome, any reality, that did not include William—a healthy and fully able William. She petitioned God every night and every dawning and throughout the hours of her busy days for such. And in her heart, she had the confidence of a trusting child that her prayers would be answered. For up until this moment, all of her prayers had been answered.

When she looked back upon the past, she could trace the patterns that God's faithfulness had drawn on the tablet of her days. She recalled his presence with her during the echoing loneliness after her mother had died when she was a young girl. God had given her the gift of Mrs. Cole, the loving head of the Broadwinds kitchen, who was there to give the vibrant child all the nurturing love she needed. Mrs. Cole had been sent to her once more and was with her now, for God must have known Kathryne needed her again.

I thank thee, dearest Lord, for always knowing what to give me before I even ask, she prayed.

When Kathryne went off alone at the age of sixteen to London to attend the Alexandrian, the school for young noblewomen, God had given her the gift of Lady Emily Bancroft. He knew that without a mother, young Kathryne needed a strong mentor in her life who would be the model of a successful, godly woman. Kathryne knew Emily had the openness to accept her as she was, and the power to understand her completely, for at times she felt as if her very thoughts were being read. Emily discerned Kathryne's talents and spirit, lovingly opening the tender petals of the girl as if a flower—seeing into her very soul, it seemed—then having the courage to guide Kathryne into the unconventional path that she was meant to walk, training her to be a successful businesswoman.

Such a gift, Kathryne thought. *Such a precious gift.*

She looked back upon the days of indecision when three men were in her life, all vying for her attentions as the best suitor. She had struggled with the choice being in the hands of her dear father and not her own and had fervently prayed for the grace to allow her future to be decided by another. Her prayers were answered in a most unusual way, for God brought her the gift of William, a man not of her class, whom most considered an unlikely match for the Lady Spenser. She knew it was a difficult thing for her father to approve of a former pirate to be his daughter's husband, but her heavenly Father had taken care of that, too.

And now, this gift of a child. How her heart longed for motherhood. The Almighty had blessed her yet again with this little life that even now grew within her.

Yes, God has answered all my prayers, she thought, *but not always in the way I have prayed them.*

She closed her eyes once again and directed her mind and heart to God.

I will trust thee to care for Will, my heavenly Father, for thou knowest best. Thou knowest best of all.

⬛⬜⬛⬜⬛

It was late in the evening when Kathryne slipped back into their bedchamber. She carried a tray of flannel cakes and tankards of cider—both favorite foods from Will's childhood.

"Will?" she whispered as she stepped in. "Darling? Are you still awake? I have a great treat for you."

The room was dim, for Kathryne had left a single candle flickering in the main room of the cottage, near the great stone fireplace. The moon was out and nearly full, and its silver light mixed with the golden illumination of the candle, filling the room with a burnished glow.

Will turned from his side and propped himself up on the bed. He struggled to smile, for every day brought such little improvement to his leg that discouragement and flashes of fear lurked in the dark corners of his thoughts. Many nights, until the dawn came, he lay awake in the darkness, imagining his leg to finally be healed. He would arise, lay both feet to the floor, and attempt to stand and walk. And every morning the outcome remained the same. The leg, now weakened further by lack of use, would simply crumble beneath him, and he would tumble to the stone floor. As he lay there, feeling the stones' uneven coldness against his back, he would bite his lip, resisting the urge to cry out in frustration to God.

"A treat?" Will replied. "It be treat enough to have you here. That is all the treat I need."

She smiled and sat next to him on the bed. "Mrs. Cole has managed to produce a passable batch of flannel cakes. She claims that on this island the flour is different than what she had employed at Broadwinds, as well as the butter. She continues to despair for good English firewood for the oven. Yet, I think that these cakes are every bit as pleasing as were those of my childhood. And the cider is most tasty, almost like the Somerset cider I loved at Broadwinds."

Kathryne prattled on, her words edged with a slight tint of false cheer. The days had gone too long for her joy to be totally honest and free. And Will recognized the truth of this masquerade, but had grown to accept it and to expect it as well.

"Well then," he replied, edging his own words with a hint of false optimism, "let me try them and determine the quality myself. I remember that I was quite the expert of what made a good flannel cake when Mrs. Cavendish was in the kitchen."

Kathryne picked up the pewter plate and was about to hand it to William when it tumbled from her grasp and clattered to the floor, spilling the thin, small cakes in a dozen directions. She froze for a moment, a most bewildered and astonished look filling her face.

Will called out, alarmed, "Kathryne!" He elbowed his way to a sitting position.

She did not answer but grabbed at his right hand and took it firmly in hers. She spread out his fingers and placed his palm hard and tight against her belly, against the textured damask fabric of her gown. Her eyes were first locked on William's, then her gaze drifted off, her eyes unfocused as if they sought out something that was not yet visible.

"There!" she whispered loudly. "There it is again!"

William was befuddled. "What is? What are you attempting to tell me? What is it you are showing me?"

She pressed his hand tighter against her.

"There!" she cried out again.

Will stopped moving and sat rigid, pushing himself further upright with his left hand. His eyes widened in the darkness.

"What was that?" he called out. He looked into Kathryne's eyes, and suddenly, as if the sun had slipped from behind a cloud, his thoughts were flooded with the illumination of insight. He knew the import of that small but powerful nudge against his palm. Will had been told that such movement was not expected for weeks, but he was sure he felt a soft pressure against his hand.

"It is your child, William," she whispered softly in the night. "Your child."

And in the space of a single heartbeat, Kathryne began to weep, tears spilling from her eyes in a deluge. Will knew she was weeping for the joy over her child's first felt kick within her womb, as well as for her husband, whose crippled leg prevented his getting out of bed and walking.

Though William was a man and such powerful emotions were often alien to him, this was a torrent of emotions that he clearly understood. He knew their true origin. If it was a tiny foot that kicked against his palm, he felt that movement echo and reverberate down to his very soul. He felt it in the deepest passages of his heart. If such a kick could be so overwhelming to him, he knew that Kathryne was near to being drowned by those feelings.

He pulled himself up and embraced her as tightly as he could. She continued to sob against his shoulder. He whispered to her as she cried. "Everything will be accomplished as the Lord wills it, my darling Kathryne. All is well. All is well."

Until this night, she had shed not a tear for Will's wound, nor for the fatigue caused by the additional work his condition forced her to undertake, nor for the strains of the growing child within her. It was not until this night were the emotions let loose.

Perhaps a full half an hour later, Kathryne's crying began to cease, and Will loosened his embrace. He leaned back and kissed the salty tears from her face.

"Kathryne," he said, his words free of the small traces of self-pity that had begun to creep into Will's speech, "my heart has never been as full as it is tonight. My child exists. I felt it with my own hand. It is as if God himself touched me at that moment."

He placed his hand under her chin and lifted her face to his. Her tears were still wet on her cheeks. Her lips trembled slightly, and Will could see the fear and concern clouding her features.

"Kathryne, I am sorry that our lives have been made so complicated by what has befallen me. I never thought the Lord would allow this to occur—after all the disappointments in my life."

Kathryne was about to speak, but Will held his finger to her lips.

"But God has given me what he desires for me. I will accept this. I must accept this."

Kathryne looked as if she might be nearing tears again. "Oh, William," she said, trembling. "I have prayed so much for you and . . ." Her words trailed off, lost in a sob. William hugged her again, holding her close.

"Kathryne," Will said, a firmness in his voice that had been most clearly absent for the past months, "this child will need a father who can leave his bed unaided."

He spun his legs out of the bed and placed his feet firmly on the floor. "I hope that the crutches John made for me are still here."

Her eyes widened.

"Please, my darling, would you get them for me? There is more than one way for a man to walk. There is more than a single method that a father can use to train his son to walk in his footsteps."

"I tell you, Lord Willougby be no better than any of the others," Gleeson hissed. "He be puttin' the screws to you as soon as look at you."

"He seems to be patient and fair with me," Taylor Bullock replied, taking a long draw off the rum jug that Gleeson had placed before him. "Never been one to punish much, nor praise, but he seems to be fair and all."

The two men, both field overseers, huddled outside one of the slave huts at the Carruthers estate. Bullock was the newest man at Lord Francis Willougby's neighboring plantation, and Gleeson had invited him to Carruthers's for a taste of some new rum.

Bullock was a small-framed man with ragged teeth and a thin thatch of red hair that whisked into tendrils at the slightest breeze. He had been on the island for only nine months and had yet to endure the backbreaking work of a cane harvest. Currently Bullock had his gangs of slaves doing the preparation work in one of the three huge fields owned by Lord Willougby. They were halfway through the field, holing the thick, dense red soil. The men, in precise rows, would each dig first a hole a half foot deep, as wide as a man is tall. A few cane tops would be added and covered with a thin layer of soil. As these sprouted, mold and manure would be added to make the field level. For the next five or six months, each would need weeding and thinning. The soil was baked hard by the sun, and only the fittest were up to the task of holing the soil. It was the old men and women who carried the manure and weeded.

"Maybe," Gleeson snorted, "but you've not yet seen a harvest. That be the hard work. The darkies be out there from sunrise to darkness, hackin' away at the cane with their machetes, cuttin' and strippin' all day."

Bullock nodded and drank again.

"Then they be draggin' it to the mill to be crushed and all, then cooked. It be so hot in that sugar mill, I be sure hell would be a most cooler place," Gleeson cawed. "You'll lose more than a handful of darkies when you start the boilin'."

Bullock shrugged and dipped to the jug again.

"Why you be tellin' me all this, Gleeson?" he said. "It be no jam off your toast if a few of my darkies pass over or I have to work harder for a stretch."

Gleeson smiled, his yellowed teeth barely visible in the pale moonlight. He picked up the jug, wiped at it with the palm of his dirty hand, and swallowed.

"Ah, but there be a good reason." He belched. "There be a most powerful good reason to listen."

Bullock waited in silence for a long moment. "And what be that reason?" he asked evenly.

Gleeson smiled again. "Freedom," he hissed. "Freedom, pure and simple." Gleeson belched again. "And gold . . . more gold than you kin imagine."

CHAPTER

5

30 June 1644

The dawn had just arrived to the island of Barbados. The sun grew bright, and the air grew hotter than it had been in weeks. With only a few minutes into the day, sweat dripped from William's forehead, and his shirt clung to his body, stained dark with moisture up his back and across his shoulders.

Every day for the past month, Will arose early from his bed, slipped his feet to the floor, took up the two tamarind wood crutches that lay beside him, and as quiet as he could, thumped and shuffled his way to the kitchen, where he would grab something to eat—a biscuit, a wedge of cheese, or a sweet left over from the previous night's dinner. He gobbled it down before Mrs. Cole or Kathryne had a chance to scold him for not having a proper breakfast.

Munching on his purloined items, he would make his way to the crest of the bluff, through the thick pangola grass, to the very edge of the sea. He would practice walking and getting by on crutches well before anyone else was awake to watch his initial clumsiness.

Navigating on crutches had been difficult and most frustrating at first, but now Will was becoming most adept at maneuvering with them. His left leg was in fine health and was growing stronger with each day. His right leg down to the knee appeared to be normal in all regards. He could feel pressure and pain, hot and cold. The flesh responded to the touch of a hand. But the flesh below the knee seemed connected to a different body than the rest of William's frame. At first there was pain, culminating with Luke's surgery on the decaying flesh surrounding the wound. Then the leg grew less and less sore. But along with that, to his dismay, all other sensations grew less and less prevalent as well. Will simply could not issue any control over his leg below the knee. The foot would not bend on his command, nor would his knee lock in place to support his body. If he dropped his crutches, he would tumble to the right, spilling himself in a heap.

This day marked an entire month since Will first slipped the sturdy crutches under his arms. It also marked the first day Will attempted to carry himself to the very edge of the sea. The tips of the crutches sank deep into the fine coral sand, and Will had to lurch about on his good leg to make progress to the water's edge and the softly rolling surf as it hissed toward his feet.

Will turned and looked over his shoulder. He saw no activity at the cottage, but he knew looks could be deceiving. Mrs. Cole clattered out of bed at all hours, seeming to need to have her hands in flour and butter as the sun rose. However, on this day all looked silent.

Will turned about again, took the crutches from under his arms, and tossed them a few feet behind himself while balancing on his good leg. He bent down and allowed himself to fall the last foot or so to the soft sand. He looked over his shoulder again. The cottage was now out of view behind the dune and windswept grass tussocks.

It is time to try it, he told himself in the firmest voice he could muster.

He pulled off his shoes, his doublet, and his breeches and tossed them into a pile by his crutches. He left his drawers on for modesty, for he was not sure if what he was attempting could be accomplished without calling for assistance. Using his hands and good leg, he dragged and pushed his way to the warm waters and rolled into the surf. Within a moment he was in deep enough to begin to stroke into the waves.

How delicious this feels! he thought, rejoicing. *How long I have denied myself this pleasure.*

He paddled out past the first small reef and the waves that grew and tumbled over it. His arms did most of the work, and he could feel the broad sinewy muscles across his back and chest tighten and pull with each stroke.

I have remained inactive for too long, he told himself, *for I know I shall be stiff and sore on the morrow.*

He continued to stroke through the surf, quiet this day, for the winds were slight and from the north.

How good it feels to be in the sea again, he thought. *I must never let myself be so fooled by my weakness again.*

He turned and laid on his back, buoyed by the warm salty waters. As he moved his right leg, the portion below the knee still showed little, if any, response, yet by moving his thigh, he could produce a passable means of paddling through the water. He had to swing his right hand a bit more often than his left as he lay facing the sky, for his right side had a tendency to dip more than the left. In no more than a few moments he had the rhythm set, and he floated, weightless and buoyant.

He closed his eyes to the sun and began to pray.

Dear Lord, I thank thee for all thy blessings. I thank thee for Kathryne and the child that she carries. I thank thee for the financial blessings thou hast bestowed upon me. I . . . I thank thee for allowing me . . . for allowing me to be wounded as I was. I struggle with this lesson, but it is a lesson that will not depart until its import is recognized. My God, watch over Kathryne and bless her with the health she needs. I thank thee for allowing her to come into my life. I ask that thou wouldst watch over and guide us, and keep us protected as thy children. Show me the way of thy plan, Lord, for I seek to serve thee.

He floated there in the surf, quiet and serene, the waters gentle about him, the soft, warm, lapping wavelets caressing his body, soothing all portions of him. He lost track of time as he immersed himself in the great floating saltiness of the sea. At the corner of his hearing, he thought he heard a cry and dismissed it as the cawing of a gull or pelican who inhabited these shallow waters. Then, a moment later, at the edge of those shrieks came a deeper call, deeper than any flying creature Will had ever heard.

What could be causing that sound? Will thought to himself, almost perturbed that his drifting and dreaming was being interrupted by such raucous cries. Then it came again, a deep rough sound.

It sounds like English bullfrogs in May, he thought, and smiled at the memories of his childhood by the river Taw as it meandered through Hadenthorne in Devon, England.

Will leaned his head back into the surf to clear the hair from his face, then splashed upright into the waters, wiping the salty wetness from his eyes. From no more than a dozen feet came the source of the deep booming calls. It was Bo, the golden-haired dog that had adopted Will so many months prior. He was stroking toward his master with a most desperate look upon his canine features. With every stroke the dog made with his forelegs, he would bark, as if calling out to Will. And just as Will's vision focused on the dog, he looked up to shore and an even more bewildering sight filled his eyes.

Kathryne was in the surf to her waist, her arms held out as she walked and paddled toward the sea. Her face was twisted into a mask of terror as she stroked into the water. Behind Kathryne, Mrs. Cole stood at the edge of the dunes, first waving toward the house, then spinning to face the sea.

As the water splashed from his face and ears, he could now hear Kathryne's frenzied calls of "Will! Will!"

He was at once befuddled. Turning to the open sea, he expected to see a large sea beast bearing down on him. Why else would these women be so troubled and frantic?

Kathryne cried out again, "William! Do not leave me!"

In that instant, the puzzle became clear. Bo was at him then, splashing and barking and nipping at his hands.

"Good dog!" Will shouted, tussling at the dog's ears. Will smiled, shook his head, then dipped his shoulder into the surf as they both began to stroke toward the shore.

By the time he reached shallower water, Kathryne had waded in so the water was lapping at the bodice of her gown. She was both standing and bobbing in the light rolling surf, finding it now difficult to move forward, for the waves lifted her feet from the sandy bottom. As he neared, he could see how distraught and shaken she had become, her face ashen, tears streaking her cheeks. Mrs. Cole, on the bluff behind her, mirrored Kathryne's distress.

"William!" she shouted, her voice trembling and hysterical as she extended her arms to him. "We thought you had drowned yourself. We saw the dog barking at the shore, and we ran to the bluff to find you adrift in the sea! I thought you were leaving me! I thought you were trying to end your life! And all I could do is wade to this point! I was helpless to come to your aid!"

Will bobbed in the waters. Bo splashed in circles about him, finding this new game most pleasing. "Kathryne, how could you think that? I could no sooner leave you than I could take up wings and fly away. I was just seeing if this leg allowed me to continue to swim."

By that moment, they were face-to-face, at arm's length. Kathryne's tears mixed with her great relief, and as Will floated close to her, she clenched her fists and began to hit him solidly on his chest and shoulders.

"William Hawkes!" she cried, both laughing and crying. "Never do this again! I thought my life was ending when I saw you floating out there as a dead man. How could you? How could you do this and not tell me of your plans?"

He caught her fists in his hands and pulled her close, the salty water splashing and tumbling about them. "Kathryne, darling, I simply wanted to test my leg in the water. And I am most gratified to report that swimming is one thing I can do equally as well this day as I did before."

She embraced him tightly, holding him as close as she could. Bo, tiring of this game, ran from the water and hurried to the side of Mrs. Cole, where he shook himself from head to tail, drenching the woman in a salty spray. She almost fell in the moist sand as she attempted to avoid the dog's wetness.

In the surf, Will could hold Kathryne lightly in his arms and carry her expanding body with as much ease as he had done on their wedding night. Her feet simply dangled in the warm waters. He lifted her and began to turn in circles, feeling her arms tight about his neck, her body against his.

"It appears that there are other benefits to bathing in the sea," Will added as he spun her about, hopping gracefully, balancing on just his good leg. Kathryne looked up into his eyes. In their deep blue, she saw a sparkle that had been extinguished for so many weeks.

Kathryne laughed as she circled him. The dog began to bark at the water's edge, calling them back.

"Perhaps we should return to dry land, William," Kathryne whispered. "After all, we haven't had our breakfast."

William nodded and pushed toward the shallower waters. "But perhaps I shall let you leave the water first and . . . and I would advise taking Mrs. Cole back to the cottage before me."

"But why?"

"Do you see the bundle of clothing on the beach?" Will asked with the hint of a smile.

Kathryne nodded.

"Did you think whose they might be?"

Kathryne peered at the shore, then back into William's face. She leaned back and at that instant realized that he had stripped to his drawers. Her face turned scarlet, and she turned her eyes downward, hoping that the normally crystal clear waters would be murky this morning. They were not.

"I think that civility and modesty commands that the two of you leave," William whispered into her ear.

Kathryne, blushing harder than she ever remembered, simply nodded and began to wade and paddle toward land. She stopped when the waters reached about her knees, the heavy gown draping about her form most intimately. William had to remind himself that he was indeed a gentleman and averted his eyes, but only slightly. When she turned, he could see the gentle swell of her belly, now grown more pronounced.

"Perhaps, William," Kathryne called softly back to him, "perhaps you may teach me how to swim in these waters? It is truly a delicious sensation."

William's smile took a moment to build, but it broke broad and loving across his face. "Perhaps I shall, dear wife. Perhaps I shall."

As Mrs. Cole helped Kathryne climb the slight, sandy bluff, Will continued to float in the sea for a long moment.

Dear God, he prayed, *I thank thee for allowing me this pleasure. It feels good to know that the limitations of this injury are not complete. I thank thee for reminding me how a man feels when he holds his wife in his arms. I know now that I simply need to persevere and that thou wilt show me the way.*

During the next several weeks, Will became as a man reborn. While still hobbled and required to use crutches for mobility, he began to reassume all the duties that he had forfeited since his return to Barbados.

He resumed his duties at the fort, committing his energies to seeing the damages of the pirate attack repaired and rebuilt. He resumed friendships with those he had not seen in months. He resumed his rounds of the town, visiting with new merchants, meeting new settlers, and feeling, for the first time in many months, that he had found again the pulse of the town.

For journeys longer than a mile, he borrowed Kathryne's horse. Will, with some manipulations and a short ladder, could mount the horse alone, then lean over and with his hands place his right leg into the stirrup. He would tie it in place, snug and tight, with a short leather thong. And, in an effort to make amends for not having the skills to heal him, Luke fashioned him a leather weaving that held his crutches at the rear of the saddle. The more he walked and rode, the stronger his arms and good leg grew, and the more adept he became at managing life with one useless limb.

Kathryne watched as he rode off in the mornings and thanked God that he had granted her request that Will be healed. It was not a physical healing she was thankful for; she knew that his body was still fettered by his injury. But it was his soul that had been healed.

While William weathered through his despair to find a brighter day, Vicar Thomas Mayhew at first struggled with much the same malaise.

He had been held captive in the hulking Spanish prison in St.

Augustine for so many months, yet he had found there a balm for his pain in sharing the Good News of the gospel with fellow prisoners. He took pleasure in that both he and St. Paul accomplished much while in chains, and Thomas remembered with deep affection the dozens of souls he had led to knowledge of Christ's love. He prayed every morning and every evening that the seeds he planted within those dank and vile prison walls would bear fruit and blossom in the darkness with the light of God's love.

And when exiled to the small island of Guajiro, Thomas had spent long and pleasant days learning the rudiments of the native language and telling them about his God. To his surprise at first, and then to his wonderment, many in the village began to accept his words as the truth. A few days before Will's rescue, Thomas had had the honor of leading the village chief in accepting the gift of salvation through belief in Christ Jesus.

The vicar knew that the words were not all properly Anglican and correct and that most of those young believers had a slightly skewed version of the foundations of the faith—but despite that, they truly believed. Those simple villagers accepted the Son of God as their Savior and Lord. And for that Thomas rejoiced.

But now rescued, safe and secure on Barbados and living under Will and Kathryne's roof, a certain restlessness, a feeling of disheartenment, began to creep into the vicar's soul. He greatly enjoyed ministering to William, though he had seen little impact of his words while Will lay prone in bed. And now that William had picked himself up and returned to as much of a normal life as he could manage, Thomas felt most adrift. Becoming more acquainted with Kathryne and Mrs. Cole was pleasant indeed, but those women did not need him nor his services as a man of the cloth.

∎ ▢ ▢ ▢ ∎

His wounds healed and his deprivations now surfeit with food and shelter in abundance, Thomas dressed in the best of his two new cassocks and breeches and paid a call on the island's acting bishopric, Vicar Giles Petley of St. Michael's Church in Bridgetown.

Their meeting was most cordial and comfortable, Giles welcoming him into the sparse study of the parsonage. As he sat in a most rickety and threadbare tapestry chair, Thomas explained that his original assignment was the mission on St. Lucia's but that a second vicar had been sent to replace him more than six months prior.

Giles nodded, knowingly, as Thomas continued his tale of imprisonment and exile. He concluded his history with his rescue at sea, first by William, then Kathryne.

"And now that I am on this wonderful island and sufficiently recovered, I seek to again become a practicing vicar. I seek to serve him, to be wherever God calls me to be and to do whatever he calls me to do," Thomas said, having practiced this ending line for some days.

Giles nodded again and sipped at his tea, now grown cold.

Thomas's cup stood nearly full, for one sip convinced him he was not sufficiently thirsty to partake of such a badly brewed drink.

"Well then, Vicar Mayhew," Giles responded, leaning back in the one leather chair in the study. The chair, creased and worn, with small tufts of stuffing poking out at the arms and seat, groaned under the strain. "It appears as if you have been somewhat adrift these past many months."

Thomas nodded. "But not by my own choosing, of course."

"Of course," Giles replied. "But nonetheless the bishopric in London will need to be informed of your present status and availability. I agree that to travel to St. Lucia to fill a vacancy that has now been filled is unwise."

He paused, tried to smile, then continued. "And St. Michael's parish, while we continue to grow as new landowners arrive, is currently fully staffed—by myself and Vicar Coates. We shall need to plant a small church in some of the other eleven outlying parishes in the future, but not until our population increases sufficiently to warrant such."

Thomas nodded.

"And we have no room on the staff for unexpected arrivals, you see. There are no funds available to pay such staff, unless London would see fit to provide such additional remuneration."

Thomas nodded again. "But perhaps there is something else I may do while I await word from London?" he asked, for he did not take well to inactivity.

Giles screwed up his face, as if in deep concentration.

"Alas, Vicar Mayhew, I am at a loss to consider what that might be. I have written to London, and the letter was shipped out a fortnight prior to today. I would anticipate the bishopric taking no more than a month, perhaps two, to make a recommendation as to your disposition. After all, they did consider you dead for all these months. Now that you are not, well . . . all sorts of paperwork will need be corrected. You understand, of course, that not only does God move in mysterious ways and in his own time—the same applies to our humble leaders within the church."

Giles nodded again, yet Thomas could not decipher his reason.

"I do not intend on raising false hopes, good Vicar Mayhew. It may take them more time to reach a decision than I have assumed—what with the political turmoil and all that grips our country these troubling days. Can you imagine—our dear Bishop Laud still imprisoned in the Tower? I understand that zealots in Parliament are resolved to reform the church and have imposed the most uncompromising . . ."

Vicar Petley continued with a long litany of news and complaints regarding the Puritans and their threat to the church and the tightening association of Oliver Cromwell and Sir Henry Vane, the famed orator Sir John Pym's successor. Giles continued to nod after each statement. He paused and let several long moments of silence fill the room. He finally broke the silence by nodding and clasping his hands together, almost as if clapping aloud.

"So then, Vicar Mayhew, I am glad that we have had a chance to clear this matter up." He stood, as if dismissing Thomas.

Thomas was too polite to remain seated, so he stood as well. "But, Vicar Petley, what shall I do until London responds? I am still a man adrift."

Giles appeared puzzled, as if he had never considered that as problematic. "Well, we should hear in no less than two months from today. . . . And I am sure that no more than a year will pass until you receive new instructions."

A year! Thomas thought, nearly incredulous over Giles's matter-of-fact dismissal. *I cannot simply sit and wait an entire year with nothing to do!*

Giles began to walk his guest to the door. "You will see. A year passes most quickly on our pleasant island. And you should be thankful that you have such a friend in William Hawkes, who is gracious to give you a place in his home in the interim." Giles leaned in close to Thomas. "I understand that Mr. Hawkes has become quite wealthy with his shrewd trading and through his days as a royal privateer. It will not hurt to have a patron such as him offering you protection."

Giles pulled hard at the doorknob, the door squealing in protest as the swollen bottom stile bit into the floor, leaving a wide, scraped arc in the pine boards.

"This humidity does horrible things to wood," Vicar Petley complained as Thomas walked into the brilliant sunshine. He blinked several times, as much in reaction to the brilliance of the day as to the surprise of having his problem unresolved in such a cavalier fashion.

Set to push the door closed, Giles stopped, thought for a long moment, then added, almost as an afterthought, "Vicar Mayhew, there is that . . . group of . . . well, that group of assorted . . . people that Mr. Hawkes taught the Scriptures to at the fort. Since his absence, they have been without a proper leader. Perhaps . . . since the fort is under the jurisdiction of Mr. Hawkes, you might become its de facto chaplain of sorts. Since you are staying under Mr. Hawkes's roof and all. . . . Perhaps it might be something that could occupy your time until we hear from London."

Giles nodded again and smiled, more to himself than to Thomas, and pushed the door with a shrieking squeal, splitting the silence of the day. Just before the door was completely closed, Giles added one last thought.

"I would prefer if those people were taught at the fort—as they have been in the past. Some of them have actually tried to attend services at St. Michael's, and I do not need to tell you, Vicar Mayhew, that such a practice will simply not do. Not with St. Michael's under my jurisdiction, that is."

With that, Giles shouldered himself against the door and shoved it closed with a final screeching shriek.

Thomas stood on the walk, feeling properly dismissed and challenged. *A chaplain at the fort,* he began to think. *Perhaps . . . yes, perhaps so. It does sound as if no one else wants the task.*

And as he began his walk back to Will and Kathryne's home, his steps quickened.

CHAPTER

6

Sunday afternoons were a most quiet and still time on the island. Slaves were not required to work and could do as they pleased. Many worked the small plots of land by their quarters, raising yams, cassavas, sweet potatoes, or beans. Women sat and sewed coarse fabric into crude shirts and breeches.

On this Sunday, Herbert Gleeson sat on a mangrove stump at the edge of the clearing, watching the bucolic scene before him, hating everything his eyes took in—the long, lanky slaves as they rested in the shade of their crude huts; the women, clad in sparse rags, who were busy sewing or weeding the small gardens. Gleeson hated everything that morning except the full tankard of amber liquid he cradled lovingly in his hands.

Gleeson appeared to have an unlimited supply of potent refreshments, almost straight from the boiling syrup at the end of the sugar refining process. He himself helped skim the clotting juice from the surface of the boiling cane syrup, pouring it into earthen jugs to quickly ferment in the hot tropical sun. Refined once more, the golden liquid became a smooth and tasty rum. But some preferred to drink it as Gleeson did—rough and unrefined. That first pressing of the cane was called *mobby,* a heady and powerful drink. It was most suited to a man of Gleeson's sensibilities.

He snorted, then rummaged through his pocket, pulling out the stub end of a clay pipe. He filled it with a shock of tobacco pulled from his other pocket; it was a mixture of tobacco leaf, dust, and linen threads from his breeches. Gleeson seemed not to notice as he tamped it down, lifted a coal from the fire, and began to puff like a drowning man.

The clouds of acrid smoke all but enveloped his head and shoulders, and he coughed several times, a gurgling, watery sound coming from his chest. He thought back to a meeting a month prior—a meeting in the dark recesses of a dank and dingy public house in Bridgetown. Nestled in the darkest corner of the room, at a tankard-filled table, sat a one-eyed man whose face was marred with a long jagged scar.

By the time Gleeson had downed his second mobby, he had found himself sitting next to this stranger, who introduced himself as Captain Forge Bliss, "the most skilled sailor and trader in all the Antilles—the most powerful ally any man could desire."

Gleeson had not known who this man was, nor where he came from, nor anything of his standing or history. But the one-eyed stranger had had a willing ear and appeared to be fascinated by the slurring talk at the table.

Their conversation had begun innocently, but powered by the thick, potent liquid, it had soon descended onto more intimate and dangerous ground. Gleeson tried to remember exactly what Captain Bliss had inquired about that day, but his recollections were clouded by the fourth, then fifth, then sixth tankard he had happily quaffed that quiet Sunday afternoon.

There was an oily, almost twisted smile on the crusty sailor's face as Gleeson recalled his litany of grievances against the titled landowners and the wealthy—his master Peter Carruthers, Governor Spenser, William Hawkes. Gleeson blamed every one of those noble fops for making his life a tropical nightmare and for exchanging his life for a mere slip of paper. Bliss had smiled as Gleeson's anger intensified, nudging him into ever-increasing rancor and bile.

At the hour when Gleeson had taken his leave, the sun had all but dropped into the western sea, and he had stumbled through the growing darkness, his heart curiously warm with the thoughts of revenge. Had those thoughts originated with Bliss, or had they laid dormant in Gleeson's tiny soul, waiting for the chance to surface and fester? As he had fallen facedown on his bed that night, Gleeson had claimed them as his own.

Gleeson shook his head to clear the foggy image from his mind and smiled. He leaned back, took a huge swallow of the mobby, and waited. From the sun he reckoned it was nearing noon, the time Taylor Bullock, Ian Tafert, and Jenkins O'Reilly were to gather. Gleeson peered up the north road that wound along the coast and led to the most recently cleared land on the island. In the distance came two figures, slowly pacing along the dusty way, one short and one tall. It could be no other than Bullock and Tafert. To the south, on the road that led to Bridgetown, Gleeson could see three men winding their way up through the narrow valley. It was a white man—O'Reilly, no doubt—with two black men a half-dozen paces behind.

"Gawblimy!" Gleeson spat. "Why in blazes be that stupid Irishman bringin' darkies to our meetin'? Blasted sods ain't got an ounce of common sense—not like us English gents, anyhow."

As they approached, Gleeson fortified himself with several long drinks from his mobby jug, making sure he had three more jugs, full and ready for his new friends and . . . *partners*, for lack of a better term.

Within the hour, all four white men were well into their cups. They had allowed the two darkies to finish off a half-consumed jug, all unwilling to share a cup with a black heathen.

"We'll toss it aside after they be done," Gleeson giggled, "for I be sure not wantin' to drink from the same vessel as them." He pointed his elbow at the two sullen black men squatting a few paces apart from the crowd. The rest laughed, and the two black men attempted to smile.

Soon Gleeson began to spin his plans, a word or two, a wink or two, a nudge or two at a time. If it be presented in all one sum, Gleeson thought, it would be too big for men of small minds such as these to grasp. *No sense in frightenin' 'em off afore we gets started,* he thought.

"I tells you, none of this be possible," Gleeson said with a sweep of his hand, taking in all the valley before him, thick and green with cane and tobacco, "if it ain't be for us. Be not one of the fancy noblemen who know how to raise a hoe or cut a cane. It be us and us alone that be the reason for them makin' the gold that they make."

The rest nodded, grunting their assent with his thoughts.

"Now I ain't sayin' that they be without use at all." He smiled. "After all, somebody has to drink all this rum and fool about with all that bloomin' Roundhead and Cavalier nonsense."

O'Reilly began to giggle, and his mobby sloshed in his tankard and spilled over his lap, which caused him to laugh even more.

"So, Gleeson, what is it you be tellin' us? What you be wantin' from us?" Tafert asked, his eyes becoming glazed and watery.

Gleeson stood up and let a few deep breaths in and out. He looked fully at each of them before he spoke.

"I ain't tellin' you to do anythin'. I don't want nothin' from you but to ask you t' think 'bout what I'm talkin'. We be doin' all the work on this blasted island—us and the darkies. And we be gettin' nothin' for it, save chopped-off fingers, fevers, sweats, rotten food, bugs everywhere, and most of us be dead by the time we be forty. All the while, the rich noblemen sits in their fancy houses, kissin' their prissy wives in their fancy dresses, drinkin' their costly wines, arguin' 'bout who be king of England."

He paused for a long moment. No one else spoke, for they were most unaccustomed to such long speeches.

"I ain't sayin' t' make no changes this day. But I wants you all t' think 'bout me words. It ain't right that they get rich and all we get is poor and dead. It ain't right, and I believes it be comin' on the time that we be doin' somethin' to make it change."

He paused again.

"That's all I be sayin'."

He looked about, and while the faces he saw were drunk on the mobby, he also saw in each face a hint of interest, a hint of agreement, a hint that they would consider the next step. It was all he wanted to see this first day.

"And be rememberin' that it ain't just me who be feelin' this injustice. It be plain as day to others, too—powerful men who be wantin' to help us right these most horrible wrongs." Gleeson coughed once, and his chest felt as if a wave had crashed through his lungs. "I be talkin' to others who be willin' to aid in this. They sees that we be wronged men—and they be willin' to see all the wrongs be righted."

Gleeson then nodded to himself, as if closing the discussion for the time. His eyes went to O'Reilly, then to the two darkies, who had said no words at all the entire time, not even among themselves.

"O'Reilly, you stupid git," Gleeson asked, slipping back into a more adversarial tone. "What possessed you t' bring the darkies with you?"

O'Reilly was nearly prostrate on the ground and wearily raised his head to look at Gleeson, then his slave companions, then back to Gleeson. "I be knowin' what you be sayin'," he replied, his voice wandering about in the wind of mobby. "And I be agreein' with you before you be speakin'."

"So why the darkies?"

O'Reilly belched loudly and then giggled and fell back to the ground. "They be wantin' to offer to help if we be needin' it," he said, then added with a smile before his eyes closed, "They be most expert at concoctin' poisons that leave a man dead in minutes. I know, 'cause I be seein' 'em do it. A few minutes is all it took."

And with that O'Reilly passed out as Gleeson's jaw dropped open.

▪ ▫ ▪ ▫ ▪

Aidan stood on the front porch of Shelworthy and watched William, perched, awkward and unsure, on the back of Kathryne's horse, Porter.

The horse and rider disappeared into the afternoon sun, a thick cloud of dust pluming up behind them. He looked to the east, toward the coming night, and his vision encompassed hundreds of greening and sweet acres of tall sugarcane waving as the sea in the afternoon breeze. The boughs of the royal poinciana, now bathed in the deepening golden light, unfolded as a scarlet umbrella above the hills. He breathed a great sigh of relief as he made his way back to his office.

He and his son-in-law, William Hawkes, had spent a most pleasant afternoon together. William had laid out his plans for rebuilding the fort and had presented him with a manifest of the materials that would need to be ordered from the foundries and craft guilds of England. William had a crew assembled to begin the repairs—his team of blackamoors and an additional two dozen laborers, mostly from Ireland. Aidan had offered, at the Crown's expense, to purchase up to a dozen strong slaves from the next slaving vessel that disembarked on the island, but Will had been most adamant in opposition to the offer.

"I will not be wanting to offend you, sir, but I would think that the fort can be rebuilt without using the labors of men who are bought and sold. I do not think I could use labor so purchased. The Scriptures and all . . ."

Will had not finished his statement since Aidan knew full well of his views. Aidan looked at the man before him with a curious expression, then shrugged.

"If such a task can be done, William, and if the costs are kept in line with your drafts and proposals, then I shall urge you to do so." Aidan hesitated for a moment. "I do not like this slaving business, William," the governor confided, "but I scarce know how any planting and pressing can be done on the cane without their labors. It seems as though any planters wishing success must concede their lofty moral stance if they desire to turn any profit at all. It is a most troubling conundrum, I must admit."

William had nodded, but did not add comment to Aidan's position.

After discussing the fort, Aidan had inquired, most solicitously, as to the state of William's recovery. Both crutches had been evident as they lay on the polished oak floor by Aidan's elaborate mahogany desk. Aidan had noted that Will seemed to glide about with ease on them and hoped that use of his leg was returning. If his observations proved accurate, a heavy cloak of guilt could be lifted from Aidan's heart.

"Every day I grow stronger, sir," William had replied. "The lower part of my leg is still lacking in feeling, but the flesh is firm and pink. Luke's surgery seems to have prevented any further decay."

"Most providential, my son," Aidan had said, "that he was skilled to recognize such symptoms."

Will had glanced about the cluttered room, stacked with documents, land plats, and royal decrees from London written on thick vellum and rolled in tubes tied with satin ribbons. He had seemed to be looking to see if anyone might be close enough to overhear. He had lowered his voice and had spoken in a most confidential manner.

"I must tell you, sir, that it was again your daughter who rescued me from my ignorance and folly and despair. I was lost, sir, upon my return, and Kathryne showed me the way. I do not know if you took such liberties with your departed wife, but Kathryne forced my hand to her belly, and I felt, against this palm, the foot of my child as it kicked in her womb. I will never forget that moment."

Will had held out his right hand, open and near trembling, offering it as evidence to his testimony. "I felt it, sir. I felt it hard and solid and strong. It was as if the Almighty used that tiny foot to . . . to boot me from my despair. I had allowed myself to sink in self-pity over my injury. But if that small child could learn, untaught and uninstructed, how to use its limbs, then I was duty bound, as its father, to at least try to learn how to use my limbs again. And from that day forward, I commenced to live as I had lived before the injury. I believe it is what the Almighty desires of me."

Aidan had smiled at Will's explanation, feeling vaguely uncomfortable about the mention of his daughter's belly and the child's movement in her womb and all. To Aidan, an old-fashioned man fond of the proper practices on the other side of the ocean, it did not bide well to have such free and open expression. To him, a woman with child was best left alone and sequestered until the child was presented at baptism. That was when Aidan first spent time with Kathryne as an infant— some four weeks after her birth. That was the proper way to handle this whole matter of procreation.

Yet if this liberal attitude and practice of his daughter helped send William on the road to recovery, then perhaps it was a good thing—for Will and Kathryne at least. Seeing William active again and resuming his functions as captain of the harbor defenses did much to wash away the guilt Aidan carried for his role in William's accident.

"Very good, William," he had replied. "A most inspiring story."

Aidan had changed the subject directly and whispered a small prayer under his breath that Kathryne would attempt no such intimacies with him. The thought of an unborn foot touching his hand sent shudders through his body like a chill.

And yet, when he had looked at Will's beaming face, he had felt a small twinge in the opposite direction—a feeling he quickly dismissed.

■ ■ ■ ■

When William would head off to the fort or to town in the morning, Eileen was often making her way to the cottage from her small room at the rear of the ship chandlery. If Will saw her as she walked along the wide dusty path to the house, he would smile and wave, sometimes stopping to inquire as to her plans for the day or speak in general pleasantries of the weather or the progress of the work upon the cottage.

Eileen looked forward to these small snatched moments of civility. Because of her years spent in such an amoral and base life, she had few if any contacts with men that were simply friendships. The past several years had robbed her of the ability to deal with men on a civil level—for all her relationships had been centered on one thing and one thing only.

But Will was different. He had never spurned her in the past, before her life changed. He had refused her attentions, of course, but was polite and kind and always most solicitous. And now that Eileen had turned from her sinful ways and turned to a life of serving God, she struggled greatly with simple relationships. She found knowing how to behave with them much harder than it had been before. Now she most often felt ill at ease around others, thinking that they were judging her present in light of her past.

Kathryne was different, too. There were times when she stumbled over the right words, knowing of Eileen's history. Most of Kathryne's unintentional malapropisms would culminate with both women collapsing into fits of giggles and blushing.

This day was no different. Eileen was dressed in her most proper blue gown, laced nearly to her neck, and sleeves stretched nearly to the wrist. She had instructed the seamstress to construct the garment more to the loose side than the tight, for she knew how the smallest hint in such matters could inflame passions in men. She pulled her straight, red hair back to her shoulders and let it drape over her back. Her skin remained a most pale shade of ivory, lighter than Kathryne's, and she took steps to prevent the sun from reddening it, carrying a delicate parasol when the light became too intense.

She was now at the rise in the road as it curved out of town, following the geography of the shore. The sweet scent of frangipani filled the air. To her right was the fort, and no more than three-quarters of a mile ahead was the cottage of Will and Kathryne. She squinted into the distance and could see the team of craftsmen already at work hefting the large stones into place, sawing at thick blocks of lumber, and carrying buckets of mortar and sand.

At the front of the house, she saw Porter standing there, dappled in the morning sun. She watched as Will maneuvered himself to the horse's side, his crutches under his arms. He grabbed the saddle and hoisted the crutches into their holder. Then with a most fluid and practiced move he grabbed at the top leather cinch, and with a springing jump with his good leg, lifted himself up and into the saddle, almost with ease. He bent and tied off his bad leg, then pulled at the reins, turning the horse about and setting him toward town.

In no more than a moment or two, he would pass her as she walked. Without thinking, she raised her hand and smoothed at her hair, adjusted her waistline and smoothed her gown, glancing down to ensure that all folds and pleats were in their proper place.

Will pulled back the reins as Porter drew beside Eileen. He bent to his side, gripping at the saddle.

"Good morning, Miss Palmerston. It augurs to be a most pleasant day, do you not agree?"

His voice was warm and happy, she thought, and she tried to respond to him in kind.

"Indeed, Mr. Hawkes. I trust that the work on the cottage progresses to your expectations?"

Will turned in the saddle, the leather straps creaking in the quiet morning, to look at the walls beginning to take shape and definition.

"Indeed it does, Miss Palmerston. The work that you and Kathryne have undertaken is most admirable and worthy of my great appreciation. I trust that such work, so often reserved for a man, has not proved too taxing for you?"

Eileen felt a blush coming to her face and tried her best to prevent it. "No, Mr. Hawkes. And to be true, it is Mrs. Hawkes who has the tremendous abilities and creativity. I am simply her scribe and assistant."

Will laughed, and Eileen felt the blush arrive, wanted or not. "'Tis not how Kathryne describes your tenacious abilities, Miss Palmerston." He leaned down even further and almost whispered, as if passing on words of great confidence, "You must promise me one thing, Miss Palmerston."

She was nodding before he finished. "I will grant you any request I am able to, Mr. Hawkes," she replied, hoping that her words were not too bold.

Will seemed not to notice and continued.

"You must promise me that Kathryne will take the rest she needs. I am told by many that I am a most foolish man for allowing my wife to work as she does—in light of her impending motherhood and all. But to be truthful as well, Miss Palmerston, I scarce think I could stop her from building this nest of hers. She is driven to have these chambers completed before the child arrives. But I implore you to see that such work does not tax her too greatly."

Eileen nodded vigorously. "I will indeed."

William smiled down at her, wide and full of grace. "Thank you, Eileen," he said, employing her first name, which he seldom did. "Thank you for all your assistance."

With that, he pulled himself upright and nicked at the horse's side with his good foot. Porter snorted once, then began to canter toward town.

"Until this evening then," Will called out.

Eileen remained motionless for a long moment, watching him ride away. After that moment, she took her hand from over her heart, shut her eyes tightly for a moment, then resumed her walk to the cottage.

Would that other men be as gracious as Mr. Hawkes, she thought. As she held that thought close, a sidelong, secret sort of smile slipped across her face.

7

After his somewhat unsatisfying meeting with Vicar Petley, Thomas arose early one morning and accompanied William to the edge of the sea. They waved to some of the blackamoors from the fort who were harvesting oysters among the submerged branches of mangrove trees in the shallow salt water, the blades of their cutlasses catching the sun's rays as they hacked away at the encrusted branches.

Thomas held Will's crutches and helped him walk into the water. He watched Will with some envy as he stroked boldly into the rising surf, tossed heavier by the brisk offshore winds.

Will reached the shallow reef where the waters boiled and tossed. He turned on a line parallel with the shore and stroked for several long minutes, then returned against the current. Thomas could almost feel the waters pull and urge at Will's skin, resisting his advances with a thousand tiny shoves.

"Such a strong swimmer you have become!" he shouted to Will.

"Come join me!" Will shouted back, but Thomas only smiled.

Within the half hour, Will was back in the shallow water, where the vicar waited for him with a large white cotton sheet for drying. Thomas helped Will to a small outcropping of smooth black rock. He stood a few steps from Will, looking first to his old friend, then to the gray restless waves of the sea.

"William?" he said, posing the name as a question. *How do I ask to take over his mission, O Lord?* Thomas asked in prayer. *How can I take his position with his congregation? I do not want to insult my old friend.*

Will looked up, his hair looking like a tangle of corn silk in the wind. "Thomas?" he replied, smiling.

"William, I have a question to pose to you—and I am not sure how such a query will be received. And as such confusion reigns, I have struggled to formulate the most conducive manner of phrasing such a request. Granted, I am not struggling as if with a knotty theological question, but a struggle ensues nonetheless. It seems that—"

"Thomas!" Will laughed, interrupting his old friend. "You appear to have been taken with the spirit of befuddlement. You are as a father to me. You may ask anything. Please, ask your question before the tide pours in on us."

Thomas, flustered into silence, looked down at the sea as it broke upon the rocks and sand. "William, under your tutelage there developed a small group of men and women of faith who gather on the Sabbath at the fort to hear the Scriptures presented. Is not that correct?"

Will turned about, the cotton sheet draped over his head like a cowl of a monk's habit. "Yes, Thomas, that was true."

"*Was* true?"

"Since my wounding, and the attack, I have not yet been back to continue such meetings. Until only a short time ago I had not the determination to continue. And now that I seem to have found my resolve again, I fear that my weakness of the spirit has crippled my witness—at least for the short duration."

Thomas looked at him, puzzled. "But, William, a man cannot lose his witness through a simple bout of weakness."

Nodding, William replied, "I know that I have not relinquished my faith. That transcends all. But those who have been in attendance hold less stick in the words than they do the actions of the one who speaks. I feel as if I have betrayed their confidence in me."

Thomas took a step closer.

"William, what you say is in error. I have had failures of the flesh. If we are human, we have experienced failures and sin. Yet I continue to provide witness to the Lord. It is what he commands."

William looked to Thomas, the sun flashing about his face. "Thomas, . . . could you . . . ? Perhaps . . ."

He let his voice trail away, then turned from the vicar.

"What is it you ask, Will?"

Will reached out and slipped on his doublet, then grabbed at his crutches and faced Thomas. "Thomas, . . . could you teach those few who had been attending? You are much more skilled in teaching the

Word than I. They need training and encouragement—more than what I can offer, Thomas. Could you be their vicar? Could they be your congregation?"

Thomas smiled.

How wonderful thy work, oh Lord. How wonderful is thy plan, he rejoiced silently.

21 July 1644

A huge pile of blackened stones and boulders, twisted metal, shattered timbers, and tattered and burnt cloth and canvas was piled in the middle of the parade grounds of the fort. Laborers had spent the period following the pirate attack clearing debris from Fort Charles.

Armed conflict wreaked havoc not only on people, but on their material goods, their homes, and structures as well. Explosions and cannon fire tore hulking gaps in walls and foundations; timbers and supports were set to the torch, buildings and sheds reduced to rubble.

It was hardly what Vicar Thomas Mayhew, ordained of the Church of England, would have ever imagined as his cathedral. Yet during life as a man of the cloth, he had preached in a humble country church, on a bleak and barren Scottish isle, within the blackness of a prison, under the open skies of a jungle island, and now, in the debris-strewn parade grounds of the fort at Bridgetown, Barbados. "The surroundings make little difference to the Almighty," he whispered to himself.

Church services were being resumed in the fort—services for those who would not usually be welcomed among the more refined and cultured members of Barbados society who met at St. Michael's. Thomas asked if Luke would spread the word among the poor whites, called "red legs" on the island, and the blackamoors, the small coterie of ex-slaves, and the mulattos who scratched out a living. Thomas asked William to inform all others who had at one time been in attendance at Will's services that they would be resuming on the Sabbath.

The bell of St. Michael's rang out for the Matins service on Sunday. Thomas decided that its clarion call would be his call as well. He stood in the mottled sunshine, holding a thick copy of the Scriptures in his hands. Will had surprised him with a gift of a full set of Anglican-styled vestments made by Johansen the tailor—a new cassock and surplice of a lighter fabric for his outdoor church. Will had even procured a somewhat rustic metal cross from a forge tradesman who worked at the chandlery so Thomas would have a new cross to wear for communion.

"A man works best in attire that fits the task, good Thomas," Will said as he presented the gift. "I think it be time that these folk see a proper vicar before them. And that means the garb must be included."

Touched so by the gesture, Thomas had trouble finding the correct words to offer thanks. William had provided so much already that Thomas knew he would never fully be able to repay his generosities.

Before him that day, nearly three dozen black men, red legs, indentured servants, women of dubious repute, and grizzled and weathered sailors sat before him, spread out in a ragged and loose semicircle. William sat at the very edge, his crutches crossed before him. Thomas first thanked them for their attendance and then led them in a spirited rendition of the hymn "All Praise to Thee My God." The proper words were not always employed on the first three verses, and Thomas was sure that blackamoors were simply making them up as they journeyed through the song. But when they came to the familiar last verse, their voices rang out clearly with the words:

Praise God, from whom all blessings flow;
Praise him, all creatures here below;
Praise him above, ye heavenly host;
Praise Father, Son, and Holy Ghost.
Amen.

When the sound of the hymn ceased to echo about the walls of the fort, Thomas began with a short reading from Paul's letter to the Corinthians, which was written in a Roman prison, and tried to explain the theological nuances of the apostle's exhortations. From the glazed and puzzled looks on the faces of the gathering, Thomas realized quickly that such instruction was well beyond their simple needs. Without much of a pause, he began to tell them of his own imprisonment, the peace of God that sustained him in such a circumstance, and what he had tried to accomplish. When Thomas's life became the illustration, he noticed several men leaning forward, as if to catch all his words.

A man within earshot whispered to his friend, "He speaks the truth of that prison—I've seen its bleakness from the St. Augustine harbor."

Within the span of a half of an hour, the vicar finished his talk. He looked about at the faces before him. He closed his eyes for a long moment, then blinked them open.

"Would any of you desire for me to pray for your needs? I would be most gratified if I could take your petitions to God."

He stood, and the loudest noise was a trio of pelicans cawing and swooping down to the beach.

"Uh, . . . Vicar?" one man called out. He was seated near to William. Thomas nodded. "Do you mean, do we have somethin' to ask the Almighty?"

Thomas nodded again.

"I be likin' a prayer for me wife back in England. Be it too far for it to reach and all?"

"No, our prayers will reach that far, for with God all things are possible."

Another man called out, "Could you be offerin' a prayer for me son? He was quite poorly last I saw him."

Another called out, then another, then silence returned.

Thomas bowed his head and began to pray in a loud, clear voice, calling for God's blessing and divine intervention in the requests presented that day. He mentioned each by name and held them all up to God. It may have been the first time any of these men had had such a prayer delivered for them alone—by an honest-to-goodness vicar—in his whole life. When Thomas finished, he stood and waited for a long moment. He saw tears on several faces, glistening in the sun before the men reached up and wiped at their embarrassment with their sleeves.

"Then the grace of God be with you this day. Amen."

It took another dozen moments until they began standing and whispering to each other.

Luke came up to Thomas first, his long, thin fingers offered out in a handshake. "Be good words, Massa Mayhew."

"You may call me Thomas, if you prefer, Luke."

Luke shook his head quickly and sharply. "You be preachin'? I be callin' you Massa." Luke shook the vicar's hand with vigor. "Tellin' 'bout dat prison be most good. Don' trust de words from dem dat ain't been to places."

Thomas watched as Luke strode off, his long legs slicing through the thick grass.

A fine compliment indeed, Thomas thought. *I thank thee, Lord, for this day and the opportunities thou hast granted me.*

■ ■ ■ ■

Vicar Mayhew gathered up his copy of the Scriptures and the single page of notes he had used for the service this morning. For nearly an hour he spoke to those around him, adding explanation to what he had said, speaking of the weather, talking of favorite hymns, discussing from which town in England he had come and where he had served. It was a delightful way to spend the afternoon, in the company of those who were seeking or who had found the Lord. Perhaps their conversation was not as literate and polished as that of St. Michael's, but to Thomas the words uttered by these simple folk were more honest and real than one might hear in a month of Sundays at a more proper and refined church.

What problems these poor people face are not imagined, Thomas thought, *such as where they may find their next meal and if they will ever live a day in freedom again. They are not trivial issues of inconsequential import.*

As Thomas spoke, he had noticed two tall, very thin black slaves who had huddled together at the far edge of the gathering. He had never seen them prior, and he whispered to Luke who they might be.

Luke peered over, craning his neck. "Be from Massa Jewett's," he replied. "Dey be new to de island."

Thomas nodded and made his way toward them. He held out his hand, a gesture most foreign and unexpected between a black slave and a white man.

But I shall not treat them as slaves, Thomas promised himself. *If any man should regard them as brothers, it should be a man such as I.*

They shook his hand with an air of surprise and intimacy.

"You are new to Barbados?" Thomas asked. "And you work on Master Jewett's land?"

Both men nodded.

"And what do they call you?"

The men looked at each other and then back to the vicar. They both gave their names, an odd combination of sounds and clicks, Thomas thought, that he would never be able to duplicate.

Perhaps they will be given names more suitable, he thought, *for I know Jewett's Irish overseer, O'Reilly, would never be able to pronounce these names—sober or otherwise.*

"I welcome you both. I am glad that you have used your precious free time to attend this church."

Both men smiled and nodded vigorously.

"Massa Vicar," the taller man asked, his voice round and soft, laboring to pronounce the English words correctly, "be it true 'bout dis Jesus—dat he want ebery man to be free?"

Thomas nodded in return. "Christ did come to earth to set us all free from our sins. We do have freedom in his love."

"He be wantin' to have de heart free?"

Thomas screwed up his eyes tight, trying to understand the question.

"Well," he replied, "that would be correct. Your heart has to be free to find his love. Yes, that would be the truth."

The taller man turned to the other and chattered at him in a high-pitched series of sounds, whistles, and clicks.

They both nodded again.

"Massa Vicar, dat what we want. Be free wit' dis Jesus. Set us free. Dat what we want."

Thomas looked surprised. *Two converts—so soon?* he thought.

"Now?" he said, pointing to himself and then the pair of them.

They looked confused, then smiled.

"Not dis day, next day we here. Dat when."

Thomas extended his hand again and shook both of their hands vigorously. "Next Sunday, then. We can set a baptism service for next Sunday. That would be simply wonderful."

"We be free den dat day. We be free."

■ ■ ■ ■ ■

Aidan, using his fork and knife almost as if they were surgeon's tools, pushed at his meat with a fussiness that Emily found curiously charming. They had returned to Shelworthy after spending their Sunday together, first at St. Michael's, then at Will and Kathryne's cottage.

"It was good to spend time with them," Emily stated. "It appears that the additions to their home will be done well before the child arrives."

"Indeed," Aidan replied as he shoved an errant piece of roasted pork to the far side of his plate, behind the boiled turnips. Aidan was a most focused man at the dinner table.

"And it was so good to see Mrs. Cole looking better. I was worried for many weeks following the attack, as she appeared most wan and fragile."

"Indeed," Aidan replied again as he sliced off a very thin morsel of meat, then picked at it, looking for fat.

"And it was nice to see that Luke has found a home at the fort—and that he has doctored so many so successfully."

"Indeed," Aidan replied, gingerly lifting a turnip and peering at its underside.

Emily turned her head and tried to hide the smile that began to creep onto her lips.

"And it was so nice to know that Kathryne plans to take up riding her horse again, as well as bathing in the ocean," Emily added, watching Aidan studiously eye his plate.

"Indeed," he responded, leaning forward to sprinkle salt on his turnips.

Emily smiled, folded both her hands in her lap, and waited, a thin smile on her lips. After nearly a half-dozen silent moments, Aidan looked up, his eyes filled with surprise.

"Horses! Swimming in the sea! When did this happen?" he sputtered. "Why would she attempt such foolish activities—being with child and all?"

Emily suppressed a giggle but let a wide smile light up her face. "Aidan, when at table, you are the most preoccupied man I have ever met. I merely wanted to gain your attention."

Aidan, flustered for that moment, relaxed and smiled. He laid down the heavy silver utensils with a thump against the table, then reached over and took her hand in his.

"And now that you have garnered my attentions, what do you wish to do with them?" He smiled as he squeezed her fine hand with the slightest of pressures.

"Aidan," she began, "I have been on this island for many months now."

Please allow my words to be correct, Emily prayed quickly. She had worried over this speech for weeks and greatly desired to phrase it correctly.

Aidan nodded, assuring her he was indeed paying attention.

"And I have been overjoyed that God has led the two of us together. I can think of no happier choice in my life than when I agreed to marry you."

Aidan smiled again. He had proposed the union nearly a year prior.

"And I have understood both your reluctance and history's intervention that has prevented setting a date for this event—Kathryne's wedding and the unfortunate pirate attack and all." Aidan had explained to her that he was unwilling to so closely follow his daughter's nuptials with those of his own. It would be like lessening their import, he felt. And after the attack, well, no one could be expected to make plans while the rebuilding of the island was going on.

Again Aidan nodded, for he agreed with her words to this point.

"And I understand there may be hesitation even now on your part because of the heavy press of your official duties," Emily said with a low coolness in her voice.

Aidan hesitated and nodded slowly.

"But, Aidan, time is a luxury best spent by the young. When people of our age waste it, I think that practice borders on squandering a precious resource."

Aidan had let his eyes drift back to his plate of roast pork, only half consumed, and just as quickly as he did so, he refocused on Emily's face again. "Squandering a resource?" he asked, a bit puzzled.

"Yes, Aidan—squandering," she replied, the edge to her words growing harder. "We have not the luxury of years and years facing us as do Kathryne and William. The Scriptures speak of redeeming the time, Aidan. I know that this may not exactly apply to our situation, but I am growing . . . *impatient* is not the word I seek, but it is very much akin to that."

Aidan sat up straighter in his chair. He brushed at the crumbs on his brocade doublet. He leaned forward as if to begin speaking, but no words came from his mouth.

"Impatient?" he asked a moment later, now more than a bit surprised. "Impatient?" he repeated again.

Emily took back her hand and folded it primly in her lap and averted her eyes from his.

"Emily, my dear, I am a bit taken aback at your words. Do you not realize that there are so many raging fires on this island in which I can be consumed? I move from one crisis to another, it seems. Keeping the Cavaliers from the Roundheads is problem enough; couple that with the immense task of overseeing the rebuilding of Bridgetown, and add in the nearly insurmountable task to ensure that all taxes and import levies are collected properly. And then there are the land grants to wade through. I daresay I have matters of great import that have taken my attentions. And now, young Kathryne is to bear my grandchild. Would you think I have excess time to debate a wedding date? I think waiting until the birth of the child and its christening would be early enough to begin the discussions."

Aidan snorted quietly, waited a long moment heavy with silence for her reply, then picked up his fork and stabbed at a small crispy piece of meat. He chewed noisily.

Speaking with mouth still full, he added, pointing his fork at her, "I will decide on a date when that time is right and not before, Emily."

He looked hard at her. "It appears that you have spent too much time with Kathryne and have allowed the proper following of English civility to be corrupted. Honestly, Emily, I am much surprised by all this."

Emily did not look at him, merely twisting her lace handkerchief in her hands. She felt her eyes grow liquid and salty. *This was not at all how I planned the conversation to unfold,* Emily thought, her heart racing. *But I speak honestly of how my soul feels. What else could I have stated?*

When she heard his fork hit the plate a second time, she pushed back her chair with a rough, wooden squeal and ran from the room, her flowing gown twirling about her legs, leaving a most befuddled and rattled Aidan and his plate of pork, now grown cold and mottled with grease.

▪ ▪ ▪ ▪ ▪

Later that evening Aidan made his way into the drawing chamber where Emily was carefully stitching a small section of beige linen. It had the outlines of a map of Aidan's home shire of Dorset, and she was finishing up the letter *S* done with a curling flourish. A trio of candles flickered at her shoulder, a reflecting sconce amplifying their thin light.

Aidan stepped into the middle of the room as if he were being announced at a royal outing.

"I have come to a decision," he called, "after thinking about this problem all evening. It has vexed me so that I thought a solution was unattainable."

Emily dared not rise yet, but let her hands and her needlework drop to her lap. She leaned forward.

"You heard me speak at dinner of this nasty business at keeping the Roundheads and Cavaliers separate and appeased on this island?"

Emily began to slump, for she knew that he was not solving their problem, he was solving one of his.

"I will announce tomorrow that a new policy is being made effective. I will call it the . . . the Treaty of Turkey and Roast Pork."

Aidan was smiling and did not notice Emily's crestfallen face.

"Anyone on this island of Barbados who mentions either the word *Cavalier* or the word *Roundhead* will be obligated to provide a young hog or turkey for the consumption at his house by all those who had heard him pronounce the forbidden word."

He looked at Emily, who obviously did not share his enthusiasm.

"I think it a grand scheme," Aidan explained. "It inhibits such seditious discussions, and if they do occur, a party and dinner then ensue. A grand way to keep this ferment from boiling over and scalding this pleasant isle. Do not you think so, my dear Emily?"

And for the second time in a single day, Emily stood up and ran from the room, leaving a most befuddled Aidan in her silent wake.

CHAPTER

8

15 September 1644

Eileen curtsied as Will rode past her, sitting high and handsome on Porter. Will waved a cheery hello but did not stop to chat as he did most mornings. She fought the urge to turn about and stare after him, knowing that such thoughts were to be avoided at all costs. A simple glance, she had found, could lead her into the most serious temptations, especially with one so handsome as Will. She simply shut her eyes tightly for a dozen long heartbeats and tried to clear her mind of the vision of his muscular frame as she listened to the horse's hooves growing softer along the dusty path behind her.

In a few moments, she tapped softly at the front door frame of Kathryne and Will's cottage. She heard no one inside and had yet to assume such intimacies as entering unannounced. She stepped back a few paces and peered in the window of the bedchamber. She saw no movement in the open kitchen window either.

Most curious, she thought. *There has not been any confusion, has there? I am sure Kathryne did not state she would be out visiting this morn.*

From the rear of the cottage, where the final touches of the servants' quarters and kitchen were being completed, Eileen heard a most grating, splintery screech, then a dull thump, followed by a gale of laughter. The obvious joyful enthusiasm could be authored by no one else than Kathryne Hawkes.

Eileen tiptoed around the back side of the house, searching for the source of the amusement. As she turned the corner by the kitchen, she saw Kathryne and Mrs. Cole leaning against the wall, laughing and red in the face. Before them, lying half on the matted grass and half on the stone courtyard, was a wooden sign, the size of a small child.

Kathryne held her hand to her mouth, holding in her laughter, as she saw Eileen come around the corner.

"Eileen, come here and lend us assistance before we dash this placard to bits," Kathryne called out, her words dancing with happiness in the quiet morning. Eileen hurried to their sides. The sign, much like the quarterboard of a ship made from a thick plank of dense cypress, had been carved with boldly scripted gilded letters. The inscription read *Hawkes Haven.*

"I had it commissioned," Kathryne said proudly. "As a surprise for William."

Eileen bent down and took a heavy corner and lifted. It was no wonder to her that it had fallen from the grasp of the two women. As she hefted it upright, Eileen gasped, "Kathryne, you should have no dealing with this type of labor—a woman in your condition and all."

Kathryne stuck out her lower lip and puffed a stray wisp of hair that had tangled in her eyelash. "If I were to listen to everyone's admonition concerning motherhood, I would scarce find the wherewithal to leave my bedchamber. That is what ladies do in England, and we are not in England now, are we?"

The three women crab-walked their way around the servants' quarters and stepped and slid the heavy sign toward the front of the cottage.

"But, child, you try to do too much," Mrs. Cole cautioned. "I tried to tell her, Miss Palmerston, that such activities are just not suited to a mother-to-be. Regardless of the locale."

Eileen nodded and was about to agree again when Kathryne said, "Pshaw, I will do what my being allows me to do. Motherhood or not, I will not sit by and pretend that I am an invalid."

After a moment of silence passed, she added, "My husband has refused to let the wisdom of the day keep him captive as a cripple and has pursued his vigorous activity in the sea. I choose to follow in his example."

The trio stopped for a moment to catch their breath and readjust their handholds on the piece of wood.

"But, child, even the good Mr. Hawkes," Mrs. Cole scolded, "has said that you should restrict such foolishness."

Eileen looked at Kathryne's face and found little to warn her of any dangers. This activity was obviously having no harmful effect upon her as of yet.

As she stared, Eileen realized she had never seen a more stunning transformation on a human's features than with Kathryne over the past months. It was most evident that Kathryne was soon to be a mother— her body grew round and full, and her dresses strained to keep pace with her frame as it adjusted to motherhood. Yet it was Kathryne's features that had undergone the most startling metamorphosis. The sparkling green of her eyes had taken on a deeper, more brilliant shine. Her cheeks were rosier, rich with pink and red hues, with the hint of additional fullness. Her smile, quick to radiate even before conceiving, now seldom left her face. It was a hundred subtle small changes in her bearing that caused Kathryne to no longer be considered a striking woman, or even a handsome woman. It was apparent to all that she was now a beautiful woman, beautiful in the most classic sense and by the most objective of standards.

As the three women finished dragging the sign to the front door, Eileen recalled the import of Kathryne's transformation. Just a week prior, Will had returned for his midday meal and took it on the courtyard overlooking the sea. In the open window frame sat Kathryne, her dark hair lit to a reddish glow by the noon sun, her hands resting in the most maternal way on the growing roundness in her belly, her green eyes reflecting the turquoise waters of the bay before her. Will looked up and, as if seeing her for the first time, stared deeply at her. Eileen, even from her vantage point in the kitchen, could see the love and desire well up in William's eyes as he gazed at the woman he cherished.

Oh, to be adored in that manner, Eileen prayed.

Kathryne's melodious laughter called Eileen back to the present.

"Come on, you two, a few more steps," she laughed. They maneuvered the awkward sign to the side of the door. "Perhaps after the midday meal I can talk one of the craftsmen into abandoning his tasks for a moment to install this above the doorway," she added, stepping back to admire her handiwork.

"Won't William be pleased," she said with a note of finality. After only a moment, she took Eileen by the hand and pulled her toward the door. "We have much to accomplish this morning, and we had best be about our work."

■ ■ ■ ■

By late that afternoon, the fancy new sign hung over the front door to the newly christened Hawkes Haven, Eileen and Kathryne had plowed through a foot-deep stack of orders and ship manifests, and Mrs. Cole was busy preparing a half-dozen spring fowls for dinner and had just begun to stoke the coals in the kitchen fireplace.

The warmest period of the day seemed to affect every resident of the island in much the same manner. Most physical work slowed or ceased, with workers finding a cool patch of shade and resting or dozing until the heat had passed and the shadows began to lengthen.

Eileen and Kathryne rested in the main room of Hawkes Haven, sipping on strong, honey-laced tea that they had allowed to cool to the ambient temperature. Kathryne had nibbled her way through a full plate of flannel cakes, only an hour following a large midday meal of veal and lamb stew, breads, and sharp English cheese.

Kathryne looked up as she reached for her fourth sweet flannel cake and saw Eileen staring back at her, eyes wide with wonder, edging on amusement. She took a large bite of the molasses-flavored sweet, smiling as she chewed.

"I know what your thoughts are," Kathryne said, "for your face betrays all."

Eileen put her hand to her throat. "My thoughts? I was thinking only of the work we have to finish by this eve."

Kathryne tilted her head to the side and narrowed her eyes, grinning widely.

"Honestly, Kathryne," she added, "'twas all I thought."

Kathryne leaned forward, then in a slow sweeping gesture, took the half-eaten flannel cake in a wide arc from her body and aimed at her mouth. As it neared, she opened wide and managed to insert the entire wedge, munching it down with a wide grin. She tilted her head even more, as if asking a question without words.

Eileen raised her hands in surrender and in laughter. "'Tis true, Kathryne, I was not thinking of orders and invoices, but you . . . and your newfound, hearty appetite that causes me great wonder."

Kathryne began to laugh in response. Crumbs of the flannel cake found their way to her lips, and she daintily wiped at them with a small lace serviette.

"As I guessed, of course," Kathryne called out, trying to swallow the last sweet crumbs. "Motherhood has increased so many special abilities in me."

The smile quickly left Eileen's face to be replaced by a more somber, more inquisitive face. Her eyes narrowed in earnestness. She reached out and took Kathryne's hand.

"Tell me about it," she asked, a note of pleading in her voice. "Tell me what this motherhood feels like. I see in your face this . . . glow. I know the Scriptures warn against the sin of jealousy . . . and I fight it so . . . but here I am watching you expand with so much love. . . . I see you with William, and I see his eyes watch you. . . ."

Her voice trailed off to be replaced by a silent, tiny sob. She would not let tears form.

Kathryne pulled Eileen close and embraced her, cradling her head against her shoulder. She stroked the back of Eileen's head and whispered small words of comfort to her.

After a long moment, Eileen leaned back and wiped at her eyes with the back of her hand.

"I am most sorry, Kathryne, for I have no right to be this bold and forward."

Kathryne took both her hands and looked at her most sternly. "Eileen, do not speak in such terms. You have become my friend. And as my friend, you may feel free to enter into my confidences."

Eileen sniffed loudly. "Do you truly mean it, Kathryne? That I am your friend?"

Kathryne nodded. "And a most precious confidante."

As Kathryne spoke those words, at first simply to offer comfort and succor, she realized that they were indeed true. Over the past months Eileen had become a most treasured friend. The dawning of that awareness surprised Kathryne, for at one time she would have thought that becoming intimate with a woman with such a past would be an anathema, and a situation that any woman of breeding would have run from in shock and disdain.

But it was true. Eileen's open and honest ways and her earnest desire to see her life transformed into one of service to God had changed all that. Kathryne looked at her friend's eyes, liquid with tears and longing. She took Eileen's hands and placed them, almost reverently, on her swollen belly, palms flat against the roundness. In a moment, Eileen felt the kick of the child growing in Kathryne's womb. Her reaction, like the reaction of Will so many weeks prior, was that of eye-widening wonder.

Eileen's eyes crinkled into a smile. "Does that happen often?" she whispered.

Kathryne leaned forward and whispered back, "All the time. The movements of the child awaken me from the deepest sleep."

The two women huddled together in awe, almost as if two siblings whispering girlish intimacies to each other.

After a moment of silence, Eileen's face grew serious. She blinked several times, formulating the question that had been burning inside of her. "Kathryne, I do not know how such things be phrased, for I fear that my past has coarsened my behavior and thoughts."

"You may ask in any manner, Eileen, for such freedom is the domain of friends."

Eileen swallowed once and then took a deep breath. "I have felt your unborn child, and an ache tightens my heart."

Kathryne nodded.

"Can a woman of my past ever consider being in such a position as you are—that is to say, with a proper wedding and faithful husband and a home built on faith and all those things? If God has forgiven my past sins, will he allow me to live out my future as a noble-born lady, at the station to which I was born?"

Lying behind Eileen's question was a vast reservoir of hurts, insults, criticism, and outright mean taunting she had endured because of her past style of life. Both Kathryne and Eileen knew that it was a rare woman who could leave such a profession and carry on to anything else, for such a woman was most often branded with her past forever.

Kathryne blinked several times, attempting to formulate a proper response.

"All I want," Eileen whispered in a tiny, choking voice, "is to know what it is to be truly loved."

Kathryne pulled her tight again and whispered into her ear as an older sister, "You can indeed have all that, Eileen. God has forgiven you. You have experienced his love. You know that he, as well as I, have forgiven you. You have been reborn. You can know that God has in mind for you a life that is full of honor in serving him. Perhaps God has much more in store for you, Eileen. You must pray for guidance in finding the proper path."

Kathryne held her close for a long moment, hoping that her face would hide her thoughts. Eileen knew of God's love, it was true. But she desired to know the true love of a man—a flesh-and-blood, living, breathing man.

A deep cloud quickly passed over Kathryne's thoughts. The entire island knew of Eileen's past, and any new settler with the slightest interest in her would be informed in a trifling that she had come from a brothel to this place.

For a man to overlook such a wanton history . . . well, such a man would be a rare man indeed, Kathryne thought.

Mrs. Cole was quietly stirring a large pot of stewing tamarind pulp to make jelly. She could hear Kathryne's and Eileen's voices in the next room. She removed the spoon from the syrup and, from the shadows of the kitchen, peeked in on the two younger women.

In her deepest heart, she knew that Kathryne was still her charge— just as it had been back in England, and Eileen, in spite of her past, had found a place in her heart as well. She dusted a thin coating of flour from her bodice. She remembered her late husband calling her an *enthusiastic* baker, and such a smile she had from his accurate assessment of her personality.

She stood there in the cool shadows and watched as Kathryne and Eileen whispered and giggled and sipped at their tea. The plate of flannel cakes was empty.

No doubt Kathryne's handiwork, Mrs. Cole thought.

She stepped back and leaned against the rough stone arch that framed the expanded pantry, the gnarled rocks, cool and hard, edging sharply against her back. She let her hand slip to her side, and she pulled in on the tight, angry coiled ache that spread from that spot. Her teeth clenched together, tight and quick, in response.

Lord, she whispered aloud, *I beg thee to allow me to see Kathryne's child enter the world.*

She lowered her head and let her hands fall to her side. Looking up into the dark of the kitchen rafters, she added, *Lord, if it be thy will.*

■ ■ ■ ■ ■

Herbert Gleeson was in a most euphoric mood. He had strolled through the slaves' quarters on a Sunday evening one week ago, attempting to be on his best behavior, making sure that he did not snap or shout at any of the darkies that cowered as he went past. He had wanted to hear what they were speaking of and had sat at the far end of the huts, leaning against a palm tree and smoking his pipe. In time, several of the slaves came out and, owing to Gleeson's most convivial nature that night, began to talk softly among themselves.

What had so gladdened Gleeson's heart was the subject of some of their conversations. A few of them, the more able-bodied and strong, would make the long march to attend the vicar's service in the fort, the only place on the island where a darkie and a white man might sit together for any reason. Gleeson saw no harm in allowing them, on their only free day, to go to a church of sorts.

And, he reasoned, *how smart are these darkies? How much of what is spoken can they understand?*

Yet what he heard that day caused his smile to tremble and lengthen. They had talked of the service, of the man in the black robe and his message. They kept talking about being free and how that man in the robe kept saying that Jesus will set men free. As the darkies spoke of that freedom, their faces lit up and almost glowed.

If he be sayin' they can be free, Gleeson thought, *then I'll be tellin' them that I can help set them free. They be listenin' to that—for most certain. It be a sign for them—from the Lord up above, to be sure.*

On and on they had talked, their words faster and filled with deep yearning—a yearning for liberty.

And today, when Gleeson, Bullock, O'Reilly, and Tafert gathered again in the shade of Gleeson's hovel, it was Gleeson who held sway again.

"I tell ya," he said, "these darkies be on our side without no one pushin' 'em. It be the fear of the Lord that brings 'em there. And all to our benefit."

Gleeson related the slaves' conversations he had overheard on the topic of a promised freedom. He told the others that Vicar Mayhew was doing them a world of good by simply raising their expectations and making it so much more simple to lead them to rebel.

"And that be our only job," Gleeson concluded, "to get 'em to put action at the foot of their dreams. They rise up, and we shall be lords of this island in a heartbeat—and we'll sit pretty on top of all that gold."

Bullock asked, "Wot ya mean, the vicar be spurrin' 'em on and all?"

"Ain't ya been listenin'?" Gleeson replied. "It be that the vicar be sayin' that all men should break the chains that be bindin' 'em. I believes the vicar be meanin' breakin' the chains of sin and all—but the darkies don't know that. All they be hearin' is to break the chains. To a darkie a chain is a chain—it not be a sin, for sure."

O'Reilly rubbed his hands together as if in anticipation of counting a treasure chest full of gold sovereigns. Yet it was Ian Tafert who spoke first. "Bein' that I be master at the Spenser lands," he said, his voice throaty and rum-laced, "it be only proper that we look to there for the best spot to raise our hands in battle. If we be takin' control of the gov'nor's own fields, who be then ready to stop us?"

The rest nodded.

"Since it appears that William Hawkes still be a cripple and all—and now with a wife fat and full of child—they'll be no one on this island t' stop us," Tafert added, an unexpected venom in his voice. "No one indeed."

■ ■ ■ ■ ■

That same evening, darkness covered the shanties by the harbor, and Tafert made his way slowly, carefully placing his feet among the ruts and muddy pools that dotted the road. There were no torches lit in this part of town, and he had brought no lantern to light his way. Clouds covered the face of the moon, and Tafert walked, arms outstretched, hoping that he could puzzle his way to the Fields of Eton, the public house favored by his friend and confidant Captain Bliss.

The establishment was woefully misnamed—even a crude man like Tafert saw as much. The interior seldom saw the light of day, nor was any surface inside ever graced with a damp rag or mop. This Sunday eve, after the tenth bell sounded, Tafert slipped in, blinking his eyes several times to accustom his vision to an even gloomier view. When his pupils adjusted, he found Captain Bliss in his private corner, leaning against the rough wall with two full tankards of mobby set before him, waiting for the arrival of his friend.

Even through the most pitched darkness, Tafert could see the twisted smile on the face of Captain Bliss.

"Ahoy there, me good friend Tafert," Bliss whispered. "Take up a chair and be havin' a mobby with me."

The inside of Tafert's heart, dark and black as it was, trembled in the presence of this man, almost to the point of recoiling in fear. But the lure of the drink and the intoxication of revenge muted that small voice.

The chair squealed as Tafert sat down and reached for the tankard, sloshing some of the thick liquid on his soiled hand. He bent down and licked the warm drink from his thumb and forefinger. He avoided looking into the one good eye of his drinking partner. In that darkened room, that single eye grew darker still, luring him deeper, and its black depths often left Tafert gasping for air.

"And how goes the life of an indentured man these fine days?" Bliss oozed. "Be the days filled with pleasant sunshine and the nights with clean linen sheets?"

Tafert winced. He hated being reminded of his desperate and deplorable life, yet Bliss seemed to take great pleasure in posing such bitter questions.

"They be not fit for a dumb beast nor a heathen from Africa—and you knows how I much I be despisin' it all. Why be you askin' every time we meets? You knows it be troublin' me so."

In a heartbeat, Bliss half stood and leaned across the table, spilling his drink with a slosh to the floor. He paid it no mind and grabbed at Tafert's dirty collar, pulling him to within an inch of his own angry face.

His voice was cold, even, and full of vile venom. "You not be thinkin' too much now, Mr. Tafert," Bliss whispered. "You not be callin' me a fool for exchangin' pleasantries. You not be takin' old Captain Bliss for a feebleminded nobleman."

His fingers uncoiled and he slowly sat back down. "I don't take kindly to bein' insulted. By no man, Mr. Tafert, by no man at all."

Tafert's face had blanched. From the corner of his vision, he had seen Bliss's hand slip, with a graceful arc, to the long dagger he kept sheathed at his belt. If anger had been allowed to build for a second more, the blade could have found easy purchase in his gut. Tafert smoothed at his collar, took a deep breath, and tried to relax his knotted shoulders.

"No harm, Captain Bliss," he stuttered. "I be meanin' no harm. It be a long day is all . . . and I be tired."

Bliss's sneer never left his face. "And you be dreamin' of those sheets again, that not be the truth of the matter?"

Tafert nodded, hoping to defuse the man's anger.

Bliss smiled. "I be right again, Mr. Tafert. I be right again."

Tafert nodded again and looked away into the darkness.

Bliss pushed the spilled tankard to the side of the table, then pushed his full vessel toward Tafert. "You can be havin' mine this night, for I haven't the thirst for it now."

Tafert grabbed at it and downed half the tankard in a single swallow, feeling the liquid burn at his throat and welcoming its warming glow that spread in his belly.

Leaning forward, Bliss whispered, "I haven't much time this night. I be sailin' on the dawn's tide. Hear there soon be good huntin' up to St. Kitts." He looked around, making certain that no one might overhear his next words. "I be thinkin' 'bout the plan," he whispered. "And for certain I'll be helpin' as I can. I have sailors who can help do the fightin', and muskets to lend, and swords. But the plans be missin' a few necessary details."

Tafert looked up from his tankard.

"Ye and yer louts say you be takin' over Spenser's lands first. That be wise, him being gov'ner and all. But you must be takin' a nobleman as well as the land. You be needin' one of their own as hostage. Then the Royal Marines won't be stormin' the house with muskets and all, for fear of sendin' a musket ball through a fancy nobleman's weskit. And maybe a noble lady's bodice as well."

Bliss sat back with an evil grin and waited. Tafert listened hard, but was often slow on acknowledgment of any new idea.

"You be sayin' we be takin' noblemen . . . and noble ladies . . . as hostages? Ain't that a hangin' offense? . . . I mean, kidnappin' and all?" Tafert asked in a small voice.

Bliss's eye widened, then his lips curled into a wider smile. Then, without any hint of warning, he swung his right hand in a short arc and cuffed Tafert with the back of his hand across his forehead. The smack of knuckle to skin sounded loud and angry in the dark room.

"You stupid git," Bliss cursed. "You got less sense than a nanny goat. Everythin' you be talkin' 'bout for the last months be a hangin' offense, you toady fool." Laughing now, Bliss continued, "It be fine, Tafert, that you got no sense, for I have sense enough for the both of us. You be listenin' to what I tells you, and we both be gettin' what we be after from all this."

Silence filled the room. Bliss leaned forward as Tafert rubbed his purpling forehead.

"You be understandin'?"

Tafert waited a full dozen heartbeats, then slowly nodded.

"And now," Bliss added, "we be drinkin' to our new plans."

After he swallowed, he added, his voice barely above a whisper, "And you be thinkin' 'bout which nobleman . . . or noble lady . . . might be easiest to come upon. You be understandin' that as well, Mr. Tafert?"

Tafert swallowed the last of his drink and nodded glumly.

9

25 November 1644

A warm, humid wind rattled through the high grasses, now green and lush, carpeting the meadow in front of Hawkes Haven and sweeping down the slopes of the fort and the harbor. The long green blades rustled together in a low murmuring. The clouds grew thicker and slipped from white to gray to hints of black and purple. The wind lifted sand from the edge of the sea and blustered it into the walls and windows of the cottage with a gritty hiss. The morning sun gave way to the dense scud of rain clouds, and an eerie, dusklike darkness settled over the island of Barbados.

Luke poked his head out of the small building nestled against the lee wall of the fort. He squinted into the dim light and sniffed deeply, as if sampling the weather.

"Be rainin' soon," he spoke softly, though no one was near. He looked back at the darkness of his home and softly closed the door behind him, feeling an odd comfort at the solid metallic *snick* of the door latch. It was the first time in his life that he had a dwelling to call his own—a dwelling that was clean, dry, and had a door that closed tightly.

Will had insisted that Luke take over the small two-room stone-and-mortar dwelling originally designed as a depository for the fort's stores and supplies.

"We will not require that space for some time, Luke," Will explained, "and you need a place to do your medicine and healing. It does no one well to have to search you out when they're ill. And it will be a fine dry storage for your herbs and powders."

Luke was not comfortable as the recipient of such generosity, but he knew that what Will said was the truth.

The island now boasted four individuals practicing the healing arts. A barber and surgeon, recently arrived from Kent, had placed his striped pole by a small shed at the harbor and set out to cure most ailments by his well-practiced method of bloodletting. He had learned his trade, it was said, by first practicing on a regiment of Roundheads in London. There was a round, red-faced doctor, Delvin Delberts, who claimed to have attended the Royal College for Medicine in Oxford, but no one had yet seen any diploma or certificate. Dr. Delberts, as he called himself, had taken a room above the Pelican and carried his heavy black bag of saws, knives, and powders with him as he visited his patients. And there was a female healer, a big-boned, cheerful woman from Ireland, Margaret Hughes, who claimed midwifery as her specialty. Only two months on the island and she had already assisted in seven births. Four of them resulted in fine healthy babies, and only one mother was lost during her labors.

And then there was Luke, the first true healer on the island and whom many considered the best of the group. He had not taken to the practices of bloodletting and leeches or of drilling holes in a man's head to let out the evil humors and vapors of the blood.

A steady stream of patients visited Luke in his tiny two-room dwelling. Most of them were of the common folk of the island—the indentured servants, the freed slaves, the sailors on leave. Luke was happy to have the other physicians care for the planters and owners, for he never liked having to slip into their fancy homes under cover of darkness to prevent the wagging tongues that would start with a vengeance if a black man treated a white man.

Luke would seldom even ask for payment, for he had food and shelter in abundance. Just beyond his door was an island growing full of the raw materials for his medicines and poultices. But grateful patients left him what they could—most often in produce or fish, often a chicken or even a goat, depending on the seriousness of the illness and the success of Luke's remedies. In a rickety corral to the side of the house was one of the island's only cows, growing fat and heavy on the thick grass. As a calf, it had been given to Luke when he successfully ministered to a young girl, the daughter of a large landowner, who had been taken with fever.

And now Luke was standing in the wind as it rustled his tattered coat about, snapping the loose ends with a muted slap. He swiped his hand across his face, as if deep in thought, then set out toward Hawkes Haven only a few moments to the east.

He paused halfway between the fort and William and Kathryne's home. The wind whistled past his ears, and he tilted his head to find silence in the breeze. To his left were the harbor and waterfront. On the half-dozen ships riding at anchor sailors scrambled up rigging to tie off sails and batten hatches in preparation for the rains. Carpenters and laborers gathered in saws and hammers, dusted sawdust from leather aprons, and sought out a dry place. Repairs needed after the pirate attack were nearly complete on the waterfront, and three new buildings were being built at the north side along the river.

Luke leaned into the wind now, feeling the sand peck at his cheeks and forehead like gossamer bees. He squinted toward Hawkes Haven. The small original structure was the same as it had been before, a tidy stone home with thatched roof and a robin's-egg blue door. But now, behind the original space, grew two large wings, each a story and a half, built with thick stone foundations, and timber and beam above. The top of the eastern wing, completed all but for windows and paint, held rooms for Mrs. Cole and Jezalee, the new nursemaid, and a nursery. Below were rooms for stores, a cool larder, and the kitchen. The western wing, only partially completed, would hold stables below and living quarters above for servants and family. Will and Kathryne continued to live in the three smallish rooms Will had originally constructed for himself.

With his fingers spread over his eyes to shield him from the sand and wind, Luke loped away, covering the final few yards at a run. A half-dozen steps before he appeared at the front door the large, wet drops of warm rain began to splatter against him.

Kathryne looked up from the bench by the fire and saw Luke's face pressed against the windowpane by the front door. She smiled, waved, and called to Will to let their guest in. Luke whooshed in, followed by a small hurricane of wind, rain, and bits of grass and leaf.

"Be rainin'," Luke declared. He looked about the room, then sniffed deeply. He craned his neck to the side and in a smaller voice asked sweetly, "Be time for food?"

Kathryne giggled. She knew that if Luke ever visited them it was the few moments before the midday meal or just before dinner. His cooking abilities were adequate, but he had the most extreme fondness for Mrs. Cole's culinary skills. Whenever he could he would sit and watch as she prepared her dishes, asking questions, trying to sneak tastes when her back was turned. During his first visits, she was nervous, or befuddled, or a little frightened of Luke and his strange language and ways. But now she regarded him with a disguised affection, treating him like she might a favorite family dog—a dog who at times was underfoot, who didn't really understand much of what she said, who loved being in the midst of things, and loved the people who busied themselves about him.

"Luke, you have timed your entrance well, as usual. Mrs. Cole has just announced that William and I must eat before the storm is upon us." Kathryne leaned forward as if sharing a great confidence. "I do not understand why we may not eat when the wind and rain begin to blow, but that is her judgment."

A loud "I heard that, little missy!" came from the kitchen.

Kathryne giggled again, then winced theatrically. "I believe Mrs. Cole has the best hearing of any woman I have ever known," she declared. She held out her hand to Will. Her time was measured in days now, perhaps hours, and she felt large and lumbering, requiring assistance when leaving either the vertical or the horizontal plane.

Will expertly slipped the crutches under his arms, stood, and took his wife's hand, gently helping draw her to her feet. He had become so adept at using the crutches, with his good leg making such adjustments to his gait, that he often made his way using only a single one. It was but a matter of practice, he said, until he could simply use a stout walking stick. But that was not today. Kathryne was more than a handful, indeed, and might even have been called ponderous. It had taken the best efforts of the new tailor in Bridgetown to keep expanding her gowns so they might fit with some degree of style and proper fashion. Just the day prior, he had delivered two fine silk damask gowns—one blue and one yellow—into which he had added panels on either side for Kathryne's additional girth.

Will held her hand and lent his assistance as they made their way to the dining alcove. She as much as waddled next to Will as he lifted and set his crutches down. The small area now boasted a fine round table, its polished wooden top made of English ash, and its finely turned legs from a length of English oak. Purchased at Kathryne's insistence, it provided her a fond reminder of a formal dining chamber at Broadwinds, her home in Dorset, England.

Luke grabbed at a chair and pulled it up to the table with a great happy grin on his face. He stared hard and joyfully at Mrs. Cole, anticipating a well-prepared and tasteful repast. Will had grabbed at his chair as well and was only a second away from sitting when

Kathryne, standing still at the side of her chair, caught his eye and smiled sweetly.

Will winced and jumped back to her side, where he withdrew her chair from the table and helped her sit. Kathryne had been training Will in the proper table etiquette and other rules for living as a man of class, and he, for the most part, was making great progress in shaking off his customs of the sea. After one particularly frustrating lesson, Kathryne remembered, Will had remarked, "Becoming a gentleman is a more difficult task than I ever imagined. No wonder so many noblemen cease doing any work. It takes all their time to observe their manners!"

After he had helped Kathryne draw close to the table, he then sat, slipping his crutches to his side. Luke watched them both with great eagerness.

Mrs. Cole tottered away from the stove, carrying a great pewter tureen filled with a thick, steaming fish stew. She would have preferred to produce more typically English dishes of roast mutton, baked venison, stuffed rabbit, and chicken, but she had nowhere near the abundance of provisions on Barbados that she had had in England. It might be weeks between fresh beef at the small butchery shop in Bridgetown, with the scarcity of cattle upon the island, so she was forced to adapt to the vagaries of the island's food supplies. She ladled out generous portions, then returned with a plate of cheeses and breads.

Luke wolfed down his food, as if there were a time limit on consumption. Will would have followed suit, but was deliberately measuring his bites and swallows, pacing himself with the small, dainty bites and swallows of Kathryne.

Luke would not speak until finished, perhaps not even until he finished his second or third helping. And on this day, both Kathryne and Will were quiet as well. Will had stayed at home to complete drafting plans for an extension to the harbor and docks. There was no one yet on the island with the skills of a fine architect, and Will found himself the de facto designer of much of the civil works for the shipping requirements of the island.

Luke lifted his bowl to Mrs. Cole with arched eyebrows and a most pleading look in his eyes. "Most powerful good, Miz' Cole," he said, uttering his first words since sitting at the table almost a half hour prior. "Is der more?"

She rose and nodded, taking his plate and returning to the stove. She slipped the ladle into the broth and stirred it, knowing that Luke greatly enjoyed the meat part of the stew more than any other. She lifted the ladle out, filled to overflowing, and reached down to take Luke's plate from the warming nook. And at that moment a pain flashed through her heart like a bolt of lightning on a hot dry night, crackling and hissing through her. She dropped the ladle back into the cauldron, and the plate slipped from her hands, clattering with a crash to the stone floor.

"Mrs. Cole!" Kathryne shouted, as she watched her oldest friend begin to teeter and sway by the hot coals of the oven. Luke was up in less than a heartbeat and grabbed the older woman about the shoulders, pulling her back. Her face had gone pale and sweaty, and her eyelids had begun to flutter.

"Mrs. Cole!" Kathryne shouted again. She looked down and saw that the older woman's hand and fingers were twitching as if responding to the heat of an unseen flame. She tried to push herself away from the table, but the chair legs caught on an uneven stone in the floor and held her firm where she sat.

Will had jumped up and watched as Luke carried Mrs. Cole, now growing limp, to the nearest padded settee in the great room of the cottage. Will got a thick blanket and covered her with it.

"Mrs. Cole!" Kathryne shouted one last time. The legs of the chair screeched shrill and splintery in the adjoining room as she pushed back from the table, the chair tipping and crashing hard to the floor. She stood at the archway to the great room and watched as Will slipped a firm satin cushion under Mrs. Cole's head and Luke knelt close, staring into her eyes, holding one of her eyelids open.

"Is she . . . ?" Kathryne whispered, afraid to complete the terrifying thought.

Will shook his head no. "She has just fainted, I am sure, Kathryne. Luke, she is still breathing, is she not?"

Luke nodded. "It be faintin'. Dat's all it be," he declared, hoping to convince himself as well. "Luke say it be faintin'."

Will put his hand on Luke's shoulder. "Luke, run to the fort and fetch Toller and Salis and Mooren. Bring a stretcher back with you. We will need to carry her up to her bedchamber."

Luke nodded. "I fetch my bag, Massa Will. She be needin' medicines now."

Luke slipped out the door into the rain, now falling faster and harder in heavy, thumping drops.

Will cradled Mrs. Cole's head in his right hand. He took her hand in his. Bending close to her ear, he whispered, "Mrs. Cole? . . . Mrs. Cole? Can you hear me?" He felt the barest of squeezes against his hand. "Squeeze my hand again if you can hear me."

Again she responded with a weak grip about his hand.

"Is there anything that pains you?" Will whispered.

She turned her head from side to side with an agonizing slowness, her eyes still tight and closed.

"Luke will be back, Mrs. Cole," Will comforted the old faithful servant. "He will have medicines with him. You will see. You will be fine."

All the while William knelt there, Kathryne remained standing, her fingers clenched about the stone arch, her knuckles near white from the pressure.

At first, Will did not hear the words. They were like a whisper from across a vast room.

"William . . ."

He did not leave Mrs. Cole's side.

"William . . . ," came the voice again.

In the time it takes a flash of lightning to spark, Will's head spun to the left. It was Kathryne speaking in a mouse-soft voice, calling his name. Her one hand was clutching fiercely at the archway, the other hand cupped her protruding belly, trying to draw it closer.

"William . . . ," she called again, her eyes growing hazy and unfocused. "I think the baby is coming."

She winced, her eyes tight and closed, her brow lined with pain. Despite the chill in the air, small beads of sweat began to glisten on her forehead. She began to bend at the waist, as if a deep part of her was twisting, coiling and uncoiling. Her hand clutched harder at the stone, her delicate fingernails scraping and tearing at the cold rock, as they scrabbled to maintain the grip that held her upright. Her shoulders began to weave, and her knees trembled beneath the folds of her elegant blue gown.

"Kathryne!" Will shouted, looking helpless and confused.

The small feminine hand in Will's, lined with evidences of age and work, squeezed his fingers so tight that his vision spun. Mrs. Cole was mumbling, her lips moving like an aspen leaf in a faint breeze.

Eyes wide and panicked, he leaned closer.

"Go to her, William. I am in no pain." Her words were barely audible over the wind and spattering of the rain. She was pleading with her eyes that Will leave her and tend to his wife.

"William . . . ," Kathryne moaned, her voice frightened.

With a gentleness, Will laid Mrs. Cole's head down, letting it rest on the fine pillow, and leapt to the side of his wife. But he did not hear the last few words Mrs. Cole uttered before she closed her eyes again.

"Lord," she called out, her voice no louder than the beat of a moth's wings. "Let my old eyes see that child before I go. Please, Lord, this is my last prayer."

A clap of thunder boomed across the ocean and rattled against the roof.

"I beg you."

Luke and three blackamoors charged through the rains, now whipping about the open field with a hostile fierceness. The three men carried a large stretcher while Luke carried a heavy bag filled with every potion and herb he knew to be effective with such collapses as he had just witnessed.

They reached the stone porch of Hawkes Haven, the rain already puddling about their ankles, then stopped. It was a startling sound that stopped them—a screech, like the noise that God might make as he ripped through a celestial curtain.

Luke shuddered, a thin sliver of terror shooting up his back, and he launched himself at the doorway. He threw it open and could see Mrs. Cole, lying on the settee, still and at rest. That was not the source of such a scream. Luke's eyes darted about the room. In the archway were two huddled figures, and in an instant Luke's heart jumped hard in his chest. Will, on his knees next to his wife, turned to Luke. His face was a blank mask of panic. He lifted up his hand in a gesture of supplication.

"Luke," he choked out, "you must help."

Will stopped, frozen. His eyes fell to his own hand before him and stared at it for a long moment. As if powered by another being, he drew the hand slowly across his chest, across the light fabric of his doublet. Each finger left a thick trail of blood.

"Luke, . . . please . . ."

Luke called out to Toller and Mooren while pointing to Mrs. Cole. "Take dat lady to her sleepin' room." To Salis he handed a heavy pouch of red, coarse leaf and bark. "You boil dis in water till it sink. Den you make dat lady drink!"

As they hurried about to complete their orders, Luke knelt beside Will and Kathryne. Kathryne was crying out softly, her hands clenching and unclenching.

"You be fine, Lady Kat'," Luke sang out. "Dat baby be comin', dat's all."

Luke leaned to Will. "Massa Will," he whispered, "she best be put in de bed. No baby wants be born on dis cold floor."

Luke slipped his arms under her and scooped her up. *She be so light an' frail,* he thought. *Dis be too much for her.*

He settled her on the bed as Will busied himself lighting candles to add illumination in the murky light of the storm.

"Massa Will, she rest some now. I fetch dat healer lady to help."

Will's face sheeted white with alarm and panic. "But you know what to do, Luke!" Will hissed through clenched teeth as he grabbed at Luke's arm. "I have never been in this . . . situation."

"Don't know dat word, Massa Will," Luke replied, trying to pry Will's fingers from their tightening grip. "You be fine. Dat lady be in town. Dat lady will help Lady Kat'."

Luke was edging out toward the door of the bedchamber, but Will had not yet loosened his grip.

"But you are a healer, Luke! You stay with me," Will whispered. "You must stay here with me."

With a last yank Luke wrenched his arm free from Will's octopuslike grip and grabbed Will's shoulders, pushing him back to his wife, who began to call Will's name louder.

"I has to, Massa Will. I do healin', but birthin' babies scare poor Luke. I knows little 'bout what needs be done."

Will's jaw dropped. "And I am to be here alone? With my child on the way?"

Luke nodded.

"William!" Kathryne called out, so loud that both men jumped.

"But, Luke, the blood! What do I do about the blood?" Will hissed, hard and desperate.

Luke shrugged, helpless to offer comfort. For the first time since he had been with Will, Luke now couldn't keep fear from his deep-set eyes. In dozens of battles, in a hundred episodes of broken and torn limbs, Luke had always been unflappable. He had been without fear or trepidation. He could sew up a gaping gash from thigh to knee using a delicate fid and needle, blood spilling warm in his hands, and not so much as flinch. But this day, as the thunderheads rolled above them, and the lightning crashed into a roiling sea, Luke couldn't keep away his fright.

Luke closed his eyes, and his thoughts rolled a thousand miles to the east and a dozen years distant, to the dense greenness of his jungle home in Africa. He saw that image again, the horrifying image he struggled daily to prevent from creeping into his thoughts. He shuddered as his mind now refused to obey his commands and recalled it in full vividness—his wife, lying on the pounded-dirt floor of his hut, a deep red liquid stain spread out underneath her. The baby, Luke's first and only child, had been positioned wrong, and after an agonizing dawning, both mother and unborn son perished. Luke could only kneel at her side, holding her hand, and watch as her life and love slipped away from him.

He knew that his hands could not perform this day, that his eyes could not see past that horrible vision, that Kathryne's blood yielded too great a hurdle for his heart to leap.

"Luke be back wit' dat healer lady. She help Lady Kat', not Luke."

And with that he turned and ran through the front door, his doublet flapping in the gale, as he loped off toward town.

"William," Kathryne called weakly. "It hurts so much, William."

William blinked, then turned back to his wife.

Lord, let me see this child, he prayed, his words the most earnest and heartfelt he could ever recall thinking. It was as if his soul had cried out to God in its own language, for he knew with an absolute certainty that if Kathryne were to perish that day, his own heart would simply cease to beat. *Lord, I ask that thou protect thy faithful servant Kathryne.*

"Kathryne," he called out softly, sitting beside her and taking her hand. "I am here."

She took his hand and clenched it tight, so tight that he could feel the bones in his palm grate and grind together.

"William, why does it hurt so much?" she called out, then screamed so loud that the hairs on the back of Will's neck stood and prickled in response.

CHAPTER

10

As Luke ran to town in search of Margaret Hughes, a bolt of lightning bit down from the heavens and crackled to the top turret of the fort at his right side. The white heat sparked and charred so loud that Luke stumbled and fell to his knees, rolling in the rain-softened mud and pangola grass. He turned on his back, shielding his eyes from the rain pelting down in a torrent now. His vision was still glazed from the first flash when another thunderclap sounded from just overhead, thumping him hard and fast on the chest. His elbows flew from under him, and he lay flattened on the ground. He raised his head only inches from the mud when a second lightning bolt shot from the dark canopy of the clouds and exploded in the exact same spot on the fort's tower. The sound rolled over and away from Luke like a wave on the ocean, and for an instant Luke felt no rain, nor fear, nor wind. His eyes opened wider, blinking to clear the ghostly image of the lightning from them. He shook his head to clear the ringing of his ears. And after a second silent moment, the wind and the rain and the gale returned about him in a downpour.

Luke felt about himself and knew that he was unhurt. And just as sure was he that he had seen a sign from the Lord. *Be two bolt on the same spot. I nebber seen such a thing,* he thought. *Thank de Lord for dat sign.*

He stood up, wiped at his mud-caked knees, nodded to himself, then resumed running toward the harbor.

I sure do hope de Lord tell me what dat means.

The streets of Bridgetown were empty, deserted. The citizens of Barbados had long since learned that a rainstorm on this island was much different than a pleasant shower on St. James's Court in London. Rain and leaves and branches and sand would lash about, biting at eyes and cheeks, chiseling at foliage and paint. During a hard summer blow, the sand borne in a blowing gale could strip trees at the beach to bare limbs in a few hours. When the winds rose and the sun withdrew, everyone— save the slave in the field and the sailor on the open sea—sought solace indoors, away from the gritty gusts.

Luke pounded on the doors at three public houses facing the harbor, calling for Margaret Hughes. At each stop, the results were the same. She had not been seen for more than a day.

"I heard she be at the Carruthers place, midwifing two darkies who be in the family way," gulped one patron at the Pelican. Another offered that she might be at the Lewis plantation; another said at York's.

Back into the gale he ran, a more desperate look upon his face than anyone had ever seen.

She be in bad trouble, Lady Kat', and if I don' find dat lady . . . his thoughts raced in a tumult. *Dat bleedin' not be right, dat's fer sure.*

He was now at the northern edge of town, by the chandlery. The windows were shuttered and dark, and Luke banged and banged. From the small linhay at the edge of the building came a feminine voice.

"Who are you looking for?"

Eileen lifted back the heavy canvas drape that kept the rain from the two tiny rooms she called home.

Luke sort of bowed, half at the waist, half ducking his head. Miss Eileen was a most beautiful woman, and her ivory whiteness had startled him more than once. It would be, he thought often, how an angel would look, her curved smile as gracious as if from heaven.

Luke pawed at the ground, his bare feet covered with mud to midcalf. "Miss Eileen, where be dat midwife lady?"

"Margaret Hughes?"

"Dat be de one."

A palm frond, carried by the wind, clapped loudly against the roof of the chandlery and fell with a swish between them. Eileen stepped back further, out of the downpour.

"Luke, I am certain I do not know."

"Massa John be here? Massa John know?"

Eileen shook her head no. John and Missy had been invited to the Merriweathers' small plantation for last evening's dinner and had not yet returned. The rest of the chandlery crew was either not working that day or on board the chandlery's new ship, just completed, on her trial voyage around the island.

"Luke, they are all gone. There is no one here save myself. What troubles you? What has happened?"

Luke had turned and started to go, but he stopped for a moment and turned his face over his shoulder, the rain pelting his features.

"It be Lady Kat'. The baby be comin' wrong and she be bad."

He looked one more time into the shuttered chandlery, as if, hoping beyond hope, Margaret Hughes had hidden herself away in the darkness.

"Luke has t' find dat lady, or Lady Kat' be in bad trouble."

He faced the gale and began to run to the north and was soon engulfed by the wind and rain.

Eileen's hand went to her throat in fright. She knew quite well the dangers of childbirth. She knew of a score of problems that could end both lives in a few terrifying and pain-filled moments. Having spent years in the business of providing pleasure for men, she had seen too often the results of that pleasure. Women, often no more than young girls, whose clumsy attempts at ending the life within them left them bleeding and dying on blood-soaked pallets. Women, all bringing illegitimate children into the world, thrashing about in fetid back rooms of public houses. Not all births progressed as nature intended. Or perhaps it was nature's way to allow an escape for those whose dreams and hopes were so muted, so slight, that either their birth or their death provided no great difference.

But this matter was different, Eileen knew. This child was born of love and would grow in love. This child would be different. It was wanted. It would have a future. She clenched her eyes tight.

This child must not perish.

She let the canvas draping fall, and the two dark rooms grew still, save the patter of the rain on the thatching.

"Dear God," she prayed aloud, "let me see this child be born. I ask for thy protection on Kathryne. I ask that she be guarded by thy angels."

She opened her eyes, took her one thin cloak from the wall hook, put it on and tied it about her neck, and lifted the canvas curtain again.

Rain stung at her face. She felt the sand grit against her skin. She blinked, tried to shield her eyes with her hand, and began to take that familiar walk to Hawkes Haven. In a moment the speed of her steps increased, and the cloak billowed out around her like that of a cavalry rider charging into battle.

Luke ran to the north. He was not certain, in the darkness and the rain, of which road led to the Carruthers plantation, but he knew the governor of the island lived only a few miles further.

It be fer his daughter, Luke thought. *He tell me where dat healer lady be.*

And as the rain buffeted him from all sides, he reached the fork in the road—one road leading by the shore, the other leading to Shelworthy. His eyes squinted, filled with the sting of the rain and sand, and his long legs quickly took him past that point of departure from the main road.

It was a mistake that he would not realize for perhaps a full hour.

■ ▢ ■ ▢ ■

Vicar Mayhew stood, miserable, wet, and alone, on a sodden, muck-filled, trenchlike path, a half-dozen miles south of the harbor. Leaving Hawkes Haven only moments after dawn, he had set out to survey the southern coast. Never having walked this route before, he relished the wide expanses and vistas the scalloped shoreline offered . . . the scent of the ginger lilies . . . the profusion of orchids that grew wild under tulip trees . . . the emerald-green, turquoise-blue, and ruby-red hummingbirds darting among the bougainvillea, stopping to feed now and again on the tender yellow blossoms. . . .

The time alone provided him a perfect opportunity to rehearse his Sunday message. He had been meditating on a passage from Ecclesiastes, chapter one, verses thirteen through eighteen, which read:

And I gave my heart to seek and search out by wisdom concerning all things that are done under heaven: this sore travail hath God given the sons of man to be exercised therewith.

I have seen all the works that are done under the sun; and, behold, all is vanity and vexation of spirit.

That which is crooked cannot be made straight: and that which is wanting cannot be numbered.

I communed with mine own heart, saying, Lo, I am come to great estate, and have gotten more wisdom than all they that have been before me in Jerusalem: yea, my heart had great experience of wisdom and knowledge.

And I gave my heart to know wisdom, and to know madness and folly: I perceived that this also is vexation of spirit.

For in much wisdom is much grief: and he that increaseth knowledge increaseth sorrow.

He stopped in the middle of the path, lowered his head in thought for a long moment, then raised his face to the heavens. It was then that he noticed the iron-gray clouds rolling in from the ocean like a waterfall. At the very moment he paused and looked up, the skies opened upon him, drenching him.

He turned and began a much speedier march home. The road quickly descended into a sucking, clawing quagmire of mud. He pulled himself to the side, where a thick copse of tamarind grew. He crawled under the archway their branches created and pulled the hood of his cassock over his head.

"A fine way to spend a Saturday," he said, laughing, wiping at the rain on his face and head.

From the north a thunderclap sounded, followed by another, then another, a great angry beast of sound scudding along the hills, rolling over Thomas.

As the staccato rhythm of the rains increased, Thomas felt a most decided tug at his heart, as if someone, somewhere, was calling to him. He closed his eyes.

There it is again . . . and it is a tug . . . from above, he thought, without truly thinking of the origin, just knowing it was heavenly in its formation. *But does this still occur?* he asked himself. *God does not work that way in these days . . . does he?*

Thomas opened his eyes and looked up through his leafy canopy into the darkness of the noon sky.

"Do you want me to listen, Lord?" he called out into the rain.

That is not it, I am certain.

"Do you want me to pray, Lord?"

Yes, that is what my heart is being told to do.

"For whom do I offer these prayers, Lord?"

And in that instant, in the span of a lightning flash, he saw Kathryne's pale and drawn face before him—but only for an instant.

Without hesitation, he bowed his head, closed his eyes, and began to offer his supplications for Kathryne's protection against an unseen enemy.

■ ■ □ ■ ■

Eileen had not run so far and so fast since the days of her childhood in Taunton, growing up among the privileged and noble born. She was panting hard as she cleared the last small rise that opened onto the wide, flat plateau where Hawkes Haven stood. Winds pushed and riffled at her gown and cloak, the soaked wool weighing on her shoulders. She stopped, her chest heaving, and gasped for air. Her arms battled with the cloak, draped wet about her.

It is heavy with too much water, she thought to herself, and she undid the ties around her neck and let it fall in a sodden heap at her feet. She picked up the hem of her gown, blinked her eyes, and started again to run, her dainty boots slipping and straining in the oozing mud.

Almighty God, let me not arrive too late!

The pelicans and gulls screamed and cawed, flapping in an angry, feathered confusion over the water as Luke made his way along the deserted path that snaked along the shore of the Caribbean Sea. Waves crashed against the rocks, their hungry tongues hissing toward the softer shore where Luke stood, hands on knees, panting, confused, scared.

I be runnin' too long. Don' know where dat house mus' be.

He looked up and crawled over a steep, slick outcropping of sharp-edged coral. Standing at the top, his toes curling around the sharp rocks, he scanned the shore to the north. The rain and mists obscured most of the view, yet he knew this to be wrong, that he had taken the wrong road. Chest thumping, he turned around, toward the south. Rain and wind ripped along the shore, blocking his vision from more than a few hundred long steps.

His heart felt thick and leathery.

I not be doin' what be right, he thought, shutting his eyes to the pain. *Lady Kat' be needin' me, and ol' Luke be scared of a little bit of dat blood. Dat be wrong.*

As he tried to force his thoughts to apologize, the deathly still image of his wife and son flooded back at him, seeping into his chest with such power that he grasped both hands across his heart. Huge tears formed at his eyes and coursed down his cheeks, mingling with the drops of rain. Instead of fighting the image, he let it be, let it hover in his mind's eye, looking at it closely for the first time in decades.

It be time to talk, Luke thought and swallowed deeply. He blinked tight once and knew what he had to do. He must ask for forgiveness. The huge gulf of the past suddenly narrowed, and he was within an arm's length of that pain.

"I be most sorry, Wife. I be most pained dat Luke let life leave you dat day," he whispered over the rising waves. "I be most sorry for dat child. He should be livin'."

Despite the scream of the winds, Luke's thoughts were lost in that swirling, dark image. His wife, just before her last breath, had reached up and touched her finger, wavering and slight, at the spot just above his heart. Her hand fell away, and that slight pressure had branded his soul forever.

"Lord, I be sorry for lettin' dem die. Luke be most sorry."

He could not stop, nor did he try to, the tears that poured from his eyes like a flood.

"O Lord—you be forgivin' Luke for dat?"

For the first time in decades he allowed his heart to interact with the past. Until this day it had been a dull pain there, hidden, scarred over with the years. Yet after all that time, God Almighty reached down and took the hurt from him, and in that moment there began to beat a peaceful rhythm, a rhythm of forgiveness. He gulped, then wiped his face with the flat of his hand.

He knew in that moment that he was indeed given God's forgiveness. He felt it cleanse his soul with a white-hot, searing goodness.

He gulped again and looked to the heavens

"My Lord, Luke be thankin' you. I be thankin' you most kindly."

He lowered his hands from his chest. It no longer hurt. There remained no jagged, spiny thorn gouging in the delicate folds of his soul. He felt at peace.

In a gale, especially in a gale in the warm waters of the Caribbean, all manner of oddities can exist—waterspouts, tidal waves, rip currents, deadly surges sweeping along a shoreline. It was at that moment of forgiveness granted that such an anomaly arose. A sea swell, triggered by the strong, persistent offshore tracks of the wind, pushed a wall of water at the western coast. Luke blinked his eyes through his tears and saw the sea heave and buckle to the west, like a blanket tossed and smoothed upon a bed. The swell grew as it tumbled toward land, grumbling low, marching to the shore. He knew what it was; he had seen it before as it swept driftwood and longboats into a boiling surf. He had seen men swallowed whole, and he had seen men struggle through the fluid walls.

He looked to heaven at the last second.

"Thank you, Massa God, for makin' de pain go," he called out over the incoming roar. "Luke loves you. You 'member dat!"

And with that, the wave crashed first at his feet, then surged over him with a wet beckoning. He felt his feet leave the purchase of the rocks, and he was carried in the sea's liquid enfolding, as if by angels, into the tumbling, swirling intimacy of the sea, into the great, gray, encompassing ocean. He raised his arms over his smile as his body twisted out to sea, as if offering to embrace the Lord of the heavens in gratitude.

Off in the distance, to the west side of Barbados, sailed the *Ivory Queen,* a hulking galleon that leaked more water than she displaced. The captain, an angry, sputtering man from Amsterdam, fumed over bad weather and every natural calamity. He stood at the helm, cursing in several languages at the growing darkness of the clouds. Every bolt of lightning that flashed across the sky would elicit a new string of invectives from the man.

He turned to his port side and peered through the mist and rain. His eyes could barely discern the western shoreline of Barbados. This western passage often offered the calmest waters, so he slipped a few degrees to the east, a few leagues closer to the shore. He paced the wet deck, sliding ever so slightly with each step. His rich red captain's coat, now drenched and heavy, clung to his ample frame like a second, thick skin.

As the boat, heavy with a hold of five hundred slaves from the African coast, plowed through the churning waters, the captain cursed again, looking skyward. He was scheduled to bring his cargo to St. Kitts by the full moon. He had but three days to make his schedule, and this storm was slowing his progress. And every day at sea brought the deaths of another few souls—every one a piece of precious and expensive cargo. He had started west with nearly a thousand of the heathen black men and women and, as of this day, had lost almost a full half. Sharks and great sea creatures followed his ship, feasting on the trail of bodies left in its wake across the ocean.

He cursed again as the ship rolled into the wind. Glancing toward the island, he made certain that his ship did not slide closer than two leagues' distance from shore. And as he looked south, he saw a large log roll at the crest of a wave. What made the sight so curious was the fact that clinging to this log was the form of what appeared to be a gangly black man.

He called to the helmsman to slip a degree further south.

It be only a single blackamoor, he thought as his crew threw a thick rope to the bedraggled man, *but I not be a captain who overlooks any means of increasing my cargo—or my wealth.*

This was no time for polite tapping. Eileen took the door latch and flung it open at a run, charging toward Kathryne and William's bedchamber.

"Luke?" Will called out, desperation clinging to his words. "Have you found the midwife?"

As Eileen stepped into the room, the candles flickered from the wind, the shadows dancing on the dark walls like specters in the night. Kathryne lay sprawled on the bed, her face white, nearly ashen, coated with sweat. Her hands were clutched at the wool coverlet, each grabbing a fistful tight enough to draw out the muscles in her wrist like thick cording, taut below her skin. Her eyes were clamped shut.

Will sat at her side, his hand resting on her brow, his eyes like those of an animal ensnared in the teeth of a trap.

"Eileen!" he called out in a loud whisper, hoping that his tone would offer no further anxiety to Kathryne. "Have you passed by Luke? He is searching for the midwife." Eileen was now at Will's side. He looked up, his eyes pleading. "I pray that he returns soon. It appears that Kathryne requires her assistance."

She sat on the other side of the bed, leaned to Kathryne's ear, and whispered, "Do not worry, Kathryne. I am here. I know something of such things as the arrival of babies. You must relax now."

Kathryne opened her eyes. Eileen could see the fear and the pain there.

"It hurts so much," she moaned softly.

"We will see to that pain in a heartbeat," Eileen said. She stood and looked about the room, then she stared hard at William. "Will?" she asked.

He did not respond.

"Will!" she called out, louder than needed. She wanted to be certain that he paid close attention.

He shook his head as if to clear it from a fog, then looked up.

"Have you ever attended a birthing before?" she asked him.

He shook his head no. "I have been nearby as horses and cows gave birth," he offered, hopeful that such experience might be beneficial.

Eileen narrowed her glare at him, and he near winced in response. "Kathryne is neither a horse nor a cow, is she now, William?"

"I did not mean—"

"I am sure you did not. But that is of no matter now. We must do what we must do."

William's relief was obvious. Someone was taking charge.

"I am sure that neither of you fully prepared for this arrival—for if you had, the midwife would have remained in attendance at this house until the child came."

A sheepish look swept over Will. "But we thought there were many days until . . ."

Eileen fixed him with a second baleful stare. He stopped speaking and lowered his head.

"Since you did not," Eileen continued curtly, "we must act quickly."

Eileen commanded William to fetch a stack of clean linens, some torn or cut into large squares. She ordered a pail of fresh water, a ladle, and a thickness of cotton batting. She told him that she would need the sharpest knife he could produce.

"And it needs to be clean—very clean!" she barked. "And boil a pot of strong chamomile tea—strong enough so you are unable to see to the bottom of the tankard. Do you understand?"

Will nodded, closing his eyes as he reviewed the list.

"And send a darkie to town to fetch a Miss Glenna Heelis. She was in my employ . . . and short of a midwife, she is the most skilled in these matters."

Will was at the door when Eileen called out again. "And say a prayer for this, William. You must do that as well."

He nodded; without saying, his prayers had not ceased the entire afternoon.

The room grew quiet save for the labored wheezing of Kathryne as she bore through the pain. Her breath seemed to match the gusts of wind outside that banged against the roof and shutters. Eileen cooed in a singsong voice and stroked Kathryne's forehead, whispering softly to her.

"Do not worry, dear friend. We are in God's hands."

Kathryne gritted her teeth and nodded. "I need to confess a matter to you, Eileen," Kathryne said, her voice weak.

"You need confess nothing now. You have no sins to confess to me."

Kathryne nodded. "I must. You asked William if he had attended at a birth before, and you scolded him for not having done so." She winced after speaking.

"It was a trifling matter," Eileen replied, ashamed that she had so brazenly scolded Kathryne's husband as if he were a servant that needed upbraiding. "But this is no place for those with such inexperience."

Kathryne managed to wince out a thin, tight smile. "Then I must leave this room as well, dear friend," she whispered.

Puzzlement spread over Eileen's features.

Kathryne clamped her eyes shut for a moment, then blinked them open. "This day marks the first time *I* am in attendance at a birth." She tried to laugh, then gasped as another wave of pain tightened her body, her arms going rigid with the agony. She panted a few times, then whispered out, her words tight and coiled, "I am so frightened, Eileen."

Eileen took her hand and held it firm. "Kathryne, all will be well. I am most certain. We shall make it so together."

As Kathryne closed her eyes again in pain, Eileen fought the fears rising in her throat. She prayed her own demeanor would not cause Kathryne further dismay.

Lord, allow my words to be true this day. Allow them to be true.

"Let us talk of England, of days past, of our growing years at home, shall we, Kathryne?"

"Yes," she whispered as the wave of pain receded.

"Tell me of your time in London, at Lady Emily's."

"It was called the Alexandrian. A most lovely townhouse on Lenox Street, with the most exquisite furnishings," Kathryne whispered. "My days were filled with new experiences—tea parties, even attendance at a coffeehouse, studies, church . . . charity work."

"Charity work?" Eileen prayed her attempt to defuse the pain through idle talk would work. For the moment, Kathryne appeared calm, at ease.

"One harsh winter, we all bundled up to distribute cloaks to the poor. How the cold whipped along those narrow streets."

Kathryne paused, wincing a bit, and tried to lift herself higher onto her pillow. Her words came shorter now, clipped and reedy.

"Lady Emily knew that few of us had rarely, if ever, dealt with the poor. And she was determined that we all would help stem the misery of London's most vile and neglected."

Kathryne stopped speaking and ran her hand over the quickening rising and falling of her belly as her breaths began to come quicker. She sat up a bit and looked in panic at Eileen's face.

"Go on, Kathryne. Take my hand. Don't think about the pain. Tell me about London."

Kathryne laid back down and ran her tongue over her lips. She swallowed once and continued. "We walked over London Bridge, through a mass of shanties and hovels, to an almshouse near the river. The faces of the children made it all worth it."

Kathryne clamped her eyes shut, her jaws clenched together tight and hard.

"The pain is worsening, Eileen," Kathryne hissed between her teeth. "Where is Luke? Where is the midwife?"

"Luke is on the way. He will fetch the midwife with him. And I am here. I will help. Just lie back and listen. I will tell you a story. A story about my home in Taunton . . ."

And as she spoke, Eileen silently prayed that Kathryne could endure the next bout of pain and that she herself would receive wisdom.

I must keep her thoughts occupied, she told herself between prayers. *Oh, Lord, help Luke find the midwife. Help Glenna to come quickly. Please calm the storm—outdoors and within me.*

After sending Toller in search of Glenna Heelis, Will plodded about the rooms of Hawkes Haven, his crutches clattering and clicking, gathering what was needed. On a shelf in the kitchen he pushed and slid jars and small wooden boxes about, shuffling them in his search. He found what he had been seeking tucked behind an earthenware jar filled with sweet clover honey. Nestled in his hand was the small silver blade, given to him by John Delacroix. No more than a hand's width wide, it had been crafted with lethal pride by a skilled blademaker in Toledo, Spain.

"Is this as sharp as required?" Will asked the empty room and drew the blade lightly across the meat of his thumb. Almost without pain a thick rivulet of blood followed the blade's path. He looked at the sticky redness on the gleaming sharpness.

"It be sharp enough," he replied to himself, then felt his heart tighten, for the only purpose of a blade such as this was to separate flesh from flesh.

And Will's flesh began to ache and throb in sympathy, for it could only be destined to be used on the tender flesh of his dear sweet Kathryne.

The storm continued to howl and shriek over Bridgetown and Barbados. Good citizens closed shutters and latched doors and gates. A few souls ran through the rain, dodging from one doorway to the next, hands held above heads, trying to shield at least part of their person from the downpour. The streets were awash with the rain, and mud oozed, thick and viscous, where there was just before a dusty lane.

A small pinnace broke free of her anchorage and crashed with a wet grinding into the far dock of the harbor. A trio of sailors, passing their time dry and drunk in the Pelican, ran woozily to the ship in an effort to tie her to the moorings before she broke apart or demolished the dock as she was pushed and shoved by the winds and tide. Laughing and belching, they managed to rope the stern lantern mast and haul it to relative safety, tying it to the dock. Thoroughly drenched and muddy, they made their way back to the public house to dry out their clothing and finish drowning their cares.

Vicar Mayhew remained under the protection of the tamarind tree as the storm blew about him. Just above his head, tucked into a dry wedge of the tree's trunk, was a nest of vireos, and they chirped and cackled as he prayed. With each thunderclap, they grew silent for a long moment, then doubled and redoubled their calls, as if warning the storm not to draw near this nest of safety.

■ ■ ■ ■

At Shelworthy, Aidan spent most of the storm pacing his office, going back and forth in front of the large windows overlooking the sea. He ignored Boaz's warning that the rain or lightning would streak in an unshuttered opening "jes like dat" and wreck havoc on the structure. The storm and caterwauling of nature had unnerved Aidan and had set his thoughts whirling in a great agitation. His hands clasped behind his back, he paced the dozen steps from end to end of the spacious room. When he walked to the south, he faced the small, delicate portrait of Kathryne as a young girl. He knew not the reason, but this day, gazing at her faint happy smile brought him no peace, only troubled thoughts instead. When he turned and walked the paces to the north, his eyes were pulled first to the angry sea, then to the miniature painting of Lady

Emily that rested on his desk. Prior to this day, the image of any one of these things would have brought a smile to his mouth—but today each brought only a most unsettled, anxious feeling.

Outside Aidan's office, Emily stood by the closed door. Her hand actually rested on the brass knob, and she was but a heartbeat from tapping, announcing herself, and entering. She heard Aidan's footsteps echo in the room, sounding loud, then soft, then loud again. She hesitated again, then let her hand drop. She sighed softly to herself, then turned away and silently slipped down the darkened hallway.

■ ■ ■ ■ ■

". . . and I had a dress of nearly every color imaginable, with lace and—" Kathryne's face twisted tight with pain. "It's coming again, Eileen. Oh, it hurts so."

"Hold my hand, and squeeze it as hard as you must. And think about England."

Eileen continued to pray while she spoke soothingly of the past. *Dearest Lord, I am afraid. Please guide my hands and my mind, and allow me to help my friend this day.*

Eileen could see from the lack of color on her face that Kathryne was becoming weaker and weaker. Despite Eileen's great fears and trepidation, she knew that she had to act within the next few moments if her prayers were to be answered in the manner in which she voiced them to God.

If I am now a servant of God, then I must serve him in whatever circumstance I find myself, she thought to herself, attempting to steel her emotions against the panic where they would have turned without God's guidance. *And to serve him now is to do what I can with Kathryne.*

Within a few moments, the knifing stab of pain subsided somewhat, and Kathryne laid back against the pillows. Eileen removed most of Kathryne's bulky and now soiled clothing. She left what undergarments she could, for modesty's sake. Kathryne, as meek and subservient as a child, allowed her friend to do what she would, then closed her eyes and dozed. Eileen pulled the thick wool blanket from the bed, leaving only a cool, clean linen covering.

Will scurried back in with an armful of linens, the pail, and the ladle, and after depositing them all at the side of the bed, he handed Eileen the knife, handle first.

"It has a most keen edge," Will cautioned. "It is easy to wound with."

Eileen nodded and placed the sparkling silver blade on a small table near the bed. Will took one look at Kathryne, her most beautiful face now bathed in pain. She looked lost and alone, and he hated that he could not offer her comfort and solace. He could protect her from harm in so many ways, but this was a journey only she could make.

Eileen took him by the arm and guided him out the door. "You wait for Glenna. Call out when you see her drawing near."

Eileen returned to Kathryne's side and with the cotton batting and water swabbed away the blood. In only a few moments the cotton and the water in the pail were a deep scarlet.

Will stood, leaning on his crutches, holding the door open a hand's width. He stared out toward town. As each moment passed, he imagined that Toller and Glenna would that instant clear the top of the rise. But all was empty—the tall grasses bent by the wind and rain, the skies dark and growing darker.

Oh, God, Will prayed, *thou cannot allow Kathryne to suffer in this manner. Please, Lord, let this birth proceed. Please, Lord . . .*

His thoughts trailed off and became lost in a whirlwind of images and emotions. He could never describe the terror he had felt as the warmth of his wife's blood had darkened his hand. How totally and absolutely helpless he felt. What was a matter of such immense joy only hours prior—the impending birth of a child—was now a storm of pain and regret. Every moan and cry from the darkened bedchamber felt as if a sharp iron pike were piercing the sensitive flesh of his heart.

This should never have happened. Luke should never have run. What could have scared him so as to cause him to flee in that manner?

Will edged the door open with the heel of his crutch. The wind blasted at his face, and he hopped forward, into the rain, for a better view of the path from town. No one was yet on the way.

O Lord, please help.

He closed his eyes to the storm, the drops pecking at his face, and swore to himself that from this day forward he would never take his next breath for granted. From behind came a shuffling and a hesitant cough. Salis, head bowed, hands folded at his waist, waited until Will acknowledged him before speaking. His face was drawn and somber. Will slipped back inside.

"Is Mrs. Cole . . . ?" Will asked, not wanting to voice his true concern. He spoke her name and felt a sharp twist of guilt, for he had not even thought of her since Kathryne had fallen in pain.

"Dat lady not be dead, Massa Will," Salis said, as if afraid that the truth would be most distressing to William. "She not be dead, but she not be well."

"Did she take the medicine Luke gave her?"

Salis nodded. "It be makin' her jes sleep now."

Will put his hand on the man's shoulder and squeezed. "Thank you, Salis. You have done a good work. I am pleased."

A smile broke on Salis' face. "Dat lady ask . . . ," he said, struggling with the words. "She want to see de baby."

Will tried not to grimace. "If Mrs. Cole should awaken, tell her that when the baby comes, we will bring it to her."

Salis nodded vigorously.

"Dat make happy in her. She be stayin' not dead for dat baby. I jes knows it."

Kathryne licked at her lips, parched to a dry cracking from her labor.

Why does this birth pain me so? Others said the pain is unbearable just a short while and then forgotten. I am certain that this hurt could never be forgotten.

She searched Eileen's face for a sign, an indication of her state, but discerned no panic in her visage. Nor did she discern any encouragement either.

I cannot imagine that a woman would choose to do this a second time—not if she is guaranteed such an experience.

She cried out again, and the pains pushed out in a desperate spiral from her very center.

▪▫▪▫▪

A blowing darkness settled over town. Toller had run from public house to public house, banging on doors, calling out the name of Glenna Heelis. At the Pelican he was told she was at the Hound and Whistle. At the Hound and Whistle, they laughed and claimed she had gone to the Publican. At the Publican, the barkeep, Ellis Smithson, a round and grizzled man with only two teeth apparent in his smile, guffawed, then appeared puzzled and claimed she had been seen at the Rose and Thistle down toward St. John's Bay. Toller ran from the smoky room in a panic.

St. John's Bay be a powerful way up dat way. But if Massa Will say I to fetch dat lady, I best be fetchin'.

What Toller did not hear as the door slapped shut after him was the raucous and coarse laughter of the men who found great sport in their cruel amusements.

Had any of them known it was for William Hawkes that Toller searched that night, their answers would have been most different.

"After all," they would defend themselves later, "it was just a darkie that be askin'. Who be knowin' he was sent by Mr. Hawkes? I thought it just be a darkie lookin' for a whore. And that just ain't done on this island."

12

Eileen wiped at the sweat gathering on Kathryne's forehead like the dew on an English meadow. Another wave of pain broke over Kathryne, and she nearly doubled up in response, groaning and calling out. She grasped Eileen's hand so tightly that she, as well as Kathryne, whimpered through the onslaught.

"This birth is not as God intended; I know that," Kathryne stated, her breath coming in fast gulps. "You must be truthful with me, Eileen," she said, gripping her friend's hand tightly. "Hours have passed. It is now near dusk, and I have no child. Only more pain."

"It is fine, Kathryne," Eileen soothed, her voice unnaturally calm. "Each child enters the world in a different manner. This child has chosen to be most deliberate about its entrance, that is the difference."

Kathryne tried to smile, yet every time she did, another pain stabbed at her insides. Eileen knew that the birth was wrong, but valiantly attempted not to let Kathryne draw any true hint of her grave concern. The baby was positioned wrong. Eileen felt that clearly as she washed the blood from Kathryne and checked on the baby's progress. Eileen had been at more than a dozen births and knew that babies should enter the world headfirst and crying. This baby would not enter the world in that manner, and would tear and rip at its mother. She shuddered. Perhaps nature was choosing not to let the birth proceed at all.

Eileen closed her eyes, trying not to remember two births that had ended abruptly as wakes, neither mother nor child surviving the process. The vision of a large and a small casket flashed before her. It was all too common, she knew, and she felt that her prayers were falling short of God's hearing.

She looked up and saw the edge of the short dagger glistening in the candlelight. Eileen knew that a deep cut into Kathryne's flesh—just above her navel—might provide an opening for the child to come through, but she chilled at the prospect. She knew only the barest of the physicians' arts—and slitting into a woman's stomach was beyond Eileen's practical skills.

She watched, feeling helpless and alone, as Kathryne winced again, her muscles tensing, her arms pulling taut at the linens. She bit hard at her lip as the pain reached a crescendo, and her teeth dug into the flesh, leaving a thin trickle of blood.

Eileen rose up and looked to the window. It felt as if the sun had never arisen that day, the skies graying from pewter to silver. *It must be dusk,* she thought, *for even that slim light has begun to fade.*

And still no sign of Glenna or the darkie. Kathryne screamed once again, and a chill crawled up Eileen's spine.

I cannot wait any longer, she told herself. *I cannot wait for Glenna.* She turned back to the bed and knelt beside it.

Lord, I am so afraid, I do not want to make this decision on my own. But there appears that no other alternative exists. Please, Lord, guide my hand.

She swallowed deeply and stood, taking Kathryne's hand in hers. She sat near her friend and stroked at her hair, now wet and slick from her sweat and tears.

"Kathryne," she began and then grew silent, not knowing which words might lessen her fears.

Kathryne blinked and whispered loudly, "Eileen! I order you to tell me the truth. If this birth is not right, I demand that I be informed." Her eyes blazed with a combination of pain and determination.

Eileen felt her soul loosen, as if freed from her body's constraints for an instant. Her eyes closed for a moment, and her head dropped—almost as if in defeat.

"Eileen!" Kathryne hissed, now edging to anger. "You will tell me the truth!"

She gulped. "Kathryne, forgive me for what I must say."

Kathryne gritted her teeth. "Just tell me. You must."

Eileen blinked again and spoke with her eyes firmly closed. "The baby is backwards. Babies should come headfirst, and this child is not."

Kathryne panted, "And that is troubling?"

"Indeed, sweet dear friend." She thought her heart would break. Without even a conscious thought, Eileen's tears began to flow. "The baby stops, and the mother cannot push it from her. If that happens, then all is lost."

The wind clattered at the shutters. The rain rushed against the windows with a velvet, liquid rattle.

Kathryne looked up. "There is nothing to be done?"

Eileen looked into Kathryne's deep green eyes. Then her vision darted to the sharp glint of silver that rested on the nearby table.

"No . . ."

"What then, Eileen?" Kathryne cried out. "You must tell me!"

"I have seen, only once, a physician take a knife and cut through the mother. The baby is then taken through that cut."

Kathryne tried her best not to show alarm, but her eyes could not hide her abject fear.

"A slice through the stomach . . . with a knife?"

Eileen could only nod. Kathryne knew better than to ask of the probable fate of the mother. A cut such as that would mean only one thing—a sentence of death to the mother for the life of the child. A stomach wound was so often the last wound any soldier or sailor would receive. A gash on the arm or leg oft recovered with scarring, but a blade to the belly was a wound that provided no hope.

"But is there no other way?" Kathryne wheezed. "With every push, the pain seems to double . . . but the finality seems to draw closer. My soul has told me that the ending is near."

She propped herself up on her elbows. Her hair, tangled and wet with sweat, clung to her forehead. Her skin was ashen, yet her eyes blazed with the deep turquoise intensity that rivaled the deepest ocean pool.

"I will not let such a minor thing as pain stop this child from being born. Let me redouble my efforts."

She extended her hand to Eileen. "Help me, Eileen," she whispered. "This child wants to be born. I know it. Let us try one last time."

In her voice was a hint of hope, a hint that Kathryne, in her heart, knew a slim glimmer of a future existed for her child.

Eileen nodded and stood beside Kathryne. "Then, dear friend, let us try together."

She placed her hands on the first swelling of Kathryne's belly, up toward her chest. The flesh felt hard and thick and warm. She spread her palms out wide, encompassing the roundness there.

"Kathryne, when your body next calls out for you to push this child, you must do so with all your power. I will push from here as well. Perhaps the two of us can birth this child."

Kathryne nodded. "We will need wait a moment, I am sure, for the last wave just swept over me." Her breath was labored and rattled in her chest. In a small voice she added, "Perhaps we might pray one last time?"

"I have scarce ceased, Kathryne, but yes, let us pray one more time together."

It was not a time for prayers loud and formal, yet each woman, lips moving, mumbled a most fervent petition to God, a petition asking for the blessing of a new life.

Kathryne began to pant. "Eileen, the wave is come upon me! It is time!" she screamed, bending her head toward her belly, her shoulders arching up off the bed.

Eileen drew in a huge breath of air and, with all the power she had in her arms, pushed hard at Kathryne's belly, harder than she had ever pushed in her life.

Louder than the wind and the gale was Kathryne's voice as she shouted out an unintelligible scream.

"Yes!" Eileen shouted out in encouragement, her hands still pushing, guiding, directing. "It is near! Once again!"

And once again, Kathryne bent into her pain and pushed, a great gasp of air exploding from her lungs as she could push no further.

"Once more, Kathryne! It is near! Once more, please God, once more!"

Kathryne opened up her eyes. The room was darkened, and the candles flickered and swirled before her eyes. For that brief moment, she was not sure if it was the light of heaven she glimpsed or merely the candlelight. Eileen's strong, insistent voice urged her back to her task.

"Once more, Kathryne! You must push once more!"

Kathryne wanted to lie back and let the wave of unconsciousness simply wash over her and carry her to a softer, quieter place with no screams, no pain. She wanted the agony gone and the sweating done and the fear to be put away. But Eileen's voice cut through the fog and smoke of her thoughts. "Once more, Kathryne! You can do it! You must!"

She clamped her eyes shut, felt the linens under her arms, and fought the fear. She gritted her teeth, bent forward, and screamed out one more time.

For a long moment there was silence. So still was the room that Kathryne could hear her heartbeat above the now gentling rain.

And from someplace far away came a bubbling, crying, whispering, excited laughter. It was a heady mixture of every emotion that was common to man, and Kathryne felt incapable of sorting it out.

After a long moment, Eileen's giddy, weeping laughter was mingled with that of a sharp new cry. It was the angry, excited cry of a soul just entering the world, upset that it had suddenly gone drafty and rough.

"You have a son! Kathryne! It is a son!" Eileen's voice was quivering and excited.

Kathryne looked up and saw Eileen wrap a clean linen about a tiny, bloody bundle. She could not keep the smile from her face. She let her elbows drop to the bed.

"A son," she whispered. "Won't William be proud."

She felt detached, as if the pain had been happening to someone else. She knew that the child had torn at her, but her body had ceased to feel that pain. She felt afloat in a cottony sea. Sounds grew fainter and distant, as if she were riding away on a silent steed.

But yet . . .

Another nudge . . .

She placed her palms flat on the bed, ignoring the warm stickiness there. It felt so welcoming to leave the fingers unclenched.

But yet . . .

A nudge again . . .

She turned her head and from the smallest slit in her eyes saw Eileen wipe and caress that small bloody bundle. She could now see the face, clean, wrinkled, and red. It was William, she was sure. It was William's face as an infant.

It was a peaceful time, to simply lie there, the pain drifting away, her mind slipping to nothingness.

But yet . . .

A third nudge . . . this time stronger and more edgy.

No, she thought, it was just the reaction to the pain. It was nothing but normal.

But yet . . .

Another nudge . . .

It took all the effort she could muster just to open her lips wide enough to wet them with her tongue. They felt as dry and thick as the leather of an old bull. Drawing up all her strength, she whispered, "Eileen?"

She felt the bed creak and valley next to her as Eileen sat near. She had not the strength to open her eyes again.

"You have a beautiful son, Kathryne," Eileen said, her words hard to understand through the tears.

"Eileen . . ."

Kathryne turned her head to the side. She felt the smoothness of the linen against her cheek. It felt damp from her sweat. "Eileen . . . there is . . . I feel a strong . . . nudge."

"Nudge?"

"Like there is . . . something not finished . . ."

Eileen stood, still holding the small bundle to her breast. The child had cried soundly for only a moment, then as if it too were worn out from the birth, fell immediately to sleep.

Eileen took a candle and carried it closer.

"William!" she shouted, loud and demanding, so loud that Kathryne arched up a few inches on her elbows. "William! You must come at once!"

In only a breath, William was at the bedside, his crutches under each arm.

"Will, I have no time to explain. Take your son! Keep him warm! Now!"

Will placed the small bundle in the bend of his left arm. With his right, he grabbed at the worn and smooth handgrip of his crutch. He had practiced often with one crutch alone, tucked under his right arm, yet had never felt stable or secure trying to navigate and stumbled and tripped as often as not.

But he knew that this night was different. There would be no stumbling nor dropping of parcels. At this, Will would be offered no second chances.

He kicked at the bedchamber door with his left foot. It slapped open and barked. Will almost stumbled backward. The door had never barked before.

In a flurry of golden hair, Beauregard the dog crashed out from behind the swinging door and bounded back, his tail tucked underneath him.

"Bo!" Will called out, "Go and sit!"

With a careful step and slide, Will traveled the dozen steps to the padded bench near the fireplace and lowered himself down. His crutch fell to the floor with a bang.

The light was dim. The fire had burned to a crush of red embers, and the candles had long ago flickered out. Will turned to the side so the coals lit the small package in his arms. He looked down at the linen covering, searching out the end flap. He felt the tiny person breathe and then wiggle inside its delicate wrapping. At the top of the bundle was a corner of linen, folded at an angle. He lifted it back, and underneath it was the face of his son. It was red and puckered and wrinkled, and Will's heart began to break into small pieces as he first gazed at the tiny and perfect features. He was looking at his son. A breeze slipped past and brushed against that small face. The baby's eyes were unfocused, yet knowing.

Will felt the power of speech leave him, the power of movement halt. It was as if his heart stopped its beating.

The child blinked, and his head turned an inch to the side. William took a breath, finally, and pulled back more of the covering. The child's hands were balled into tiny little fists no bigger than an acorn, it seemed. Each perfect finger was capped by a perfect nail, so small and pink, Will thought, that God in heaven would smile at such a creation.

The child blinked again, and Will bent closer, staring into those deep-green pools. They were the eyes of his mother. Will and Kathryne had been two, and now in a heartbeat their family had grown to three. His heart expanded in his chest to accommodate the love that blossomed there, like a field of lavender after a spring rain, fragrant and reaching to the sky.

"Little one," William whispered, "welcome to Hawkes Haven."

The child snuffled and yawned. Will felt his heart leap as the tiny face wizened tight, then relaxed. The dog, lying at Will's feet, turned his head to the side and cocked his ears.

"We have waited for you. We have prayed for you. And now you are here, little one."

Will reached down and smoothed at the child's downy cheek, the roughness of his forefinger barely touching the ultimate softness there. The child startled an inch, then relaxed, as if he knew the hand of his father upon his skin.

Bo whimpered at William's feet.

"Sit, Bo."

The dog scrabbled to his feet, then lowered his hindquarters to the floor and waited.

"Bo, meet . . . meet . . . Samuel," Will whispered, struggling to find the words. "Samuel Hawkes, meet Bo." He turned so the dog could see the child's face.

Will could not contain his tears at the sound of his father's name. Bo arched his head forward and sniffed at the air about the child. He cocked his head at Will, then back to the baby, then almost nodded and slipped to the floor again, his head resting on his paws, his tail sweeping the floor with a deliberateness.

"Samuel Hawkes," Will whispered, his words soft and slurred with tears and tenderness, "welcome to your home."

He bent and kissed his son's forehead. He felt the child yawn again as his whiskers touched Samuel's skin.

Will believed his heart could grow no fuller. And it was at that instant that the bedchamber door banged open again, setting Bo to scrambling to Will's feet as he lurched upright.

Eileen stood in the doorway, silhouetted by the dozen candles still lit in the bedchamber. It appeared that she had in her hands a small bundle of linens and bedclothes.

"William Hawkes, I suggest you open your arms wider."

Will looked up, not comprehending any of her words.

"William," she demanded, her words filled with care, "I suggest that you indeed follow my request and open your arms."

Will looked down to the face of his son, sleeping in the bend of his left arm.

"William, you will need both arms," Eileen said with a huge smile. "Please, if you would, greet your daughter."

Will's eyes opened wide.

"D-d-daughter?" he stammered, fussing with the linens around the baby in his arms. "But this child is a male. . . ."

Her voice tinted with loving laughter, Eileen walked to his side and sat next to him. "Do not inspect the child, William. It is for certain a man-child."

"But . . . ?" his voice trailed off in wonder.

"*This* child is your daughter," she said as she slipped the bundle from her arms into his. She pulled back a fold of the linen, and before him was the face of Kathryne as a baby, tucked and wrapped into a tight bundle, squirming ever so gently in his arms.

He looked first at Eileen, then at the girl child in his right hand, then to his son in his left, then back to the face of Eileen. She smiled and placed her palm on his cheek.

"God has graced you with twins, dear William."

◼◻◼◻◼◻

The sea gathered Luke to its watery arms and took him in a liquid embrace, pulling him from shore and carrying him to the north. He had no recollection of how he found the log in the heavy surf, nor could he remember how he found the strength to hold on as the waves crashed about him.

And now, a rope fell to his side, and he looked up at the looming presence of a ship, no more than a stone's throw from him. He heard voices shouting to him, and he reached and took hold of the rope.

It would have been best, Luke would tell himself later, to simply have let go of everything and to slip beneath the waves and find his peace.

But he could not know that now, and in a moment he lay wet and nearly naked on the deck of the galleon. The ship pitched and rolled in the tall waves as the winds grew stronger.

The captain nudged at the prostrate form with the toe of his black boot, softly at first, then harder. Finally Luke's eyes fluttered open, and he coughed out a great deal of seawater.

Managing to lift his head slightly, he called out in a weak voice, "Dis be heaven?"

The captain was puzzled for a long moment, then began to laugh, in rough, angry ripples. "This not be heaven for no man," he called out. A sailor knelt beside Luke and fastened a thick iron ring about his neck and snapped a lock into place. A short length of chain and cuffs was snapped on his ankles and wrists, and he was jerked roughly into a standing position.

"It not be heaven fer certain," the captain laughed.

And with that, Luke was pulled down a narrow gangway, past a deck of moaning and wretched men, all chained together, until he reached the bottom hold. Water splashed at his ankles, and he was locked next to a thin shivering boy, only the whites of whose eyes showed in the dank, fetid air.

The sailor stood and laughed as he turned away. "Welcome to the *Ivory Queen,* ye godless heathen. Welcome to hell."

26 November 1644

As the sun crept into the eastern sky, Margaret Hughes traipsed along the muddy path leading from town to Hawkes Haven. She slipped from side to side, trying her best to avoid the largest puddles. Any heavy rains and the roads and paths became quagmires, trapping carts to their axles and leaving those on foot to scramble through the thickening brush at the road's edge.

Margaret cursed and beat at a thorny, prickly pear cactus that blocked her progress. She swung out with her staff and succeeded in knocking the brambling plant to the road, its fragile yellow blossoms graying in the mud. Nodding in satisfaction, she stepped over it, only to sink, up to her calf, in a hidden pool of gray tropical ooze.

She looked up at the sky, at a clean bright day, and shook her tight fist at the heavens.

Only a few minutes prior, she had stopped in at the Publican for breakfast after a long night at the Carruthers' slave quarters. Most plantation owners would not have spent their coins on a midwife for a slave, but the Carrutherses were different. True, they saw it as an investment. Soon, they would have more slaves at no cost to them. And, as proper Christians, they saw it as their duty to provide what comfort they could to their darkies.

Ellis, the barkeep, looking as if he had slept in his clothes for a fortnight, greeted Margaret with a wide, near-toothless grin and began to pour her a shandy ale. He belched loudly, then began to guffaw, as he told her of the darkie Toller seeking out Glenna Heelis during the darkest of the night's storming.

Margaret's eyes widened, and then, with no warning, she reached out with her long, knobby walking staff and clubbed Ellis square on the temple. The blow raised a welt within a moment or two and was sure to be leaving a snaking, purpled bruise by afternoon.

"You stupid git! You loony buffoon!" she shouted, gathering up her bag and staff. "Toller be looking for Glenna to help with the midwifery tasks, you simpleton! Mrs. Hawkes bein' in a family way and all, and you dinna realize what that poor darkie be askin' fer?"

Ellis, rubbing at his head and now feeling a bit lopsided, began to tremble with the growing realization that Margaret was correct.

"I pity ye drunken louts who be sending poor Toller on a wild goose chase!" she shouted. "Ye best be prayin' that Mrs. Hawkes ain't doin' poorly . . . or worse. I know what Mr. Hawkes can do to the sodden likes of ye."

Margaret stormed out, her stomping sounding loud and angry on the wooden planking.

"Wait!" Ellis shouted after her, scared and nervous. "You be tellin' him 'twas but a poor amusement. It only be for a laugh is all. We meant no harm."

Margaret threw her hand in a curt, dismissing wave as she stalked off, not bothering to look back.

"You be tellin' him that, won't you now?" he shouted louder, rubbing at his temple, his voice cracking. "You be tellin' him it all be in good fun. You tell him that!"

In the far booth, in the darkest corner of the room, in a cloud of tobacco smoke at the back of the Publican, sat a stupefied Herbert Gleeson and

Ian Tafert. Both had slipped away from their plantations last evening and spent the entire night, through the darkest hours, drinking and plotting, plotting and drinking. As the dark hours wore on, the blearier did their plans become, the more fanciful and grandiose the schemes.

But upon Margaret Hughes's noisy entrance and exit, both lifted their drunken frames from the table and struggled to gain an upright stance. Gleeson clasped his arm about Tafert's shoulder and came close to kissing his cheek with joy.

"Taffy, me mate," he whispered, his words slurred into a paste. "'Twill be drawin' close to the time. Ya heard what that lady said—the Hawkes child is due soon. We waits until it be here, then we makes our move. I bets Captain Bliss be happy with our choosin' of who we need be kidnappin' and all. I bets he be most pleased with us plannin' to take Mr. Hawkes. I bet he be most pleased indeed."

Tafert did not say a word, but simply slumped to the floor in a wrinkled, boneless heap.

"Soon 'twill be the time," Gleeson said, then tripped over his fallen companion and fell to his knees in a sprawl.

◼ ◻ ◼ ◻ ◼

Will had nearly fallen asleep holding his son and daughter that first night, until Eileen gathered them up and slipped them back into the bedchamber.

"I trust they may be a bit hungry, and Kathryne needs to be seeing them," she had explained as she took them in her arms.

And from that late hour until Margaret Hughes appeared at their doorstep with the dawn, the house slept, still, quiet, and ever so grateful.

13

Margaret strode up to the front door just as the first glints of dawn arrived. She bustled into Hawkes Haven with barely a knock, issuing orders to her left and right. Will nearly fell from the bench in response, trying to rub the sleep from his eyes. Eileen slipped out from the bedchamber, her gown wrinkled, her hair sleep tousled. Two servants and three blackamoors slipped in from the kitchen, hearing noises and voices.

Margaret surveyed the assembly with a most stern and disapproving glance. She clucked her tongue, cleared her voice, then began to tick off her requests—demands, if the truth be told. She called for a breakfast to be prepared in quick time. A proper breakfast with eggs, biscuits, cheeses, cured meats, ale, coffee, and teas. The blackamoors scurried about the kitchen, pulling out tins of meat and boxes of flour, and seeing to the oven's fire. She ordered that the shutters be opened and the rooms aired out. The two servants ran around in a great hurry. After seeing the blaze of activity about herself, the woman nodded and then scurried off to the bedchamber to be at Kathryne's side.

Will stepped to the fire, and as he poked at the embers, the door swung open to reveal a bedraggled and muddy Vicar Mayhew, looking as if he had spent the night in the downpour.

"I have heard, William!" he cried, brushing an errant leaf from his hair. "The child is coming. I passed your blackamoor Toller on the road."

Will stared at his old friend's appearance. Thomas saw his stare and looked down as well. He was most muddy and wet. He held up his hands in surrender.

"Do not ask, William. 'Tis a long and pointless story."

Margaret stormed out of the bedchamber with a great handful of linens and cotton batting in her arms. She was about to speak when she saw the vicar, looking every bit the unkempt country rube. Her jaw dropped; she gulped, closed her mouth, then started again. Passing the linens to the vicar, she called out, "See to it that these—as well as yourself—are boiled clean. We need a new supply in the bedchamber, as well as fresh water and candles. Mr. Hawkes, we will need the breakfast brought into Kathryne as well. I think one of you should send word to her father, who is now a grandfather twice over."

"Twins!" Thomas exclaimed excitedly. Will nodded, beaming.

"In fact, both of you should wash. I would not let either of you in the same room as those beautiful babies," she said, coolly eyeing Will as well.

"How is she?" Will asked, getting to his feet, slipping just the right crutch under his arm.

"Weak as a sick yearlin'," Margaret said. "More women than not would have given up and died last night. She will require her rest, to be certain. But her spirit be that of a fighter. Not many women could I say that about. She'll be makin' a fine mother. A fine mother indeed."

Margaret stopped, almost in mid-sentence, and narrowed her eyes, looking like a hawk about to pounce on the unsuspecting mouse. "I suppose you have made arrangements for a nanny and wet nurse and all?"

Will looked to the vicar, who simply shrugged. Margaret lowered her head and shook it slowly, as if in disgust over Will and Kathryne's lack of planning.

"Mr. Hawkes," she inquired, "did you both realize a child was on the way? Did you fathom any hints that it be comin'?"

Will nodded, silent, unwilling to speak.

"And, perchance, did you think that such timin's are . . . expanded in some way for those in your situation?"

He shook his head no, like a scolded child.

"Then perhaps 'twould behoove you to make such arrangements this day, would not you agree?"

Will hoped she was finished and nodded enthusiastically.

"I trust the immediacy of the situation will give cause to add speed to your steps." Margaret remained silent for a moment and then muttered out, almost as an oath, "Men!" She shook her head and then made her way into the kitchen to supervise Kathryne's breakfast.

Will's eyes were wide as he slipped toward the bedchamber, hoping he could see Kathryne for a moment before Margaret returned. With a quiet step he entered and stood beside his wife. She was wearing a fresh nightdress, and her hair was tied back with a ribbon of green, the same color as her eyes. And now the same color of Samuel's eyes. A second pillow was under her head. She held both sleeping infants in her arms. When Will knelt by her, she smiled. Her face was wan and tired, yet radiant. He put his palm against her face and smoothed an errant curl from her forehead.

"I love you, Kathryne."

She smiled in response.

"The children are the most . . . beautiful I have ever beheld in my life."

She smiled and nodded again.

"Kathryne, we have not spoken of this . . . but may we call the boy Samuel, after my father?"

Kathryne adjusted the boy child in her arms so she could see his perfect sleeping face. She nodded.

"Samuel will fit him well. 'Tis a strong name—for a strong child."

Will leaned over and kissed her forehead. She smiled back at him.

"And what of the girl child?" Will asked.

Kathryne smiled down at that smaller, tinier bundle in her left arm. She turned her eyes to Will.

"We shall call her Hannah," she stated, her voice soft, yet strong. Her voice told him it was a decision that she did not want questioned.

"Hannah?" Will replied.

He knew of no Hannahs in his family or hers, but knew that now was no time to disagree about one name over another.

"Hannah is a wonderful name, sweet Kathryne," Will said firmly. "'Tis a wonderful name for a beautiful child."

And for the next few moments, until Kathryne's eyes fluttered shut, Will knelt there, worshiping at the side of his new family.

■ ▨ ▨ ■

Will had marshaled his servants, as a soldier might, sending one to Shelworthy with the news and one to fetch the physician in town. At the behest of the midwife, one was sent to the Carruthers plantation for the solicitation of a wet nurse, and another was sent to the chandlery to have a second cradle made up in a hurry. His friend John would build it quickly, he knew.

He also sent his two most trusted men from the fort on a mission to find Luke. The black man's absence was most uncharacteristic. Will chose not yet to worry, but knew that virtually nothing could keep Luke from delivering on a promise.

As they all scurried about their tasks, Will slumped to the back stairway and lifted and pulled his way up. It was hard work for a man with only one good leg, and this morning the journey was even more wearisome. He did not want to face the cold reality of the ailing Mrs. Cole.

Once upstairs, he stood quietly by her bedside. She seemed in no pain, and her breathing was slow but steady. He touched at her shoulder, at first gently, then with a firmer hand.

She blinked and struggled to rise, for it had been more than four decades since she had slept past the first light of dawn. Will smoothed at her shoulder, attempting to reassure her.

"Do not rise, Mrs. Cole, for breakfast is being handled."

She struggled to rise on her elbows, caring not that a man was in her bedchamber and she in her bedclothes.

"Mrs. Cole, you must rest. We will handle such details."

She tried to speak. Her mouth moved, but the words seemed lodged in her throat, unable to be brought out. Will knelt at her side and leaned closer.

"Mrs. Cole," he explained, "you were taken ill yesterday with some sort of passing malady. You have rested till now, and I am sure the physician will have you stay abed until recovery comes."

Her face was drawn tight into a twisting of pain and frustrated effort. "Kathryne . . . ," she managed to garble out. "How is . . . ?"

"Kathryne is fine, Mrs. Cole," Will whispered. "She had twins—a boy and a girl."

If smiles could effect a cure, Mrs. Cole would have taken to her feet that morning, for she beamed so bright and fully that Will thought for a moment that her malady had indeed been only a temporary passing seizure. Yet she did not rise further, but fell backwards after only a moment.

"Kathryne is very weak, but she is sleeping now," Will added.

Mrs. Cole was moving her lips, hard and tight, yet only a small groan was audible.

"Names?" she questioned.

Will nodded. "We will call the boy child Samuel, after my father," he said proudly. "She said it was a strong name for a strong child."

Mrs. Cole nodded, trying to smile again but failing. "And . . . ?" she whispered.

"We will call the girl Hannah. Kathryne insisted on it."

At the mention of the name of Hannah, Mrs. Cole stiffened, and in the briefest moment tears began to well at her eyes and cascaded over her cheeks, falling on the coverlet at her neck.

"What is it, Mrs. Cole?" Will called out, louder than needed. "What is the matter? Are you in pain?"

She managed to shake her head no.

"Why are you crying?" Will asked as he took her hand in his and stroked at her frail, graying skin.

"Hannah . . . ," she croaked. "Hannah . . . my name."

───────

The sun had cleared the eastern horizon. The day would be fine and fair. Will took a single crutch and walked his normal path to the shore. He thanked God for every step, for it was the first time he had made the journey using only a single crutch. He had not fallen, nor even stumbled. It was as if those few steps with the child in his arms had taught him all that he needed to know of the process.

As he swam in the chilly waters this morning, he did not cease giving God the glory for such a help—as well as offering his praises for the safe birth of two children.

It proved to be a most tiring day. Aidan and Emily arrived, celebrated, and returned home by midafternoon. Missy and John came, carrying a hastily assembled cradle. Missy began to weep the moment the first child was placed in her arms, and her tears did not cease until she was halfway home to Bridgetown.

The Vicars Petley and Coates made an official church visit and suggested on the morrow, or as soon as Kathryne was well enough for the trip to town, that arrangements be made for the children's baptism. "After all," Vicar Petley said in a cheery voice, "not all infants live their first week. And while these two appear most hale, haste is a most important consideration," he cautioned.

By nightfall, only Mrs. Hughes, Eileen, and Vicar Mayhew remained. Each sat silent, nearly asleep, about the fire in the great room. Kathryne had slipped into a slumber only a moment or two after consuming a large portion of lamb stew.

After supping, Will made his way to Mrs. Cole's room. She showed no improvement over the morning. While in no discernible pain, she could not be roused for more than a moment or two. She whispered a few garbled words, indicating that she would like to see the babies. Will promised that on the morrow he would bring them to her. She smiled a wan smile, then drifted back into a most unconscious state. Will chose not to inform Kathryne of the full extent of Mrs. Cole's condition—at least not yet. He merely reported that she was still unwell, yet resting comfortably.

CHAPTER

14

29 November 1644

At the dawning of the fourth day, Kathryne struggled to sit more fully upright in bed. She winced several times as she did, but a look of determination was most evident on her face.

"I want to see Mrs. Cole," she said. There was no mistaking her words for a request—this was an order.

Mrs. Cole had not improved since that first day. She could manage only a few words, and she had consumed only the barest amount of food since first spilling to the floor. Will had guarded his comments concerning her true condition, not wanting to cause his wife any undue worry or heartache.

Will had seen men on ship take to their pallets with much the same symptoms as Mrs. Cole. Without an exception, each one of those sailors perished within a fortnight of losing the ability to speak or walk. Perhaps the conditions at sea were harsh and more unforgiving, but Will thought the time drew close for Mrs. Cole.

"Perhaps she is not quite well enough, Kathryne," Will said in explanation. "The good doctor Delberts said that rest is most warranted in such situations."

Kathryne snorted. "I would not trust Dr. Delberts to care for Bo."

Will turned and stared at his wife. "Kathryne," he replied, shocked, "that is most unlike you. To have such an adverse opinion of any man."

She continued to gather herself up and was poised to swing her feet to the floor for the first time in nearly four days.

"Forgive me, dear husband," she stated, her voice edged with a new hardness, "but I believe the good doctor has less of an idea of what birthing requires than . . . than . . ." She struggled to find the proper comparison. ". . . Than does Vicar Petley."

Will stared for a moment, then broke into a fit of giggles. It was the first time he had truly laughed in what felt like a month. Kathryne watched the laughter erupt from him and giggled a little as well. As she did, she reached about her belly, smiling and wincing at the same moment.

"Is he that untrained?" Will asked.

Kathryne placed both feet on the ground, looked up at him with a very stern look and nodded.

"That is all I will say about the good doctor, save to prohibit him from returning to this house."

Will nodded.

Kathryne extended her hand and stated again, firmly and precisely, "I will now take my babies and visit Mrs. Cole."

Will was about to protest again, stating his case for rest.

"Now," she said evenly.

Will stopped for a moment, shrugged, and extended his hand to his wife to help her stand.

▪▭▭▭▪

It must have been a curious procession, Kathryne shuffling across the floor of the great room, Will only a step behind, with one crutch under his arm, his other extended for balance. Behind them walked Mrs. Hughes and Eileen, carrying a single child each. And as if forming a gauntlet, there were a dozen servants and blackamoors to each side, holding their breath, waiting to leap to anyone's aid should they stumble or fall or cry out in pain.

As Kathryne reached the foot of the steps that led to the upper floor chambers, she turned and faced the sea of anxious faces, each red with held breath. She was tempted to stamp her foot, though she knew it would be too painful an act to do convincingly.

"Honestly," she exclaimed, "I will not tumble to the floor in a heap. It was just a birth. Do not treat me as a porcelain vase."

The crowd withdrew only a half step. Kathryne turned to the stairs, and they all crowded in after her.

All she could do was sigh loudly and carefully lift one leg at a time up the steps as if mired in a great liquid thickness, her movements slow and most precise.

"Mrs. Cole!" Kathryne called out as she sat on the edge of the bed. "Mrs. Cole, it is me . . . Kathryne."

The room, no bigger than five paces of a tall man, was neat and tidy. Through a small window, light filled the space. A spray of frangipani flowers lay limp on the sill in curly clusters, their fragrance warming and heady.

Kathryne halted the rest of the procession and shushed them back from the room, save Margaret, Eileen, and the two babies. She could hear the small crowd shuffling about in the narrow hallway.

"Mrs. Cole?" Kathryne whispered again as she stroked her cheek with a velvet touch of her fingers. "Can you hear me?"

Mrs. Cole's eyes snapped open, and Kathryne's heart twinged. Her eyes looked like that of a captive, trapped behind a wall that the body could not penetrate. They were the desperate eyes of a prisoner.

But when they focused on Kathryne's smile, a sense of relief and happiness appeared as well.

"It seems like we have not seen each other in a month of full moons," Kathryne confided. She bent down and whispered in her ear. "I have become a mother, and I am most frightened, for I do not have your help and guidance."

The old woman struggled to speak.

Kathryne stared, trying to catch the import of her few strangled words.

"Nonsense . . . be fine."

Kathryne sat back up. "Would you like to see them?"

Mrs. Cole nodded her head a fraction of an inch, her mouth desperately attempting a smile.

First Samuel was placed in Kathryne's arms, and she turned and bent so the tiny new face was no more than a hand's width from Mrs. Cole's lined face. The baby began to coo soft, pleasant sounds. The old woman's eyes traced over the small body with an infinite care, drawing in every feature, every shading, every sound.

Kathryne turned and held out her arms for her daughter. She fussed for a moment, setting the linen blanket just right, adjusting the lace snood on the child's head.

"And this is . . ." Her voice began to crack. "This is Hannah."

Tears again began to swell in her eyes, and Mrs. Cole tried to nod and widen her smile.

Kathryne embraced the old woman, holding her daughter between them so that both could feel the warmth of the infant, the sweet baby fragrance tight to them both.

"I had no other name selected, save Hannah, Mrs. Cole." Kathryne sniffed, trying not to weep. "For I have had no better example of a godly woman than you, my sweet, dear friend."

She struggled, trying to raise her hand to touch the child. Kathryne could see the muscles in her shoulder jump and twitch. She took the limp, immobile hand and stroked it against Hannah's cheek.

"Love God . . . ," she spoke, the words thick and garbled.

"She will, Mrs. Cole, she will," Kathryne assured her. "If there is no other thing I do as a mother, it will be to teach her of God's love and how to serve him, as you have taught me. I promise you that."

"Love you . . . ," she whispered, her voice fading, tiring.

Kathryne handed the baby back to Eileen, then embraced Mrs. Cole fully and totally.

"I love you, Mrs. Cole. I always have and I always shall."

She leaned back up.

"You will get better soon. The doctor says it as well." She wiped away the tears on her cheeks with her palm. "I shall need your help in raising these children."

Mrs. Cole's eyes fluttered. Her head turned slowly back and forth. She was trying to tell Kathryne no.

"Love you . . . ," she said again, the words struggling mightily to escape.

"You will be up in a few days, Mrs. Cole," Kathryne said as she stood. "You will. You shall help raise these children."

And as Kathryne voiced those words, she realized that Mrs. Cole would indeed help with raising her family—for she already had, by providing the example to follow.

Kathryne stood and then reached out suddenly, her arm swinging as if for balance. Margaret caught her and pulled her close. She was dizzy and heartbroken. She was faint and as sad as she had ever felt in her life, staring at the face of her truest friend and teacher in the world.

"I will see you tomorrow," Kathryne said firmly, choking back tears. "We shall talk then."

The old woman tried to nod, and her eyelids fluttered closed. She could not say the words, but would have scolded Kathryne for telling such a falsehood. As true as a bell tolling in the distance, both women knew that Kathryne had spoken only the truth as her heart saw it, not as the way it would be.

A sweaty and tired Ian Tafert, late of the Dover hills off the coast of England, stood and watched as the gang of slaves began their harvest of the cane. Bending at the waist, they raised the sharp machetes over their heads and swung them down with a hiss until they *humphed* into the green stalks. Then they stood and chopped at the leaves and fronds. The cane shoots were as thick as a man's arm and as tall as two men together. The young men would swing the cane to horizontal, then lash out into the air with the blades, cutting each sugary limb into arm's length segments. The women and the old men would scurry out, grab each segment, and carry huge armfuls back to the crushing wheels and the boilers.

Ian hated what he was doing—hated the heat, hated the smell of the sweet, sickening sugar, hated the blackness of the slaves, hated their smell and twisted tongues. He wiped at his brow and spit into the dust.

The only thing that was worse, he often thought, was staying back in England and dying at the hands of some stupid Cavalier defending the king or a Roundhead posing for the honor of the dour braggart Cromwell.

Tafert picked up his thick walking stick and made his way over to the slave closest to him. The black man cringed without knowing why, and Tafert lashed out at him with his stick, catching him soundly in the ribs.

"Faster, you stinkin' vermin!" he shouted. "You be rememberin' that I don't provide no beatin' that ain't been approved by the governor. Remember that for sure."

He swung the stick and hit the slave again, a welt forming across the man's shoulder blades.

"It ain't me doin' the beatin'," he called out again, "it be the governor."

And then he smiled. *In a few months we'll rise up and I'll take what be due me. And these stupid darkies be the key. And that Mr. Hawkes and the rest of those fancy noblemen will be gettin' what's coming to them, fer sure. Won't that be the most pleasant of days.*

15

21 May 1645

Will edged the front door of Hawkes Haven open and wiggled through the narrow opening to the outside. His face winced up as if eating a lemon as the hinges creaked and rasped, filling the dawn air with a rusty squeal. In the humid climate, metals cleaned and polished one day would be rusted by the next. As he eased the door shut behind him, he prayed that the metallic clicking of the latch would not awaken anyone in the house. The metal finger snapped down and Will held his breath. He counted to ten before taking up his walking stick and making his way to the edge of the sea.

No cries, no stirring, no whimpering. He nodded happily to himself and set out with a smile for his morning swim. He walked slowly, but more sure of foot than he had in months. The improvement had been gradual, and Will attributed it to two causes: necessity and practice. Keeping up with the demands that twins, now nearly six months old, had placed on his household was no job for a man who was slow and hobbled. Carrying a child was nearly impossible with crutches, but with a walking stick it was achievable. And Will maintained that his daily swim in the ocean helped strengthen what remained of his damaged muscles. He knew he would never run powerfully again as he once had, nor lithely climb the rigging of a ship under sail, but short of those activities, he endeavored to do all that he had done prior to the bullet tearing into his calf.

He stroked out past the first shallow reef and plowed through the breakers, enjoying the ability to swim through their liquid power. The swells crashed and swirled him about, and he stroked hard, the muscles of his chest pulling taut. He rode a swell back into the small bay and let himself float, face up, his hands slowly stroking the water.

It had been a hard six months, and just now Will was beginning to feel that life was returning to a natural, more ordered existence. The death of Mrs. Cole, so soon after the birth of the children, was difficult for everyone who knew her. She was, without a doubt, the most beloved servant in any house on the island. Kathryne did not cry at the wake or burial, but attempted only to remember the goodness of Mrs. Cole's life and the towering impact she made on one young girl's tender heart. It was a comfort to know that she was at home now in heaven. Yet Will woke a dozen times in the following weeks to his wife silently sobbing in bed, the tears flowing in great volume.

"I have been orphaned twice," Kathryne had wailed one night and collapsed into his arms. At those times, all he could do was soothe and whisper comforts to her, telling her that the godly woman was now living in her reward, without pain, without heartache, and no doubt wishing that who she left behind would pick up their courage and carry on.

Kathryne would always sniffle and nod, then add in a hurt, small voice, "But I miss her so, William. I miss her so."

And then Will's heart would break, and tears would come to him as well.

Now Will turned in the waters, trying to clear that image from his thoughts, and stroked parallel to the shore.

What made the nights so thick with grief was that the sadness over Mrs. Cole's passing was magnified and doubled by the disappearance of Luke. After he had not returned home, Will sent out every available man to scour the island. For weeks on end, every corner of Barbados was searched. No slavers had been in port or near the island that day, so it was most unlikely that Luke could have been spirited away as a runaway slave. No trace had been found of him—no body, no possessions. There had been talk of a series of unusually high waves along the coast that night, and while Luke had had no reason to be that close to the sea, he could have been.

Will's heart remained troubled and hurt; the pain of not knowing the truth of what had become of Luke was indeed a most vexing and disturbing matter. Yet as the days slipped past, the hurt in his soul began to gradually lessen. And while he would never forget his wonderful friend, he was slowly accepting the reality of his disappearance. As sadness broke Will's heart in pieces, God seemed to fill those hurtful fissures with a calm and a peace that Will scarce understood. Yet he knew God's love would heal all, in his own time. And Will would accept that as he attempted to make his peace with Luke's absence.

Will rolled over onto his back again and looked toward shore. He sat upright in the surf and shouted a cheery hello and waved. Thomas was at the beach, bare feet, breeches pulled past his knees, and his white, skinny legs covered to mid-calf by the water. At his side was Bo, who bounced at his feet, barking and pleading with him to throw the stick he had found.

As Will watched, Thomas attempted to placate the excited animal and bent to retrieve the thick section of driftwood. Will smiled, hoping that Bo would not see this as part of their daily game. As soon as Thomas bent to retrieve the stick, Bo lunged and pulled at it. Footing in the shallow cove was never that sure, for the rocks were often coated with a heavy greening of moss and sea grass and would often roll and relocate themselves under a man's weight. Bo leaped, got a mouthful of stick, and pulled. Thomas did not know enough of the routine to let go and held on tight. In an instant, Bo pulled again, and Thomas lost his footing and tumbled headfirst into the calm waters, all the while shouting at the dog in Latin. Will strained to hear the words, but only a few sounded familiar. He smiled when he realized that none of his words were the least bit polite, scholarly, or even repeatable, especially coming from a man of the cloth.

Will turned and stroked toward the shore and in a moment was at Thomas's side, helping the sputtering vicar regain his footing.

"Your beast has attempted one more time to do me in, William," Thomas said as he tried to wipe the stinging salt water from his eyes. "I would venture to think it be at your behest . . . some sort of tropical vendetta against me."

Will laughed, bent to Bo, snatched the stick with a quick hand, and tossed it far down the shore. Bo barked happily and bounded in the shallow water after his prey.

"Nonsense, Thomas," Will laughed. "It is a simple matter of the dog knowing how better to play the game. He knows a vicar is slow and methodical, not bold and quick, like his master."

Thomas was ankle deep as Will spoke, and he laughed in return. When he was at last on drier ground, the vicar turned to face the sea.

The sun spilled its first golden rays from the east over the small bay, and the choppy waters broke the gold into a million separate twinkles and glints, each sparkling as an individual diamond.

Breathing deep, Thomas placed his hands on his hips and smiled.

"Someday, William, I will have you instruct me on the mechanics of locomotion in the sea. It is most intriguing."

Will nodded and smiled broadly. "Perhaps I will simply let Bo give you the proper teaching. He seems to be accomplished at ridding you of your fears of the water."

Thomas sat at the edge of the sea, the small waves curling about his feet. "It is good to see you laugh and smile, old friend," Thomas said.

"It is good to be able to do both," Will replied.

"Truly, a more difficult six months I could not imagine."

"Yet I am sure all has been God's design," Will answered. "For Kathryne and I to weather twin tragedies as we have done—without having the twin delights of Hannah and Samuel—well, Thomas, that course would have been truly through a dark and trackless valley."

"And Kathryne," Thomas asked. "How is she feeling, Will? Truly feeling?"

Will paddled close to shore and extended his hand toward his walking stick, planted in the sand at tide's edge. Thomas stepped toward it and handed it to Will.

"There are times when her joy is complete, as she is with young Samuel and Hannah—feeding, playing, holding. But such low valleys follow those highs, and it is all that she can do to roust herself from the bed in the afternoon." Will sighed as he toweled the water from his hair. "And I have made certain that it is not from fatigue that she suffers. We have the nursemaid Jezalee and servants and maids for all the household tasks. And the children are most pleasant—save for their cries at night."

Will limped toward his clothes. "I am at a loss, Thomas, as to what I shall do. This is most unlike Kathryne."

Thomas shook out his dark cassock, trying to dry it in the early sun. "William, I would not yet be overly concerned. Not that I have much experience in these matters, but back in Hadenthorne, such emotions were most frequent in new mothers. And she did have a most troubling time—with Mrs. Cole, and Luke, and all. I would simply urge you to be most accommodating and kind."

"Thank you, Thomas," Will said as he slipped on his doublet. "That is most cogent advice. Now, will you accompany me back to Hawkes Haven for some breakfast?"

"I would be delighted," Thomas said. He then added quickly, "I trust that you do not consider my appearance here as a request for such an invitation. Though I live alone, cooking skills are not so foreign to me that I must cadge sustenance from a friend."

Will placed his arm around his friend's shoulder. "Thomas, you are family to us. And I must add that I *have* eaten your cooking. If I were you, I would await every morning at this beach for the likes of me!"

Thomas was about to react with shock, but seeing Will's great smile, he laughed and admitted, "You speak the truth, dear friend. You speak the truth."

Halfway to the house, Thomas, without breaking stride nor appearing too interested, asked of Will, "Will Miss Palmerston be in attendance this morning?" He did not look at Will when asking, and his tone was even and calm.

How odd for Thomas to ask such a question, Will thought.

"I am not sure, Thomas," he replied, then after a few more steps in silence, added, "she has been supervising the construction of some furnishings for the great room and has told Kathryne she may be in attendance this morning. Why do you ask?"

Thomas's answer came too fast and too practiced. "She was not at the service last Sunday, and I thought she may be ill and might require a pastoral visit. I merely asked, for I noticed her absence."

Will nodded. "I see."

Thomas stared straight ahead and did not speak again until they reached the flagstone veranda of Hawkes Haven.

Why would he want to know of Eileen's whereabouts? Will wondered, dismissing the first thought that came to mind. *No, that cannot be correct. After all, he is a vicar . . . and she a . . . fallen woman.*

"After you, good friend," Thomas called out, opening the front door.

To Will, the vicar's tone was a few degrees too cheery and bright for the occasion.

■ ■ ■ ■

After a most delightful midday meal prepared by the recently hired cook staff, Thomas returned home, his heart buoyed by the evidences of returning cheer at Hawkes Haven. And curiously buoyed also by the thoughts of a certain Miss Palmerston as they entered and stayed on his consciousness.

Thomas had spent scant time in her presence since the arrival of the twins. He knew that she had taken charge during the birth and had stayed on, on a near-permanent basis, following their arrival to assist in all manner of household duties. In the wake of Mrs. Cole's passing, she was doubly needed and appreciated also as a companion for Kathryne. Because of such duties, her appearances at Thomas's Sunday services were at best sporadic. However, the next Sunday found her in her familiar spot, to the right of the vicar as he spoke.

Thomas found her presence oddly comforting and reassuring, and he felt as if his message was more animated and dynamic than had been the truth previously. After the service, he made a most deliberate point of seeking her out.

"Good day, Miss Palmerston," he said. "It is so nice to see you with us again. Are your duties at Hawkes Haven lessening? Have they secured additional servants and help?"

Eileen, at first averting her eyes, looked up with a dawning smile. "Yes, Vicar Mayhew," she replied, her voice as soft as a stream in summer. "I have wanted to slip out many Sundays before this, but was unable until the new nursemaid was found."

Thomas nodded, noting the steel blue in her eyes as the noon sun caught her face. "Well, Miss Palmerston, I am most certain that the Almighty had you in mind all this time, for as Will tells the story, Kathryne may well have perished if it had not been for your capable ministrations."

Eileen looked away again, uncomfortable with such praise. She mumbled softly, "Thank you, good vicar. William is most kind to have said such a thing . . . and you are most kind to tell me."

The crowd thinned, and most crewmen had gone on to their midday meals or back to their posts and positions. Thomas felt his heartbeat quicken as he looked upon the face of this woman.

"Well then, Miss Palmerston . . . ," he said, then paused as if searching for the proper words to use, finding his thoughts most alarmingly empty. "I . . . I . . . I am most . . . gladdened by your presence."

He then smiled, a frantic tight smile that he held until hailed from behind by the three men who were in charge of storing the vestments and the like. He nodded and half bowed as he made his exit, leaving Miss Palmerston standing alone in the noonday sun.

As he hurried away, unwilling to look over his shoulder for fear that she may still be staring at him, or worse yet, may not be staring at all, his thoughts were a muddied torrent of conflicting pushes and pulls.

Why did I say that? he thought to himself. *Why did I say she gladdened my day?*

He joined the three other men and issued quiet instructions on what should be taken to where.

I do not understand the workings of the human heart at all, he thought, *yet there is a . . . a certain . . . something there. Perhaps I shall inquire of this to William. It is a most puzzling experience,* he decided and determined he would think no more of it until he found suitable advice from one more experienced in such matters than he.

▪ ▫ ▪ ▫ ▪

Her journey from the fort to her small living space would normally be no longer than half of one hour. This day, it was more than an hour in duration, for Eileen stopped and thought, walked, stopped again, gathered some flowers, looked about, sat, walked, puzzled, and slowly, very slowly, made her way to her home.

She so enjoyed the church services at the fort. It was there, on Sundays, that she felt most accepted and least judged of all her days. It was a most freeing experience to worship God with others who cared not about her past but only about the present. Vicar Mayhew had done such outstanding work in making all feel welcome and loved.

But today was different, she felt. *Today was different indeed.*

She saw his face before her. He was not a tall man, so the image did not hover above her like other men's images had done. His eyes were soft and kind, and the lines that grew about them as a spider web were from smiles and laughter and not from anger. She saw his hands before her—thin fingers, gesturing into the air, sweeping through the space to make a point. She could watch just his hands and gain the import of his words.

But this is not what he meant at all, she thought, scolding herself for imagining that such a man could have the slightest interest in her for reasons of her past. *He is a vicar,* her thoughts called out. *And I am not worthy.*

Yet her heart had turned toward him, and she felt its beats increase, bolder than it had been only hours before. *And why would he have said he was gladdened by my presence? Do men such as the vicar say such things without measuring their import?*

Her hand fluttered to her throat and stayed there for a long moment, like a butterfly seeking refuge from the rain.

16

25 May 1645

The carriage clattered to a stop on the eastern side of Hawkes Haven. The two Belgian draft horses snorted from the dust, pawed at the ground, and shook their heads. Boaz set the brake and jumped to the ground, reaching for the carriage door with an ebony fluidness. Aidan Spenser unlimbered himself from the cramped interior, squinting into the bright afternoon sun. He turned quickly, and from the darkened carriage a gloved hand appeared. He reached up and offered his in return, and in a moment Emily stood before him. She fretted for a bit as she attempted to raise her parasol to shield her fairness from the harshness of the sun. Boaz, the tall, ebony driver, waited until the taciturn couple turned the front corner of the house and then closed the carriage door, shaking his head.

It was not until the end of the ensuing meal that Emily actually addressed a comment to Aidan, asking him if he would not mind waiting until she and Kathryne withdrew from the table until he lit his pipe.

"On a hot day as this," she stated evenly, "the smoke simply casts a pallor about the room. Perhaps William and yourself might be refreshed if you adjourned to the rear courtyard."

Aidan looked at Emily with a mixture of surprise and a hint of exasperation. Yet he nodded in a civil manner, pushed his chair back, and motioned for William to accompany him.

As the two men left the room, Kathryne turned to Emily, her eyes opened wide, her palms spread flat and open on the white linen tablecloth, now dotted with tiny spots of consommé.

"Emily, what has occurred between Papa and you?" Kathryne whispered. "Do I feel a note of tension between you?"

The older woman looked at her young friend and tried to smile convincingly, a task in which she was not nearly successful. "Of course not, child," she replied. "All is well."

Kathryne leaned forward and took Emily's hand and squeezed. "This is me—Kathryne—that asks you such a question," she said softly. "You may feel at complete liberty to respond in truth, dear Emily. I am most afraid that I have noticed a brevity in your conversations."

For a single moment, Emily narrowed her eyes. Then with a note of forced brightness, replied, "Why, Kathryne, there is no need for concern. I would state it so if your worries had validity. But they do not. Your father and I are most content."

Kathryne swallowed again. "Has he spoken of a specific date for your wedding? Have you discussed such a matter in recent days?"

This time as Emily narrowed her eyes a darkness swept over her expression. "He has not, Kathryne," she said with a cold finality. "And I shall speak no more of it on such a lovely, bright day as this."

"But, Emily," Kathryne rebutted, "there is need for—"

Emily stiffened and stood without hesitation. "There is no need for concern, Kathryne," she replied. "No need at all."

▪ ▫ ▪ ▫ ▪

Will sat on a rough bench and leaned against the warm stone wall that separated the small stable and paddock area from the rear courtyard and porch behind Hawkes Haven. The two wings of the house formed a protective enclosure about the pleasant space. When the days grew moist and hot, the stillness of the air amplified the heat. Today was such a day, and Will felt the sweat immediately begin to bead on his forehead and gather between his shoulder blades. It had been so many years since feeling the chilling, gray winds of a rainy English spring that Will scarce recalled what it was like to have a shiver jump along his back. He blinked into the sun, closed his eyes, and smiled as the warmth seeped into his muscles.

As a man ages, such warmth feels most refreshing, Will thought to himself.

Only three steps away, Aidan stood fussing with a satin and leather pouch filled with fine tobacco grown on his acreage. In his hand was a fine clay pipe. He tamped and filled and tamped again at the rough-cut tobacco leaf. When he was finally pleased with the arrangement, he touched a glowing coal to the leaf and puffed noisily, the tobacco emitting a tiny hiss and spark. Within a breath, a cloud of smoke enveloped his head in a swirling thick whiteness. After several moments, he stopped, took the pipe in his hand, and turned to William.

"Has my daughter spoken to you of . . . ," he began.

Will blinked, looked up, and hastily replied, "Spoken of what, sir?"

Will, despite everyone's assurances to the contrary, often felt tongue-tied and ill-spoken when engaging in polite conversations with the governor.

Aidan looked up into the sky before responding. "Spoken of Emily and myself and our . . . arrangements?"

"Arrangements, sir?"

Will panicked a bit. He knew that Emily now occupied one wing of Shelworthy, and Aidan the opposite wing. He knew that some viewed the arrangement as chaste and decent, yet there were others on the island that saw it as a stepping-stone to an illicit affair. Will, Kathryne, and anyone who knew either or both Emily and Aidan would soon concur that there were no morals ever in violation, or even near to that.

Did he desire me to comment on who sleeps under which roof? Will asked himself.

"Yes, William, our arrangements."

Will sat forward, then stood and paced, his walking stick clicking with a loud snap against the flat stones. "Well, sir," he began, "of course, you must understand that I know what decent Christian people you and Emily are. You must know that I am assured that you would do nothing that might compromise that standing."

"William," Aidan called out, sharp and edged. "Those are not the arrangements of which I speak. Though I am most gladdened," he said with a slight trace of caustic tone, "that my activities meet with your moral approval."

He brought the pipe back to his mouth and puffed again until a cloud hid his face.

Then what does he require me to answer? Will mused, his thoughts in a jumble. *What do I say?*

"Has Kathryne ever mentioned Emily's stance concerning our nuptials?"

Will opened his mouth, then closed it, then stammered out a reply. "I believe Kathryne has stated that Emily was in favor of them."

The smoke cleared from Aidan's face, revealing a bemused expression. "No, William, that is not the question I need answered," he stated. He puffed again, then continued. "Has Kathryne ever said that

Emily is . . . disconcerted, perhaps, or even unhappy that we have delayed the proposed date?"

Will blinked again, several times in a quick flutter. *Kathryne did speak on more than one occasion that the date has been delayed—but did she ever mention Emily's response to such news?* Will tightened his face in thought and said, "No, sir. I have no recollection of such a concern made public."

Aidan puffed again, nodding to himself, with almost a smile on his face. That is, until Will added, "Though such matters are often not discussed in my presence. I am most often unaware of the more feminine concerns. I suppose I could ask Kathryne if you desire."

A little cloud drifted over the two of them, slipping a darkness about the courtyard. Aidan swept his hand in a small arc.

"No, William, that will not be required," he said as he puffed on his pipe. "Perhaps it might be better if I asked her myself."

17

29 May 1645

Thomas took a short, stubby, nearly dull knife and stabbed at the hard edge of the cheese. It started to skitter from the table, and he held it firmer with his hand and pushed hard until a wedge the size of his fist was cleaved off. There were two plates and a tankard resting at the corner of the table, but Thomas ignored them. He hefted the cheese in his hand and bit hard at the edge, gnawing his way through a very simple breakfast.

He stood in the dim coolness of his two rooms, set at the western edge of the fort's parade grounds. It was a most simple dwelling, of rough wood with an amber and gold color in the planking. The roof, of long thin poles woven with palm fronds, was just at the far reach of his upstretched hand. Opening the door, he looked over at the empty shed in which Luke had lived. He looked to the main gate, open in invitation on this overcast Sunday morning. The bell at St. Michael's had not yet pealed, and Thomas thought he may have nearly a full hour until the first of his motley congregation would arrive.

He chomped again at the cheese and chewed noisily, not caring for manners this early and this alone. As he ate he walked about the living chamber. It held a rough desk of planks with trestle legs. A candle, half burned, sat in a tarnished brass holder. To his left, by the door, hung a simple crucifix, given to him by one of the blackamoors who had carved a simple figure prostrate against the wood; a jagged gash sliced into the dark wood by the figure's face was an expression of Christ's agony. Thomas looked at it as he chewed, then turned back to his desk. There was a well-worn copy of the Scriptures open there, a gift from William and Kathryne upon their return to Barbados. A quill, an inkwell, and a few sheets of coarse vellum also occupied the desk. A three-legged stool was at the right, comfortable for only bouts of short duration. He looked out the window at the shadows chasing across the grounds, bathing the walls and buildings in a colorless gray. A blue bottle, chipped at the edge, rested at the sill of the single window in the main room of his quarters.

Picking up the papers in his left hand, he took another bite from the cheese in his right. He held the papers closer to his face in order to make his thin scribbles visible. Such measures were becoming more frequent to Thomas. He knew his vision had softened over the years. He reviewed the Scripture he was using for his text and read quickly the notes he had drawn. He had chosen a passage from Paul's letter to the Philippians about finding joy in all circumstances.

He finished his review and his breakfast at the same time. Taking only two steps, he entered his sleeping chamber. A small rope bed was tucked into the corner, with a thin canvas and straw mattress covering the roping. Over that was a fine, delicate woolen coverlet, a gift passed on from Kathryne, who claimed she no longer needed the bed covering. A small bedside table held a metal lantern. A four-drawer chest sat on the opposite wall under a small looking glass and held his washbowl and pitcher. A few wooden clothing pegs lined the wall by the door.

He dressed quickly. The cassock that he chose, of the three he owned, slipped over his frame like a loose glove. He knotted the cording at his waist, adjusted the collar and hood in the looking glass, and walked to the front porch, closing the door behind him.

He had still heard no bell and walked to the far edge of the fort, closest to the sea, and climbed up the stone stairway to the top rampart. He walked down the narrow passageway until he came to a gap in the outer wall, to be used as a shooting position if an attack occurred. Thomas used it for a much more spiritual reason. He sat in the gap and tucked his legs up under his wiry frame. For hours he could sit there, unobserved, with a view of the ocean, the harbor, the fort itself, and Hawkes Haven. It was as if all of what was dear to Thomas, all the people and places that he loved, were nestled within the scope of his vision. It was true that his vision now rendered most locations into a softer, hazy image, yet Thomas loved the peace that these few minutes offered him. It reminded him of his practice back in Hadenthorne when he would spend the morning in the church tower, reviewing the expanse of his parish, praying about the boundaries of his little world.

How long ago that all seems, he thought, *and how different a world I now inhabit.*

He began to pray for everyone within the realm of his vision, as well as for all those beyond it. Every Sunday morning, for as long as he could, Thomas prayed and petitioned the Lord on behalf of the people on the island. He spent precious time with his God, speaking to him about those he knew well and those who needed the Lord's hand in their lives.

He prayed for each member of his odd congregation, listing through the soldiers, the blackamoors, the servants, the sailors, the ex-slaves— each person who sat on the grassy hillocks as he preached from God's Word.

As he mentioned the name of Eileen Palmerston, his prayer stopped for a long moment. It was her face that came before his thoughts—her ivory skin so fair and luminescent against the vibrant red of her hair. Thomas blinked, then closed his eyes, his prayer temporarily abandoned. When she was able to attend services she would sit no more than a dozen paces away from him as he spoke. She would stare up at him and nod ever so slightly as she agreed with his words.

Snapping his eyes open, Thomas looked to the gate. He saw no one enter, nor near.

Lord, I ask that a blessing be given to Miss Eileen Palmerston. She is trying to be thy faithful servant, and I ask that thou wouldst give her wisdom and strength.

He paused for a long moment, then bent his head again and continued his prayers about the boundaries of his heart and all that resided within them.

▪ ▪ ▪ ▪

Will never swam on Sunday mornings; he never left the house early to ease away the painful cramps in his legs with a stroll to the fort or the sea. On that day, Will knew better than to abandon Kathryne with all the tasks that the day required.

Standing in the middle of the great room, he was in a quandary over which way to turn first. Should he rush to the kitchen, where little Samuel was screaming at his breakfast despite Jezalee's best efforts to have him consume a third spoonful of porridge, laced heavily with the cloying sweetness of black molasses? It was perhaps an early age to offer solid foods to such a child, but the twins' growing appetite necessitated such an adaptation. Will looked about, puzzled. Instead of offering aid to Jezalee, should he first enter the bedchamber, where Kathryne's voice could be heard, nearly in tears as she struggled to dress Hannah in a proper lace and satin gown?

Both women called for each other, nearly in unison, then after only a heartbeat of hearing no response, called out louder and more insistently for William's attention. He actually took one step toward the kitchen, knowing that feeding his son was much easier than dressing his daughter. But as soon as the step was made, Kathryne called out again, her voice most frantic.

"William!" she called. "Please, I need your assistance with your squirming daughter!"

Will stopped and turned back. *Odd,* he thought, *how the primary parentage of each child shifts on an hourly basis at times. The only time they are both* our *children is that peaceful moment of first slumber.*

"Jezalee," he whispered loudly to the energetic and cheerful nursemaid, "please, if you would, assist your mistress with Hannah. I am no use in tying fancy ribbons and bows."

The nursemaid wiped her porridge-stained hands on her apron and smiled, her wide, white smile against her dark face lighting up the room. "Massa William," she said, nodding as she passed a porridge-encrusted spoon to him, "dat be powerful good news. It be dat lil' Samuel has taken a dislike to what he most liked dc day past. Maybe he eat for you. He be starvin' wit' me dis morning."

And with that she scurried into the bedchamber, her nervous laughter ringing in the morning light.

Will sat in front of his male child, whose face was a pasty smear of porridge and molasses. His tiny eyes glared out at his father, his mouth set into a tight little grimace, his fists clenched tight as a trap. There was porridge and cream spread all about the table and chairs, and it appeared as though a large dollop of his breakfast meal was being worn that day as a hat.

Will bent to his son and eyed him with a sideways glare that soon broke into laughter on both faces.

To most of the nobility on the island, and indeed, most of the inhabitants in general, what William and Kathryne were attempting to do was odd at best—most curious and strange. "Imagine," Will had heard others whisper, "that people of their standing and resources actually are attempting to raise their children in such a manner." If a family of means, such as William's, had children, those children would be the complete responsibility of nannies, nurses, tutors, servants, and cooks. That a member of nobility such as Kathryne would allow herself to be demeaned so far as to attempt to dress her own daughter for church was most unthinkable. For a father to attempt to feed his child breakfast was ludicrous.

Even John Delacroix had questioned Will one evening, asking him if his fortunes had suffered a loss. For why else would Will have deigned to bathe his son in the evening and place him in bedclothes for the night?

Will had smiled and replied in a most good-humored way that no calamity had befallen them. This was simply a matter of choice. To be parents, Will and Kathryne decided, was to be parents in all matters. They had help to be sure—servants and cooks and the like—but as parents they would be involved in the care of their children, not as overseers, but as participants.

"How else would I see the love shine through their sweet faces?" Will asked John. "For if others perform these tasks, I scarce would know my children at all. And it be a scriptural injunction for parents to teach their children. How can I teach my son if I do not participate in his life?"

John nodded and hummed an affirmative response, indicating clearly that he did not understand a word of his friend's explanation.

Will blinked and returned to the task at hand—placing sustenance into the closed mouth of his son, whose demeanor at the moment was anything but lovable. He took a damp linen cloth and wiped at the food on his child's face and then bent to kiss the child's soft forehead. Patiently, Will tried odd clucks and animal noises, soft orders, and whispered commands into his child's ear. Soon Samuel was grinning and laughing a gurgling giggle, spreading his cheeks wide with a smile, his arms waving, his fingers performing a complex wiggling dance in the air. Within a dozen moments the food was gone, the child was full, and William basked in the unabashed, unspoken love of an infant.

It was at that moment that Kathryne appeared in the doorway holding little Hannah in her arms. Both were gowned in white, trimmed with scarlet ribbons and lace. The sun streamed through the window and lit Kathryne's dark hair with a velvet glow. Hannah, with Will's blue eyes and his golden curls, laughed and pawed at the air when she saw him. There was a certain tiredness in Kathryne's eyes, yet what diminished the physical weariness was that light from within as she held her child in her arms, nestled to her shoulder, smiling down as her daughter reached out for William.

"She seeks the arms of her father," Kathryne said, and held her out for William to embrace.

How more fortunate can a man be? Will thought to himself as he embraced the tiny laughter of his most perfect daughter.

As the bells rang for the morning service, William, Kathryne, Jezalee, and the twins were at the steps of St. Michael's. The Hawkeses had been welcomed back into the graces of the official church of the island. Vicar Petley had sent word through Vicar Coates that he had ceased all formal opposition of their union and that he would be honored if they attended Sunday services again.

William argued against their return for several weeks, claiming that the message and the acceptance at Vicar Mayhew's curious congregation was more biblical and proper than any they could expect to experience under Vicar Petley.

"But, William," Kathryne explained, "the Almighty can be worshiped the same in any location. I admit that I value Thomas's messages more, for they are more practical. But we must think of the children. I want to impress on them early the importance of attending church. Going to the fort will appear to be a picnic to them and they will learn nothing."

It was not a position to battle upon, Will realized. And he also knew that despite his absence from the pulpit of the fort church for so many months, many of them saw Will as the true head of the body, leaving Vicar Mayhew in a disquieting position. If Will remained absent for several more months, those attending the gathering would have no choice but to view Vicar Mayhew as their true parson. It was the right thing to do, Will knew, but it hurt him to leave those whom he had first discipled. Yet he knew in his heart with no doubts that Thomas was more able than he could ever be. It would be Thomas who would lead them from darkness to light. It would be Thomas who would become God's vicar to those who saw the fort as their one true church—and the only church that would have them.

After the service concluded, the twins were sent back to Hawkes Haven with Jezalee and a second nursemaid. The four were bundled in the carriage, leaving William and Kathryne to stroll back at their leisure. The weather was warm, not yet hot, and these infrequent constitutionals were often the only quiet time the pair had to spend alone in each other's company. Their walk took them down the main promenade of Bridgetown, past the courthouse, now nearing completion. They passed several new shops and establishments on the main street. Kathryne was taken with the recent addition of a seamstress and cloth merchant with a wide window facing the harbor. In the window were displayed bolts of delicate Belgian lace, plush velvets in a dozen colors, and gauzy silks. She asked Will to remind her that she would need to send Eileen to inquire as to costs and availabilities. Since the birth of the twins, Kathryne had yet had time to acquire many new items of apparel.

As they walked slowly, both were stopped a dozen times by citizens inquiring as to their health, the state of the children, progress on the fort, local gossip, and, perhaps most important, news from England.

Just a fortnight previous, William had received a most welcome letter from Captain Waring, his old friend and business partner. The merchant captain and his lovely young wife, Alicia, still lived in their cottage just outside of Weymouth. Along with reports of their business dealings together, Captain Waring had written news of the war that continued to rage between Parliament and King Charles, although there was no fighting near their home. The war had done little to hinder their still-successful shipping concerns, he wrote, though internal trade and distribution had been affected, with the sacking of vital market towns, including Leicester. In Somerset and Nottinghamshire, the whole of Oxfordshire and Berkshire, and in Lancashire and West Yorkshire, which were continuous war zones, the rival armies' need for food and an ongoing supply of fresh horses were putting the farmers of those lands under a severe strain. Captain Waring had recently heard of an association of peasants in Will's home shire of Devon and other West Country shires, calling themselves the Clubmen, who, arming themselves with clubs, were grimly determined to keep both armies off their land. Will wondered how the Browns and the two sons of Mrs. Cavendish were faring in Hadenthorne and if demands on their farms by the war had caused them to join such a group.

Will had heard whispered talk in the dark corners of the public houses of Bridgetown that the lightly armored and poorly disciplined Royalist forces stood little chance against the New Model Army, led by Oliver Cromwell. The islanders knew it was forbidden for them to speak of their allegiances in the war at home in England, but they all eagerly awaited some news of a deciding victory that would end the conflict—a most harrowing experience for a nation that had enjoyed almost uninterrupted civil peace for 150 years. So any news from home was most welcome, and Will and Kathryne shared what they had learned from Captain Waring's letter.

Within no more than a half hour's walk, they were at the shore path, where the clatter of town was replaced by the gentle crashing of the waves. Walking in sandy loose soil was harder for Will, who had to swing his injured leg wider and higher to maintain his balance. His cane sank too far into the soft surface to be of much assistance. Kathryne extended her arm, and Will leaned heavily upon it. Halfway between town and home, Will halted and stepped over to a large smooth rock and sat for a moment, bending to massage the muscles in his good leg.

They did not speak, for Will would admit to no pain or discomfort. It was a most brief play that had been so often rehearsed in the past. Kathryne asked if Will wanted assistance. Will would smile and indicate a momentary cramping is all that troubled him. Given a moment's rest, he would recover. Kathryne then worried in silence, and Will suffered quietly.

Kathryne came behind him and placed her hands on his shoulders and gently caressed the tight cording of his muscles. She gently kissed the top of his head and nuzzled her face into his golden hair. He turned and looked into the deep green of her eyes, and their lips met for many precious moments.

Kathryne moved to sit down at his side, and as Will wrapped his arms around her and pulled her near, she rested her head on his shoulder. Both stared out to the trackless sea, smooth this day like a rippled silver plate, extending to the horizon. After several long moments of silence, Kathryne looked into Will's blue eyes and took his hand in hers.

"Do you miss him?" she asked.

"Miss who?" Will asked, instantly then knowing of whom she asked.

"Luke. Do you miss him?"

A catch formed in Will's voice, and he had to swallow hard to answer. "I do," he replied in a whisper. "I thought the pain would be diminished, but it has not."

Kathryne nodded and squeezed his hand.

"To not know hurts so," Will said, his voice now edged in tears. They had yet to fully speak their hearts about this loss. "If I had seen a body, had evidence, perhaps then I would feel settled."

Kathryne nodded, then leaned her head on his shoulder once more.

"I do not understand why he was so frantic to leave. I do not understand his fear. We had faced death together on dozens of occasions—muskets, cannon fire, cutlass, and ax—and never did I see such a look of panic on his face." He swallowed hard. "Why did he leave like that, Kathryne?"

She shook her head. "I do not know, dear William, but I know that if Luke perished from this life, he is alive in a far better place."

Will nodded. "I know that as truth, but I . . . I miss him so. I look to see his face each morning at our door, and when he does not arrive, my heart hurts."

He felt a warm wetness on his shoulder and realized that tears were streaming down Kathryne's face.

"I miss Mrs. Cole so much, William. I miss her every moment. She had only a few moments to see my children." She sniffed loudly. "Why did our Lord take her so early? Why could she not have enjoyed Hannah and Samuel? Even for a little while?"

Will reached up and stroked at his wife's cheek with his rough hand, trying to be as tender as he could. "Kathryne, do you remember the words you spoke to me so long ago when I had taken you captive? The day by the ocean when I spoke of my mother's death. Do you remember how you comforted me?"

Kathryne looked up, wiping at her tears. "William, my thoughts are too jumbled. What words did I say?"

"You told me that the legacy of my mother lived on in me. You told me that I must take refuge in the fact that she was in heaven at the Lord's side and that her goodness and honor would live on in me. You told me that she was looking down and would be in pain to see my anger and hurt."

Kathryne sniffed and nodded.

"That is what I must tell you—and myself as well—this day. The love that Mrs. Cole showed to all must now live on in you, Kathryne. She would have it no other way. And Luke's dedication to serving others must live on in me. If I ignore that, Kathryne, I am sure I will need answer to the flat of his hand in heaven. I wish not to experience that again."

Kathryne giggled through a tear, sniffed again, and nodded.

"We can do that, can we not, my darling? They will never be gone if we let their example live in us," Will said, his voice a velvety whisper. "If they are looking down on us, let us make them smile."

Kathryne nodded, her lip trembling, her eyes small puddles of tears. "I shall," she whispered, her words edgy in a sob.

They stared into each other's eyes deep and long. It was the most intimate that Will had ever felt with another person his entire life, that moment of drowning in the depths of his wife's soul.

She blinked once, then dove into his embrace, her tears flowing again. "But I miss her so. I miss her. I miss Luke as deeply."

He stroked her flowing hair against her shoulder. "As do I, my darling," Will whispered in reply. "As do I."

And the ocean hissed a silent sob to the edge of where they sat as the tide slowly rose to the shore.

■ ■ □ ■ ■

Aidan and Emily sat at the far ends of the long polished table in the dining chamber of Shelworthy. Crystal glasses graced the lustrous surface, drops of moisture forming on their sides, dripping with an elegant silence to the wood below.

Emily lifted a heavy silver knife and edged a boiled potato to one side of the gold-rimmed plate. For all her activity, Emily had eaten no more than three bites of food. She looked up and watched as Aidan fussed with the contents of his plate, carefully trimming and slicing, segregating different foods to their own sections of his platter. Emily stared hard at him, knowing he would be most oblivious to her as he dined. She let her knife down, clicking hard against the plate, and took up her goblet of wine and swallowed a third of its contents. She seldom partook of more than a genteel, ladylike sip, but today her heart had banged in anger and she spent a most uncomfortable church service being civil and polite. The wine, she knew, was ill-advised to calm such emotions, but she cared not for what was proper and correct this particular afternoon.

Emily had waited through three postponements of their now seldom-discussed nuptials, and she could wait no longer to speak of the matter. It would be today, she had decided. Today. She would speak from her heart today as they dined, regardless of its consequences.

"Aidan," she said, her voice even and controlled.

She waited in silence, his only reply the quiet scraping and cutting of silver to plate.

"Aidan," she repeated, the volume the same as before.

Again, the hiss of metal to meat was her only reply.

She stiffened in her chair. "Aidan," she called out, her voice nearly a shout.

Aidan jumped, his left hand flailing in surprise, his fork actually flipping from his hand and skittering across the room to land with a faint click against the far wall.

"What is it? Where is it? Is it on me?" he called out.

"Whatever are you talking about?" Emily replied, her tone one of confused agitation.

"The mouse . . . the lizard? Where is it?" he shouted, his voice thin and reedy.

Emily squealed back her chair, her hand racing to her throat. She despised both mice and lizards, and now it appeared they had invaded the room just as her courage had risen.

"What mouse?" she cried back. "What lizard?"

Aidan spun about, this time knocking his knife to the floor, catapulting a small piece of roasted beef, drenched in Madeira sauce, across the floor toward the butler's pantry.

Emily shouted and pointed, her hand to her mouth, "Over there! By the door!"

Aidan, not brave with such creatures either, knew that Boaz, whom he normally called upon to administer justice to such invaders, was away for the church service at the fort. The cooks were no good in such matters, so Aidan would have to attempt this himself.

Knowing that it could not bite through his boot, he jumped up and hopped to within a stomp of the rodent. Leaning back, holding as much of his body as far from the peril as he could, he stomped down several times. The last stomp from leather to hardwood resulted in a flattening of the offending piece of beef. But the slippery Madeira sauce was not well suited for traction, and Aidan's stomping foot slid out from under him, toppling him to the floor in a frenzied heap as he struggled to avoid all close contact with the rodent. The beef slipped as well, and as Aidan fell, he propelled it to the tall window before him, where it struck the glass with a sticky, liquid sound, then slowly slobbered down toward the sill, leaving a greasy brown track on the pane as it descended.

Emily took one look at the glass and shut her eyes to what she thought was a mutilated rodent, and one hand went to her mouth, fearing that she might become ill. Aidan scrabbled backwards, getting his footing, jumping to his feet and brushing off the dust from his backside. He was gasping from his efforts, yet a thin smile made it to his face, as if he was proud of his manly accomplishments.

Emily, without truly opening her eyes, turned and fled the room, knowing that her emotions and sensibilities were too disrupted to ever hope of returning to a serious discussion on any matter that afternoon. She prayed that Aidan did not hear the sob that escaped from her breast as she ran out.

Aidan first peered closer at the window and realized what had indeed been stomped upon, for no mouse left a trail of Madeira sauce. He then turned and looked at the open door through which Emily had fled, and wondered why the death of a mouse would have caused her to cry.

"You be puttin' too much stock in that Captain Bliss! I say it ain't proper that an outsider be makin' such decisions. We be waitin' too long to act, you harebrained lout," shouted a very tipsy Herbert Gleeson as he launched himself against Ian Tafert. In the time it takes a fist to land on a cheek, both men were rolling in the mud and dust outside Tafert's small hut on the far southern edge of Governor Spenser's estate. Tafert, less from ability and more from not having consumed quite as much mobby, managed to wrestle Gleeson facedown in the muck and tightened his arm about the man's neck and pulled.

"I'll not be forced into a muddleheaded action listenin' to the likes of you!" Tafert shouted into Gleeson's ear as he forced his face deeper into the black and red ooze. He waited a long moment as Gleeson's flailings became less angry and more desperate. Then he pulled his head out and sat on his haunches as Gleeson gasped and panted, clawing the mud from his face.

Tafert turned to the other four overseers gathered in a wide circle about them.

"Any of the rest of you care to debate the issue with me?" he shouted, pointing his hand at them.

To a man, they all took a half step backward, some holding their palms up in supplication.

"Good," Tafert exclaimed almost as if a curse, and spit in the dirt. He paused a moment to catch his breath, then grabbed at Gleeson's muddy shoulder.

"Come on, you stupid oaf. It be not yer fault that you be dense and dull witted. It be the fault of your poor mother, no doubt."

By the time the sun had set, Gleeson had washed most of the mud from his face and frame in the small stream that bubbled nearby. The water was clean, to a point, yet smelled foul. He stumbled back to the small cook fire and sat down with a wet slump.

Tafert motioned to O'Reilly, who passed the jug around the circle to Gleeson. The man smiled at being forgiven and took a long, silent swallow.

"Now as I be sayin'," Tafert continued, "before we was so rudely interrupted, the time be drawin' near when it be best suited for us to make our move. And blast that poor excuse for an ally, Bliss. He be talkin' more than he be doin'. I know it be months now since we first talked on this, but it still not be the proper timin' to make the move."

Gleeson belched, and the rest of the circle laughed.

"But when will it be the right time?" O'Reilly asked. "None of us be gettin' younger, you knows that, and a bunch of me darkies that would have followed an order without askin', well, they be dead now."

Bullock looked up as he took the jug. "That be the truth. If we wait too many months more, we be runnin' the risk of bein' dead as well."

Tafert wiped his face with his hand, then leaned forward. "We need to wait till all the nobility be noticin' somethin' else. If we get that to happen, then it be easier for us to take over."

"But weren't the birthin' of the Hawkes twins such an event?" Gleeson asked.

"'Twasn't at all," Tafert replied. "Only took a day or two and all was back to normal. I say we be waitin' till old Governor Spenser and the Lady Emily be gettin' married. That be the time when no one be payin' attention to what us slave masters and darkies be doin'."

Gleeson laughed. "That old goat will not be gettin' married." He lowered his voice and leered. "The way I hears it, is why should the governor be buyin' a cow when all the milk he wants is free for the askin'?"

The rest of the men added a gale of coarse laughter. Tafert held up his hand to silence them before anyone in the main house drew a suspicious glance at the group.

"They be gettin' married. I heard it from that darkie cook in the main house. Hattie be her name. She be tellin' it true, no doubt." He leaned closer in. "When that be happenin', it be time indeed."

Gleeson, red-faced and wheezing, nodded mutely in agreement.

"But we still be agreed that Hawkes be the man we take first in all this. He be the one who could most likely spoil the day," Gleeson muttered. "I not be sure of all what Captain Bliss be plannin', but I knows that he be correct on this matter."

Tafert nodded. "Be that true indeed. We take Hawkes first, and the rest of these addle-brained nobles be fallin' over their feet tryin' to stop us. Hawkes be the first in front of our muskets for sure."

A coughing fit rattled Gleeson's lungs, watery and painful, and he held his hand up in agreement.

"I wants to be the one who be pullin' that trigger," he wheezed. "That be all I be askin' for."

Tafert smiled, and after a long moment, he nodded. "If you wants that pleasure, you can have it."

Tafert's grin widened, and he took in a deep breath of fetid air. It was the first time that such a breath caught in his lungs and rattled there for a moment, bringing pain that spread across his chest and heart. He closed his eyes tightly for a moment, in an attempt to deny the pain. He had seen it all too often, that watery, rattling cough that led nowhere but death. Even though he was not a praying man, Tafert looked up and muttered a few words in Latin—words that had echoed in his soul from childhood.

Please, Lord, do not be takin' me breath jus' yet. There be work to be done, he thought, fighting the lonely, desperate feeling in his soul.

CHAPTER

18

3 June 1645

"A full pulpit? With carving and steps and all manner of decoration?" asked John Delacroix. He brushed the wood shavings off his leather apron and picked up a scrap of paper and a thin sliver of charcoal. "Like this?" he said as he began to sketch a towering pulpit that could easily hold a minister and a portion of a heavenly choir.

Vicar Mayhew peered over John's shoulder as he sketched away, and he shook his head. "No—not like that at all, John," he said. "First off, what you've drawn might fit in well with the likes of the archbishop of Canterbury, but I daresay that most of my fledgling flock would be more than a mite intimidated by such opulence. And it would not be right to spend such a sum on a pulpit without having a cathedral to put it in."

"Ah, good Vicar," John said as he stopped his drawing, "there be your first mistake. You have the best cathedral in the world—out under God's own creation and the sun and the sky. Your cathedral puts any other to shame."

The vicar nodded and smiled. "You are correct, John, but until I have some sort of roof to protect it, I shall insist on a smaller version that be more portable."

John grinned. "You needs to dream bigger, good Thomas. You must start at some point. You start with a grand pulpit such as this," he said, holding the sketch out for both to admire, "then the building will just follow along afterward. You can be sure of that."

Thomas draped his arm over John's shoulder. "I understand that you're encouraging me to have more faith. Well, that is not my problem.

For even if you build the simplest pulpit, I must have the faith that money will be found to pay for such a project."

John looked surprised. "Why not ask William for the funds, Vicar? William is a very wealthy man, after all."

Thomas nodded and replied, "I understand that, but it is not William's church. It is God's. If God wants us to have a proper pulpit, then God will provide it through the hands of those who attend. It would not be right if I leaned on a single wealthy patron for all our needs. How will the flock develop their faith if I do such a thing?"

John rubbed his chin in thought. "I suspect that you be correct in that, Vicar. And if that be the case, if your congregation be the ones paying for this piece of furnishing, then indeed I shall need to simplify my plans. By the looks of most of them, a farthing be a fortune."

By the time Thomas left the chandlery, he had assurances that John would construct a most simple lectern on which the vicar could place his Bible during his sermons. Thomas was most frustrated as he tried to hold the Scriptures open in the wind, losing his place a dozen times in the process. Also, a lectern or simple pulpit would help to make his open field seem a more proper church.

Thomas stood at the entrance to the chandlery for a much longer moment than was needed. He knew that Eileen had taken residence in the small space of two rooms at the rear of the building. John, her landlord, had added a third small room and tidied things up for her after her place of business and residence, the Goose, had been burned in the pirate attack. It was not what one could call a spacious home, but it was dry and clean and provided her a fine view of the waterfront and harbor.

And between her home and the waterfront is where Thomas stood, debating on what to do next. Should he return to the fort and prepare for the following Sunday? Should he see the butcher for something for the evening's meal? Should he make a pastoral call on Miss Eileen?

After all, she had been at the church service for at least two months of Sundays, always coming and sitting to his right side on a small square of canvas laid precisely upon the ground, squared to the walls of the fort. She watched him most carefully as he spoke, always participated in the singing, always listened to the points he made in his sermon.

Thomas turned to the water, then back toward Eileen's home, then back to the harbor, pivoting on that one spot. As he faced the water, he heard a door creak open, and a smile bloomed on his face as he turned back again. Yet the door to Eileen's home remained closed. He spun around again, perplexed.

"Up here, Vicar," called a voice. It was Missy, who had come from the first-story residence nestled over the chandlery. She smiled and waved to him.

His face fell, the smile simply vanishing, and Missy's expression soon matched his.

"I did not mean to disappoint you, Vicar," she said as she glided down the steps carrying a small basket.

The vicar shook his head, "No, I am sorry, Missy. . . . I was looking for . . . it was just that I did not expect to see . . . and I must be getting back to the fort . . . then. . . ."

She placed a hand on his forearm and squeezed it tight. She leaned closer to his ear, and he noticed the fragrance of lavender and violets filling the air around her.

"She is at Hawkes Haven," Missy whispered.

"Wha . . . wha . . . who do you mean?"

"Eileen," she said again. "Eileen Palmerston."

The vicar looked on the verge of panic.

"She is at Hawkes Haven. I spoke with her this morning," Missy said.

"But I did not say . . . I mean that . . . ," the vicar stammered.

Missy smiled a most knowing smile. "Thomas," she said confidentially, "your secret is safe with me."

"Secret?" he mumbled. "Secret? . . . there is no secret . . . I mean to say . . ."

Missy looked up at him, the full strength of her deep blue eyes bearing in on him. Never a man to be most comfortable in the company of a woman, he felt his heart begin to beat fast, not from excitement by any means, but from fear.

"Thomas," she explained to him, her voice low, even, and patient, "you may think that no one else sees your eyes on Sunday. And perhaps most do not. I know that John would not . . . and to be honest, most men would not. But I see them."

"My . . . my eyes?" he stammered.

"You look to your right more often than your left. It is not because of the sun; it is because of the view. That is where Miss Eileen sits."

Thomas felt an overpowering desire to run, to avoid having to think that others could read him that well. He thought little of Eileen's past, save when it came to times like this.

Thomas took a step back and edged as if to turn to the harbor. "I must . . . I must be returning to the fort," he said, attempting to keep his voice smooth, without trembling. "I have set apart this afternoon to work on this week's sermon." He stepped to the wooden walkway that led around the harbor front.

"Vicar," Missy called out softly, "do not be so terrified of such feelings. They are not wrong."

He stared back at her as a wild animal might who is surprised by hunter and musket. "I . . . I . . . I must be going," he finally said and turned on his heel and quickly walked away, sweat having formed in a heavy beading on his brow and upper lip.

Thomas wiped at his forehead several times as he marched along the rickety harbor decking, his boot heels echoing woodenly.

I must control myself in the future, he ordered himself, *for if it is apparent to Missy, who else might be noticing the same sort of . . . partiality?*

He kept up his quick march until he was well clear of the town and its confining atmosphere. Slowing his pace on the path that led along the shore, from town to the fort, Thomas attempted to rein in his galloping thoughts. He reached a small outcropping of rock and smooth stone, worn slick and comfortable by centuries of wind and surf. He stepped over, carefully picking his way through until he at last reached the edge of the bluff and a large smooth boulder, shaped much like the throne of a monarch.

He lifted up a few strands of dried seaweed and driftwood and tossed them aside and swept out the sand from the seat of the rocky chair. He sat back, the sun warm on his face, the breeze from the sea whistling past his ears like the gentle hum of a mother bending to her child. To his left stood the fort, a quarter hour's walk away. Behind him and to his right was the town. And it was here that he could find solitude.

How is it that Missy commanded me to not be terrified of such feelings? How could she have seen my heart so clearly? How could she have discerned where my thoughts are? And how can I let myself descend into this gulf? Am I not a man of the cloth? Do I not attempt to honor God in all that I do? Does not that mean living a life above reproach and condemnation? It must, or I do discredit to all that I believe and honor. Miss Palmerston is a most beautiful woman, to be sure, but how can I ignore her past? A woman of easy virtue could never be considered fit for a man of my position!

He picked up a small piece of mangrove branch, bleached to whiteness by the sun and the sea, feeling its smoothness against his palm and fingers. He tossed it out into the surf, half expecting the dog to lunge out after it. If he craned his neck from where he sat, he could just make out the top roofline and chimney of Hawkes Haven.

Looking up into the afternoon sky, he attempted to settle his thoughts and clear his mind. He would need to focus his energies on the sermon. He would need to concentrate on the Scriptures. He would need to place aside his personal distractions.

But how can I ignore the stirring in my heart? Did not Christ forgive the sinner, the prostitute, the thief? Am I above Christ's station that I offer no such forgiveness? His thoughts echoed all about him.

Thomas stood, an energy forcing him up and forward. He had sat for only a brief moment, yet realized that he could remain motionless no longer. He carefully stepped back to the path and began to walk. Hawkes Haven came more into view with each step. The path came close, then veered back toward the sea, and back to the fort.

She is a harlot . . . or was a harlot, and I have no right to subject the church and the holy Scriptures to such an association.

He stopped, several hundred yards from the entrance of the fort. He turned around and began retracing his steps as his mind raced.

But if I fail to show mercy and love, what sort of example am I? Do I think others will see Christ's love in me then?

He was no more than a musket shot from Hawkes Haven when he stopped again. He looked at his feet for a long moment, then looked at the stone and thatch house that sat before him. In it this day were the people whom he held most dear and close to his heart.

He sighed, dropped his head to his chest, and turned back toward the sea.

I have no right . . . I cannot do this. She is from too sordid a past, and the gulf between us is too wide for even a foolish old man such as I to cross. I must think of what is best for the church and suffer what loneliness I suffer without complaint. That is what I am sure is the right path to follow.

His steps grew slower and more deliberate the further he walked. He turned once and looked back at Hawkes Haven as he entered the cool shadows of the fort. He sighed again, blinked his eyes shut for a long moment, then stepped within the walls of his church. Hawkes Haven and all the rest of the world disappeared from his view.

20 June 1645

The vicar stood behind the new pulpit, which smelled strongly of pine resin, and looked out over the small congregation. More than fifty faces beamed back at him, each one proud of that first purchase, financed as a result of their giving. For most, it was the finest, most ornate piece of furniture that they had ever had a part in owning. The lines of the pulpit were clean and simple, and the only concession to ornamentation was a cross, chiseled into the wood, with the rays of a sun behind it.

Thomas spoke that morning about the responsibilities of a church, of caring for one another, of sharing one another's burdens. He told them how proud he was of them for all donating from their meagerness to purchase such a fine pulpit. He promised them he would do nothing to dishonor the trust they placed in him, and as he said those words, his eyes darted for the shortest moment to Eileen Palmerston, who sat in her normal location. If she had received any hint from those words, she did not show it, for she smiled and nodded again.

After the service, after the somewhat warbly singing of the benediction, everyone came up to inspect closer the marvelous new pulpit, touching the neat edges, running their fingers in the deep grooves of the cross.

Simbro, a mulatto who had received his freedom while on the pirate island of Tortuga, knelt down and looked closely at the chisel marks in the wood. "Be dis de shape of dat cross dat dey used for Jesus?" he asked.

Thomas nodded. "I am sure it looked much like that—only much larger, of course."

"Simbro see men strung up on cross before, but dey look like—" He crossed his fingers in the shape of an X.

"Well, yes," Thomas replied, "I am sure some looked as that, but this is the shape of Christ's sacrifice, and of our hope, our future," he said, pointing to the carving.

"Dat be a good sign," Simbro said, smiling. "I be glad you be usin' Simbro's gold to buy dis. I be most glad."

As the crowds thinned, Thomas looked around, looking for Eileen's face. His heart held a mixture of relief—for he did not know how he would even speak to her this day, what words to use—and sorrow, for he wanted, in some small way, to hear her voice and to look into her eyes.

But this was a good day, he thought, *a good day, and I know our Lord is pleased.*

▪▫▪▫▪

Ian Tafert sat alone and still in the doorway of his small hovel. If he looked to his right, just at the edge of the palms, he could about see the shadow that Shelworthy made in the setting sun. He spit into the dust, clearing his throat. His boots were off, and he leaned against the rough door frame smoking a pipe. Nestled between his legs was a half-full bucket of rum, an oily coating floating on the surface, the handle of a ladle just below the surface. Despite the fact that he had consumed most of the top half of the bucket, he felt no drunkenness in his bones. Angry men such as Tafert often showed little effect of alcohol; it simply seemed as natural to them as water was to drink.

Tafert's mind raced this day, spinning more complex and convoluted schemes as to how he would take over the Spenser plantation once the rebels had succeeded in killing off the noblemen.

He spoke aloud, though no one was in attendance, his voice low and guttural. "Be a fine day when the gov'nor dies and I rise and take over this land—land I be slavin' on harder than the darkies. I ain't gonna work my flesh till I die in another man's employ. I be smarter than all them rich, slimy noblemen put together. And I deserve this more than they, with their lily-white hands and fancy velvet coats. It be men like me that be deservin' this land—not some fancy coddled wealthy boy who be handed his money on a silver tray. It be belongin' to those who be workin' for it—not sittin' about on their backsides, ringin' for another pot of wine to be brought to 'em by some poor white lout or darkie."

He slipped his fingers into the rum, fished out the ladle, and brought it to his lips, swallowing several times till he was finished. He wheezed from the potency of the drink, licking his lips, exhaling hard.

"Be not at peace, Gov'nor Spenser, for it be your time a-comin'. It be comin' faster than you might imagine. And Mr. Hawkes as well. Yer days bein' numbered, too—you best rest not easy a'tall."

Tafert began to laugh, then cackle, until he near collapsed in a fit of coughing. It was halted only by another long draw on the bucket.

23 June 1645

The moon lay hidden behind the night's thick blanket of storm clouds, and the drumming of the rain turned the island's trails and paths into mire and muck. Gleeson and Tafert sloshed through the mud, skirting the deepest puddles, and wading in when the path offered no alternative. Within a half mile of town, both men were caked to mid-thigh by the viscous mud.

They spoke very little on their journey that night, laboring to breathe as the mud pulled at their boots. Wheezing and gasping for air in the humid darkness, they clutched at each other for support. At the tenth bell, they were only a hundred yards from the public house Fields of Eton.

"Why he be preferrin' that nasty hovel be beyond me," Tafert gasped. "He claims he be a man of breedin', yet he be pickin' the worst of the lot."

Gleeson, too winded to speak, nodded in the darkness.

Bliss was at his expected station, sitting with his back to the wall at the small table, a trio of full tankards awaiting his guests.

"Gentlemen," he called out, his voice an evil, whispery rattle, "I hopes ye've not had a rough time in the rain and all. But we need be meetin'. We need be speakin' of many things this night."

Tafert sat as far from him as possible. There was something about Bliss that felt so completely wrong, Tafert thought, and he wanted no part of that evil. But as unsettled as the man made him feel, he also knew that it would take his help to achieve success in what they planned.

Gleeson was the first to speak. "We thought you be huntin' up north, Cap'n Bliss. Is not that what you be tellin' me last time we met? We be not expectin' you to return for a fortnight."

Bliss smiled, and Tafert felt a chill course along the bones of his spine.

"I be huntin' for certain, me friend," he said. "And I be findin' prey sooner than expected. A fat, lumberin' slave ship . . . called the *Queen* or some sort of royal appellation. Slim pickins, but slim pickins be better than none. A few doubloons, a cask or two of wine, and a bunch of sick and bony black heathen. But I be happy with it."

Tafert leaned back, a few inches further away. He knew this man was a pirate. He knew that he stopped at this island for only a day or two at a time, for Barbados was not kindly to pirates using their waters as a safe harbor.

Bliss was a smart, clever entrepreneur. He made no mention of his nefarious activities and never tried to sell his ill-gotten cargo in Bridgetown. He needed Bridgetown Harbor as a port for replenishing and purchasing supplies. He would not jeopardize his thin veneer—the veneer that showed him to be an honest merchantman.

Bliss was not the only pirate who called upon these waters. If a ship and its crew participated in no illegal activities while lying at anchor, British law made no provision for the harbormaster to prevent them from anchoring. Bliss kept his men confined to ship while in Barbados. His true safe haven lay several days' sail to the south, and there his men had free reign while in port. It would not be wise for Bliss to let a stupid, drunken sailor tip his hand.

Bliss brushed his oily hair from his face and tucked it behind his ear. Tafert looked over and saw, for the first time, that his ear was missing a large V-shaped wedge. The cut ran jagged, almost to the point where ear and scalp met.

Bliss narrowed his eyes. "It be from an old fight with an English sailor who be wantin' to press part of me crew. I took his insults for a moment and then drew the cutlass," he explained, feeling Tafert's eyes on his deformity.

"And he cut you?" Tafert asked.

Bliss cackled. "If I draw me cutlass on a man, that man be dead. He not be the one doin' the cuttin'. 'Twas his friend who took me from behind." Bliss closed his eyes as if reliving the battle, a smile etching his face. "And now both of them lie at the bottom of the sea, as well as the rest of their mates and their stinkin' ship."

Opening his eyes with a snap, Bliss cursed, then added slowly, "So don't be thinkin' of crossin' me. For men don't be breathin' long if they be crossin' me."

Gleeson nervously giggled, then coughed.

Bliss placed his hands flat on the table and eyed them both. "I hear ye be waitin' for the nuptials of the gov'nor to be settin' up the attack. That be a good time, indeed."

Tafert and Gleeson exchanged surprised looks, for they had not discussed this plan with Bliss.

Bliss snickered and said, "I have me ways, gentlemen. That why I be tellin' ye not to be crossin' me."

Gleeson gulped and took a long swallow on the mobby from the tankard before him.

"It be a fine plan indeed. And me and me mates will be back in harbor a day, maybe two, before the blessed event, whenever that may indeed be. We be providin' the muskets and blades and sailors to help ye. I be findin' ye both when I sail into harbor."

Tafert took a swallow on his drink, hoping the blazing warmth might settle his jangled nerves.

"And on accounts of our help, we be takin' a wee bit of the gold on this island. That's all we be askin' for."

Tafert and Gleeson exchanged looks and nodded.

"We not be after the gold, Captain Bliss," Tafert said. "It be the land that we be takin'."

Bliss shook his head, almost as if in disbelief. "I can't do much with a field, gentlemen, so ye be welcome to all of this acreage. Do with it as ye please."

"And Hawkes be the right man to be takin' first?" Gleeson asked.

"Hawkes be the right man," Bliss said firmly. "If the head of the snake be chopped off, then the snake dies. Simple as that, gentlemen, simple as that."

CHAPTER

20

Will stroked in from the turquoise sea, puffing hard through the white surf. He swam, then waded the last few yards. Thomas was there, a toweling cloth in his outstretched hand.

"Thomas?" Will asked as he dried himself.

There was no answer, for Thomas's eyes were focused on a faraway point out to sea.

"Thomas?" he asked louder, and still no answer was forthcoming, no movement of any type.

Will smiled and scooped down into the sea with his hand. A small splash of water drenched the vicar's side. He reacted with a yelp and danced to his left.

"Thomas!" Will shouted playfully. "Where had you gone? Sorry for the sprinkling, but it seemed the only method to gain your attention."

Thomas looked back, a most perturbed and distant look upon his face. As he saw William's smile, he smiled back. "You must pardon me, Will," he said, "but I must have been distracted by . . ." His voice faded off as his gaze focused into the distance again.

"Thomas?" Will asked as he worked his way to the shore, hopping on his healthy leg. His walking stick was firmly planted at the water's edge, thrust deep into the sand as he first dove in. "Thomas, come here and talk to me. I have never seen you in such a befuddled state."

Will sat on a large stump that had washed up in the previous storm and finished drying himself. No longer did his skin have the typical English pallor, but was nearly bronze in color. Though the sun made his skin darker, it made his hair lighter, now a velvety shade of blond.

"So what is it, Thomas?" Will laughed. "A woman?"

Will had thought he had picked the most remote possibility of concern to Thomas, and his friend nearly tripped over his feet as he spun about, his feet splashing in the surf.

Thomas stared hard at his friend, at his smile, at his nonchalance, and realized, as his heart thudded in his chest, that Will was jesting and meant no truth to his question. He stood there, at the edge of the sea, watching the waves slide toward his bare feet, as Will waited for the vicar's reply.

Thomas gulped and turned to Will. There was no sense, the vicar thought, in beating about the bush any longer. "When did you know in your heart that you were in love with Kathryne?"

William let the towel drop into his lap, and his hand fell limp to his sides. "What was your question, Thomas?" he asked in a most slow and paced tone, thinking that he had not understood the true meaning of the vicar's words.

"I asked when the time was that you knew of your love for Kathryne. Did it happen all at once? Was the movement gradual? Were you surprised by such a turn? Was she?"

William's jaw fell open in obvious surprise. Thomas knew that such questions, such personal questions, were most unusual for him to pose, even though he was Will's oldest and closest friend.

"Thomas," he replied, slipping his doublet over his head, "I . . . I am surprised by your inquiry. May I ask why you seek such answers?"

Thomas looked hard for a moment at Will's puzzled face, realizing in a heartbeat that a threshold of intimacy must have been crossed.

Thomas replied, "It is simply that . . . that I have no understanding of such . . . things of this nature. If I am to teach my church about such matters, I must . . . I must have a broader knowledge of such subjects."

Thomas smiled but quickly hid it again, pleased at his nimble response.

Will looked up and nodded, as if the explanation was most sufficient. "Well, . . . I was simply . . . simply surprised by the question, Thomas. We are as family to each other, after all, but I do not think we have ever discussed such topics."

"William," he replied, "do not feel obligated to answer. I am curious, is all."

William slipped on his breeches and stood to fasten his belt. "Well, since the question has been raised, I think I can supply you with an answer. But let us do so over a warming breakfast. This swim has made me famished."

I should never have asked such an impudent question, Thomas chastised himself as they made their way back to Hawkes Haven. As usual, Thomas was several feet behind Will and puffing hard, despite the fact that the younger man had to make use of his walking stick with every step.

Now that I have asked, all sorts of conjecture will be forthcoming as to the whys of my question and to the reason for my interest. Thomas shook his head, almost hanging it in shame as he walked. *If only I could ignore what I feel. I know it is not right for a vicar to feel these things.*

And as he walked, he tripped over a tangled root and tumbled to his knees, sprawling on the ground. Will, so far ahead already, did not hear the fall nor stop to offer help. So Thomas lifted himself up with a quick lurch and ran after his crippled friend, his arms pumping and his breath coming in short gasps.

■ ■ ■ ■

The breakfast platters had grown cold and were near empty. A huge platter of fried fish and rice quickly disappeared, as did a mound of biscuits and a full plate of oranges. Will did seem to have a most prodigious appetite for a man so slim.

Thomas picked and poked at the victuals this morn, for he was most perplexed and troubled. It was as if he searched for an answer to a question that never stayed the same from moment to moment.

Will smiled over his shoulder as he heard the twins laugh and babble away in the nursery. Jezalee had taken them, with a helper, to be bathed and dressed. It was an activity that consumed most of any morning, and it was one task that Kathryne was most pleased to allow others to perform.

"So, dear wife," Will said, his hands resting on his full belly, "Thomas has been quizzing me this day as to the time when our love for each other first entered our lives."

Kathryne turned her head to Thomas, a most curious stare in her eyes. "Indeed, Thomas?" she asked, holding back a giggle. "You ask of love? And you ask William before myself?"

Thomas opened his mouth to reply and moved his jaw, but found no words there to speak.

"Yes, darling," Will said. "He inquired from me first, for in me he must see a gentleness that does not occur in other men. Why else and who else would he ask?"

"William, you are a most sweet man." Kathryne smiled back, continuing, "And the dearest of husbands. But you are a man, and as such do not truly understand the enormity of falling in love."

Will played at being hurt. "I daresay that is untrue. I have a most romantic heart indeed."

Thomas's eyes bounced back and forth between the two, following the gentle words and observing the obvious love that flowed between them.

"Then shall you answer the vicar's question?" Kathryne teased. "When was the time that you first knew of such a love as we have? Was it on the *Plymouth Spirit* when you first encountered me, trapped in the captain's cabin?"

Will sat back and laughed, slapping his knee. "I think not, Kathryne," he said through his smile, "for if the truth be told, had you a blade that day, I would have found myself skewered and writhing on the floor."

Kathryne played at being shocked, a hand fluttering to her throat. "William!" she called out. "Such a thing to say of your most civil wife. Remember, it was you with the pistol, not myself."

"And you did not find love in your heart for me that day?"

Kathryne giggled. "You may have swept me off my feet, but it was with a faint from fear, not from a matter of the heart."

"Then was it at the waterfall? The day we first kissed, when you told me of God's love?" Will asked, a more serious note in his voice.

"Not even then, dear Will," she replied. "'Twas true that I was captivated by your charms and attempted to show you Christian love, but my heart was not yet turned to you in completeness."

"Then when?" Will asked, his elbows on the table, cradling his chin at the apex of the V they created, his blue eyes almost piercing.

Kathryne dropped her eyes to her lap and pursed her lips, as if thinking a most complex thought.

"It was . . . ," she said, her voice but a whisper, "it was as I left your ship to return to my father. It was at the moment I stepped into that small boat that would take me away from you. I knew at that point that my heart would break if I could not have you." She looked up, her green eyes clear and bright. "I know that I spent many more months telling myself that it was untrue, that it was only a moment of passion and surrender. But I told my heart falsehoods. I should have listened to it then. Perhaps we would have all been spared the pain that followed."

Will's face softened and looked close to tears, yet he smiled and reached out his hand, which Kathryne took and held tightly.

"Never apologize for such things, dear wife," he said, "for each step in our history has led us to this most perfect point. If we had not so endured, then would we be here this day? Only the Almighty knows, but I must say, I approve of his timing."

Kathryne nodded, swallowed, then spoke again. "You have never said as to the time you first knew, William. When was that moment?"

"I do not know if I can tell you . . . for you will not believe my words, I am sure."

Kathryne turned her head, her dark curls sliding from her bare shoulders to hang like a thick vine against her back.

"I will not believe? You say I will not take my husband's words for truth? I think not, William," she said, a hint of backbone increasing in each word. "Pray tell me. Tell us both of such a time."

Will opened his palms, as if giving up, and looked to Thomas, then to his wife.

"I believe that her words require an answer, William," Thomas said.

William sighed and laid his hands flat to the table. He looked down for a long moment, then back up, and then stared directly into Kathryne's luminescent eyes.

"Do you remember a foxhunt on the estate of the earl of Hadenthorne—in the fall of the year 1630?" Will asked.

Kathryne looked puzzled. She glanced over to Thomas, who shrugged in response.

"I know the date well, for it was the season of my father's death," Will stated softly.

Kathryne's eyes dropped again, for she knew the pain that his death had caused Will.

"I was a young boy, helping my father, aiding in the preparation for the foxhunt. There was a moment when I watched a young girl descend from a most elegant carriage. A young slip of girl. I did not know her name, but I saw her eyes. They were deep and green, like a cooling pool of turquoise. I inquired of my father as to the name of the family. He said it was the Spensers, from the shire of Dorset."

Will stopped talking for a moment. First there was silence, then a long peal of an infant's laughter from the nursery. Then a splash. Then another peal of the laughter of a babe. And then silence returned.

"I did not know the name of that girl, but it was as if her eyes had never left my heart, for in all the years hence, I have never forgotten those eyes, telling myself that someday I would love the person behind them, telling myself I should search for that . . . that deep window into a woman's soul."

Tears had begun to form in Kathryne's eyes. "It was you I saw that day. I looked into your eyes . . . and I saw you." She paused and sniffed. "But I never thought that one look meant anything to you. I never thought you would remember such a fleeting glance."

"I have never told you of this, Kathryne," Will whispered, "for I did not want you to think I was foolish or misguided. But it was then. It was then that I first loved you. I have known since that moment that it would always be you."

The wind hissed through the room and gentled the lace curtain at the window in a soft dance with the sun.

"For so long, I also told my heart lies, told it I was silly or mistaken. But it was not."

Kathryne sniffed and squeezed her husband's hand as tightly as she could. "I am sorry, dear William," she said. "I claimed you knew nothing of the emotions of falling in love. I have misspoken. It is I who know so little."

It was silent for a dozen long moments, as both their eyes searched the other's face, until a second noisy splash echoed from the nursery and a doubling of the laughter of a child spilled out of the room. Kathryne smiled and rose to go.

It was then that the door opened and Eileen entered, a beatific smile on her face, her arms full of bundles of cloth and velvet and a bag full of threads and cording.

"I have attended the milliner's as you asked, Kathryne, and have returned with treasures!" she exclaimed.

Thomas blanched white upon her entrance. Within only a moment, Thomas jumped to his feet, knocked over the chair in which he was sitting, and tripped on his way to the door.

"I simply must be going," he called out. "Many thanks for the breakfast and the answers to my queries."

He nodded, made a half bow toward Eileen, and added as he stumbled through the doorway, "Miss Palmerston, always nice to have seen you again."

Thomas then lurched from their presence and set off to the fort, almost at a dead run.

■ ■ ■ ■ ■

It was nearing noon, and the twins had settled in for a long nap. Will had been gone for hours, settling up accounts in town and then heading off to Shelworthy. Eileen and Kathryne had spread the fabrics and cording across every item of furniture in the dining chamber of Hawkes

Haven, attempting to determine the proper colors and fabrics for various pieces, both current and envisioned.

Kathryne held a long draping of a rich damask with a light rose tint against the window, allowing the sun full play on its surface. She looked first to the fabric, then to the chair on which it was to be placed, then back to the fabric again.

"Is this too muted?" she asked of Eileen. "Or will this subtle patterning be visible in such a large space?"

Eileen stepped back and cocked her head to one side, narrowed her eyes, then stepped forward. "Indeed it will, Kathryne. It looks most settled in this place. A most becoming choice."

Kathryne laid the bolt over the chair and sat in the folds and creases, as if it would be an approximation of how the finished product might look. She fingered the coarse edge with her hand and watched Eileen as she spread other samples and fabrics out, holding one to another, selecting and rejecting one after another.

"Eileen," she asked, "have you spoken recently to Vicar Mayhew?"

Eileen spun about, a few samples flapping from her grip and settling at her feet. The lines on her forehead appeared furrowed with concern, but only for a brief moment. "Other than this morning?" she replied quickly.

"Yes," Kathryne responded, "other than this morning."

She placed her finger to her lips in an attitude of deep thought. "I do see him on Sunday mornings, and on chance we share a word or two of greeting then . . . but there have been few other occasions for us to speak at length."

"He has never asked for your company at a dinner, perhaps?"

Eileen narrowed her eyes. "No," she replied, "he has not. Why, if I might ask, do you ask?"

Kathryne looked back at her, her eyes filled with an innocent stare. "Oh . . . there is no reason. Mere curiosity is all." And then she smiled at Eileen with a most open and accepting expression. "Just curious is all."

■ ■ ■ ■

An uneasy quiet settled about Hawkes Haven. Kathryne had left the dining chamber to attend to her children, leaving Eileen alone with her spinning thoughts.

Why would Kathryne have asked of myself and the vicar?

She sipped at her tea, now grown cool, the temperature of the morning. She fussed with some fabrics piled on the table before her, holding first a blue to the light, then a red, then a light linen, then all three together.

I will never grasp the complexity of colors displayed together, she thought, and tossed them in a gentle heap before her. *Kathryne thinks I possess more skills than I truly do.*

She turned to the large window facing the sea and watched the clouds roll from the east and sail across the ocean's face in a soft parade.

The vicar? she puzzled, returning to her curiosity of a moment before. *Why would Kathryne inquire of his actions to me?*

She picked up a broken honey cake and nibbled at the edge, not from hunger but driven by a feeling of anxiousness. She fought the thoughts that were slowly forming in her mind, attempting to dismiss them as the most fantastic and far-fetched that any woman could devise.

It sounded as though she thought the vicar might be interested in me—or be planning to ask for my company.

She shook her head to clear that thought. *Preposterous,* she decided, *that a man of the vicar's stature and morality could have any interest in a woman like myself. Simply unthinkable.*

She nodded, agreeing with her own internal assessment of the questioning. A thick, gray cloud slid past the window, and the sun was covered for a long moment, then returned with a blaze of intensity. Eileen blinked in response and held her eyes closed for a long moment, listening for sounds and hearing nothing.

It simply is fanciful talk and nothing more, she said again to herself. *A woman like me has no right to think further on this than I already have.*

And as she blinked again, there was a fleeting image of Thomas's face in her thoughts, a smile on his features, a curious questioning smile.

The image was at once so real and so distracting that she dropped the honey cake, and it rolled with a crumbly bounce across the floor. In less than a heartbeat, she heard Bo jump to his feet and pounce on the unexpected treat dropping from the heavens, as it were, to his waiting appetite.

■■■■

His legs were pumping quickly, his arms flailing in the air as he ran back to the fort and back to the solace of his small few rooms. The vicar grabbed at the back of a chair to hold himself upright as he panted for breath, sweat clouding his eyes.

It was nearly afternoon by the time his heart regained its normal rhythm.

This cannot be! he insisted to himself, his inner voice demanding and stern. *I must not ignore my duties again in this most undisciplined manner! She cannot occupy my thoughts in such a way. I am an old foolish man and must not allow this to happen!*

He sat at his small plank desk and stared at a blank sheet of vellum, his hand holding a feathered quill, the ink slowly dropping from the nub in tiny dark rings.

I must be strong. I must.

Thomas puttered about in his small darkened rooms that afternoon, first lifting one possession, then replacing it in another location. Then the action would be repeated again with another curio, until by the time the evening shadows began to lengthen and draw across Fort Charles, he had touched every movable object in his home at least once, and often twice. A small crucifix had been relocated more than a dozen times, from desk to windowsill, from windowsill to door frame, and had made that journey more than three times alone.

As he wandered about the small space, his thoughts were a tangled storm of fleeting, snatched images that appeared for a moment, then slipped from his mind's eye. He made no real attempt to slow the flood, but allowed himself to go where the current led. He often remarked that such unstructured thinking was most conducive to settling worries and discovering new approaches to thorny problems. Back in Hadenthorne, what now seemed a lifetime ago, he would walk along the river, not thinking, waiting for his mind to locate the source of his heart's questioning. Often he would arrive at a place several miles up- or downriver, having no idea of how he had come to that place—and often would not recognize his location. It was a fact he seldom revealed, but he was often lost on these rambles and would need seek a farmer's direction to point him back to the parsonage of St. Jerome's.

On this island he attempted less of that, for the heat was often so beastly that he was afraid he would expire as he walked. More often he would pace inside his house or walk along the outside of Fort Charles.

Yet this day he realized that he could pace till he reached London and the conundrum he faced would not be resolved. He felt a nagging, looming fear that the answer was lost or hidden and he would breathe his last before he would find the solution.

Dark stretched its dim fingers into the fort and blanketed Thomas. He sat, at long last, and looked about. He blinked, for he scarcely recognized his home anymore, such was the extent of his rearranging and replacing. He put his elbows to his knees and cupped his head in his hands and sighed. He had no alternative save to pray, for his human abilities were failing him.

"Dearest God," he began, his voice soft and humbled, "I am lost. I am a foolish old man, and I know what I am thinking is wrong. A man such as myself who is in thy service cannot think of a woman such as Miss Palmerston—at least not in the manner of which my thoughts are taking me. I cannot overlook her sordid past. I cannot . . . can I? It is too great a gulf for any man's love to cross. And I must think also of thee, whom I represent here on earth. Wouldst thou have a man such as I linked with a woman such as that? I know that by thy grace the vilest of sins are forgiven. I know that regardless of the blackness of our soul, thou alone offers forgiveness and the erasure of all the past. But man is not as forgiving. If I were to imagine such an . . . arrangement, how damaging could that be to my witness for thee here? How many of these sinners would turn away from thy Word because of my actions?"

Thomas stopped and let silence again flood into the room. His ears heard the rolling and rumbling of the sea, and the far-off caw of gulls. He could discern a most polite scratching that may have been a mouse in the far wall. He heard the sound of his own breath as it filled then emptied from his lungs.

He sighed again, having no words to use that felt to him as correct. "Lord, please show me the way. Guide my heart. Set my steps to thy path."

And then, most unexpectedly, a tear formed in his eye and splashed in a dusty puddle at his feet.

CHAPTER

21

25 July 1645

The morning sun gleamed off the exterior walls of Shelworthy and illuminated the cracks and peeling paint from the north side of the structure. No paint yet formulated could withstand the harshness of the tropical sun and the rain and the heat and the dampness. Ian Tafert stood there, his hands on his hips, staring up at the walls, tapping his foot with great impatience.

Early that morning he had called for a dozen darkies to be brought up to begin to scrape away the damaged paint. It was now nearing midday, and not one person—slave, servant, or nobleman—was stirring outside. Save himself, that is. It was always Tafert doing more, working harder, struggling longer than anyone else on the island. He still owed Governor Spenser a full two years of service, until his meager freedom dues would be paid. The few indentured workers that had been paid off in the last months had found their allotted acreage to be at the very farthest corner of the island, well into the area called the Scottish Highlands, and so far from town and the harbor that many simply took the money alone and sailed back to England.

Since no one was in attendance that morning, and since Tafert was not about to begin any of the hard, manual labor himself, he looked about, pulled out a plug of tobacco, gnawed off a mouthful, and sat in the shade of the governor's home.

He closed his eyes, and a thin, brown dribble of juice from the leaf coursed down his chin, staining the stubble there a rich ochre. He smiled, recalling the conversation of the previous day, the conversation he had with Gleeson at the Publican.

Gleeson, ever the impetuous fool, had been ready to give the word, to attack the noblemen as they slept, to slit throats and set fire to all the proper, mighty plantation houses he could.

"Now's the time to set our plans into action," he had wheezed, finishing off his fourth rum flip, using his greasy and matted sleeve to wipe at his mouth. "I got more than a dozen darkies who be with me and be doin' my biddin'. They be tired of bein' slaves, and I be tired of bein' their master. We be wantin' our freedom now! Gawblimy, I cannot see why there be a reason for further delayin'. I don't give a tinker's dam 'bout Cap'n Bliss and waitin' for the weddin' and all. I says we take action now!" Gleeson had gasped as he finished his tirade and had fallen into a fit of coughing.

Tafert had twisted his face into a smile. "It be that you haven't got the patience that be needed for such things," he had explained, careful to keep his voice low and even. While the Publican had been nearly empty, a few drunken sailors and two women of dubious virtue had loitered at tables at the far end of the dank room. Tafert had been concerned about placing his future in jeopardy by boastful and loud talk he had no intentions of showing his hand in front of some old salt who may repeat their words to Captain Bliss the next fortnight. "We have no problem with the recruitin' of darkies. That be easier than froggin' in a barrel. We have no problems with enlistin' us proper Englishmen to the task. We have more than a dozen who be sympathetic to our plans."

Gleeson had snapped his fingers in the air, indicating another round of drinks was desired. As the barman delivered two full tankards, Tafert had waited in silence before continuing his argument. "But listen, you low-witted clump—it not be for lack of manpower that these things fail. It be from bad timin' is all. You think the good king or Cromwell— whoever wins the bloody war back home—be sittin' idly by whilst we be takin' over these lands and estates?"

He had leaned forward and had rapped his knuckles against Gleeson's head, who had responded by yelping and almost falling from his stool. "They not be that stupid or forgivin'," Tafert had gone on. "We needs to do it big—we needs to do it on every estate on the island. By the time we be done, we be in every one of these fancy houses. And if the dim-witted king or the scoundrel Cromwell be wantin' our sugar, then they be forced to be dealin' with us. We need to wait for the proper moment. We can't be doin' it one at a time, you stupid git. And that be the reason we need be waitin' for the muskets and men that Cap'n Bliss provides. I not be sayin' I trust the man, but he has weapons—and we don't."

Gleeson had snarled, "I not be takin' kindly to all your insults and names, Tafert. This be my idea from the outset, and I be askin' you to remember that. Bliss or no Bliss, I be owed respect fer what I brought and what I thought."

Tafert had smiled again, thin and tight. "Oh, Mr. Gleeson, I do apologize for besmirchin' your fine family name. And be most assured that I will never be forgettin' whose grand idea all of this was. It be yours, plain and simple, and I be meanin' to tell all when the time be nearer."

Gleeson had glared at the wiry man for a long moment and then had reached out a muddy palm and offered it. "I be forgivin' you, then, Tafert," he had said as they shook hands. "As long as you be aware of who be responsible for all this. That be the important thing, eh?"

Tafert had smiled, a free and clear smile, for the first time the entire evening. "Indeed, Mr. Gleeson," he had oozed. "It truly be the important issue."

"You there!" Aidan presently called out from the porch. "Tafert! What are you doing simply sitting here this day? Do not you have some specific duties to perform?"

Tafert fell to his side, having dozed off with a smile on his face during his musings. He rolled to his knees and stood in a jumble, brushing away dust and leaves from his backside, spitting a prodigious volume of tobacco juice from his mouth, wiping at the excess with the back of his hand.

"Yes . . . my lord," he stammered. "I be waitin' for the crew of darkies to commence the scrapin' of th' paint from this wall. They to be here by this hour, and I be set to wait for 'em, Gov'nor, sir."

Aidan scowled at him for a long moment. "Well, if they do not arrive by noon, I would strongly suggest that you abandon your unproductive waiting and tend to some real work. I am not employing you to simply sit on your backside for an entire morning."

Aidan turned and walked back to the front door, unaware of the baleful glare and the impudent gesture Tafert leveled at his back.

CHAPTER

22

28 July 1645

Vicar Mayhew entered the public house Cross and Arms and blinked in the dimness. He sniffed the stale air, filled with smoke and the aroma of rum, brandy, and ale spilled on the rough wooden planked floor in great abundance.

On most days, the vicar would hardly have considered this a proper respite for a man of the cloth. But many of his congregation frequented the establishment, and several of the women in residence here had come, on occasion, to a Sunday service.

Yet the vicar was not making a witnessing call, nor was he in the habit of inhabiting such places. If the truth be told, it was that he was hungry. He had tired so of his own efforts at setting food upon his meager table. He had awakened with a gnawing in his stomach that no amount of hard cheese could satisfy. In fact, the vicar wished never to view cheese again, so frequent had been his consumption of it. As the sun had neared noon, the vicar had gathered his pride and begun to stroll toward Hawkes Haven with the hope of being invited to share their noon meal.

But when coming within a hundred yards of the front door, he spied a woman's head and torso through the open window of the great room, holding some sort of fabric to the very top of the opening. It was not Kathryne, he knew, for the hair was red. In a sudden jolt, he realized that he was staring at Miss Palmerston, and before he could form a cogent thought, his feet turned and propelled him toward the harbor.

He was overwhelmed by his sudden nervousness. True, he had recently been near to Miss Palmerston and had actually shared more than a few words with her on the past two Sundays. But such conversations were with a large group of others standing in close proximity, and the themes of such talk focused on his most recent message or the duration of the very hot weather or the likelihood of a storm brewing in the east. He had hoped that she had not noticed his nervousness or that his laughter was more forced and pitched than was his norm.

If she had noticed anything out of the standard, he thought, *she was gracious enough to simply not respond visibly.*

And so Thomas had found himself hungry, frustrated, and walking along the crowded streets of Bridgetown.

In the months that Thomas had been on the island, the town seemed to expand like a fairy circle of mushrooms after a warm summer night in England. Almost like magic, new structures appeared, shops opened, merchants set out wares, competing for the farthings and shillings of customers. What once could be traversed in a matter of moments, the town now was a warren of streets and alleys and turnings, each lined with the facades of shops and homes. Planking was laid out as a walkway about the town, for the rains would leave the streets a muddy quagmire in a matter of moments, sucking off men's boots and swallowing them whole.

Thomas had not spent much time exploring the new streets, and despite Bridgetown's small size, he quickly became disoriented. He sighed, looked down at the ground with resignation, and felt his stomach grumble again, louder and more angry. He sniffed the air, which smelled of a pungent roasting—young fowl perhaps, or a guinea hen, he thought—and his stomach rumbled again, even louder.

It was then that he entered the Cross and Arms, after spending a moment to closely examine the freshly painted sign hung over the front entrance. Thomas puzzled that while the facade looked less than a few weeks old, the interior looked and smelled as if it had been here for decades. He looked about in the dimness and saw an empty table by the front window. Dusting the crumbs off the stool with his hand, he sat and stared out. Through a gap in the buildings across the street he could see the harbor and the dozen ships lying at anchor, rocking gently on the azure waters.

Within a moment or two, the barman shouted from across the room, "What be yer pleasure, Vicar? Be hidin' from some'un, or be ye lookin' for a wee drop to slack ye thirst?"

Thomas startled upright, shook his head to clear his thoughts, and replied, "What might be that most pleasing aroma? Is it roasted fowl?"

The barman grinned wide, revealing a mostly toothless smile. "Ye be a man of proper tastes, then, wouldn't ye? It be a couple of fat and juicy guineas—just waitin' for a man like ye to eat 'em."

Thomas nodded. "That is what I would like, and perhaps a small flagon of wine as well."

The plate on which the roasted fowl was delivered looked none too clean, but it was heaped with the roasted bird and all manner of side dishes—potatoes, turnips, yams, and beans. The barkeep set down a huge linen square under the plate, nearly a yard in width and length.

"Be not fussin' with them fancy forks or knifes, Vicar. Eat like the Lord intended—the fingers be most satisfactory, if ye be askin' me."

Thomas thanked him, bowed his head, and offered a heartfelt prayer of thanks for the meal. All the while he prayed, his stomach rolled and rumbled, anxiously awaiting its due. The food was even better than it smelled, and before noon had slipped past, Thomas emptied the plate, leaving only a bare carcass of bones in his appetite's wake.

He pushed the plate to the far side of the table, poured the last of the wine, and let his body slump in the chair, feeling at last fully satiated and comfortable. The sun had cleared the top of the building where the vicar sat and now played upon his face, warming him and nearly lulling his body to sleep.

"Vicar Mayhew!" a voice barked out, strident and grating. "My heavens! To see you in such an establishment. Do tell me that I am mistaken and that you are not a regular patron of this . . . place."

Thomas sat upright, almost spilling the wine into his lap as he bounced against the table. He blinked his eyes in the sharp sunlight. Slowly a face came into view, sniffing the air, its nose tilted up, the sun radiating out from behind like a moon during an eclipse. It was Vicar Giles Petley, carrying a stack of letters in one hand and under his arm a large bolt of fabric so black and thick it seemed to soak up the sun.

"Ah," Thomas said as he tried to gather his wits, "Vicar Petley, how nice of you to drop by. . . . I mean, how nice to see you."

"Do you know you are in a public house . . . of dubious patronage?" Giles asked, leaning forward at the waist, unwilling to draw any closer than necessary.

Thomas looked about, as if really seeing his surroundings for the first time. "It was for an afternoon meal, is all, Giles. I had tired of my own cooking, and the fare here is most tasty."

Giles sniffed again as if he had stepped in a fouled puddle. "All well and good, Thomas, but a proper vicar—such as myself—would never deign enter such a place. We have a reputation to honor. We must avoid the appearances of evil, to be certain." And then he took a small step back, distancing himself even further, so that the heel of his boot was no more than a hair's width from the edge of the wooden walkway.

"What a day today has become!" he rattled on. "First, I receive news that the beloved Bishop Laud was tried for treason, found guilty, and executed. That such a tragedy should befall the church, who could have imagined? And now I see you here—in this place—flaunting the holiness to which you were called as a vicar of Christ! What can possibly happen next?"

Thomas held his ire in check. He paused for a heartbeat, but could not hold his tongue any longer. "I am most sorry to hear of the unfortunate death of the bishop. But, Giles, do you not think that we should go to the places where the sinners are? How else will we afford them a view of the Almighty? I daresay most of these men would never darken the entry of a church."

"So?" Giles responded. "I am sure that through a birth or a marriage or a funeral they will hear of God's kingdom in some manner. I simply would not lower myself to such a level as this," he said, indicating Thomas's position with a dismissing wave of his hand.

It was such a flippant gesture that Thomas felt his face redden with anger. "Does that mean I should never aspire to becoming close to a man or woman who has sinned—who has fallen and now attempts to regain their footing with God? Would you have me ignore them, Giles?"

Giles opened his eyes wide, as if in great surprise by Thomas's words. "I do not intend to stand here and debate such issues, Vicar Mayhew. I simply would suggest that you be on guard to protect your image. After all, is not your image the most important element of your person?"

And with that he looked away, stating very firmly without words that this conversation had ended. He took a step backward, unaware of how close to the edge was his foot. He slumped from the footway and descended with a syrupy *splash* into the mud, puddled there nearly to the depth of a man's knee. Giles had the presence of mind to toss the fabric he held to the safety of the wooden walk, then he tipped backward with his fading scream of indignity—the last sound Thomas heard as Giles disappeared below the walk and into the muck.

Thomas, as he arose to offer help, told himself that he could not smile. And he knew that he had at last an answer for his most puzzling question concerning Miss Palmerston.

▪ ▪ ▪ ▪

Emily slid her teacup to one side and her plate of biscuits to the other. She then smoothed a wrinkled paper with a firm push of her hand. When a letter spent a month or two in its journey from England to

Barbados, despite the expense of the posting or thickness of the vellum, the letters most oft arrived creased and smudged.

Emily took great care in her handling of this letter, for it was from her solicitor in London, and he had never been known for his extravagance in paper or of letters. So even if a single word became illegible, it might have rendered the entire document useless for the economy of his phrasings. Emily pulled the candelabra close to provide adequate reading light.

Aidan looked up from his plate of meat and fruits. "I heard the messenger bring the posting, Emily," he said. "May I inquire as to its import?"

Emily did not speak. With each turning day, she had grown more resolved that unless Aidan were to suddenly change his spots, she would have to seek out other arrangements on this island. For she felt her heart tighten harder each day that Aidan delayed, and she did not want to become an embittered old woman and knew it best if she could escape before the process was too entrenched. She had spent hours upon hours in prayer over her dilemma. Should she become insistent and thus drive a wedge further between them? Should she demure and wait—and wait—and wait for Aidan to decide on the proper timing of their proposed nuptials? The very word *marriage,* or *nuptials,* or *wedding* would spread tension through the house like a winter storm— so much so that Emily had scarcely uttered those words in months. It would be to God's timing, she felt, and not hers, if such an agreement was to be reached.

"Emily?" Aidan asked again as he placed a very precise dollop of jam on his biscuit, "What is in the letter?"

Emily heard his request, of course, but chose not to answer until she had determined if it was a proper message to share.

In a cramped style, her solicitor inquired as to her health. The climate on Barbados and on all the Lesser Antilles was often so vile, he wrote, based on the rumors in England, that settlers died faster than could be replaced by English shipping. He then inquired as to her plans for the future. Was she to stay in the islands? He mentioned that she was of an age when such matters as travel could not be considered lightly. Her days of mobility, he wrote, might be limited.

Emily smiled to herself. *He must mean well, and I am sure his intentions are noble,* she thought, *but a more dour and depressing letter I can scarce imagine receiving.*

"Emily," Aidan asked again, "will you inform me at some point this morning as to your letter's contents?"

Aidan's tenacious pursuing of his goals, whether they were small, such as this, or large, such as bringing English respectability to all of the Caribbean, could be viewed as charming and noble. However, this day Emily found his dogged pursuing so maddening and so vexing that she chose to ignore him entirely.

She read on, silently, peering closer to the page. He wrote that her townhouse in London, once run as a finishing school for young ladies of the peerage, was once again empty. The tenants, in the diplomatic corps of the French king, whom Emily had selected before she left for the Caribbean, had recently been recalled to Paris. Her solicitor remarked, with a hint of pride, Emily noted, that they had paid for the full year yet only made use of it for six months. There would be a sizable savings, he wrote, because of reduced needs for servants and upkeep. The savings, of course, would be added to Emily's accounts in London.

But that was not the true crux of the letter. He wrote that despite the political turmoil of the times, business and commerce flourished as never before. It appeared that the war was coming to an end, with Cromwell's New Model Army destroying the king's main army at Naseby and Langport. So merchants, shippers, and trade guilds all the more clamored for a bigger share of the market and sought to increase their holdings—and thus their influence—in the post-war period.

Emily's townhouse was extraordinarily well suited, he said, being in close proximity to Parliament, Buckingham Palace, the city, and the river docks. Houses up and down that street had sold and resold at doubling and tripling of their value. Emily owned the land on a freehold basis—it was hers to keep or sell—so no leases would encumber the property. The solicitor wrote that a certain syndicate of bankers had approached him with a purchase price that he was faint to write on paper, lest it fall into the wrong hands. Suffice it to say, he continued, that her accounts, of which she was aware of the total assets, would be fully tripled if he was allowed to offer the property for sale.

Emily sat back and ceased reading upon that report. *A full tripling!* she thought, amazed. *That would make me a most wealthy woman indeed.*

She could authorize him to proceed with the arrangements, or Emily could sail home and do so herself, for an additional two months of wait will only increase the buyers' appetite, the solicitor was certain.

"Emily," Aidan repeated again, this time a shade louder and edging on a peevish tone, "I have inquired as to the subject matter of your letter, and I have not received an answer. Is it bad news? Is it good news? I should think I warrant your reply."

Emily scanned the last few paragraphs, an assortment of trivial details. She smoothed the letter once more, with a most deliberate slowness. *Was this the answer for which I prayed?* she thought. *If not, why now? If not, why at all?* She folded the letter once along its original crease and slipped it back into its envelope.

"Why, Aidan," she replied, her voice cloyingly sweet, "it is an inconsequential matter after all. Nothing to be concerned with," she bubbled cheerfully as she turned from her chair and rose to exit the room. "It is simply a matter of real estate. My solicitor has requested that I sell the Alexandrian. He is such a dear man that he has insisted that I return to London at once to attend to all the details."

And with that she slipped out the door. As she exited she noticed Aidan sat still, his jaw gaping wide, his hand poised in midair, holding a fork with a morsel of roast pork skewered on its polished prongs.

* * *

Vicar Mayhew did not laugh as he helped extract Vicar Petley from the mud and muck. He borrowed a twig broom from the barkeep at the Cross and Arms and within moments had succeeded in scraping and brushing away most of the dirt caked on Giles's backside and legs. A small pile of mud clumps grew about Giles's feet. With each brushing, Giles grew angrier and his face grew redder.

To his credit, though, he did not speak above a normal tone, nor did he utter words that might be construed as curses or blasphemous talk. But neither did he offer thanks to Thomas; he simply stomped off, the planks beneath his feet reverberating with his enraged steps.

Thomas settled his bill for his meal, thanked the barkeep for the broom, and began to make his way home. His heart was lighter and of better cheer than it had ever been, he felt. It was nothing that Giles had said in particular that turned his thoughts, but he knew that what he inferred was very wrong and against how a Christian should act and feel. While his judgment may have been endemic to the clergy of the Anglican church, Thomas knew in his deepest core that it was not as the Almighty desired.

He had denied the urgings of his heart for too long. He would take a chance. He would do what his soul had called out for—to connect with another on a deeper level than he had ever experienced.

He stopped at the rock outcropping where he had prayed so earnestly only days before. His prayers this day were much more direct, much bolder, much more focused.

Dearest Lord, I ask for thy blessing and thy guidance. Thou knowest

*my heart better than I and knowest how this old man yearns to hold
someone close. Thou hast provided my soul that wonderful blessing,
but my arms yearn for the same as well. I pray that this is not
displeasing to thee, for Eileen has been forgiven by thy miraculous
power and yearns to serve thee. If a woman or man turns from their sin
to follow thee—am I not obligated to honor that change as well?
Cannot a man, a sinner such as I, seek love with such a person? I pray
that thou wilt guide my words, as for the first time in my life, my heart
trembles at such a task. I was not afraid of death in prison, though I
faced it every day. Yet this task brings my knees to shake, O God.
Watch over me and protect me, Lord, as I seek to do thy will. Amen.*

Thomas looked up, expecting to view a restless sea, only to find the
wind diminished and a smooth surface, the color of polished silver,
stretching as far as his eye could see. He touched at his chest, for his
heart beat so softly and with such peace that he scarce recognized its
rhythms.

Aidan lowered his arm at a rate slower than a feather falls to the
ground. The pork cushioned the fork's landing on his plate so no sound
was heard. The house grew as still and quiet as a graveyard. Aidan
looked down at his plate, his appetite now departed. He put his hands
flat to the table to help stabilize his spinning thoughts and calm his
quaking stomach, which roiled and tightened in fear.

*Go back to London? Have I heard correctly? How could that be?
Did we not agree that a marriage would be our destiny? The sale of a
property can be handled by others with ease. I know, for I have bought
and sold dozens of things without being in attendance.*

He turned to look out the window. The sky was a brilliant blue; a
thin sparkling of clouds dotted the heavens. It was no match for the
blackness that now poured over Aidan's world.

*This cannot be. She cannot leave, for we are to be married. Has she
forgotten her acceptance of my request? She could not have.*

His thoughts swirled. Should he arise and take steps to follow her
and insist that she abandon such a foolish plan? Should he demand that
she stay and fulfill her promise?

After all, I have never indicated any other course than to be married.
He stood and took a few hesitant steps to the door. *Other than once
asking for a delay in the date. . . . Or twice . . . or has it been thrice?*

He reached the door, his hand on the latch, and a great dawning of
awareness swept over him, like the tide rushes to the shore.

It took Aidan a full half of one hour to navigate the journey from the dining chamber to the outer door of Emily's suite of rooms on the far eastern wing of Shelworthy. He paused at each step, considering and reconsidering the truth of his inaction these past months. He formulated one apology on the first step, only to reject it and rework the words by step two. Each small ascent marked a different thought, a different tack, a different reason to be sorry, a different reason to feel guilty and ashamed.

By the time he had climbed each of the twenty-four steps, each inlaid with hardwood patterning, he had formulated and discarded a full dozen varying approaches. At the top of the stairs he stood, confused, his heart aching, as if part of it were dying. He put his hands on the polished railing and bent slightly at the waist, closing his eyes and lowering his head. He was not a man of prayer and had never been an exceedingly devout Christian. He believed he knew of God's gift and fully accepted it as his own, yet he had never allowed the fullness of salvation to be interspersed in his daily activities. Even this act, a prayer of desperation, felt forced and awkward. He worried that the Lord of heaven would see this action as a last resort—to petition the Almighty when the skies looked their blackest. Yet even if that is how the prayer appeared, Aidan could not help prevent it and mumbled softly in the quiet house, pouring out his hopes, his dreams, and his fears.

Could he be a good husband again? Could he be head of a household once more where it was most obviously the wife who was the one with the stronger faith? Could he ever forget the past and let his heart follow the future as it should be?

He paused for a moment, looking out on the great hall below him.

It is most odd, he thought, *for in all these months I have never considered these truths. Only now that I am at risk of losing her do they flood my soul. I am perplexed . . . yet so much at peace as well.*

He stood up, straightened his doublet, smoothed his hair, and tidied the bow that held it tied at his neck. He set his lips tight, turned, and marched in long, deliberate steps to Emily's door. He raised his hand and hesitated a moment, his knuckles only an inch from the ivory-painted wood panel.

He gulped, breathed in deeply, and prayed for guidance . . . or strength . . . or wisdom . . . whatever it took, he petitioned the Lord to provide him.

Then he drew back his hand and rapped at the door, a hollow, empty sound reverberating through the warm rooms of Shelworthy.

At first, Emily did not notice the rapping at the outer door. She was sitting in the window seat, the glass sash drawn up, letting the fragrances of the lush island wash into the room. Intermixed with the scents of bougainvillea and frangipani, the sweet scent of sugar wafted through the warm air.

How I will miss that intoxicating scent, she thought as she cradled her solicitor's letter in her hand. *But I see no future here. I have asked for a sign, and I believe the Lord has provided me with one.*

The rapping, louder now, brought her back to the present. She stood up, placed the letter on her bed, and went through the small corridor from her suite of three rooms to the door that faced the main upper hall. She opened the door to find Aidan standing there, his hand poised in midair.

"Emily," he finally said, then stopped and just looked into her eyes.

"Aidan," she replied even and cool.

No words were spoken for a long series of moments, Aidan seemingly content to look into Emily's face, Emily searching his face for his reason for being there.

"Would you like to come in, Aidan?" Emily finally asked.

Aidan mutely nodded and followed her into the small sitting area outside her sleeping chamber. Emily chose the smaller chair and sat down, adjusting her gown as demurely as she could. Aidan hovered above the remaining chair as if he could not decide whether to sit or stand.

It was another long moment until Emily spoke again. "Aidan, is there a specific reason that brings you to my room? For if not, I have a myriad of preparations to attend to prior to my voyage."

Aidan sat at those words and placed his hands on his knees. He looked to the floor, then back to Emily's face.

"I am not a romantic man," he began.

Emily nodded, ever so slightly, but was willing to agree with him in full measure on his assessment.

"I am not so skilled in the social niceties, Emily. At first it was Beatrice who smoothed my rough edges, and then Kathryne."

Emily nodded in agreement again, this time even more pronounced.

"And here I am, attempting to fight for the person I love most in this world, and I have no words to use. Were I a court poet, I would not know how to utter the loving words."

Emily had been looking down as he spoke, but then her head snapped back to seek his eyes.

"I have no rights, Emily, to forbid or instruct or demand on how and where you go or buy and sell. If your estate requires your presence in London, then how can I prevent you from—"

"Aidan," she interrupted, "what did you say?"

He looked as frightened as a rabbit caught in a woodsman's snare. "I . . . I . . . I said that if you require to travel to London—"

"No," she called out, "before that."

He tightened his eyes. "That I have no rights or demands?"

She smiled and shook her head. "Before that, Aidan."

He tilted his head to the side, trying to recall his exact words. "That . . . that . . . ," he stammered, then suddenly realized which words had caused her to startle. "That I am fighting for the person I love most in this world?"

Tears formed in Emily's eyes. "Yes, Aidan, those are the words. I truly believed you when you first said those words, but you have uttered them so seldom since that date that I have begun to doubt their truth."

"But I have always felt that way," he explained. "I have loved you from that day—and before, if the truth be fully told."

"But I am not a magician that I may read your thoughts."

"Ah," he uttered, suddenly contrite. He blinked his eyes several times. His voice was hushed as velvet. "When I heard that you might leave this island—that you might leave my side—my world suddenly grew bleak and empty. I cannot bear to lose you, Emily. I do love you. You may need to urge me to repeat that sentiment, but be assured that it is in my heart."

Emily nodded, not yet willing to stand and embrace the man.

"And what of our future, Aidan?" she asked. "We shall soon be growing old. You have grandchildren now. How many more seasons will the Lord grant us? Do you not understand my anger in your delays? Every morning that we wake in separate rooms is a morning never to be recaptured. We may have wealth and titles, Aidan, but we cannot afford to squander our days in fear."

Aidan stood, then knelt before her. "You must forgive me, dear, sweet Emily, for my distractions. I am a foolish old man who has been too accustomed to thinking only of himself. I have been too foolish to admit that I am alone."

She placed her hand on his shoulder. "There is nothing to forgive, darling Aidan."

He looked up into her eyes again.

"And you love me as well?" he asked.

She smiled and graced his cheek with her fingers, a long trailing sweep along the lines and edges of his face.

"More than life itself."

"Then will you marry me, in a fortnight's time from this date?"

Emily sat back an inch or two. "Only a fortnight to plan all the details of a wedding?"

Aidan smiled. "I would have said a week, but I was attempting to be most gracious."

Emily smiled and nodded. "Yes, Aidan. Yes."

And in the warm silence of that room, their lips met in a long, restrained joining. The kiss spoke of a dignified passion, of a proper and civilized love. Yet a moment passed, then two, and the duration of the kiss began to speak as loud of their hunger, only now being made evident.

■ ▪ ■ ▪ ■

Aidan had never been sure of how it happened or of what means the chambermaid used, but within moments of any important decision being made at Shelworthy, Hattie would shuffle past the room, hover in the background, then ask Aidan a question regarding the outcome that he had only moments before decided.

She knew of Kathryne's impending motherhood before anyone else, apparently, though Aidan claimed that it was simply a matter of a woman reading a woman's face. Such a feat was beyond most men, he reasoned. She knew of his proposal to Emily for her hand, so many months ago now, within an hour of the question being asked. At the time, he was puzzled over Hattie's lack of enthusiasm, yet it must have been that she had also divined that he would hesitate until this very moment.

So it was this afternoon that her being outside Emily's bedchamber caused Aidan no great surprise. He fully expected to see her standing there, though he had misjudged the breadth of her smile. For this day, her beaming countenance seemed to fill the wide hallway with joy and celebration.

"It be certain, Gov'nor Spenser?" she asked, as she nodded and near quivered with excitement.

Aidan, whose heart felt more buoyant and free than it had felt in decades, was not about to give in without a playful tussle.

"Certain about what, Hattie?" he asked, his face a serious mask.

Hattie threw her hands in the air. "You be knowin', Gov'nor. It be Lady Em and you? It be the time?"

Aidan smiled as well, then took her hands in his, plump and covered with a thin dusting of flour, and held them, joining nobleman and slave in a most childlike manner.

"Hattie," he asked, making his voice grow serious, "how is it that you know before I what I will be choosing? Do you spend all your day listening at keyholes?"

Hattie looked shocked. "Dat not be true a'tall, Gov'nor. You know dat. It be dat you don' be keepin' secrets, dat's all."

"How can that be, Hattie?" he said, pulling her hands together. "For I have not spoken to you this day until now."

Hattie pulled one hand free, then flagged her finger at him in a girlish wave. "Dat not it, Gov'nor. It be yer eyes an' all. Dey be tellin' on yer heart. I kin read yer eyes. Dat's all."

Aidan smiled, let her hand drop, and finally admitted to her, "'Tis true, Hattie. You have two weeks to prepare a feast for our wedding. A fortnight from today, I shall be united with Lady Emily."

Hattie's eyes grew round and wide as saucers. "You be sayin' two weeks? Not two months?"

"Two weeks. I shall not wait any longer, now that I have seen the error of my ways."

She hung her head and sighed, swinging it from side to side. "A man be takin' forever to be sayin' yes, den he do an' he be sayin' two weeks." She held a finger up to him, scolding him. "It not be nuff time a'tall. But I be likin' Lady Em, so I be workin' hard."

She turned and stepped toward Emily's room. "I not be doin' it fo' no man," she whispered just so Aidan could hear, "but I be doin' for Lady Em, fo' sure."

▪ ▪ ▪ ▪ ▪

As quickly as Thomas's thoughts had become settled over Miss Palmerston, as he walked home to Fort Charles that night after another delicious meal from the Cross and Arms, they became unsettled, as if being scattered with the evening breeze. Thomas padded homeward along the darkened lane, picking his way among the ruts and puddles of High Street. His stride became even slower and more meandering as he turned onto the narrow path that led along the shore.

How many questions have been debated here? he wondered as he passed the smooth boulder outcropping that overlooked the gently rolling tide. He stopped out of habit and looked to the sunset, across the darkening Caribbean Sea to the hidden and exotic lands to the west.

Thomas turned about to see if any person was nearby. He knew it was an affectation, but for some problems he had to voice the words, as if in a discussion with an equal. Hearing the words aloud gave credence to the process.

"Thomas," he spoke, addressing himself, "you are simply a man with frailties. You desire comfort and companionship. That is not evil nor unwarranted. It is good for man to have a wife, for God designed that relationship to avoid all manner of sin and illicit thoughts. But, Thomas, why Miss Palmerston? There have been others in your past that could have posed as potential mates, yet you ignored them all, and often in the face of some surprising accommodations and urging. All were overlooked till this one woman."

He bowed his head and shook it sadly, then looked back out to sea. "Thomas, you are foolish to think that she would consider you. Perhaps a sailor, or trader, or soldier might have the restless, adventurous spirit that she must like. Perhaps they know more of the way of the world. You would be as a lamb with a lion with her—a poor, uneducated, and inexperienced lamb. To think she might yet consider your attentions is as flattering as it is ludicrous."

He turned and began to walk away, then stopped after only a few steps.

"But when you heard Vicar Petley's words of admonition, it made you resolve all the stronger. Is it because you wish to flaunt convention in the face of a church and society that so long ignored you and kept you from the things you truly love? Are your feelings born of spite?"

After a few moments of thought, he began to walk again, nodded firmly to himself, as if agreeing that his emotions were not of love, but of something more base, more uncivil.

Then he stopped a third time. He turned back to the town and faced the area where he knew Eileen now lay resting. He looked at the spire of St. Michael's, the last few rays of sun glinting off the cross perched high upon the thin steeple. He looked to Hawkes Haven and knew that Kathryne and William would be there, laughing and playing with their children before the warming fire. He looked down and saw the small cross about his neck.

"Thomas, what would Christ advise? What would he say of this matter? Would he counsel you to follow your heart alone and ignore all else? Would he ignore this woman's past? Will you be able to do the same?"

He closed his eyes again and felt in his heart that, sadly, there would be no firm answers this night.

29 July 1645

"Finally!" Kathryne whooshed past Will as she spun about in the great room and landed with a thump on the chair, still draped with a score of fabrics and swatches.

Will stood in the doorway, leaning on his walking stick, having just returned from the harbor and the chandlery. He was grinning and so enjoying his wife's unabashed revelry in the good news.

She looked up. "Will, exactly how did you find out so soon? They decided only last evening? And they have sent no official word as yet. I am sure they will, and I am sure it will first be sent to me."

"Well," he began, "it appears that Hattie knew of it, even as they were discussing it."

Kathryne raised her hand to her mouth and giggled.

"And I believe Hattie told the scullery maid, who told the groomsman, who told the coachman, who told the stable boy, who had to deliver a harness to the leather maker this morning. I believe the leather maker needed a repair to his working bench, and he told John, and John hailed me in the street as I rode by, wanting to congratulate me on the good news."

Kathryne looked about ready to pout. She crossed her arms tight in front of her. "It appears that the entire island has known of this for hours. I wonder when Papa and Emily will get around to informing us?"

It was then, just as the sky grew from the gold and red of dawn to the fuller colors of day, that a tap was heard at the door. Will swung the door open to reveal Aidan and Emily standing on the porch, bathed in the warming sunlight of morning, holding hands. Kathryne launched herself at the couple before either spoke, crying, laughing, and calling out her wishes for happiness and congratulations.

After a dozen long and teary hugs, Aidan extracted himself and shook Will's hand. "How did you discover about—?"

Will held up his hand in surrender. "I do not believe I could recreate the chain," he laughed, "but suffice it to say that there are many who are now aware that they need to plan for a grand celebration a fortnight hence."

Will reached about and clasped his arms around Aidan in a fierce bear hug. The older man, back in England, would never have assumed such intimacies with another man, but he discovered that he quite enjoyed the robust congratulations.

By the time Aidan and William had settled in the great room, Emily and Kathryne were already deep in plans and preparations for the wedding, a list of tasks and requirements already filling a full page of vellum.

"And your dress simply must have that new deep lace collar style that I've heard is all the rage back home," Kathryne was saying to Emily.

Will wondered how so much could have been accomplished in the twinkling of an eye.

And by the time the first list was completed, the front door banged open again, and Eileen raced in, full of squeals of excitement and joy, with an armful of ribbons and trims. The three women gathered around the large table in the kitchen area and spread out the wares like traveling merchants.

<hr/>

Hawkes Haven that day had been a crossroads of sorts, with noblemen and their ladies coming and going in a steady stream of toasts, well-wishes, congratulations, and more toasts. Will and Kathryne, ever the obliging hosts, were gracious and welcoming, though by nightfall they were most fatigued from the constant banter and a few too many sips of wine toasts.

Night drifted over the land, and the stars began to fill the heavens with a carpet of lights. Kathryne sat at the table, her head propped up on her palms. Eileen stood, leaning heavily against the stone arch that separated the cooking area from the dining chamber. Will leaned back in his chair and massaged the thigh of his injured leg. He had not had much opportunity that day to walk—or to swim for sure—and the result was tight and creaking muscles.

The twins had been cared for, for the most part, by their nursemaids this day. Will knew that Kathryne would have preferred that she spend at least a few hours with them, but the press of the public made such activity impossible. And now both babies were asleep, as well as the nursemaids and most of the serving staff.

Will looked over to the larder in the kitchen and saw empty shelves that the dawn had found with a full complement of meats, vegetables, and supplies. During the course of the day the cook had prepared it all to feed the well-wishers. Will could but smile and shake his head in disbelief.

The house was nearly silent, save the subtle pop and hiss of the cook fire. It was then that a rapid tapping was heard at the main door. Will simply leaned back and called, "Whoever is come this night, I bid you enter. But be aware there is no food nor drink that awaits."

The door slowly opened. In the dim light Will squinted to make out the form that entered. "Thomas!" Will called out, trying to straighten up in his chair. "I have seen every other face on the island today and until this moment did not realize that yours was not among them "

"Please come in, Thomas," Kathryne called, her voice a tired lilt.

Eileen said nothing, but her eyes darted to Kathryne's face. If one were to look close, a careful observer may have detected a note of panic, or perhaps a form of worry, behind the blue of her eyes.

Thomas slowly made his way to the edge of the room, his hands clasped together, his head near bowed. "Earlier this day I passed your father and Lady Emily on the road to Shelworthy, Kathryne, dear," he said. "They have shared with me the good news, and they invited me to share in their joy that wedding day. It will be a most joyful day."

Kathryne nodded. "We are all so very happy for them."

"I could not determine why Aidan waited so long," Will added. "Lady Emily is not the type of woman a man can easily overlook or ignore."

Thomas lifted his face and stared deeply into Eileen's eyes. She returned his stare, a blush beginning to glow on her cheeks.

"Miss Palmerston," Thomas began, sounding as if he had rehearsed his words, "since I will be attending the nuptial celebration, I would like to inquire if you would consent to attend the festivities as my guest?"

Will simply stared at his old friend. Of all the things his friend could have said, this was the last that Will would have imagined.

A dozen heartbeats passed. The house remained silent, hushed, as if it too were anticipating a response. The wind slowed to a whisper. Even the roar of the surf seemed to hold for a long moment, unwilling to crash to the shore and alter the mood.

Eileen blinked her eyes and slowly stood upright, away from the wall. She lifted her chin and replied, "Good Vicar, I . . . I . . . would be so deeply honored if I could accompany you."

Will saw the wave of relief crash over Thomas's being and his consuming smile crackle at the edge of his lips. His eyes snapped to Eileen, then to Kathryne, who was smiling contentedly, then back to Thomas. Will himself could not truly comprehend the progress of the questions and answers.

Thomas took a gulp of air, perhaps the first in several moments. "Then . . . good. Then . . . then I shall call for you that day," he stammered. "Thank you, Miss Palmerston. I shall look forward to two weeks hence."

And with that he bowed and bolted out the front door into the darkness.

Will turned to look at Kathryne, whose face broke into the widest smile he had seen in months, and then to Eileen's, whose shock and surprise gave way to much the same expression.

■ ■ ■ ■

Hannah and Samuel nestled and rolled slightly, but their steady, slow, and tiny breaths told William that they were fast asleep. He marveled at the two tiny beings in their slumber, so perfect, so complex, that he knew that any man who beheld a child asleep could never deny the existence of a Creator.

Perhaps God uses children like these, he thought, smiling and joyful, *to remind older men like me of his blessings and provision.*

He made his way down the steps after bidding good night to the chambermaid. He stopped and snuffed a dozen candles in the hallway. *Despite wealth,* he always said, *it does no good to ignore prudence in all matters.*

He slipped through the kitchen and tore off a small piece of rum cake that had somehow been overlooked by the day's visitors and munched it happily as he felt his way through the darkened great room. The door to the bedchamber creaked loudly, and he hoped he would not find Kathryne asleep, as he so often did.

But this night a candle was lit and flickered at the bedside. Kathryne sat in bed, her back against a dense collection of pillows. Her hair cascaded about her shoulder like a darkened waterfall. Will, when seeing her beauty, was caught short and felt his chest tighten.

"Kathryne," he whispered as he made his way to the bed. He sat down at its edge and brushed her face with a soft kiss. "I thought you would have been asleep an hour ago."

Kathryne narrowed her eyes. "And you would expect me to tumble to my dreams on such a night as this?"

William cocked his head to the side, his eyes sparkling. "A night such as this . . . meaning?" His hand smoothed her hair.

Kathryne pursed her lips, as if about to scold a child who playfully misbehaves. "William," she said calmly, "are you most serious? Was this night not . . . different? In many ways?"

Will paused and thought quickly, for he was averse to being caught outside his wife's thoughts and considerations. "Well . . . ," he said slowly, attempting to gauge a proper response, "there was the matter of your father and Lady Emily. That was different."

Kathryne shook her head. "And that took such thought, sweet Will?"

His cane dropped to the floor with a wooden thump. "But was it not a foregone conclusion as to the eventuality of the match?" he answered softly. "Postponement occurs, but did we not all think that such an event would one day occur?"

Kathryne placed her small white hand over Will's large, bronzed one. "Dear husband, there is no such matter as a foregone conclusion when it comes to matters of the heart. Both my father and Emily had deep waters to navigate before this date. And no, it was not an absolute. Many such arrangements are changed."

"Indeed?" Will asked.

Kathryne turned her head to the side. "William, do you not remember the story of a reformed pirate and a most willful noble girl? Did this eventuality," she said with a sweep of her hand, "seem predestined to you at every moment?"

Will nodded as the full import of the impending nuptials began to dawn upon his thoughts. After a moment, he looked up at his bride's smiling face. "You said this night was different in many ways. What are the many?"

Her jaw dropped open, and her eyes arched in surprise. "William," she responded, "surely this time you speak in jest?"

Will's face narrowed and he grimaced, trying to make sense of her words.

"Perhaps we hear matters in different ways and in different languages. Honestly, Will."

He made no attempt at speech.

"Did you not hear Thomas's request?" she asked.

"Oh," he finally responded, "you mean to accompany Eileen to the wedding? Yes, I heard that. I thought it a most civil gesture on Thomas's part, to offer his arm as escort. It is difficult for a single woman at these affairs, I imagine."

Kathryne drew a long breath in and exhaled loudly. "You have failed to grasp the import again."

"I have?"

"Indeed."

"And the import is . . . ?"

"Sometimes men can be so thick about these matters."

William bristled. He did not consider himself unknowing and unaware.

"William," she continued, "Thomas asked Eileen to accompany him because he is . . . interested in her as more than a friend." She spoke the words with a great precision and finality.

"Thomas?" he said as a question. "He and Eileen as . . . romantic partners?"

"Indeed," Kathryne nodded, smiling widely.

William did not return her smile. "I think not," he replied.

"You think not?"

Will waited a full moment before speaking again. "Thomas is a vicar. A man of the cloth. He would not think of such things."

Kathryne no longer looked bemused but seemed nearer to anger.

"And besides that," Will continued, "have you forgotten of Eileen's past? A woman of her history and a vicar of the Church of England? I think not at all. The idea has no merit."

Kathryne's smile disappeared into a tight-lipped stare. "You are saying that Thomas is too good for Eileen? She has reformed, you realize. She has turned to God. She has turned her back on her past. She seeks to serve our Lord."

Shaking his head as he removed his boots, Will replied, "That may be, Kathryne, but Thomas would not be a man who would be united in any way with Eileen. This may sound cruel, but she was a harlot. And Thomas is a vicar. It simply would not be agreeable to any party concerned. And that is the truth of the matter."

Kathryne tensed as if readying to strike. "William!" she whispered fiercely. "You mean that a man may be forgiven his sins—as I am sure *you* were—yet a woman is forced to bear her shame for *her* sins for the rest of her life? Is that the truth you see? That God forgives men and not women?"

Will recognized in that heartbeat that this was a rabbit hole that offered no escape. His words did imply that, and it was a theological argument that he knew was not defensible. Yet he knew it to be true in ways not based on the Scriptures, but on culture and convention.

"Kathryne," he replied firmly and sternly, seeking to end the discussion before he became so badly ensnared that he would be impaled forever, "all I say is that Thomas has a moral standing to consider. He is God's servant and must act like God's servant in all that he does. He is taking Eileen to this celebration because he is a friend and a vicar and seeks to offer some civil comfort to Eileen. He is seeking no more than that, I assure you."

"But, William—," she protested.

Will held his hand up to silence her, and her eyes blazed at his action. "I will speak no more of this tonight. It is preposterous what you suggest. It will simply go no further than one night."

And with those words, he turned, slipped on his nightshirt, climbed under the covers, and turned from her. This was not the pleasant ending he had foreseen to this evening. He knew Kathryne was angry, but he also knew that in the light of the morning she would recognize his words as true. Yet during the long darkness, until he wrestled his mind to sleep, he felt his wife's tenseness, coiled and sharp, only inches from his being.

1 August 1645

"I told you that it soon be the proper time, din' I now?" Ian Tafert wheezed, his lungs cloudy.

Herbert Gleeson smiled, his toothy grin missing several spots of white, and nodded vigorously.

"You been right, Mr. Tafert," he called out. "You been right so far."

The two slave masters and field overseers were in a fluid, drunken march from town back to the far shadows of the Spenser estate. Tafert carried a half-full jug of mobby and intended that the two of them finish it off before the moon fully rose.

They stopped where the shore road forked, one branch leading along the surf, the other inland and past the governor's lands.

"I tol' you that Hattie be sayin' it true. The weddin' and the feasts and the drinkin' will be commencin' in less than a fortnight," Tafert gasped, straining for breath. "We be most ready now. O'Reilly and Bullocks have got their darkies primed—as do we. And Cap'n Bliss—if he be a man of his word, and I don't have the time to be doubtin' that now—he be on his way as I be speakin', with his vessel full of muskets and sailors and sharp cutlasses and the like."

Gleeson snorted and danced a little woozy jig by the side of the road. "We be livin' as kings by then," he crowed. "We be takin' over their lands, their fancy houses, them costly linens and things. It be such a day."

"We best be sharpenin' our machetes," Tafert instructed, his breath coming in puffs. "And Mr. Hawkes best be gettin' his last will and testimony all set, signed and proper."

Gleeson looked at him hard and saw the redness in his face, growing a deeper shade at his throat. Even in the moonlight his face appeared scarlet with angry blotches.

"Mr. Tafert," he called out and placed his hand on the smaller man's shoulder, "you be feelin' proper? You not be lookin' so well."

Tafert straightened up and knocked his hand away. "I be fine, you stupid git," he barked.

Gleeson could see his companion's chest expand in short huffs, then collapse as he let the air die away.

"Well, just bein' civil and askin' is all I be doin'," he said, his own voice caught in a wheeze. "Just don't want you dyin' 'fore the fortnight passes."

Tafert glared at him in the dark. *I'd rather be sliced in two than die a poor servant as I am,* he thought, his heart filled with a bitter chill. *I knows that the darkies be ready to die lookin' for freedom, but I be lookin' to lie for one night on that clean linen bed of the brigand governor. I just wants to lie me weary head there for a single night!*

He looked up to the heavens, then spit a swallow of tobacco juice to the ground. "That too much to be askin'?" he called up to the dark skies with no real expectation of an answer.

24

8 August 1645

Thomas had spent the entire week in what he could describe only as a personal fog that simply would not lift from his thoughts or behavior. Since that dark night when he finally scrounged up the courage to tap at the door of Hawkes Haven and invite Eileen to accompany him to the wedding, his thoughts had been in a perpetual whirl—a hurricane of images, warnings, admonitions, joyous releases, exaltations, and full hours when no thoughts at all existed in any form.

He managed his Sunday sermons, but the most theologically astute would not have praised him for his insights. Thomas was sleepwalking, and he knew it. He knew he was in dire straits when he rose to the pulpit and looked to his right and did not see Eileen's face there. In a moment of supreme terror, he imagined that his bold request that she actually accompany him—a vicar—to a social function had indeed terrified her as well, and she fled, never to return. He was glad that he was in the midst of a long reading in Matthew, for he could not connect more than a sentence or two of original thought in his mind. He looked up as he spoke and glanced to his left, and as he did so his heart found its home in his chest again. Eileen was there, on the wrong side, sitting with Missy and John. Thomas blinked several times to make sure and prayed that no one could see the vast pool of nervousness in which he was floundering, nearly drowning.

He marched through his message like a good soldier, faithfully illuminating each point, for he had done his preparations for this section of Scripture some two decades earlier. He knew that he had no attention for a fresh revelation this week.

After the service, Thomas, as was his custom, walked toward the front gate and tried to greet everyone who was in attendance that day. Missy and John slipped out with a cheerful greeting, and Thomas was afraid to look around in the thinning assembly for fear that Eileen was there—or was not there. The last few sailors took their leave, and Thomas closed his eyes, took a deep breath, and turned to the fort's interior. No more than three steps from him stood Eileen Palmerston, clad in a gown of deep blue, edged in gold trim; she carried a small velvet pouch, tied with a polished leather cord. Her hair, red as a robin's plumage, was pulled away from her neck and off her shoulders. The gown was open at the shoulders, revealing a deep whiteness like that of cream thick from a country farm. She blinked her eyes once, a flashing of cold and deep water.

"Vicar Mayhew," she said, her voice the rippling of a stream, "a most inspiring service. I appreciated your insights into St. Matthew's writing."

Had Thomas just then been asked, he would have had no recollection as to the book on which he had spoken, nor any of the salient points he had expounded upon. "Thank you, Miss Palmerston; you are more than kind."

She extended her hand and touched his forearm. He attempted to keep his eyes level and not let them widen as he felt his heart was telling them to do.

"Please, Vicar Mayhew, if you would . . ."

He thought, *Simply ask and I will do it.*

". . . would you call me Eileen? Miss Palmerston sounds . . . a bit too formal."

"I . . . I . . . I would be delighted." He smiled. "And if you would not think I am too forward, perhaps you might deign to call me by my Christian name—Thomas?"

"I shall, Thomas," she replied, a happier, more alive tone creeping into her voice.

"Eileen," Thomas said, as he gathered breath into his chest, "perhaps . . . since we are to attend the nuptials of Governor Spenser and Lady Emily this upcoming week together . . . perhaps . . ."

His eyes darted about, not knowing where to find their purchase. *It cannot be her eyes where I fix mine, for I will lose speech if I look too directly at them,* he thought.

"Perhaps what, Thomas?" she asked.

"Perhaps, this evening, at the seventh bell, perhaps I may call on you, and together we could take our evening meal in Bridgetown?" he breathed out in a rush.

She lowered her eyes for a moment, and Thomas was certain that she was formulating an excuse as to avoid the meeting.

"Why, Thomas, that would be most delightful. I shall wait for you then, at the seventh bell."

She turned and began to walk away, and Thomas began to breathe again. He most ardently hoped that she did not look back, for as he turned back toward the fort, he ran face first into the door and bloodied his nose in the noiseless accident, stumbling the entire way back to his living space, clenching his nose between a pinching thumb and forefinger.

■□■□■

Thomas's heart, his words, his breathing, did not appear to operate as normal until midway through their dinner together. Thomas thought Eileen ideal company, witty and charming, her laughter rising easy and often in the cool night air. But Thomas felt very much the oaf, knocking over a tankard once and stumbling through his words on several occasions. But Eileen paid little attention to any of his gaffes, he thought, and seemed to be much at ease, almost as if she was actually enjoying the experience. They sat in a small courtyard of Nelson and Sons, an establishment more noted for the taste of its food than the potency of its drinks. The night was mild; only a soft breeze blew about the harbor, and only on occasion did the candles on the table flicker.

As the platters were removed and new plates arranged for the sweets and cheese portion of the meal, along the street out front jostled a crowd of passersby. There were sailors on their way to ships, merchants heading toward their homes, strollers out for the evening air. Thomas waved to several who were often in attendance at his church, and a few stopped and chatted for a moment before continuing their journey.

But Thomas would never remember their faces from that night. All he could see was Eileen's smile, and all he could hear was her delicate laughter.

That same evening, and along that same promenade, came another solitary figure, robed in the dark and somber folds of a cleric's cassock. Vicar Giles Petley was enjoying a brief walk after vespers at St. Michael's.

He was at the far side of the wooden walkway, lost in the evening's dim light. He first saw Thomas and was near to hailing him when he stopped, his arm halfway into the air and his mouth partially open, and saw across from Vicar Mayhew the back silhouette of a woman. It took him three more steps to decide on her identity. A scarlet shade of red flushed his cheeks as he hurried past, ducking his head into the folds of his robe even further. He knew he could not trust his volatile emotions that night.

And as he paced away, he turned his head back to assure himself that what he was seeing was not an apparition. In the darkness, such a movement was unwise, for no one heard Giles as he pitched headfirst from the walkway, landing with a soft splash in the mud below.

CHAPTER

25

9 August 1645

The rapping sounded much like an incessant woodpecker searching for a meal. Thomas rolled over in his small bed and doubled the feather pillow over his head to drown out the clatter.

But it did no good, for the rapping grew louder and more insistent. It was then that Thomas fully awoke and stumbled from his bedchamber, at first looking for the bird, then, realizing he had company, looking for a dressing gown to wear. All the while the rapping never ceased in rhythm nor volume.

Thomas swung open the door to reveal a red-faced and fuming Vicar Giles Petley standing on the small porch, wearing his full array of ecclesiastical garb, including a collar, pitched hat, rope belt, and a heavy metal crucifix, which hung about his neck on a thin leather thong.

Thomas's eyes widened in great surprise.

"Vicar Mayhew!" Giles near shouted. "You will stop this at once!"

Thomas looked about the small cluttered room, looking for something to stop. "Wh-what do you mean?" he mumbled, still trying to clear the sleep from his thoughts.

"You know what I mean! Your lascivious and wanton behavior must cease!"

Thomas looked around the room again, thinking that someone had brought in revelers to his small, cramped room as he slept. But the room was as empty as he left it the night before. "But . . . I do not . . . ," Thomas mumbled again, then shook his head to clear it. "Vicar Petley, the hour is most early. I am tired, and I would like to dress. Please, if you would, tell me what I have done wrong."

And as soon as he said those words, he knew why Giles was at his door and angry.

"You know, Vicar Mayhew," Giles said in a menacing and chilled tone. "I saw you last night with that . . . that fallen woman. You were dining with her! You were laughing as if your presence in her company was of no matter!"

Giles took a step forward, and Thomas thought for a moment that he was about to raise his hand to him in anger.

"How dare you!" Giles vented. "You are not allowed to see that woman again! I forbid it!"

Thomas raised his shoulders back. He regretted instantly that he had not awoken earlier and dressed. He found it hard to be brave and courageous while wearing a wrinkled and threadbare nightshirt.

"Vicar Petley, whom I chose to dine with last night is of no concern to you. I do not need your approval to follow my heart. You have no right to forbid my actions."

"Not even if they defy all logic and the teachings of the church? I daresay I do."

Thomas was sorely tempted to slam the door in Giles's face, but did not. "I shall see whom I want and when I want."

Giles drew himself up to his full height, squared his shoulders, and glared at Thomas, his eyes narrow and glinting. "If you think you may continue this . . . this evil liaison with that . . . with that woman of the night, then you are the one who is most deluded. I have the power of the Church of England behind me! You run the risk, Vicar Mayhew," he said, his words oozing with contempt, "of forcing my hand. I shall advise church authorities and have you stripped of your title and excommunicated!"

Thomas felt a lurch in his soul. Vicar Petley was just such a man to follow through on his threat, and Thomas knew that church politics might warrant such an action. Could he risk losing all that he was for a friendship with a woman with such a past? Could he risk his standing with God to follow his heart? To knowingly abandon his calling and vocation? All these thoughts raced through Thomas's mind in an instant.

"I can see that you will never represent God to anyone!" Giles warned and then turned and stomped away.

As Vicar Petley stepped away in a huff, Thomas called out, "If that be the price of following my heart, then so be it."

He slammed the door and stumbled back into his darkened room.

CHAPTER

26

10 August 1645

Secrets were not an option on Barbados. What happened at Shelworthy would soon be known through every noble home and humble hovel on the island. What occurred in any public house in Bridgetown would soon be common knowledge throughout every plantation and parish. It took only one day for Eileen, William, and Kathryne, and all the people whom Thomas held dear, to hear of Vicar Petley's angry denunciation of Thomas and Eileen's dinner together.

Thomas did not seek anyone's advice, yet sought God's counsel in prayer and searching through the Scriptures for a resolution to his dilemma.

"Abstain from all appearance of evil," he read. "The husband of one wife," he read. "Go, and sin no more," he read, and knew that Eileen had done as Jesus had commanded and now was no longer condemned. "Their sins and iniquities will I remember no more," he read. She had confessed. She had repented. She had changed her ways and now sought with all her heart to serve the living God. That was enough for Thomas.

If Christ could forgive those who put him to death, then Thomas could forgive a woman who had turned away from her past with absolute certainty.

"Blessed is he whose transgression is forgiven," he read, "whose sin is covered. Blessed is the man unto whom the Lord imputeth not iniquity."

It was enough for Thomas, who for his entire life had preached the duty of a man to follow what God said rather than society's conventions. Thomas felt secure in the fact that Scripture did not contradict his heart in this matter.

The day after Vicar Petley upbraided him, Thomas appeared on Eileen's doorstep. He stood in the bright sun as he spoke, the waters of the harbor behind him glistening and radiating a thousand diamonds of light.

"Miss Palmerston," he began, having rehearsed his speech for hours that morning, "I do not know if you have been informed of Vicar Petley's visit to my residence." He dared not employ her first name for fear that even such an innocent intimacy may cloud his message.

The stricken look on Eileen's face told Thomas that she had indeed heard.

"He threatened me with the most severe form of ecclesiastical punishment if I was to pursue seeing you."

She nodded, fearing that he was about to insist that they have no further contact. She held her breath.

"It matters little to me as to his warnings," Thomas continued, his voice strong and confident. "I do not know your heart, but I am drawn to your presence. I shall not be swayed by any man's foolish accusations. I pray you shall not be swayed by the sins of my past, and neither shall I be swayed by the sins of your past."

Eileen breathed again and nodded.

"I expect you to attend the marriage of the governor and Lady Emily as my guest, as I offered prior."

Eileen nodded again, mute and still.

"Does that meet with your approval?" Thomas asked softly.

Eileen nodded again, then added in a small voice, "Nothing would provide me with more pleasure—or comfort, Thom—I mean, Vicar Mayhew."

Thomas nodded in reply. "Then, until this Saturday, Miss Palmerston, I take my leave."

━ ▪ ━ ▪ ━

"Emily, my dear, have you heard of all this nonsense with the vicar?"

Aidan was near buried behind a towering stack of documents and plot surveys of the new land grants issued by the king. Emily slipped into his office carrying a tray with warm, sweet, spiced tea and busied herself preparing the drink for this afternoon.

"Nonsense?" she asked with a smile. "What has Vicar Petley done this time?"

Aidan fussed with another sheaf of papers, then snorted quietly to himself. "No, dear one, not Petley—though I scarce blame you for thinking of that man first. No, this has to do with Vicar Mayhew."

Emily looked up in surprise, the teacup held halfway to her mouth. "Vicar Mayhew? Are you sure? Nonsense, you say?"

Aidan rose, took his cup, and gulped a large swallow. "Indeed," he continued. "We, of course, invited him to our wedding celebration. And it appears that he has asked for the company of a Miss . . . Miss Palmerston to accompany him."

"Eileen? The one in Kathryne's employ?"

Aidan nodded, taking a second sip and draining his cup. "Indeed, one and the same. As much as I experienced such consternation over my daughter having a woman who had run a brothel in her employ, well, I find this latest wrinkle even more upsetting. I mean to say, how far does a woman like that think she can climb in refined society? And do you not think it presumptuous that a vicar, of all persons, would ask for her company?"

Emily did not reply at once, nor did she nod, but simply lowered her half-full cup to its saucer with a faint, crystalline clinking, a shrill sound in the soft, warm afternoon. She waited, pondering, considering her reply. *After all,* she thought, *did I not say much the same to Kathryne when she first offered that woman a position in her home?*

Aidan went back to fussing with his papers, for he had spoken his mind.

Emily looked out the window, watching the clouds drift and flow past in the deep blue of the sky. "But, Aidan," she finally said, "is not that an uncharitable evaluation of any person? To strictly judge her on past mistakes?"

"Mistakes?" Aidan snorted. "The woman was a harlot. And owned an establishment of ill repute. That is no mistake, as I see it, but a choice."

He returned to his work, then looked up again. "And I see her presence among my grandchildren as most disquieting. I have a mind to mention such to William the next time he visits."

Emily chose to sit still and refrain from either a nod or affirmation to Aidan's remark, hoping that it was only a passing thought.

"Honestly, Emily, I do not think her presence will be appropriate at our wedding feast. Perhaps I shall mention to Vicar Mayhew that he has ill chosen his guest for the evening."

Emily knew now that this was not just a passing comment and that Aidan would most likely make mention of it to all parties concerned.

"No, Aidan, I do not wish you to do that," she said evenly.

Aidan looked up from behind his desk, his eyes questioning her words.

"Aidan, I will make few demands of you as a wife. I expect you to love me, as I am sure you do, and as Scripture demands. And I want you to respect me. I am sure that you will do both of those with all your heart."

"But what has that to do with this—this woman?"

Emily was as still as a bird locked in the gaze of a hungry cat.

"She has fallen, Aidan, and she has found God. That is enough. I will not humiliate Thomas for his association with Miss Palmerston by retracting our invitation. If our displeasure with a person's past was a criteria for this event, then I daresay I would uninvite a great many of the noblemen planters—and their wives—that live on this island. For, as you well know, their actions are no less reprehensible than what that poor woman did in the past."

Her eyes focused on Aidan's, hard and tight and narrow. He looked as if he were about to reply, but instead he scowled for a heartbeat and then went back to his land survey.

"Very well, Emily, I shall allow them to attend."

She smiled.

"But I shall not make such accommodations a habit in this household."

She nodded and, with great deliberation, took a final sip of her tea, the honey-sweet and thick part at the bottom of the cup.

Kathryne, holding a gurgling baby in each arm, brushed past William, taking no time as she often did to pass one to him to hold and play with. Will looked up from his chair in the great room and watched his wife and children disappear into the kitchen. In a moment, he heard her footsteps on the back staircase, the wood creaking in such a familiar tune that he could tell which step was being tread upon by the squeal it gave off.

More than a dozen minutes passed until she returned from the nursery. She would have brushed passed him again had he not called out.

"Kathryne," he said, his voice holding a hurt edge to it, "where are you going in such a hurry? It is nowhere near time for bed."

She spun about, stopping quickly. She looked hard at him, then slowly stepped back into the room and sat with a sweep into a chair far opposite her husband.

"I have not had a single chance to speak with you for what seems like days, dear wife. Please, I would like an evening of conversation with you, if I might."

Kathryne looked glum, yet nodded. Silence poured into the room like a wave.

"Well, then, how have the children been today?" he asked, attempting to sound cheerful.

"They behaved as expected."

"As expected? 'Tis an odd manner of speaking of the babies."

Kathryne did not respond.

"Has Samuel continued his crawling? It appears that he is well on the way to walking. He is growing fast."

Kathryne tried to hide her smile, but could not. "Indeed, his little feet pound and pound at the floor," she answered. "And if I let him go, he simply tumbles to the floor, both laughing and crying at the same time. It will be perhaps a few more months until he may have the ability to walk as he wishes."

"Is this early for a child to walk?"

Kathryne shrugged. "'Tis the first boy child I have had. Some say it is most early; some do not look overly surprised when I tell them of his eagerness. I think children progress at their own pace."

"And Hannah? Has she tried as well?"

A dark look swept over Kathryne's face. Will saw it and wished he hadn't asked. "No," Kathryne said coldly. "She attempted it once, and as she did, she tipped over the small table in the bedchamber, breaking that small blue glass plate."

"Was she hurt?" Will asked, alarmed.

"No, just her pride. But I will not let her do such a thing twice."

Kathryne looked as if she were about to speak again, and as if a debate raged inside her. She closed her eyes for a long moment, then looked up. That dark look had reappeared. "Though she is but a tiny girl, I cannot forgive her for breaking what I hold dear. So she will walk when I say there is reason for her to walk and not before."

Will turned to her and stared hard at her and her rash words.

And before Will could respond, Kathryne jumped to her feet, ran to the bedchamber, and slammed the door hard enough to set the plates rattling in the pantry.

▬ ▬ ▬ ▬

Thomas did not knock nor announce his coming, but swept into Vicar Petley's residence nestled hard by St. Michael's Church. He had ignored the housekeeper's calls for his need for an appointment and had barged into the smallish room Vicar Giles Petley used as his office and study.

Giles looked startled, as if awakened from a long afternoon nap, and nearly fell from his tattered chair.

"Vicar Petley," Thomas announced, hoping his voice did not slide into shrillness, "I have heard your warnings and admonitions concerning my . . . my liaison with Miss Palmerston."

Giles wiped at his face and tried to smooth his rumpled hair as he attempted to slide his feet back into his boots and stand at the same moment. It looked as if he were dancing a slow, unbalanced reel.

"Goodness, Vicar Mayhew," he muttered as he bounced about the room on one foot, "do not you believe in announcing your arrival in some other fashion? I was . . . meditating on this Sunday's sermon."

Thomas ignored his words of caution. "I have spent several days in prayer and in the Scriptures."

Giles now had both feet in his boots—almost, that is—and he nodded, more than a bit off balance.

"And you have come to ask for forgiveness, no doubt. Well, I am sure the church can be satisfied in some fashion, Vicar Mayhew, but I warn you that any more such behavior cannot be tolerated. After all, do not the Scriptures call us to be different from the heathens? Does not Paul say in the second letter to the Corinthians, sixth chapter, fourteenth verse, 'Be ye not unequally yoked together with unbelievers. What communion hath light with darkness'?"

Thomas snapped, "But she believes—perhaps more than you and I combined."

Giles snapped back, "And does not Paul also say in the seventeenth verse of that same chapter, 'Wherefore come out from among them'— and she is more *them* than any woman on this island—'and be ye separate, saith the Lord, and touch not the unclean thing'?"

Thomas held up his hand, bidding Giles to stop. "No, Vicar Petley, do not attempt to use the Scriptures to justify such an unforgiving spirit. I came here not to ask for your forgiveness. I merely came to state that I am ignoring your threat. I shall continue to see Miss Palmerston if I choose. You have no say in the matter. This is between me and our Lord." He hesitated only a moment, then added, "I know Christ came to offer forgiveness for us all, for we are all sinners. You, me, and Miss Palmerston. All of us are forgiven if we ask for such and turn from our sins. That is what she has done. Do you not remember the promise of 1 John 1:9? 'If we confess our sins, he is faithful and just to forgive us our sins, and to cleanse us from all unrighteousness.' She has asked for forgiveness. She has turned from her sin. She has been cleansed from all the unrighteousness of her past. God remembers it no longer, and neither do I."

Thomas spun on his heels and walked out, stopping only to call out over his shoulder, "If you must attempt to disrobe and excommunicate me, then I must encourage you to proceed."

And with that, the door slammed behind him.

27

12 August 1645

The governor's wedding sat at the very apex of all social affairs on Barbados. No other event so inflamed the curiosities, the passions, and the excitement of the population.

The two weeks prior to this date provided nowhere near the necessary time for all the arrangements to be made for all the parties that needed to be held. But the noble men and women tried their best, often attending two and three galas on the same day, providing every titled estate an opportunity to host a lavish celebration for the merry couple.

Aidan complained quietly to Emily only a few days before the actual day of their nuptials that the whirlwind of social affairs had been so overwhelming and exhausting that if he remained awake and on his feet until the noon hour on Saturday, it would take all his strength and then some.

Emily nodded and smiled. "Just a few more days, Aidan, and then all matters shall settle down to a most pleasant routine. Just a few more days until we shall again have our peace."

Kathryne's tears started the morning of the wedding, at just about dawn as William reckoned it, and did not cease until the final pronouncement that Aidan Spenser, Lord Governor of Barbados and all the Lesser Antilles, was now legally bound as husband to the Lady Emily Bancroft of London, England. Kathryne would later say that they were all tears of joy, but to Will, tears were tears.

All agreed that the affair, for being planned in such haste, was a most perfect and beautiful wedding, a blending of joy and solemnity, an auspicious event coupled with the most boisterous celebration Barbados had ever seen.

Lady Emily was a vision of beauty and refinement in an elegant gown of pale yellow silk taffeta. The gown was finished with a high collar and a short, high-waisted bodice that caught up the front hemline to reveal a delicately layered lace petticoat. She wore lace gloves and carried a bouquet of bougainvillea. Lord Spenser wore a brocaded weskit over a pale yellow silk shirt, tan velvet breeches, lace stockings, and tan leather shoes. From his baldric hung the Spenser family sword.

Kathryne, sitting near to where her father stood at the front of the church, could scarcely hide her sniffles when, as Lady Emily appeared at the back of the center aisle, Aidan's eyes spilled over with tears of his own. As the bride made her way up to the altar, a beaming smile never left her face and remained in place throughout the ceremony.

The first gathering immediately following the ceremony was a small, intimate, light midday meal for the Spenser family, their closest friends, and associates at Shelworthy. The dining chamber groaned with scented bougainvillea and hibiscus garlands, and the windows were nearly hidden by festoons of flowers. A special punch of rum, tea, wine, lime juice, sugar, and delicate spices glistened in a bowl of delicate crystal. Harp music colored the air with romance and gaiety. The scent of the dinner—pickled oysters, pork with currant stuffing, and potato pudding—competed with the intoxicating scents of the flowers.

Then the floodgates opened once again, and all of Bridgetown was ablaze with gay music and food and drink. There was indeed drink in most bountiful amounts. One sugar mill on the Carruthers estate, it was rumored, used its entire production of molasses to produce a wagon filled with barrels of sweet, strong rum. It was young rum, to be sure, but it was most free-flowing. There was much kissing and kicking up of heels as guests joined in dancing the gavotte, the daring and new kissing dance, set to the music of the harpsichord.

William and Kathryne swirled through the laughing and cheering celebrants who ebbed and flowed through the streets of Bridgetown. William had always avoided such affairs in the past, but this day he made a happy exception, for it was a truly wonderful experience to see Aidan and Emily joined as husband and wife. It was a privilege to share in their joy, and Will let himself be carried about by the happy current of the party as it flowed into the night.

<hr />

Vicar Mayhew had made a promise to himself to touch no drink containing spirits this night, for he was most fearful that any artificial loosening of his words would be to his grief. It was not easy to do, with waiters and servants carrying trays filled with elegant goblets of crisp wines. There were small kegs of ale and brandy. There were huge, man-sized barrels filled with new rum. At every turn another drink was being offered, and Thomas said no to them all. Eileen had taken only a single serving of wine and sipped on that throughout much of the evening.

And Thomas did not feel that he needed spirits this evening, for if asked, he would have claimed that he was pleasantly intoxicated with the presence of the beautiful woman at his arm.

He had decided, firmly and securely decided late the night prior, that the course he had envisioned so many months ago and never shared with any person—to pursue his relationship with Eileen Palmerston— would be the course that he would embark upon tonight. No decision he had ever made—not even the decision to enter the seminary at Cambridge—was bathed in as much prayer as this one had been. He asked God for guidance, he argued with God, and finally wept in his arms. To Thomas, it felt as if he had battled the forces of good and evil, fighting to know what was civil and proper and right. And in the end, Thomas began to feel a warmth and a peace in his heart as he began to embrace his decision. His thoughts slowed and calmed. His breathing returned to normal, and his sleep was no longer filled with wild thrashing and troubled dreams.

That was how he knew it was right.

Now all he had to do was carry it out. All he had to do was to put feet onto his dreams.

Daniel in the lions' den was nothing in comparison to this, Thomas thought as he looked back on his struggles. *That would be but a Sunday stroll in the gardens of St. James Park.*

In a quiet corner of Bridgetown, near where they had first shared a dinner together, walked Vicar Thomas Mayhew and Eileen Palmerston. He was attired in his finest cassock and surplice and she in a gown of scarlet with blue velvet slashed panels cut into the sleeves and full skirt. Thomas knew she was the most beautiful woman he had ever beheld and sought to memorize every inch, every breath, every moment of her.

Thomas felt most old and inadequate at her side, but her laughter and the soft touch of her arm as it slipped through his erased all that in a heartbeat. The vicar was a most childlike man when it came to matters of the heart, and he had become overwhelmed with her. He could not contain the smile from his face any more than he could stop the dawn.

Under the fluttering light of a torch, Thomas stopped and turned toward her. "Miss Palmerston—I mean to say, Eileen," he stammered, "I wish to tell you of my heart's joy at spending this evening with you."

It looked as if she had blushed, Thomas thought, but it may have been the reddish glow from the torch.

"Thank you, Thomas," she said, her voice a whisper, "I have enjoyed this eve immensely as well."

"Is that true?" he asked. "I mean, I do not know the proper words for all this. . . ."

"You have done most well," she replied.

A moment of silence slipped past them. Echoes of harpsichord music lilted in the warm air.

"I have enjoyed this single day the most of all my days upon this island, Thomas," she continued. "It has not been often in my life when a man has respected me and treated me with as much kindness as you."

Now it was Thomas's turn to blush.

"I scarce want this evening to end," she went on, "yet I have no right to tell you of this and how my heart . . ." Her words trailed off.

"Eileen," Thomas said, "please tell me. I am an old man—"

"You are not," she interjected.

"Indeed but I am, and yet I have no map to guide me in this."

She looked up into his eyes. "This evening has been perfect. I wish it would never end."

"To be the truth?"

"'Tis the truth indeed," she said most firmly.

"Then it does not require an ending," he said, his voice softer.

"But, Thomas, you are a vicar, and I am a—"

He held up his hand, stopping her words. "You told me I am not an old man. Then I shall tell you that you are nothing more than Eileen Palmerston, a noble-born woman of grace and breeding, of Taunton, England."

She smiled, her eyes flashing in the dark.

"This is all unknown ground to me, Eileen," he tried to explain, "and I am no good at poetry and such. But my heart tells me this way is correct. There is no other course."

She looked up at him, and Thomas saw the puzzlement in her eyes.

"Eileen, I possess no idea of how such things should be done. I am a poor country vicar who has no instruction in such matters."

"Yes, Thomas," she replied softly, her words as much a question as a statement.

"Eileen, would you consent to consider a proposal from this old—rather, this not old man?"

"Proposal?"

"Of marriage," he added, then holding his breath and closing his eyes as if he feared the entire night might disappear in a vapor.

"Marriage?" she whispered in disbelief.

He nodded, opening his eyes to hers.

"T-Thomas . . ." she stammered, her eyes blinking at the tears soon to start. "Thomas, I am overwhelmed."

"Yes?"

"And so overjoyed."

"Yes?"

"And the answer is yes."

"*Yes?*"

"Yes, Thomas, the answer is yes."

And as they embraced, fully and intimately for the first time, the night closed in about them.

While the nobles feasted and celebrated, an armed uprising was imminent.

Ian Tafert insisted that the attack on Shelworthy occur first. He argued that the head of power must be seized, then the rebels could move on to the rest of the estates they had on their list. He and six slaves planned to lead the offensive on the governor's residence as near to ten bells as he could determine. His small group would be joined by Gleeson and what slaves he recruited, and then by Bullock and his small force. Captain Bliss had promised that his men and weapons would be waiting for them at the north side of Shelworthy. He had said that he intended to anchor his vessel north of the harbor and bring his men inland along the coastal road. Sailing into the harbor itself would be foolhardy, for it would draw attention to the attack. O'Reilly would simply rise up and take over the estate where he worked, for the plantation was miles from Shelworthy and could not be part of a combined attack.

Tafert was as certain as the sun that once others saw how easily it all progressed, how easy it was for the indentured servant and slave to rise up, rid themselves of oppression, and take over the ill-gotten lands from the nobility, then every slave overseer on the island would seek to do the same.

Tafert spent the evening pacing about his small hovel, stopping every few moments for another long sip of his private stock of kill-devil rum. Six darkies sat expectantly, leaning against the wall opposite Tafert. They held in their hands newly sharpened machetes, the long metal blades catching the faint light of the moon. Two of them carried muskets, spirited away by Tafert from the gameskeeper, who had them locked in the stables. Besides a machete, Tafert had a brace of pistols, both loaded, tucked into the rope belting at his waist. The pistols were issued to him for control of his slaves in the event they ever became unruly. As of this night, Tafert had yet to fire a single shot. His nervousness multiplied, for he was unsure of the exact workings of each weapon.

"Ye be ready, now, hear?" Tafert called out to the silent black men who had not stirred or said more than a whisper since they had arrived an hour prior.

"We be ready, Massa," one of them said. "Been ready. And we still ready."

Tafert looked at the moon. It was still young into the sky, and he reckoned that nearly a full hour remained until St. Michael's would sound the bells marking the tenth hour. He began pacing faster, stopping only to drink and then to cough so violently that he doubled over and fell to his knees as the deep sounds wracked through his chest.

One of the slaves rose, padded to him silently, and touched his shoulder. "Massa fit to be doin' this, this night?" he asked.

Tafert responded by slapping the man's hand from his shoulder. He pulled himself upright and snarled, "I be fit, as fit as you be. Now you best be shuttin' yer mouth till I give the order."

The slave slunk back into the darkness with his comrades. Tafert had not stopped pacing, nor had he stopped his consumption of kill-devil. And at every third or fourth pass in front of his door, he would stop, pull a pistol from his belt, aim at an imaginary opponent, and mimic the roar and recoil of the pistol in his shaking hand.

He stopped, wiped at the sweat that found his brow in heavy beads, then spit to the ground. He looked up to the moon and held his hand out, splayed against its light. He paced another dozen times and stopped for a final guzzle from his jug. He hitched his breeches up, recinched his rope belt, and felt the edge of his machete one last time. His finger slid along the sharpened surface, digging into the callused skin to a depth that drew a thin bead of blood.

Tafert looked to the moon again, wiped his brow, cursed the night and the darkness and the slaves to his right, cursed his foul quarters and the coarseness of the rum, cursed the heat of the island and the bugs and gnats and merrywhigs, cursed the paper he made an X upon and signed away his life for four long years, cursed the cloudy constriction in his lungs, and finally cursed the governor and all his crisp, clean linen sheets.

He stopped his litany of evil invectives and closed his eyes. *To be asleep on clean white linens,* he thought, *'twould be a feeling like floatin' on heaven's clouds.*

He blinked several times to clear the image from his mind, then cursed yet again, blaming the world's woes on those who held power above him. He paced to the far side of his hut, kicked at the legs of the first darkie he saw, shouting at them all, "It be time, ye louts, it be time!"

The most critical assignment of this evening's attacks was being handled by one of the most recent soldiers enlisted in the cause, Ezra Trimble. Ezra was a rather dapper man, at least as dapper as an indentured servant could be. He claimed that he had spent time at Eton, before gambling and loose women drove him into bankruptcy and ruin. It was natural to all that he be the pawn to draw Mr. Hawkes from the celebration and into the revolt's violent maw.

Ezra hesitated at the outskirts of town and for the hundredth time felt for the note that was in the breast pocket of his doublet. He had written it himself and tried his best to imitate the childish scrawl of a slave just learning to write: "Mr. Hawkes, you be needed at Shelworthy. Please come at once. Hattie."

These few words would be enough to get Mr. Hawkes alone. And once alone, the small pistol tucked at Ezra's belt would convince him that it was indeed time to leave the celebration.

And with that thought, Ezra touched at the pistol as well for the hundredth time that evening. The metal had warmed from his skin, and the hardness felt most comforting. He slipped his thumb to the hammer and tugged at it slightly. *All in due time, Mr. Hawkes,* he thought. *All in due time.*

Tafert coughed several more times then stood up and shouldered his musket. "All right, ye dogs. It be time to prove the puddin'.'"

They shouldered their machetes and muskets and began to pad off across the stubble of a field only a week cleared of its crop of tall, sweet cane. The sharp edges of the cut stalks could easily puncture a man's foot, and the seven men carefully picked their way across the acres, heading north, heading toward the lights of Shelworthy, toward their destiny.

Within moments they were two hundred paces from the governor's estate, hidden yet by a sharp rise of the road. The two uppity darkies, as Tafert called them, who were guarding the drive, fancy in their blue and red velvets, would be either napping at this late hour or so unaware of danger this joyous night that Tafert knew their removal would be a simple task.

But he stopped and bent at the waist, his hands to his knees, drawing in air with a sickly, sucking wheeze, spots of colors dancing in front of his eyes from the long walk. He gasped loud and trusted that the hum and chatter of cricket and locust would drown out his panting. The six darkies crouched by him, each kneeling on one knee, their palms flat against the warm black soil.

They would wait here until the half-past bell sounded. Ezra promised to have Mr. Hawkes there at that hour, and he would be their shield.

And if Mr. Hawkes ain't here by then, Tafert thought, *we be goin' in on our own.*

One of the slaves turned and whispered, "Where be de muskets dat de pirate be promisin' to us?"

Tafert blinked as if he had forgotten about Bliss's participation. "He said he be at the north side of the house," Tafert snapped back in a whisper. "Which side be the north side, you stupid mongrel?"

The slave shrugged.

Tafert reached over and cuffed him soundly and then pointed to a place beyond the estate.

"Bliss say he be waitin' over there by them trees for us to go first. Then he and the sailors be chargin' in right behind us."

The silence was broken only by Tafert's wheezing.

"'Tis a pity ye gits be as stupid as ye is. Bliss will be there, that be sure," Tafert said, his voice fading. "The man claimed on his holy word that he would be there. And a man's word be his gold, to be sure."

■ ■ ▮ ■ ▨

Aidan swung to his left, and Emily's delicate hand, bent at the wrist, came up to meet his larger and infinitely more clumsy hand. The harpsichord sounded gay and joyful as it measured out the steps to the dance.

As they came together in a most orderly fashion, Aidan whispered loudly to his wife of now six hours, "Shall we repair to our bedchamber after this set?"

The couple parted and swung to their right, turning and then facing each other again, a few steps closer to the music. Emily leaned forward and spoke to her new husband. "As if you have divined my thoughts, my sweet Aidan." She parted again from his side, counting out her steps.

It was her coy smile, Aidan would say later, that so blinded him and caused him to stumble forward. He fell into the arms of a most dour Vicar Petley, who looked on from the far corner of the room, attempting to winnow the crowd by his glare.

"Please, Vicar, a thousand pardons, but it is not your arms I seek," Aidan laughed, and returned in great haste to his wife's side and to that bewitching smile that beckoned and spoke of a thousand moments of pleasure to come.

■ ■ ■ ■

Ezra walked through the laughing and giggling crowd with nary an eye turned askance at his presence. In the middle of the street stood a long table, groaning with hams and pork and sweetmeats. At the far side of the table rested a trio of stout barrels filled with ale, cider, and thick wine.

Ezra found William and Kathryne in that throng of celebrants, laughing and mingling with guests outside St. Michael's. William stood at the far side of the crowd, sipping on an ale, watching the dancers swirl.

As Ezra approached, Will glanced at him and nodded, having met him on several occasions prior. Ezra handed him the note, and Will read it in a heartbeat and looked up confused. He leaned toward the servant, but Ezra mimed that he would not be able to hear over the music and laughter and motioned for him to step further back into the shadows. Will followed him without question.

As Ezra turned a corner, Will called out, "Wait just a moment, sir; what sort of trouble is occurring?"

Ezra spun about on his heels and with a well-practiced move grabbed for his pistol. Despite his practice, the hammer caught on his belt and it nearly fell from his hand. He grabbed at it, steadied it, and drew a bead on Will's forehead. The barrel wavered slightly in the darkness.

"Mr. Hawkes, if you will," Ezra hissed, "do not make a sound or you will leave a most comely widow out there on the dance floor."

Will stopped, and his eyes darted about. Ezra thought he might be

looking for a place to jump out of harm's way, but there was none. He
saw Will's arm tense about his cane, and Ezra stepped back one full
step, out of range of a quick clubbing.

"Don't think about escaping, Mr. Hawkes. I do not want to kill you,
but I will if you try to escape."

Will narrowed his eyes. "What do you want? Money?"

Ezra laughed. "No, good sir. This is one predicament you will not be
able to buy your way out of." Ezra slipped around back of him and
placed the pistol barrel at the base of Will's neck. "Now if you would,
please, start walking to Shelworthy. We have an appointment to keep
there this night, and I would not desire either of us to be late."

The air slowly came back into Tafert's lungs, and in a long moment he
was well enough to stand and peer over the earthen rise of the road.

It be the time I stand and take what be due me, he thought, his mind
an angry jumble of drink and invective.

"Now!" he shouted and clamored up the crumbly embankment and
onto the dusty road opposite the brick posts and iron fence. As the
darkies climbed up, following his lead, he snatched the two pistols from
his belt and held one in each hand as he had once seen in a most lurid
engraving of a pirate. He shouted out to the night, "We be takin' over
this land and all that belongs to it, in the name of the . . . in the name
of . . ."

His thoughts remained muddied from the kill-devil, and he did not
know the words to finish his challenge. The two black Shelworthy
guards, responding to Tafert's sounds, stepped from behind the posts,
each buttoning his doublet and adjusting his belt.

Tafert knew it was time to act, and he leveled his guns at the guards.
He narrowed his eyes, his arms trembling in the moonlight, and slipped
his fingers to the triggers and pulled, closing his eyes tightly in the
process. The guns barked loudly, smoke billowing from each like a
clogged chimney. The pistol charges whistled into the dark, both
missing their targets by a dozen yards, striking the estate's facade.

The two guards ducked and gaped at the crazed white man. Behind
him they saw another half-dozen menacing black men, each with a long
sinister blade in his hand. It did not take much thought for the two
guards to turn and flee, running past the house and into the cover of
night.

Tafert blinked, trying to see through the smoke, and looked to the
ground, anticipating that his victims would have fallen at their posts.

The six men behind him ran up to his side, and Tafert, emboldened, charged the house.

Boaz, the tall, formally clad doorman, swung open the front door, holding a torch in one hand and a musket in the other.

Tafert held up his hand and demanded that all stop. "Hand over the musket!" he bellowed. In a moment he had his sights leveled against the spot of light flickering on the porch. He pulled the trigger again, and another roar erupted into the night. The musket ball hissed and found purchase in the flesh of Boaz's left shoulder. The doorman spun about, screaming in pain, dropping the lit torch at his feet.

Tafert took off at a run toward the house, knowing that the front door was now unguarded. He leaped up the steps, bowling over Hattie, who was cowering by the door. He looked to his left, then right, as the men behind him piled up in a bunch just at the inside of the elegant house. His eyes spun in a wide circle, trying to take in the opulence of the governor's mansion, yet he had no frame of reference to judge the level of riches here represented. He had never set foot in so grand a residence. Even the church in his tiny village back home would have fit inside the entry hall of Shelworthy. He stepped, almost on tiptoe, toward the main staircase.

The fancy bed be up there, that I be sure of, he thought. *And the fancy white linens. So crisp yet so soft. . . .*

He turned to the group of men following. "Ye be ransackin' the kitchens and the . . . and the fancy rooms about the place," he shouted, indicating the ground floor with a sweep of his hand, now grasping his machete. "I'll be lookin' for the riches up there," he said, pointing up the steps. He stopped and looked about, confused. "And be settin' off for the far side of the house. That be where Bliss waits. Ye tell him we be needin' his help with the battle."

The six men behind him did not move, their eyes wide and unfocused.

"Ye stupid clumps!" Tafert shouted. "We be takin' over this fine place! Find Bliss, and then ye can go where ye will." He swung his machete in a long, sweeping arc and slashed at the banister, chipping off a huge splintery chunk that skittered to the floor by the front door. All eyes followed it as it arched, as if that small desecration opened the door to all of them to rush through.

Tafert turned to the stairs and began taking them two at a time. Three of the men turned and ran out the front door, looking for Bliss. The other three slowly walked through the ground floor formal rooms, at first simply touching the colored walls, the intricately carved moldings, the elegant silver services, the delicate porcelains, the fine paintings, the thick draping, and stepping on the thickly woven and richly patterned rugs from the Far East. One of them picked up a dainty teacup and held it up to the candlelight, feeling like he had captured the moon in his hands. Another picked up a silver teapot and slipped it under his arm, never having cradled anything that polished before in his life. The others sniffed the air and headed through the rooms, making their way to the larders and kitchen. They shouted at the two cooks who remained on duty to prepare tomorrow's meals, brandishing their machetes at their menacing best. Soon the rooms were empty, save for the six black slaves, who now stood before more food than they had ever dreamed of. Certainly no man, save perhaps the chief in their villages back home in Africa, had a more abundantly stocked larder than did Governor Spenser.

Slabs of bacon, hams, wheels of cheese, bags of barleycorn, sacks of flour, barrels of sugar, and casks of molasses. Pitchers of milk and cream. Vegetables, fresh from the garden plots of the island. A half-dozen freshly killed hares. A dish filled with eggs. Piles of yams, sweet potatoes, yellow squash, and turnips. Baskets of bananas, melons, guavas, and custard apples. Golden-brown pasties of young goat, roasted chickens on huge platters, flaky pear pastries, raisin cakes, and sugary candies.

They walked about, sniffing, drinking in the air with great gulps. In no more than a few moments, their treasures of silver and china were laid aside and they began to gorge themselves on the repast that lay within their grasp.

As the six slaves set to eating, Ian Tafert was heading down the west wing of Shelworthy, kicking at doors, peering into the darkened chambers, attempting to find the most palatial bedchamber in the house— the bedchamber of the lord governor. In it, he was sure, would be the finest and softest bed on the island.

Tafert came to a set of double doors and kicked at them, splintering the lock with a brittle crack. He spun back to the hall, grabbed a candle, and stepped into the darkness of the master chamber. He gasped as his eyes took in the size of the room and the huge bed positioned on the far wall, its four posts reaching to the heavens. He walked to the side of the bed and reached out with his muddied hand, touching with the most hesitant touch the smoothly woven, hand-stitched linen coverings. They were as white as the whitest sand Tafert had ever seen. His hand slipped to the pillows, stacked in abundance at the head of the bed. His finger traced the delicate S monogram embroidered along the edges. He pressed against them and felt his hand sink into the feathery softness. He reached out and tore at the coverings to reveal the inner sheets, even smoother and more delicately woven than the coverlet.

It be as heaven to lie upon this bed, Tafert thought. Coughing, he turned and sat down, then lifted his feet, boots and all, onto the crisp white bed. He felt his body float above the downy softness, then slowly become encompassed by this vast field of cloudlike sweet cradlings.

He had been transported, and he knew that to sleep in a bed such as this would be to sleep the sleep of angels. He coughed, felt his lungs tighten and spasm, then relax, as if smoothed to painlessness by the soft velvet of this bed.

It not be right for a man to have this much, he said to himself, *whilst the rest of us haven't got but dirt and mud to be sleepin' on.* He smiled in the flickering darkness and closed his eyes.

Gleeson, two other white indentured servants, and a dozen slaves came up the road to Shelworthy at a dead run, their arms pumping, sweat dripping into their eyes, nearly blinding them in the dark.

From more than two miles distant, Gleeson had heard the shots ring out in the stillness. His pulse quickened, for Tafert had said the tenth bell would be the time and it had not been nearly an hour since he had heard the ninth chime.

"Must have been set upon by those fancy guards," Gleeson had surmised glumly, and with a wave, he had called the rest of his force to follow him at a run.

From the distance of a half mile, they saw an angry smudge of flame at the front porch and ran even faster to get there.

"We not be wantin' to be burnin' it down," Gleeson gasped, "we be wantin' it to be havin' for ourselves. And where in blazes is Bliss? His sailors were to be here by now."

They came upon the uniformed black man on the porch, bleeding from a musket wound in the shoulder, and a frantic slave woman beating at the flames with a scrap of rug and a twig broom.

Within a moment, Gleeson's men had the flames extinguished. The flames had burned a half-dozen feet of the wooden railing and porch floor. Smoke darkened the facade of the mansion like the sooty thumbprint of a giant.

Gleeson grabbed the wounded man and gave him a rough shake. "Where be the men who did this? Have you beat them off? Be the guards about?"

Boaz looked up, his eyes narrowed with pain, his jaw clenched. "Don' know where they be." He grimaced and tried to knock Gleeson's hand from his arm. "The governor be here now, and he be sendin' you all to the hangman. More guards be comin' too."

It was all that Gleeson had to hear. He turned to Hattie, who sat at Boaz's side, blubbering, her hands fluttering about her face. "Where them guards live?"

Hattie did not answer.

Gleeson kicked at her haunches. "I be askin' you a question, you stupid darkie. Where be the guards?"

Hattie cowered even more. She pointed at the front door, toward the guard quarters, which were located just at the far side of the kitchen, at the rear of the mansion.

Gleeson's eyes widened. "They be in the house!" he cried. "We got no time t' waste! We'll not be waitin' for that pirate's help. We be doin' it by ourselves."

He stood, unlimbered his musket, and ran through the front door. "Ye all follow me now."

Gleeson stopped in the front hall, the men crowded behind him, just as Tafert and his men had done only moments before. Gleeson pointed to the muddy footprints up the steps and motioned to Blane Edgars and Timmy O'Donnel, indentured servants both, that they should be investigating upstairs.

"We'll be clearin' a path to the kitchen, mates. Be back quick."

And with that Gleeson ran off, followed by the rest of the slaves, while Edgars and O'Donnel climbed the steps, their muskets to their shoulders.

■ ■ ■ ■ ■

In the darkness, the *Sea Demon* rolled and pitched in a slow, cradling arc. Captain Bliss stood at the starboard rail on the quarterdeck of his old and creaky ship and peered through the blackness toward Bridgetown. The vessel lay anchored just outside the harbor, having slipped into the waters of Barbados an hour after sunset. He could easily make out the torches and lanterns as they blazed away, lighting the dozens of street celebrations, marking the governor's marriage. The winds blew out from the land, and faint echoes of music slipped along the surface of the calm water.

"Be a good night for partyin' indeed," he cawed. "But Bliss be waitin' till the town be in flames. Then ye'll see who be the real master."

He lifted a large jug filled with an oily, sugary rum and drank several large and noisy swallows. Turning around, he called out for the first mate, a slight, pale boy from York by the name of Wincer Tellet. "Wincer, ye little squirt, where ye be hidin' tonight?" he shouted.

In a dozen heartbeats, Bliss heard a scrabbling on the deck behind him. He knew it was Wincer from the softness of his step.

"Y-yes sir, Captain Bliss?" he stammered. "You be needin' my assistance?"

Bliss turned about and leered at him, placing his greasy hand on the boy's shoulder. "I need ye to stand guard with me this night," he whispered. "Ye wants to be standin' guard with your captain?"

Wince blinked, then nodded.

Bliss continued. "We need be lookin' for flames, me boy, flames of a city on fire."

"Flames?" Wincer replied, no louder than a scared whisper.

"Indeed, little one. If them stupid gits manage to kill a few noblemen and the fight spreads to the city, then we'll be goin' in to help ourselves to some of them riches. If we see no flames, we stay here till dawn, then sail away for home."

Wince nodded again, then raised his head to face his captain. "But, sir, did not I hear you promise that our men would be joinin' their attack on the governor's mansion? I thought we had prepared for a battle tonight?"

Bliss draped his arm over the smaller man and laughed. "Wince, that be what I likes most 'bout ye—yer sense of honor. Stupid ye might be, but ye have a sense of honor."

"But, did you not say—?"

Bliss spun about and grabbed him by the scruff of his neck and near lifted him off the decking. "Listen, ye little runt. I'll not be riskin' me neck over the fool plans of some loony drunken Englishman. I doubts if them slaves have the sense to strike a flint to start a fire, let alone be takin' over some fancy estate with guards. If they be settin' the town ablaze, I be sailin' in. If the partyin' be civil and goes on all through the night, then I be stayin' where I be anchored. Me life be worth more than all them drunken louts put together."

He squeezed his mate's neck one last time and felt Wincer squirm in pain beneath his grip. "Do ye understand, my little Wince? Do ye?"

Wince nodded vigorously.

"That be most good," Bliss whispered and smiled as he relaxed his grip. "And now be a fine and cozy night fer the two of us to be watchin' the pretty lights of them parties, ain't it?"

And Wince nodded again, no trace of a smile on his face.

The darkness filled their vision, and the quarter slip of a moon provided scant illumination for their footsteps. Ezra Trimble walked a pace behind William Hawkes and kept the pistol within inches of the back of his hostage's head. The pistol was old and heavy, and with each step they took the barrel dropped another hair's width lower. The ruts and hollows in the road prevented any brisk walking, especially for a traveler unwilling to risk using a torch.

"Ezra," Will asked, "what are you planning to do? You know that you will not be able to commit a crime and go unpunished. This is a small island. There is no place for you to hide."

Ezra laughed, "Does not matter as to the size of the island. Once we have taken over, then it will be you poor noblemen that will need a place to hide."

Will kept his pace slow, feigning a greater loss of mobility than was real. The longer it took to walk to Shelworthy, the more time Will had to devise an escape.

"Once *we* have taken over, Ezra? Who is this 'we' that you speak of?" Will's voice was calm and easy, wanting to keep his abductor as calm as possible.

"You have no need of knowing who be in charge just yet, Mr. Hawkes. You will know soon enough."

"But why take me? I am not a nobleman," Will asked. "It would seem that if you wanted a proper hostage, you might have selected a titled nobleman. Neither the governor nor the king would have much use for a kidnapped ex-pirate like me."

Will felt Ezra stumble as the import of his words came clear.

"After all," Will continued, "what good would I be as hostage? I may have a pound or two stored up, but most of my funds are held with a barrister in London. Takes more than several months to get to it, and then it would be requiring my signature and all."

Ezra stopped for a moment, and Will walked ahead several steps. Will knew his words were causing Ezra great consternation, and he heard the man's steps increase to catch up. Once again the hard metal of the pistol nicked at the back of Will's neck.

"No more talking, Mr. Hawkes!" Ezra shouted. "I'll not be deceived by your logic. No sir, you best be quiet till we arrive at Shelworthy. Then Mr. Tafert will know what to do with you."

Will nodded in the darkness. *So it's Tafert that is behind some of this. I might have considered as much.*

The first time Edgars and O'Donnel had ever placed the butt end of a musket to their shoulder was no more than an hour previous to this moment. Gleeson had showed them the trigger and the rudiments of aiming. If they fired, they would have to bring the weapons back to Gleeson, for neither of them had the faintest idea of how to reload the mechanism.

They stepped into the darkened hallway, where only a few candles were still lit. Doors up and down the long passageway were left open, yet inside each was nothing but darkness. With hesitant steps they followed the faint trackings of the muddy shoe prints on the polished wooden floor.

They could see the far doorway, left open, where a candle flickered in the far distance.

"That the gov'nor's chamber, I bet," Edgars whispered, his heart pounding.

"Be he there? We be facin' the gov'nor?" O'Donnel whispered back, his words trembling. "Maybe a guard with 'im as well?"

Edgars shrugged. It was not the time to think. Edgars was told, as they were all told, that the "rich scoundrels mus' be done in, fer no other way there be fer us to take what we deserve."

And with that thought echoing in his thoughts, he stepped into the large bedchamber and shouted a vile curse, with O'Donnel only a step behind.

Tafert, startled awake, jumped bolt upright in the bed, shouting back, pulling the empty pistol from his belt, swinging it toward the intruders.

"He got a pistol!" O'Donnel shouted as he lifted his musket and fired. The explosion flashed like a lightning bolt in the room and dug through one of the four posts of the bed. Tafert pulled the trigger on the empty pistol, the hollow *click* a weak counterpoint to the bellow of the musket. It was then that Edgars lifted his weapon and fired, the musket ball catching Tafert clean in the chest, hurling him back against the mahogany headboard with a meaty thump and tumbling him in a bleeding, collapsing form on the soft whiteness of the pillows below. His eyes grew wide with surprise as his mouth moved in mute agony. No sound came, and his hands, limp and flat at his sides, smoothed against the crisp linen sheets for a long moment, until his eyes fluttered shut.

"I done killed the gov'nor," Edgars whispered, then both men dropped their weapons and fled the room in a frenzy, tumbling down the steps and out onto the front drive. They stopped for only a breath, then continued their mad run east, toward the dark jungles that lay beyond.

███ █ █ █

Gleeson had stopped in the drawing room to paw at a silver inkwell and candlestick holder. It was then that he heard the shots from upstairs, and he and the rest of the men renewed their charge toward the guards' quarters.

Gleeson jumped into the small hallway that led to the kitchen, hefted his musket, and fired it into the group of black men who were rushing toward him. One fell in a splattering heap, just as the others reached Gleeson, their machetes flashing in the dim light. To the slaves in the kitchen, all they saw was a white man with a musket. They charged back, thinking they were under attack by the governor's men.

Gleeson felt no pain as the blade entered his chest. His eyelids snapped open and shut rapidly for a moment, then the eyes went cloudy and he fell, face first, to the stone floor.

█ █ █ █

The sounds of musket fire rippled over the quiet landscape and reached those at the edges of the wedding celebrations. A few men had slipped away to investigate, and a few slaves came running toward town with crazed and frantic tales of hordes of attackers storming the fine plantation homes. Rumors, like wildfires in the dusty months of autumn, spread like a wave through the crowds. Snatches of shock and disbelief punctuated the music and laughter and clanking of tankards raised in a toast.

A friend of Kathryne's turned to her and asked if what she had heard was true—that Shelworthy was under assault by a demon horde of crazed slaves who were killing everyone in their path.

Kathryne looked at her friend, her eyes wide, not believing a single word. Yet ludicrous as it might sound, why would such a tale spread on this night?

She turned and sought Will's face. He always remained calm and always knew the truth of such situations and the proper response.

"Will," she called out, softly at first, for most often he was no more than a few steps from her side. "Will!" she called louder now, for he had not signaled his presence.

"Will!" she called out again and waited a dozen heartbeats until she called out once more, near as to shouting as was proper in such a celebration, "William Hawkes! Where are you?"

■ ▫ ■ ▫ ■

Will lifted his head and squinted his eyes. They were now no more than several hundred long steps from the road that led past Shelworthy. The span of no more than a quarter hour would be sufficient to reach the front drive. It was here that the darkness would be most encompassing, most concealing. It was here that Will would need to make an attempt to escape or place his fate in the hands of the indentured servant Ian Tafert.

Will considered every option and knew that he stood his best chance in the dark, with a single, untrained man as his guard.

"I need to rest for just a moment," Will called out. "This is as far as I might walk without stopping to work the muscles in this bad leg of mine." Will had been exaggerating his limp and his pain for the last half hour. In truth, he could have walked the entire night if needed.

Ezra pulled up short behind him, keeping the pistol aimed at Will's back. Will knew the pistol had grown heavy in his hands. No man wanted to carry a pistol at arm's length for more than a few dozen paces. The muscles soon tired, and the aim wavered in kind.

Will knelt in the moist dirt of the road and massaged at his lower leg, offering a low moan as justification of his action. He turned his head a quarter turn and saw Ezra behind him, the pistol aimed high and to the left. Will slowly extended his hand to his cane and took a slow, easy breath. In an instant he swung the cane from his kneeling position in a short arc to his back. The cane first hit the pistol and knocked it further to the left. Ezra cried out in surprise and pulled at the trigger, thinking he had no choice as a guard. The pistol exploded, and the musket ball missed Will by the span of more than a dozen hand widths. Will stood quickly and, before Ezra could raise his hands in defense, thumped him soundly, the cane making a curious hollow noise as it bounced off the man's temple. Ezra remained standing only a moment longer and then collapsed in a heap on the road.

Will grabbed at the pistol and pawed through the man's pockets, looking for extra powder and shot. To his astonishment, Ezra carried none. *He was attempting to take over this island with a single shot from a pistol,* Will thought, incredulous.

He dragged Ezra's limp form from the road and pushed it to the side. *No sense in having him run over by a carriage in the dark,* Will thought. Will slipped the pistol in his belt and loped toward the governor's home.

I may not have any powder in this pistol, he thought, *but no one other than me has to know it.*

░▒▓█▓▒░

Kathryne spun through the crowds looking for Will, her eyes becoming more frantic at every passing moment. At the end of the long street, she came upon John Delacroix, who stood off to the side with a half-filled tankard in his hand. His eyes were slightly glazed, and he had the loose appearance of a man slightly into his cups.

"John!" Kathryne near shouted. "I need your help. Will is missing, and there is wild talk of a slave uprising. You must take me to Hawkes Haven at once."

John straightened up, looked about the crowd, then called out several names. Soon an open carriage rattled up to them, and John and Kathryne climbed aboard and took off to the south as fast as the single horse could carry them.

░▒▓█▓▒░

With quick steps, Will covered the ground from where Ezra lay unconscious to the wide front drive of Shelworthy. He crouched behind the thick royal poinciana shrubs at the far edge of the entrance and stared at the house. He saw the charred residue on the front porch, evidence that a fire had threatened to consume the house. As Will made his way in the darkness, he heard the muted barks of several musket shots.

Is that a smear of blood on the front wall by where the fire was? Will wondered, his heart beating faster from the implied danger of these signs.

From behind him, there came a slight rustling, and Will spun about, aiming the empty pistol at the sound. A dark figure tossed his musket on the ground in front of him and dropped to his knees, holding his hands up in the darkness.

"Don' be shootin' me, Massa Will!", the form cried out. "It be Prichard Manning! I be Massa Spenser's man. I not be fightin' you, Massa Will."

"Prichard? What are you doing out here in the dark? What has happened?" Will whispered with an urgency.

"A bunch of crazed men and darkies came up, and dey shot poor ol' Boaz. Hattie done dragged him off. But dem crazies be in de house, doin' God know what. I done hear screamin' and muskets firin' and all sort of devil stuff." His voice sounded as if on the verge of tears.

Will reached out and put a hand on the slave's shoulder. "Steady, Prichard. You are safe now."

Will reached out and took the musket from the ground. It was still filled with powder and shot. "Do you have more powder and shot for this pistol, Prichard?"

The frightened man nodded and handed Will a powder horn and a leather bag filled with rounded lead shot. Will loaded the weapon as both of them crouched behind the shrubs.

"How many men have entered the house?"

"'Bouts a dozen, maybe more. I done run off when dey start shootin,' Massa Will." He hesitated a moment. "I be most sorry for not fightin' dem men, but ol' Prichard be most powerful scared."

"You did fine, Prichard," Will soothed. "You were here when I needed help, so you have done right." Will looked back toward the house. "Any of the governor's slaves still in there?" Will asked.

"Don' know fer sure, Massa Will. Mos' likely be sum of 'em in de house. Hattie maybe. Maybe dem cooks and Lady Em's maids and all."

Will grimaced. Women in such a situation were often most at peril. Possessions could be replaced, homes rebuilt. But the honor and life of innocent and virtuous women were items that could never be repaired. Will knew that when blood began to spill, men's baser instincts were often inflamed, causing them to do things that any civilized man would consider repugnant and evil.

"Are there any others who ran with you, Prichard?" Will asked. "Would there be any other men who might be here to help?"

Prichard looked about, scanning the darkness. "I know der be two more just in dat field," he said, pointing behind him. "Dey be hidin' fer now. But ol' Prichard kin fetch 'em fer you."

Will clasped the man's shoulder again. "Do so, good Prichard. We need to protect those left inside."

Prichard rose from his knees and ran in a low crouch in the direction he had pointed.

Now if I only knew what to do next, Will thought. He lowered his head and offered a quick prayer for safety, success, and God's divine hand of protection.

The carriage careened through the narrow streets of Bridgetown, John flailing the reins against the horse, spurring it faster. Celebrants jumped from its path, shouting and shaking their fists as the carriage passed, angry for having their revelry interrupted.

Kathryne clung tightly to the passenger seat, calling out, "Please hurry, John, you must hurry!"

In a few short moments they had cleared the city and the crowds and were on the short road that led to Hawkes Haven. Kathryne strained to see the house in the darkness, praying that she would see no flames nor hear shots fired.

Dear God, she thought, *do not let my home be ravaged a second time. And, God, protect my babies. I could not live a moment without them. Thou must send thy angels at once to guard them. Thou must, I pray, dear heavenly Father.*

The carriage became nearly airborne as it cleared the small hillock, the horse gasping and pulling for all it was worth.

The house appeared normal—no flames, no unexpected intruders milling about. In no more than a few moments, John was pulling hard on the reins and pushing against the brakes, and the carriage swerved and skidded to a stop.

Even before the carriage stopped rolling, Kathryne leapt from her seat, picked up her skirts, and dashed across the front gardens, slamming open the front door, startling the three servants and the nursemaid still gathered in the great room by the fire.

Without bothering to explain or call out, she ran up the steps, two and three at a time, and flashed into her children's room, gathering both sleeping infants in her arms and clutching them tightly to her breast.

John, now at the bottom of the steps, looked up as Kathryne appeared at the landing.

"John!" she called out. "Thank God they are safe, but you must send for a guard! I will not risk these treasures."

John thought now of his family. As he had run off with Kathryne, a dozen of John's most burly ship workers had gathered up Missy. She would be in no danger, for they would all repair to the chandlery and be on watch for any trouble.

"Kathryne, I will send a servant to guard the nursery door, and I will stay here until Will returns."

Kathryne could only nod in agreement and then slipped back into the nursery and latched the door behind her.

■ ▪ ▫ ▪ ▫

Will stood, his leg now truly throbbing from the long walk. Beside him were Prichard and three other servants and guards that Prichard had herded together from the darkened field.

"What we be doin', Massa Will?" Prichard asked, his confidence now restored from Will's appearance. "We be attackin' de house now?"

Will did not respond for a moment. The house had remained quiet and serene—no shots, no screams, simply silence.

"We may not have to raise arms at all," Will said. He knew that men's passions could be quickly inflamed in battle and just as quickly subside after a moment of calm and peace. Will prayed that such a calm had descended on Shelworthy and that the attackers would be at rest.

"But we shall not be foolish either," Will added. "Are all the weapons loaded with powder and shot?"

A small chorus of "They be loaded" was the response.

"Then let us take back the governor's house," Will stated calmly, and began to walk slowly toward the main door.

As his small squad drew closer, he saw that it was indeed a bloodstain on the front wall near the door. The front door lay open. With each step up, Will saw more and more. He saw a body, halfway down the hall toward the kitchens, hacked and cut in a dozen places. He thought he recognized the face as that of the field master from the Carruthers estate. Beyond that lifeless form lay two others, both black men, slumped in the hall, blood and entrails splattered about. Broken pieces of porcelain and china lay strewn about them.

It has been long since I have seen such carnage, Will thought. *I had forgotten how unsettled my heart becomes and how evil such bloodletting appears.*

Will held his hand up to stop his men's progress. He heard talking and perhaps laughter from the kitchens. *Why would they be in the kitchens?* Will wondered. *It offers no protection, nor riches.*

He took another dozen steps forward, his pistol held before him. He stepped carefully over the bodies and blood, seeking to remain unnoticed until he ascertained the attackers' true strength.

The kitchen doors were open, at least partially, and Will turned his head from left to right. In the middle of the room stood a large wooden table with benches beneath. The table was stacked with wine bottles, casks of ale, meats, breads, and an assortment of other edibles. And gathered about the table were perhaps a dozen men, mostly slaves and a few white indentured servants, judging from their dress and appearance. None seemed to be on guard, but were most interested in consuming as much food as possible. Nearly every man held a wine bottle in one hand and some food in the other. They were drinking, then chewing, at a fast, regular pace.

Will turned to his men, all with muskets at ready. He raised his eyebrows in surprise, then whispered, "I think they will offer no resistance. Follow me, if you would."

And with that whispered command, Will marched boldly into the room, pistol before him, calling out in a loud, but not excited voice, "All right, you men, you must stand down from your battle. The fight is over. Do not look to weapons, for this house is surrounded by Royal Marines."

A few men jerked to one side or the other, looking for machetes or clubs. As they moved, Will pointed his pistol at their frames, and within a heartbeat they sat back down, waited only a moment, then continued to eat.

"Finish your food," Will called out, "but I will allow no more aggression. Is that understood?"

They replied with nods and a mumbled chorus of "Yes, Massa."

Will motioned to Prichard and said softly, "Gather up their weapons, but keep your muskets aimed and armed."

And with that, the rebellion, at least as far as Shelworthy was concerned, came to a whimpering conclusion.

Before another hour passed, Aidan rode up on horseback, leading a full squad of three dozen Royal Marines, as well as another dozen armed noblemen and assistants. Will, still holding the pistol in his hand, greeted him as he dismounted.

"I would venture to assess this rebellion as concluded," Will announced, then told him of the recapture of Shelworthy and informed him as to the deaths that had occurred as well as the damage to the house.

Aidan listened and surveyed, his face growing more ashen and dismayed with each new revelation. Will pieced together what information he had gathered as to the identity of the leaders of the attack and what their motivation truly was.

What saved the lives of the governor, and of Lord Carruthers, Lord Jewett, and several other of the noblemen whose estates were targets of the rebels' guns and blades, was Aidan and Emily's wedding. It was the event that Ian Tafert had hoped would create the most appropriate diversion for their uprising, yet proved as much their undoing as any of their ill-thought plans.

The plantation houses were empty that night, save servants, slaves, and guards. At the three other estates the rebels attacked, the men simply rummaged through a few rooms, as had happened at

Shelworthy. But after capturing the estate, they wandered about in the darkness for a time. Within moments, they had all found the larders or wine cellars and stayed there, eating and drinking until squads of the Royal Marines were dispatched to secure the premises. Ringleaders were arrested and secured in the fort's stockade. In no more than a dozen hours the revolution had begun and fizzled out, like a cannon's fuse on a rainy day.

While the great majority of the rebels were captured easily, a handful of slaves and two indentured servants had gathered up what they could, carrying silver and gold in canvas sacks, and set out for the jungles and uplands toward the east coast of Barbados. There was still wild land there, and a wily and resourceful man could hide in the dense greenness of the hills and valleys for a long, long time.

And in such fertile lands could the seeds of vengeance be nurtured well.

CHAPTER

28

13 August 1645

Bliss blinked his eyes at the dawn and stretched, his bones creaking. He looked over at Wincer, who lay asleep next to him, and jabbed him hard in the ribs.

"I told ye to stay awake the night, Wince, ye dog," Bliss yelled. "Now how can ye be knowin' if the city be on fire last night?"

Wincer jumped upright, adjusting his doublet and breeches. "I dozed for no more than a moment, Captain, I swear it. And I saw no fires at all. The city be quiet all through the night."

Bliss reached out and grabbed the young man's wrist, hard and tight. "That be the truth?"

Wincer nodded.

Bliss looked through the bare light of false dawn and saw the city, intact as it had been the day before. "Well, it appears that ye be tellin' the truth to yer sweet captain," Bliss said. "And be a good thing that ye did."

He stood, stretched again, then called out, "Raise the anchor, lads, for we be sailin' for home."

■ ■ ■ ■ ■

On Barbados, the saying went, the skies never delivered a gentling rain but always a tropical downpour. The same was true for excitement, gossip, and intrigue. The wedding of the governor was exciting, indeed, but the revolt of the slaves was doubly so. The courtship between a proper English vicar and a woman of most dubious virtue was simply a garnishing to a meal of gossip full of enticing secrets and mysteries shrouded in the cloak of civility.

And while the nobility acted as if the events of the day were a grand adventure, a great many were shaken by what might have happened. "Could my throat have been slit in the dark?" they wondered. "Could the trusted servant standing next to me slip a blade between my ribs in silent, bitter anger?"

No longer were the secret currents of which noblemen sided with King Charles and his Cavaliers or which sided with Oliver Cromwell's Roundheads a subject of prime consideration. No longer did noblemen drag compatriots off into dim corners to enlist their aid and comfort to one cause or the other. English politics, once a most heated and debated subject, now seemed curiously unimportant. For in reality, the news from London arrived back to the island in small doses, filtered through the eyes of often ill-educated ship captains and traders. They saw the happenings most often from a purely economic position—what it meant to their purses and treasuries.

But now, the noblemen were faced with a most immediate threat— not from the king, not from Cromwell, but from the men in their own employ. The small rebellion served no purpose to the slave and servant, other than to make their lot worse. A suspicious man holds little sympathy and respect for those he is suspicious of, and treating a slave with ill temper simply increased in occurrence over the weeks following the would-be rebellion.

Emily refused to mount the main staircase the next morning. After spending the night at Hawkes Haven while Aidan and the other planters attempted to sort out what had transpired, she rode back to Shelworthy to find her new husband. She looked for a single moment at the muddy tracks in the entry hall, the thick matting of blood in the hall where Gleeson had breathed his last, the tumbled and confused piles of silver treasures, china, glass, food, wine bottles, and the linens wrapped about them in heavy bundles. She ran from the house, feeling the panic rise in her throat.

Aidan and William, with a squad of marines in tow, spent hours ascertaining that no brigands lurked in closet or stable or dark pantry. Aidan ordered servants and slaves about, barking out commands with terse, angry words. While none of them had participated in the attacks, Aidan viewed them all with a more suspicious eye and nodded to the marines to keep close watch on their activities. The slaves carried buckets and mops about, swabbing up dirt and blood. Servants busied themselves at scrubbing the governor's bedchamber walls, stripping the fouled linens, patching musket holes in the white plaster. One of the washerwomen attempted to place the bloody linens in a large boiling tub until Aidan shouted out from a second-floor window that he wanted those linens burned, not washed.

"There will be no trace of those villains in this house by the time the sun sets!" he shouted. "Not one trace at all!"

Aidan looked about his bedchamber just before sunset and still saw the traces of the attack—the splintered doorjamb, the fresh patches in the wall. And then he instructed Hattie to prepare Lady Emily's bedchamber for their temporary residence.

As he descended the staircase one final time at the end of the day, he shook his head sadly. *This is no manner in which to start our first day of marriage. No way at all.*

"Where are your pistols stored?" Kathryne asked William as he returned home after the attack.

"Why should you be wanting to know that, Kathryne?" he asked.

She looked at him for a long moment, then her eyes darted to the stairway that led up to the nursery. Will followed her gaze, and without adding another word of warning, he stood and showed her the small hidden compartment tucked into the west bookcase.

"The key is always here," Will said as he pointed to a tiny slotted opening. "It unlocks so," he said as he turned the key. The small cabinet opened to display a brace of shining, lethal pistols, nestled quietly on a bed of scarlet velvet.

She was at his side watching, absorbing each position, each placement. She did not want to ask, but knew she had to. "And how are they operated again? How are they cocked?"

Will closed his eyes for a moment, then evenly and calmly showed his wife the working of the hammer and trigger and the procedure in aiming one of the weapons. As he tucked it back into its case and snapped the lock shut, he blinked. *What has this world come to? That women need be concerned with pistols and defense.*

Then he thought of his two small babies, asleep in their soft, cozy beds. And as he did, a cold shudder spun its way up his spine.

29

15 September 1645

Thomas looked about as he stepped into the quiet courtyard of the chandlery and across to Miss Palmerston's small cluster of rooms. He had hoped that no one would see him on his journey, for he took no pleasure in defending nor explaining his doings, especially since he had done so more than two dozen times in the past few days. Everyone from Vicar Petley to Kathryne Hawkes herself prodded and queried him frequently about his personal comings and goings.

To Thomas, whether it be right or wrong, every question seemed to be edged with a nudge and a wink, a smirk, or a knowing glance.

Kathryne was one of the few who took delight in his happiness. Will remained silent on the issue. Most others looked upon a vicar in a relationship with anyone other than a virginal young woman or a shy spinster as cause for much tongue wagging and idle speculation.

The couple had not discussed another word of Eileen's past themselves, for the vicar would hear no talk of it. Nor had they discussed the vicar's ecclesiastical standing, for he would brook no words on that matter, either. And he had not told anyone of his proposal of marriage since that joyous night, almost a month ago now, under the stars.

Thomas looked over his shoulder again and, seeing no one in the near vicinity, went to her door directly, tapping softly upon it. The door swung open, and Eileen stood there, dressed in a gown the color of the sea at dusk. Her red hair was pulled back from her shoulders and tied with a doubling of golden braid.

She looked up at Thomas and smiled, then averted her eyes down, a mixture, Thomas thought, of deference, shyness, and more than a hint of shame.

"Eileen," he said warmly, extending his arm to her.

She looked back up and did not speak for a long moment.

"Thomas," she finally said, with a cool, even tone to the sound of his name, and stood there, not extending her arm to his.

He waited another long heartbeat, then asked, "Eileen, is something the matter? Do you feel unwell? We do not have to dine at the Cross and Arms if you would prefer another establishment."

She shook her head, then looked up again. "Perhaps, Thomas, . . . perhaps we can stay here this evening. I have a good wedge of cheese and fresh bread."

Thomas hoped she did not see him wince but was afraid she had. "Well, we could do that," he said with no real enthusiasm.

Upon hearing his words, she then stuck out her hand and took his arm. "No, I am being foolish. The Cross and Arms will be fine. Their fare is better than most."

And she began to walk and tug on his arm, urging him to keep pace with her steps.

"Are you sure, Eileen?" he asked. "There is no urgency for this."

"No, it will be fine," she said, averting her eyes from the third gaping couple that they passed along the walk. "I do not mind."

Thomas walked along with her, noticing her quietness and the speed of her steps, not fully understanding her altered behavior. But it was her icy silence throughout the entire meal that triggered such confusion in him. It simmered in his heart, and he knew that he must find out why Eileen was not as herself.

■ ■ ■ ■

The appearance of Thomas and Eileen as they wound their way along the narrow street in Bridgetown on their way to dinner inspired one of two reactions from most people that they met. One typical response was an overly friendly greeting, much handshaking and joviality, with great gusts of promised attention. This was most typical of the merchants and shopkeepers and small landowners. Eileen felt their reaction to be forced and false. If Thomas suspected their motives to be untoward, he never made mention of his discomfort. Others would fall into silence until they passed, then would come alive with a low buzzing and hum, reacting with shock or outrage or bemusement over the sight of a vicar and an ill-favored woman strolling together.

If they paused they could catch the words, falling just at the edge of their hearing. It seemed to Eileen that Thomas had grown used to the wave of silence that preceded their coming to be followed with a gentle hush of conversation. Apparently his heart never weakened, and he remained cheerful. But Eileen suffered from their reactions, though she tried not to allow it to show on her face and never mentioned her discomfort to him.

"The vicar be goin' round with that woman like there be nothin' wrong with it. Land sakes, what is the world comin' to?"

"The nerve of that hussy, to parade about with her head up in the air like that."

"I tell you, he be interested in only one thing, and that be what that woman be there for."

"A man of God doing what he is doing. I tell you, I have never seen such a sight since leaving London."

"I hear tell the good Vicar Petley shall toss him out from the church for good. I daresay he's deserving of it for what he's doing."

Eileen would wince inwardly, struggling to keep her face blank, and when she searched Thomas's face for any hint of anger, she always found only his soft, kind smile.

30

16 September 1645

Will slipped away from the breakfast table claiming he had important tasks to be seen to at the fort, the most pressing being a thorough inspection of the prisoners' cells. His attentions and cautions were heightened these last few days, for a whisper of gossip had swept through the harbor public houses that certain prisoners were planning to make good on an escape. Will thought the idea ludicrous, for a man to burrow like a badger through solid rock with bare hands was a feat that even the most optimistic knew could not be accomplished.

Yet he knew that nervousness on the island was at a high pitch, so he would inspect each cell for telltale signs of digging. Of course, each man would be guarded during the inspection process by a full squad of armed marines. Will would take no chances.

His departure left Thomas, Kathryne, and a full complement of servants in the dining chamber of Hawkes Haven.

Thomas had spoken but a few words during breakfast, but Kathryne chattered on, filling the spaces when Will and Thomas sat there, seemingly staring off into a great void somewhere.

After Will had left, though, Thomas pulled up his chair and sat closer to the table, looking as if he had a great burden to share.

"Thomas, you should stay away from all games of chance," Kathryne playfully scolded. "Not simply because of being a vicar, but because your face never holds a secret long enough to warrant a wager. A person seeing you at a hundred paces would know that your thoughts are troubled."

Thomas simply nodded and did not reply.

"And when I see you are troubled, I must ask you as a friend, as part of this family," Kathryne prattled on, "that you unburden yourself. When I have troubles, that is what I do with sweet William."

Thomas nodded and continued to stare ahead, a mournful look in his eyes.

Kathryne tightened up her face in response. "Thomas!" she called out, louder than needed. "Shall you sit there in silence all day and have me guess as to your problem? Or shall you tell me now?"

Thomas unlimbered his shoulders, dropped his head, and mumbled a fragment of words that Kathryne could not decipher.

"Thomas," she replied, "you must speak in English. I did not understand a word you said."

His head still lowered, he mumbled again.

"Thomas!" she shouted, almost banging her palm on the table. "You must speak up. I cannot offer advice to a situation I have heard naught about because of your mumbling."

Thomas snapped his head upright. "I have asked Miss Palmerston to marry me."

Kathryne was set to answer immediately, until the full weight and meaning of the words sunk into her awareness. "Excuse me, Thomas?" she replied, her face a curious mix of shock and joy and incomprehension. She swallowed, closed her mouth, then added, "I thought for a moment that you said . . . *marry.*"

He nodded, not knowing to grin or grimace.

"Why, that is so perfectly marvelous!" she said, a smile coming fast to her face.

"Is it, Kathryne?" he asked. "I have not been sure of many things in my life, and I have no experience with this above all."

She reached forward and took his hands in hers. "Of most certainty, this is wonderful news. It is!" she exclaimed. "How could you think otherwise?"

"Few others share anything save gossip about us, it seems," he said. "And not that it matters to me, for I am doing what my heart calls me to do, and I find no admonition in Scripture to prevent my loving this woman. And this despite Vicar Petley's warning of dire consequences if I continue to see Eileen. Regardless of all that, it is she whom I desire to have as my mate."

Kathryne squeezed his hand. "Thomas, I am so happy for you. Ever since you accompanied her to my father's wedding, at least *I* felt that the union was correct."

"Thank you, Kathryne."

"And you asked her for her hand last night over a romantic dinner?"

Thomas looked puzzled. "Well, no. . . . That is not the exact truth."

"Then as you walked along the harbor in the moonlight afterward, perhaps."

"No. . . . Actually, Kathryne," he said, a great degree of foreboding in his voice, "I proposed such a union on the night of your father's nuptials."

It was Kathryne's turn to look most perplexed. After a long moment, she asked, with a note of caution, "Was not that a month prior to this date?"

Thomas shrugged and then nodded.

"And you proposed marriage at that date to Eileen?"

He shrugged and nodded again.

"And who have you told of this arrangement since that time?"

Thomas seemed to shrink an inch or two in his chair. "Well, I have told you this day . . . and . . . well, no one else."

Kathryne narrowed her eyes. There was a hardness there.

"Was that wrong?" he asked in a small voice, growing smaller.

Kathryne closed her eyes in exasperation and shook her head. "Thomas, what is it about men that makes them so thick and clouded at times? What makes them unaware so often?"

Thomas could provide no answer, so he merely squirmed a bit.

"Perchance," Kathryne inquired, "has Eileen seemed cool to you in the last days? Has she been distant?"

"And how could you have divined such a thing?" he exclaimed. "Yet such was the problem that I came to speak with you about. Last evening," he continued, "was just such an example. We ate together, a most well-prepared meal at the Cross and Arms, and I daresay Eileen spoke no more than a dozen words to me."

Kathryne placed her hands flat against the table and looked as if she were about to rise up in great haste. "Thomas, you are a man of great sensibilities and spiritual insights. But you have no knowledge of the female emotions."

"Tell me, what have I done wrong?"

Kathryne bent forward so he could hear her words clear and plain. "Vicar Mayhew, you are most aware that Eileen has a past," she said evenly.

"Indeed," he replied, "yet I will not allow her to discuss it, for she has turned from that life and seeks to serve God."

"I know that as well," Kathryne said, "and her transformation is no less a miracle than any that is scribed in the Scriptures." She furrowed her brow. "But she shall be troubled by it for all her days. I would think that she hears others smirk and giggle behind her back. She must think that they still view her as a fallen woman."

Thomas now looked confused. "She has never spoken of this to me—"

"For you have not allowed her to," Kathryne interjected. "And you have trebled the problem by asking for her hand, then telling no one. The poor child must think that you too are ashamed of her and do not wish others to know of your plans."

"But . . . but that is not it," he explained. "I simply was waiting for a proper time for such an announcement."

"And which day would that be, Thomas? Which day is best suited?"

He looked down at his hands, then out the window to the ocean. In a small voice, he replied, "I do not know."

"You do wish to marry her still?"

He looked up, tears edging at his eyes. "More than anything I have ever wanted."

"Then you must be willing to tell the world of it. This is a special time for a woman. She needs to know that you are unashamed and joyful over what you have asked. You should not behave sad and ashamed, not acknowledging her inward pain, as you seem to have been until now."

Thomas nodded, holding back his emotions, looking out to sea to avoid Kathryne's piercing stare.

"Shall you go to her now and offer your apologies?"

Thomas nodded.

"She will accept them, you know. I am sure that she loves you greatly."

Thomas nodded again.

"Then shall you bring her back to Hawkes Haven?"

"But why?"

Kathryne smiled and said, "Eileen and I have a wedding to plan! After two, I have become quite the expert."

Thomas was about to speak and mention his meager assets, his standing as a vicar, his sense of conservatism, but could only nod in the face of Kathryne's most firm request.

"I shall bring her back."

As he slipped out the door, Kathryne called after him, "And be happy, good Thomas. Ask Will if marriage is not the best thing that has happened in his life."

Thomas waved and nodded, knowing that he would not risk being scolded a second time in as many hours. He had a message to deliver, and he was not allowing any further detours.

* * *

Will stood outside the door for a long moment, leaning heavily on his cane. He knew he would enter, but a small part of him debated the matter.

There has been little happiness here, he thought, *since this most unfortunate matter of Thomas and Eileen. Kathryne has taken it up as a cause, and I feel my home is an unspoken battlefield. I will have to end my silence on the matter soon.*

He swung the door open and entered. Kathryne stood there, holding Hannah in her arms, their smiles a reflection of one another.

"Good evening, darling," he said. "And how is my little one?"

"Full of fire this day," Kathryne replied. "She has given none of us a moment's peace. I think Samuel went to sleep out of sheer desperation."

William laughed. It seemed as nothing frightened Samuel, nothing save the angry wrath of his sister.

"And how are you, Will? Has your day been orderly?"

"Orderly?" he replied. "Yes, I could agree that today has been orderly."

"Well then, I suggest that you sit, and I will call for a cool drink and perhaps a nibble before the meal. For this day will soon become otherwise."

Will had almost sat in his favorite chair, near the fire, until he heard those words. "Otherwise?" he called out. "Has something happened? Is Samuel healthy?'

Kathryne nodded, holding one hand up to calm him.

"Are you feeling fit?" he asked. "It is not another . . . are you with . . . ?"

Kathryne looked at him with a most exasperated expression. "No, William, it is not that. Honestly, men can make such fantastic leaps of logic and reasoning."

Will was standing now. "Then what could be the 'otherwise'?" His voice was fraying slightly.

"It is Thomas," she said flatly.

"Thomas?" Will asked, not having thought of him at all, and now puzzling how to incorporate his old friend into all his most feared consequences. "Thomas? What of Thomas? Is he ill?"

"Gracious, sweet husband. No, Thomas is most fit as well."

"Then what?"

"Thomas has asked Miss Palmerston for her hand in marriage."

It took perhaps a dozen heartbeats, perhaps two dozen, until Will's jaw dropped and his chin jutted forward. He closed his mouth, then looked hard at Kathryne, as hard and as sternly as he had ever looked upon her. Without saying a word, he grabbed his cane and walked passed her, silent and angry, and without a further word, fled from Hawkes Haven.

Kathryne ran to the open door after him and was going to call him back, but he had disappeared into the thickening fog.

◼◻◼◻◼

Pounding on the door, Will stood on the small porch of Thomas's house at Fort Charles. "Thomas! Open this door! I must speak with you!"

After a long moment, Will realized that no one could have ignored his pounding. In fact, several Royal Marines leaned out the window of their barracks to locate the racket.

"He's gone into town, Cap'n Hawkes," one shouted. "Nearly before sunset, I reckon."

Will waved a recognition to him and set out for Bridgetown, to the chandlery, where he knew Thomas would have gone.

He paced out of the fort, his temper rising. *Thomas cannot do this,* Will told himself. *It is wrong. I must make him see the error of his ways. It is wrong.*

◼◻◼◻◼

They met, the two old friends, on that familiar path that led along the sea. It was the sea that had first separated them. It was the sea that had led to their being wrenched apart after finding each other again. And now it was the sea that serenaded them with its gentle rumblings and hisses, the repetitions of the sound so comforting and now familiar to them both as it sounded, softened, through the thick air.

"Thomas!" Will called out loud and curt, as he first spotted the vicar slowly walking from town. He waved stiffly, bracing himself with his cane. Thomas waved back and began to hurry his steps.

They came together at the rocks, the smooth boulders that clung there to the lip of the shore, inviting passersby to stop and sit and watch the world grow red and dim in the sunset.

"William!" Thomas called out a few dozen steps away. He was beaming. William's visage was hard and thin.

The two old friends, once teacher and student, once mentor and pupil, once friend and foe, now met in a curious, slow dance of confrontation.

"William, what brings you out here so close to the dinner hour? Has your cook left you? Or are you searching for a dining partner?"

"None of those, Thomas," William said, his words in a hurry to be uttered. "None of those at all."

Thomas nodded but did not reply.

"Thomas," Will said, first looking at his feet, then hard into Thomas's eyes, "Kathryne has told me of your . . . decision."

Thomas nodded, but owing to Will's tone, said nothing.

"I have searched for you in order to . . . to prohibit this from happening."

It was Thomas's turn to appear shocked and surprised. "Prohibit, William?"

"Indeed, Thomas, for it would appear that you have lost your senses."

"Prohibit, William?"

The winds began to increase slightly, as they often did in evening. A gentle breeze became stronger, more insistent, rustling grass and leaf in a whispering chorus in the foggy air.

"Thomas, the woman was a common whore! She has entertained countless men! How can you think of lying next to her? How can you? A man of the cloth!"

Thomas leaned forward slightly. Will saw his fists clench and his eyes narrow. "William, be thankful that I am a man of the cloth, for if I were not, I would have raised my hand to you this moment. How dare you say those words about Miss Palmerston! How dare you!"

William looked surprised. "Because it is the truth, Thomas! It is what she was. I am most concerned of this, Thomas. You have your reputation as the vicar of Fort Charles to think of."

Thomas took a step back, almost in an attempt to circle him. "So I must give up my life in order to serve God?"

Will blinked and replied, "Yes."

"And you have given up your life to serve God? Every part of your life?"

Will blinked again. He felt the theological rabbit hole, yet did not see it appear beneath his feet.

"That is not the point, Thomas, and you are aware of that," he finally replied. "You, as a vicar, cannot think of marrying a whore, even if she has repented of that and turned away from that life. You cannot."

"And you are the man who should tell me that I cannot think of being united with a poor sinner such as Miss Palmerston?"

"I am a friend, Thomas. We are family. Who else but me can speak to you of this?"

"And I should ignore my heart and follow your instructions?"

Will blinked again. He felt the slipperiness of his argument grow slipperier. "It is not my instruction, Thomas. It is from Scripture," he said, then desperately wracked his memory for what Scripture might be appropriate in this.

Thomas stepped again to his left, completing a half turn about William. William pivoted to remain face-to-face. "And so, William, you tell me that I shall not marry this . . . this *whore,* as you so gently call her." Thomas's words dripped with a venomous anger. "And you tell me it is the Scriptures that prevent a man from accepting the forgiveness and the cleansing of God."

He took another step and spoke again quickly. "Well then, William, I will follow your words if you will do the same. Would that be agreeable?"

William's thoughts raced. Kathryne's virtue was never in doubt, so this could not be a trick question, yet the rabbit hole began to widen.

"Would it be agreeable?" Thomas called out, his voice near a shout.

"Yes," William mumbled, knowing that his argument was near to collapsing.

"Well then, William, if I must be alone—according to your Scriptures—then so must you."

"Alone?"

"You must now divorce Kathryne."

"Divorce?"

"Yes, William, *divorce.* If Miss Palmerston is sullied beyond redemption, then what of you? What of *your* sin? Miss Palmerston has committed a foul sin by lying with many men—that is the truth. I know that, and I have forgiven her, as has our Lord. But you, William, say it is not enough, is that not correct?"

"Well—"

"Now you equivocate, William? I daresay the time is past. I will not marry a soiled woman—but what of Kathryne? Has she not married a soiled man? Had you not broken the king's laws for years? Have you not gained wealth through smuggling and piracy? Have you not caused the death of other souls, William?" Thomas's voice grew louder and more angry. "Have you not had the blood of others on your hands—not just figuratively, William, but literally. Your sword through another man's heart?"

Will did not answer, but stood there mute. He knew what Thomas said was the truth.

"Blood flowed over your hands, did it not, William?"

William nodded meekly.

"And since you have murdered, William—for that is what is was, murder—then you are sullied beyond redemption as well. And so violated and unclean are you that I demand that you divorce Kathryne so she may breathe clean air and live a more pure life."

William stood still and let Thomas walk around behind him in the thickening fog.

"Is that what you desire, William? That I judge you according to your view of Scripture?"

William stood still and did not reply.

"Then do not ask me to ignore my heart, William," Thomas whispered in his ear. "You, of all people, should have understood. My heart is wounded that you did not."

And with that, Thomas turned and walked sadly into the growing darkness.

There would be no sleep that night, Thomas knew, for his blood was raging over William's attempt at dissuading him from marrying Eileen. Thomas knew that William may have been rash in his actions and may have spoken foolishly, but he should have confronted him with at least a shred of compassion. William should have understood. But he didn't, and now Thomas's heart churned and ached.

I do not want to lose William, Thomas thought, *for he is as a son to me. But I shall not let him stand in my way, that is most certain. I shall not be deterred.*

In the darkness, near the twelfth bell, Thomas heard the porch board creak and groan as if someone had stepped up to the door. Then all was silent for several minutes. A knock then sounded, a quiet, humble knock.

Thomas stepped to the door, and there stood William in the fog, his head bowed, his shoulders slumped, his eyes averted. At long last, he looked up and said in the smallest of voices, "May I come in, Thomas?"

The vicar stepped back and waved Will in with a sweep of his hand. Will's cane clacked against the wooden floor, and he sat on the rough bench that served as Thomas's desk chair.

Will looked up. His eyes were red, and his face showed lines of pain. "Thomas," he said, "will you forgive me?"

Thomas made no move nor offered a reply.

"I have heard my words again and again and again, echoing about in the darkness," William said. "And I did not understand how foolish and mean-spirited and unchristian they were—until they were heard by you. I was wrong, Thomas. I was so terribly, terribly wrong."

Thomas stepped toward Will, his arms open.

"Will you forgive me, Thomas? Will you? Can you?"

Thomas engulfed him in his arms and held him tight.

"Please, Thomas, forgive me, for I cannot live without your love in my life."

"William, I had forgiven you the moment I stepped away from you. I forgive you now as well."

The two broke apart.

"You mean those words, Thomas? You truly mean them?"

Thomas nodded.

"You spoke the truth. I accepted God's forgiveness and expected others to forgive me as well. How could I not extend that grace to others? I was so wrong, Thomas."

"William, you are forgiven. If God can, then so shall I."

"Thank you, dear Thomas, thank you from the depths of my heart," William said. In a smaller voice, he added, "Please, if you would, do not tell Miss Palmerston of my behavior. I am sure it would pain her to know how cruel I was."

Thomas nodded.

William managed a smile, "And please do not mention this to Kathryne, for she might consider that divorce you mentioned if she realized what a foolish man her husband has been."

Thomas smiled, then draped his arm about his dearest friend. "Agreed, William. Your secret is most safe with me. But I caution you," he added with a smile, "that it is a matter I shall not forget, so you must behave yourself forever now."

Will laughed in reply, "Indeed, Thomas, I shall. Indeed I shall."

CHAPTER

31

18 September 1645

For most matters of truth and conviction, the test of their validity is often years in the future, or more likely, never to be acted on at all. Many a swain would vow to offer his life for his sweetheart, but how many men have truly risked their lives for a mate? A devout man may say his belief in God would allow him to die in defense of the cause, yet in truth, most men live and die with no defense required. But for William Hawkes, the defense of Thomas's right and privilege to be betrothed to Eileen Palmerston came sooner than he would have thought.

It was a bright day, clear and breezy, a light temperate tone lifted through the streets. William left Hawkes Haven in a cheery mood. Since recognizing the error of his bullheaded position, Kathryne became most appreciative of his enlightenment. And she demonstrated her gratefulness in more ways than one.

Will took his cane, his leg feeling stronger and more useful than it had in many weeks, and rather than taking a horse, he walked into Bridgetown. He had business to attend to at the courtrooms and government offices, still under construction near the harbor. A trifling dispute had arisen concerning the farthest edge of his property where Hawkes Haven stood. His plat of survey showed it extended past a small creek on the eastern edge. A new plantation owner looked to plant to the western side of the creek, and both he and Will agreed to settle the matter by resolving the conflicting boundary with a magistrate.

By the time he reached town, his leg began to cramp and pain. He knew that he had overextended his abilities, and he looked about for a place to rest and perhaps take a drink of refreshment. He came upon the Cornwall Trader, a new establishment to Will, who ventured out for a meal much less often than he used to. He stood for a moment by the door, peering in to determine the nature of the place, for there were certain establishments in town that he would not enter. As he peered in, a gale of coarse and hard laughter erupted from a distant corner. A group of sailors sat about a round table, a bevy of tankards standing about.

"And that not be the most odd part from the story," a man bellowed out. "It be that the man courtin' her be a vicar—an honest to land sakes vicar of the Church of England." He slapped at the table, nearly tipping it over, tankards sliding about, hands grabbing for the full ones, ignoring the empty.

The laughter echoed and swelled.

"A vicar?"

"A woman of the night?"

"Be wantin' to take me to confession there, to be sure."

"Be she offerin' comfort for us poor parishioners?"

Will shut his eyes for a long moment. *Can I ignore it? Should I merely let it pass by?*

He opened his eyes, swallowed once, then pushed through the doorway and walked, without looking from one side to another, until he stood no more than two steps behind the man who first spoke. Will reached out and rapped him on the shoulder with his cane, harder than called for, but softer than Will would have preferred.

"Watch out who ye be beanin' with that stick!" the man shouted as he spun about and stood. He was a very large sailor who filled up the small space about the table.

"Are you speaking of Vicar Mayhew?" Will demanded.

"And who be ye t' be askin'?"

"I am William Hawkes."

The sailor shrugged. The name obviously meant nothing to him.

"Then, Mr. Hawkes, I suggest ye be takin' yer leave, 'fore I be tossin' ye out. I don't take kindly to bein' bashed about."

William took a large breath. "The man you are laughing about is my friend. The woman is also a friend of mine. I am simply asking you to refrain from such comments."

The sailor smirked. "And if I don't?"

"Then I shall make you sorry you did not," Will said evenly.

"You? Ye little runt? Ye'll not be askin' nor orderin' me to stop talkin' about a whore and a vicar if I so chooses."

Will did not hesitate a moment, but stepped toward the man and aimed his left fist into the man's gut. As the sailor doubled over in surprise and shock, Will lifted the man's jaw with his right fist, and the man's teeth clacking together could be heard about the room. Will's fist was swung hard and full from behind his shoulder. The blow stood the sailor upright, then he toppled over backwards, crashing into the table with a sloshing clatter of ale and tankards. The huge sailor had stood for only a brief moment against William.

Will waited a moment until silence returned. "And to the rest of you—the vicar is a good man, and Miss Palmerston is a good woman. The first I hear anyone say otherwise, I shall return and do likewise to the fool." He paused for a long moment. "Are my words understood?"

No one moved nor spoke.

"Are they understood!"

The group nodded, mumbling their words to the affirmative.

"Then, gentlemen, take care of your friend and inform him of your decision. I bid you good day."

And with that Will turned and walked out into the sunshine. It was not until he reached the corner and slipped from their view that he doubled over his right hand, pulling it close to his body, trying his best not to shout out from the pain.

Through the tears in his eyes, he looked at the welt, already forming across his knuckles, and thought, *I think I have cracked a bone or two.*

32

2 October 1645

For convenience, Eileen stayed at Hawkes Haven for the week prior to the wedding. She and Kathryne sat at the large table in the dining chamber with all manner of fabric, lace trimming, ribbon, and paper and pen strewn about with abandon. Will could not imagine how a ceremony that was only a dozen minutes in duration could consume so much time and energy in preparation.

On more than one occasion Will would step quietly into the dining chamber to find Kathryne and Eileen either in laughter or in animated discussion and would inquire as to their progress or as to when they might be finished with their planning. Both would sense the intrusion, often before Will spoke, and turn, almost in unison, listen to his words, then either laugh or banish him from the room.

"Honestly, William," Kathryne said to him one evening as she playfully, yet forcibly, escorted him from their work area. "Men will never understand the need for careful preparation for events such as these, yet they always take credit for their able assistance when praise is offered."

"I do not do that," Will offered back as a weak counterargument.

"Well," Kathryne said, "perhaps not, but it is no doubt what you think. Now leave us in peace, for we still have a wedding gown to finish."

Will knew the tailor and seamstress had been in regular attendance at Hawkes Haven all week. "Why a man and woman have need to be outfitted with such fanciness for such an event seems most odd to me."

Kathryne's eyes grew wide, as did Eileen's. Kathryne jumped to Will's side in a flash. "You must fetch Thomas immediately!" she cried.

"Jezalee!" she shouted, "Make sure the tailor remains. We have an emergency! I have forgotten about Thomas's wedding coat!"

She gave William a playful but forceful shove toward the door. "William," she said, exasperated, "we need Thomas now. He and the tailor must meet at once."

William grabbed his cane and made a hasty path to the door and continued his fast steps the entire way to the fort.

I trust Thomas realizes into what he is entering, Will thought. *Such a complex world these women build.*

As he opened the gate to the fort, he turned back toward his home. Dusk was settling in like a velvet coat over the island, and Will could see the glow from the two windows that faced him. The glow could have been caused by just the fires in the cook stove and the candles about the rooms. But Will knew better. *The glow is caused by love. That is the world that Thomas will be entering.*

CHAPTER

33

9 October 1645

On the day of the Mayhew wedding, a waist-high clinging fog settled over the island. To Thomas it felt as if he was standing above the clouds, as a giant, peering down at a cottony world below. The sun was near to midmorning, yet hidden by a hazy overcast sky. It was not perfect weather for a wedding, but as Will had told him just the night prior, he remembered precious little of the weather on his wedding day.

"The weather, unless a hurricane is blowing in, will be of little consequence, Thomas. You will see the truth of my words in only a few hours," Will said to him with a wink as they took their final walk along the bluffs over the sea.

And now that the time had come, Thomas could scarcely remember his name, or how to dress himself, or in what manner did one foot precede the other.

Vicar Coates was to officiate at the wedding. Vicar Petley had categorically refused to have any part of the entire affair, claiming that it was an insult to the Church of England, His Majesty the king, and God Almighty, and had stated often that he would seek out a consideration from the church to have the wedding halted. But the time was too short, so his threats shifted to informing the bishopric, insisting that the wedding be annulled and Vicar Mayhew excommunicated.

He did not formally prohibit Vicar Coates from participating in the wedding, for he lacked the legal, theological, and ecclesiastical grounds for so doing. Of course, St. Michael's was closed to them—that Vicar Petley had the authority to do.

The wedding instead would be at the church at Fort Charles. In the fog and haze.

It was close to the eleventh bell before most of the guests had settled into the wide parade grounds. Wearing their finest, none, save a few rough sailors and ex-slaves, sat on the damp ground. Those that did sit looked lost in the fog, disappearing into the thin mist. Thomas stood near the pulpit, still the only fixed piece of furnishing that his church possessed, and William stood a few steps behind him. They had practiced no entrances nor exits, and there was no music to grace their words.

But for Thomas, the absence of such things was simply not important.

Will looked up and saw Kathryne scurry in through the fort's main gate, holding a large armful of fresh flowers, picked from the garden behind Hawkes Haven, no doubt, and loosely tied with a wide white satin ribbon. She quickly made her way up to the opposite side of the pulpit and stood, arranging herself so that she was half-turned to the gate, her smile broad and engaging. She wore a fully layered gown of muted green so as not to detract from the bride.

Kathryne looked about, made sure that all the players were in place, then nodded toward the open gate.

Eileen Palmerston appeared through the mist, the white clouding about her legs and swirling about her as she slowly made her way toward the pulpit, toward Thomas. If the sun had been shining, the gold fabric of the gown would have captured the light as a prism, reflecting and sparkling. Yet without the sun, it took on a more subtle power, softly shimmering with each step, drawing what light was available to highlight the elegant lace trimming, drawing all eyes to the bride as she came closer. She carried an armful of white jasmine and lush greens tied with a wide white satin ribbon and lace streamers, which flowed to the ground.

Her eyes were softly averted from all others as she made her walk, for she was unwilling to look at others during those few moments, for fear of what she might see. She knew that Thomas was taking a most perilous step by first asking, then actually following through on his request, to make her his bride. She knew that he had put at risk everything that he stood for as a vicar. She knew he could be stripped of that title if the church so decided. Yet she knew that he loved her, and that he would not allow another man's opinion or rough comment to turn him away from this moment.

She walked on and stopped at Kathryne's side. It was only then did she raise her eyes to gaze upon Thomas, now only a few steps from her. She held back her smile, for Thomas looked a shade uncomfortable in his fine new cassock and surplice, finished only this morning by a most cranky tailor. His smile was a mixture of pain and pleasure.

The fog muffled the noises of the world that day, creating a white, serene silence that filled Fort Charles. Everyone in the small crowd stood and watched the pair. Thomas moved forward and stood at Eileen's side. He extended his hand, and it rose from the mist like an eagle slowly taking flight into the clouds. Eileen watched his hand rise, and her own hand, like that of a dove seeking out its hunter, fluttered to meet his. Their hands came together, stumbling in the air, their fingers spread and open, seeking out flesh to hold on to. In another moment the fingers found a mesh and clasped each other, as if they had always been one. Eileen averted her eyes again and could only stare at their most recent joining, hand nestled in hand. She turned more fully to face him, her head still all but bowed. The silence and the sacredness of the moment spread a blanket of calm and peace over all who had gathered to witness the ceremony.

After a long moment, Eileen took a small step forward, their hands dropping further into the fog. She stood close to Thomas then, and she could tell that his heart had expanded in his chest, for she felt the same in her own. It was as if that vital organ had never fully beat in her before and now, after lying dormant for all these years, suddenly, with a glorious burst, began to pump life into her frame and being. It was like the soul first coming alive in a child.

She raised her face to the hidden sun and to Thomas's earnest and loving gaze. She stared hard at his eyes, knowing that to her, the gateway to anyone's soul was behind those two small portals. She looked deep into them and felt herself become lost there, knowing that she had glimpsed love in all its raw honesty and truth. She knew, knew for certain and true, Thomas Mayhew cherished her. It was not until that very moment that she finally opened that small part of herself that had forever, or almost forever, been closed. Since the death of a young man so many years ago in Taunton, England, that part had remained sealed, lost, and cold. But the warmth of the childlike love that she saw in Thomas's eyes melted that frozen part and allowed her love to flow completely once more. She felt no sadness for the years that the joy in her heart had been lost, but an overwhelming gratitude that Thomas possessed the key to give that joy back to her. Tears would not come that day, she knew, for this gratitude was stronger than simple tears, was more powerful than simple sadness, and more uplifting than simple joy. This was love.

The glow and spark that flowed between them seemed to charge the very air with a golden hue.

Vicar Coates stood a few steps from the couple, a copy of the Scriptures and the services of marriage book clutched in his hands against his ample stomach, nestled just above the tightness of his belt, cinched firm to his belly. He watched the couple with rapt attention, as did everyone else in attendance.

He coughed once, mostly to interrupt the intimacy of the couple and to begin the ceremony that would mark their new life together. He opened the small black book and began to speak the words so familiar, yet to this man and woman before him so new and so heavy with meaning and ripe with the promise of new life.

Eileen repeated the words, listening carefully to Vicar Coates's phrasings and cadence. Thomas repeated the words from memory, having said them many times before, never once imagining that he would ever be on this side of a clergyman, pledging his vows to a woman who held his hand so tight as to forever link them together as one flesh, as one heart, as one soul, as one life. Their promises were made, at once so old and familiar, at once so new and alive.

When the pronouncement of marriage was given, Vicar Coates's voice rang out over the stilled air of Fort Charles and filled the empty places with the blessings of Christ.

Eileen's eyes danced over those nearest to her. Kathryne dabbed at her eyes, her flowers by her side. Will reached up, trying his best to hide his tears as well. Even Vicar Coates seemed greatly touched by his own words and his part in this special union. It was only Thomas who stood clear-eyed, his features reflecting the greatest joy Eileen had ever seen expressed in human form. In the stillness, in the quieted hush of several dozen witnesses, he bent to his bride of a few moments and slowly, with grace and tenderness, placed his lips upon hers. Eileen would hold forever in her heart the assurance that no kiss had ever had more import, more power, more promise, than did that one brief kiss in the fog on a rough field in the middle of Fort Charles. She reached about him as he bent to her and clasped her arms about him, pulling him close, then tight, then closer yet, in an effort to draw him into her heart.

And then, without prompting, without request, the entire assembly began to applaud. At first it was polite, then becoming louder, then mixed with the cheers and hurrahs of all who had gathered.

Eileen released Thomas, and the couple stood beaming in their love and in the beauty of the mystery and the new promise that they now shared.

CHAPTER

34

10 October 1645

The loudest noise in the parsonage's study was the scratching of the quill to paper. Vicar Petley stabbed the quill into the inkwell, then jabbed it angrily against the paper, making the first word of every dipping thick and bold. The rest of the line would slowly fade to indistinctness.

Giles stopped and looked up at the window. *Not a cloud in the sky,* he fumed, *and that will serve to make the day unbearably hot.*

He scratched a dozen more lines and then sat back and lifted the paper to the sun, enabling him to admire his handiwork. He moved his lips as he reread his words.

10 October 1645
St. Michael's Parish
Island of Barbados

To Bishop Halifax,
I take no joy in writing to you of this sordid matter. You have by now received my prior letter on Vicar Thomas Mayhew's most unfortunate behavior. I am afraid that he has lost all control of his reason and morals. Not only has he continued to see the harlot in social settings, he has now done the unconscionable. He not only proposed marriage to the trollop—he actually went ahead and married her. In truth, to my regret, it was Vicar Coates who was contrived into performing the ceremony. (Do not be harsh on him, for perhaps he was unaware of the woman's background and history.) I do not write this in an air of anger, but I know that the

man can no longer be called a vicar of Christ by the Church of England. I am certain you shall seek to begin the excommunication process at your earliest opportunity. A man such as Mayhew must be stopped, or he shall make a laughingstock of all that the church holds dear.

I am trusting that this matter shall be handled with utmost expediency.

Yours,
Vicar Giles Petley

P.S. And could you see to it that a new set of complete vestments, as well as new boots, are sent to me at once. The tropical air seems to adversely affect our fine English woolens and leather.

G. P.

CHAPTER

35

15 December 1645

Thomas cracked the door of their small cluster of rooms, built in the shadow of the northern wall of Fort Charles. He stepped quietly, holding his boots in his hand, not wanting the sound of his heels to wake his sleeping bride. He sat at the edge of the porch and hiked up his feet, slipping into the worn leather boots. He could not help but smile, so great did he consider his fortune these past two months. To have Eileen at his side was a treasure so precious, so rich, that he knew that his life could not be more full and rewarding than it was at this very moment.

His boots on, he sat, staring out at the quiet parade grounds of the fort. The dew wet the grasses, and the morning sun filled his eyes with a thousand sparkling reflections. He leaned back against the rough post and tilted his head back. He thought he could just hear the rhythmic breathing of his wife as she lay sleeping in their carved wooden bed, a wedding gift from Will and Kathryne.

My wife, he thought, knowing that a smile was soon to fill his features. *Those are two words I never thought I would use in conjunction with another. And yet here I am, an old befuddled vicar living with so great a joy as to overflow my heart every day—and night.*

He marveled, every morning he arose, as to how content he was. Eileen was not the most skilled cook on the island, nor the most domestic woman Thomas had ever known, but she approached each day like it was a true gift from heaven and each night as a precious time to share unbounded pleasure, more pleasure than Thomas had ever dreamed existed. Affectionate, considerate, most often deferring to his wishes, she was Thomas's world.

Though she is most deferential, Thomas mused, *I most often find myself pursuing the course that I imagine she would find most pleasing. Perhaps that is the way of the Scriptures. A man loves his mate with such a power that he will do all he has power to do in order that she may feel loved and cared for.*

Thomas knew that his Sunday sermons had improved in a most dramatic fashion. For the first time in his adult life, he experienced emotions that had till then been only conjecture and most foreign to him. Now, his words were filled with the power of compassion, honesty, and truth.

And this I all owe to my dearest wife, he said often.

He stood and flexed his back, hearing the bones creak and snap. He stepped off the porch and onto the grass. Though his life was now filled with overwhelming joy, as a vicar he still faced sadness and anguish, for not all lives held the joy he felt. And this sadness and distress was now the goal of his morning's journey.

He walked slowly across the parade grounds, his feet leaving a silver, shadowy line in the dew. In only a moment, he came to the row of tiny cells, dug into the rock on the south and west walls of Fort Charles. There was as yet no prison on the island, so these cells served as the gaols for all the criminals of Barbados.

Most often they stood empty and cold. But for the last months, since Ian Tafert and Herbert Gleeson had led their band of rebellious slaves and servants into their failure, the cells, all two dozen of them, were filled with hollow-faced men, each confronting a most bleak future. Vicar Mayhew made this walk every other day, stopping at each cell, kneeling down to the small window, offering his prayers and concern. Most often his presence was greeted with an animal-like grunt, or a curse, or a string of excited words in a language unknown to Thomas. Yet he would make the rounds at each window, knowing that all efforts on behalf of the kingdom of God would be rewarded.

The cells were mostly underground, and the damp, fetid air closed in on the prisoners like a blanket wet with rain. The openings were barred with a thick oaken door, and the windows, which had thick bars across each opening, were no larger than a baby's head. The sun would shine through this opening for an hour, or perhaps two, each day. The rest of the day, the prisoners sat on a rough cot in a twilight of dimness.

This day the vicar had passed by the first six windows and heard no request from any of the jailed men, but he stopped and prayed for them regardless. As he reached the seventh window, two black hands grasped at the rusty bars of the small window, the fingers clasping about the rough metal as if it were a thick jungle vine.

"You de vicar, true?" the echoed voice called out from the darkness.

"I am Vicar Thomas Mayhew," he replied, his heart quickening. Perhaps after all these weeks his words had touched this man's soul.

"You be de vicar at dis place?" the voice called out with an edgy, shrill tone.

"Yes, I am the vicar who is at the church at Fort Charles."

"I done talked wit' you once at de church," the man asserted.

Thomas had no recollection of a conversation with such a man, yet there were many who visited a service only a single time and then never came again. Perhaps this man was one of those, Thomas thought.

"I talked to you 'bout Jesus," the voice explained. "You be tellin' me dat Jesus want men to be free," the voice said. "You be tellin' me dat 'bout Jesus."

Thomas's heart suddenly lurched. His words came back to him, as well as this man's voice.

"I remember you now. I did say that Jesus has come to set men free, that he wants men to be free—*of sin.*"

The man wrapped his hands tighter about the bars. Thomas could see the muscles in his hand, drawn tight below the black skin, pulling at the metal, a fierce clutching of flesh to bar.

"If dat what Jesus want—for a man to be free—den why I be in dis jail?" the voice asked, with a tone that was as near to tears as Thomas had ever heard. "Why den I not be free if Jesus wants me bein'? Why dat be? Why I not be seein' de sun? Why I not be seein' de moon?"

A long silence filled the morning. "Why I not be free?"

Thomas knelt and closed his eyes, asking God to grant him the grace and wisdom to answer this man's heartfelt question with an answer that would make sense and resonate with the truth.

◼◻◼◻◼◻

Returning after these times of prayer and anguish, Thomas was most often drained and empty. He could offer these doomed men so little— other than the freedom that Christ brings to a heart. Yet the ground was so hard, so barren, that he was sure the seeds he planted with his words produced precious little solace. And for the slave who thought Christ called him to throw down his chains and seek freedom—that brought even more pain to Thomas. He understood how the words had been confused, and he struggled to make the prisoner see the error of his thinking.

Thomas was silent for a long time upon his return, simply staring out the window to the green grass of the parade grounds. Eileen sat in the far corner, waiting for him to speak and worrying as he remained quiet.

Finally he looked up. "Dear Eileen, it is such a blessing to have you here," he said. "I look at you and my heart is gladdened."

She smiled, as if a part of her might not truly believe all his words. "Do you mean that, Thomas? Do I make you happy?"

He looked surprised. "Of course you do. How could you think otherwise?"

She looked to her hands, folded in her lap. "You often come home so discouraged and silent after visiting with the parishioners. I am afraid that people still speak of us and laugh about our union, and that their laughter causes you pain."

He walked over to her and knelt at her feet. "Nothing could be further from the truth," he said. "It is that I am troubled for the prisoners, that is all."

She looked up. "Are you certain? You would speak to me in truth if you felt otherwise about me, if you had decided that you have done a most wrong thing in uniting yourself with me."

"Do not ever think that, sweet Eileen, for it would never be true."

"But I have heard the gossip, that Vicar Petley has begun the process to have you removed from the church. I know how much that would grieve you . . . and how that grieves me that I have caused this to happen."

Tears began to well in her eyes. It had been so long that no tear could find its way from her heart. And now, in the safety of her home with Thomas, they seemed to spring up in an instant.

"Dear wife, I have chosen you above all else. If Giles gets his way, I can still serve God. I can still be a follower of Christ. Nothing will change, save the clothing I wear on Sunday."

Eileen sniffed loudly. "And you speak the truth on this?"

"I do," he said and drew her into his arms.

It is curious how well she fits wrapped in my embrace, Thomas thought, *and how often she requires such words of reassurance.*

She raised her face to his, and their lips met softly for many tender moments.

And the only sounds that Thomas heard as he held Eileen were from the crew of craftsmen testing the swing of the door of the gallows. Every time it swung, a low *swoosh* echoed across the fort.

16 December 1645

Carpenters and masons clattered about in the hot sun, attempting to finish the large, rambling building that was to house the governor's official office, the courts, and the magistrate's quarters, as well as the additional clerks and scribes that a growing colony would require. Attempting to finish was easy—actually finishing was most difficult.

The roof was in place, most windows installed, and bricking was completed, course upon course, until it almost reached the eaves. Wide-board wood flooring was hammered into place in most of the rooms and halls, and plaster was spread over most of the lath and timber. Precisely cut moldings graced the doors and windows. Paint was applied in abundance, with most walls being coated in white.

It was most evident to Aidan, as he made his way through the scaffolding, the ladders, the rubble that was a building under construction, that these quarters would never be readied in time for the trials. Under the Crown's law, more than twelve men awaited their fates in the cramped dampness of Fort Charles's cells. And they had waited there for now four months—and if their trials were to be held in this building, they would most likely wait another four months.

"Such a wait is intolerable," Aidan remarked to Quince Pallers, his new assistant and secretary, as they wandered about the site and past piles of freshly milled boards and trim. "We must proceed with the trials. See to it that those brigands face the justice they deserve by the new year."

Pallers nodded, making a mental note to scribe missives that Governor Spenser was suggesting the trial move forward and to send them to William Hawkes, the visiting magistrate to the island, and the barristers for the accused, as well as the Crown's barristers. He also would call on John Delacroix to construct a proper judge's bench, witness chair, and other seating.

To most everyone on the island, the trials would seem to be a mockery of sorts. There was no doubt as to the prisoners' guilt or innocence—all were presumed to be as condemned as the ringleaders Gleeson and Tafert had been. But after all, this small spot of land was a part of England, and there would be no lessening of the rights of the common man—despite the fact that the island sheltered no one who claimed that any of the men in chains was innocent.

Aidan stepped into the bright sunlight and gingerly walked down the rickety steps lashed to the front entrance until proper granite could be shipped to the island. As he dusted at his knees and chest, fine white plaster powder floated about in great waves. He sneezed once into a large lace handkerchief.

"Pallers," he ordered, "draw up a letter to all concerned . . . Mr. Hawkes, the magistrate . . ."

"And the barristers of course," Pallers added as Aidan struggled to complete the list.

"Ah, yes, the barristers," Aidan said, nodding. "We shall have the trials at Fort Charles—on the parade grounds. See to it that all the necessary arrangements are made. The trial will commence with the new moon."

Aidan dusted at his sleeves and sneezed once again. "And perhaps we should inquire as to who might construct a . . . temporary judge's bench and . . . a place for the witness . . . and barristers, perhaps."

Pallers nodded. "Consider it done, Governor. Consider it done."

CHAPTER

37

27 December 1645

Though it was the season of Christmas, the spectacle of condemned men, gallows, and the elegant formality of a trial titillated the entire island into a state of great, giddy anticipation. The noble plantation owners were keen on seeing the lawless brigands hung, to teach others who might be thinking of the same a lesson in the rights of authority. For months now they had been sleeping lightly, one hand reaching for a pistol or a sword at every out-of-place noise that arose after the sun set. To a man, they saw little drama in the trial and were hoping that the judgment would be swift, certain, and most deterring to others of the prisoners' ilk. But to the small but growing merchant and tradesman class on the island, the trial offered great theater to a society that was nearly devoid of culture and outside diversions.

The parade grounds at Fort Charles would be nearly large enough to hold much of the population of Bridgetown, and William was in charge of seeing that accommodations for the press of the gallery were secured. John Delacroix had done quick work in building a rough but effective replica of an English courtroom at the far western wall of Fort Charles. The joinery was simple, yet it provided the proper stage setting for all the players in the drama. John's crew had built a judge's bench, bailiffs' benches, a witness surround, railing, and benches for the jury—all the necessary trappings. The only items missing were walls and ceilings.

The afternoon before the trial was to begin, Will walked, cane in hand, with Kathryne toward the gates of the fort. William so enjoyed these rare times to be alone with her, to be able to discuss matters he faced, decisions concerning investments, matters of the future. But this day, all Kathryne inquired about was the trial. William knew that she was as much caught up in the drama and tension as was nearly every other citizen of the island.

He answered her questions concerning the judge, a short, squat, dour-looking man by the name of Bernard Muttlers. William had met the magistrate twice—once as he toured Fort Charles and on another occasion at a welcoming dinner. Muttlers spoke no more than a dozen words combined at both meetings. His small, fishlike eyes darted about, focusing then flashing onto the next face or image, never stopping long enough for a man to return his gaze. Will shuddered at the thought of a poor prisoner standing before his nervous and baleful glare, should he fix it upon one man's face. Yet the judge had arrived on Barbados with a wealth of positive recommendations about his character and abilities.

One may not judge a man by his appearance, Will had cautioned himself after the first meeting.

Will drew up close to the main gate, most recently done up with proper English oak beams and timber. The wide gate had a smaller door, secured with a metal clasp and bolt as large as a cat. It was most often left unlocked, and Will turned the handle, which squealed now from a thin coating of rust, and he allowed Kathryne to enter before him.

She took only two steps in, then stopped and stood rigid, her vision fixed not on the replica of an English court of law, but in the dark, shadowy northwest corner of Fort Charles.

"William," she pointed and asked, her voice gone thin and emotionless, "what is that?"

His eyes followed her extended hand. "At the far corner there? 'Tis the gallows," he replied, his words leaking out softly.

"Gallows?" Kathryne asked, her voice a whisper. "Have these men been found guilty before the trial? Why is there need for a gallows when their fate is yet undecided?"

She turned to face him, her features showing her fright and outrage. He caught only a thin slice of her eyes and turned away from her glare.

"Kathryne," he said, "'tis not a matter in which I have the power to choose. The gallows were ordered by the magistrate."

She reached out and grasped at his arm as he turned away. "And could you not refuse? Could you not have waited till the trial is over? 'Tis the decent thing to do, William."

He did not turn about to face her, but walked a few paces away. Her hand was on his arm until he pulled away and it fell back to her side.

"William," she asked again, "could you not refuse?"

He simply shook his head slowly. "Perhaps, Kathryne, but it would
have mattered not, I fear, for these men have already sealed their fate."

She did not move a step closer. "And this is their fate? The gallows?"

William did not move for a long moment, then nodded. He turned
back to her, his face etched with despair. His words were solemn, slow,
and deliberate. "'Tis the fate they have chosen."

30 December 1645

The sun stood overhead, hot as burning gold, and the canvas awnings
and shades erected about the fort did little to shield anyone from the
heat that gathered and rippled about the parade grounds. The crowds
that had marked the first and second days of the trial were sparse this
day. To most, the novelty and the drama of the trial had evaporated
under the furnace of the sun, as did the morning dew. The spectacle that
they had hoped for had dissipated as well. There was no articulate man
standing before them, defending his bold reach for freedom. Instead,
the drama was replaced by a parade of illiterate and ill-spoken indentured servants and black slaves. Questions asked by the barristers
gained mumbled responses of a few guttural words, at best. Each in
turn, as he stood behind the witness rail, was asked the reasons for his
actions, the reasons he took to arms. As of this third day, no man had
yet to utter more than a word or two, and most of the slaves simply
hunched their shoulders in a gesture that spoke of ignorance and
hopelessness. Their chains rattled softly in the tropical light as they
made their way, one by one, to the witness rail.

Thomas was at the near edge of the gallery. He had prayed with each
man who faced the judge and felt it was his duty to help them face their
bleak future with dignity and courage. Yet even Thomas felt a coldness
in his soul despite the heat. These rebels had no true understanding of
their actions. It was a case of the unknowing being led by a few men
with sharp tongues and an urgency pressed to action. The two men who
began the call to arms were both dead and buried in a pauper's grave
near the edge of the sea. Ian Tafert and Herbert Gleeson could now
offer no good reason as to what they had hoped to accomplish as they
took up pistols and machetes against the noblemen of Barbados and
their estates.

As the shadows shortened, the heat grew thicker, more palpable,
more viscous. The judge, complete with coiffed white wig soaked
through to the last curl by the sweat of the round man sitting beneath

it, banged his gavel down with a sharp rap. He had heard enough from the thin Irishman behind the witness rail. Danny O'Boyle stood bewildered. He had mumbled out his name, through black and missing teeth, and had been in the process of attempting to tell the judge that all he sought was fairer conditions under which to work.

"And how did you expect to gain these fairer conditions?" the barrister for the Crown barked out. "By killing your master? Is that your path to fairness?"

O'Boyle hung his head and mumbled a few words into his chest.

"What did you say?" the judge barked out, not understanding O'Boyle's thick accent.

"I be sayin' that workin' a fellow to the death not be fair, it not be fair in the least."

The judge glared at O'Boyle. He had slouched further behind the desk, so that only his eyes and the top of his head were visible. As he spoke, the wig bobbed back and forth and lifted up as he finished each sentence.

"Did you not, Danny O'Boyle, sign this document," the Crown's barrister said, whipping a thin sheet of parchment into the air, "that obligated you to a term of three years' indentured servitude?"

O'Boyle nodded.

"Did you sign it of your free will and assent?"

O'Boyle nodded again.

"Then I'll have no mention of seeking fair conditions. With this paper you were obligated to do the master's bidding—not to seek out a chance to slit his throat."

O'Boyle did not look up.

"And are you saying that it was not your plan to kill your master that night?"

He made no reply.

"I have posed a question!" the barrister shouted. "You shall answer the question."

O'Boyle looked up, his eyes narrow and his face tight and tense.

"Be what I woulda done if I coulda. I'da slit the fancy scoundrel's throat from ear to ear, if I coulda. Woulda done the deed, a big grin on me face. That's what I woulda done." O'Boyle then grinned a wide, hateful, gap-toothed grin.

The judge stood behind his desk and shouted, "Take that man away! A guiltier man I have never seen."

Thomas closed his eyes and said a prayer for the young man's soul,

for he knew that there was little hope that his life could be measured
by more than a handful of dawns and sunsets.

It was nearly done. Barbados was about to breathe one great sigh of
relief. The conclusion of the trial was not even a matter for drunken
debate. These men were all guilty. These men would all face the
gallows. Treason was a hanging offense. Murder was a hanging offense.
Insurrection was a hanging offense. Breach of a servant's contract could
be a hanging offense. Thievery was a hanging offense. Barbados would
soon witness, if conventional wisdom held true, its first executions.

Only two prisoners were left this afternoon to be brought out of their
dark, humid cells and forced to stand before the blazing sun, the searing
judge, and a smattering of their peers. One man, a foreman on Sir
Jewett's estate, was a native of the land of India, and his dark, foreboding
looks were nearly enough to hold him in permanent suspicion,
regardless of his actions. He had been found a few days after the
attacks, lugging a leather chest crammed full of Sir Jewett's silver. He
was headed for the jungles on the eastern side of the island. Even as the
Royal Marines ran toward him, he did not abandon his treasure. His
escape route was an easy matter to discern, for the marines easily
followed the deep scratches and ruts the chest carved into the soil.

The judge spent no more than a dozen moments listening to his odd
phrasings and accent before he shook his wigged head and dismissed
the accused with a wave of his hand. The barristers saw only the tips
of the judge's fingers wave about from behind the desk, and that was
enough for them. In another moment, the condemned man was led
away and back to his dank cell.

The last man to appear before the judge was a tall, chiseled black
man. It was the same man who asked Thomas if Jesus had not promised
him freedom. His chains limited his steps to a slow shuffle, and his
hands were held at his waist, his fingers gripping the chains that
shackled his bloody wrists. He squinted and blinked into the sun, but
did not attempt to shield his eyes like others had done only to have their
arms snap back with a clanking jerk before they reached their eyes. It
was a long, silent, hot wait as he made his way to behind the witness
bar.

The slave had knowledge of enough English to be understood and to
perceive the severity of the crimes of his charge. For this trial, he went
unnamed and was simply referred to as "slave of Sir Jewett."

Judge Muttlers was impatient for the trial to end. He wanted to get
out of the beastly hot sun of the island. He wanted to escape the flying,

stinging merrywhigs that seemed to be fascinated with his wig. He wanted to close this most unfortunate matter and set the Crown back on its rightful perch—a symbol of English order, decency, and civility. He wanted to see each and every man who had come before him receive the full punishment that was his due.

"You know the charges against you, and you have heard the facts of this matter," Muttlers barked out, his gaze snapping from prisoner to barrister to crowd. "And before I sentence you to your punishment, which I am sure you deserve, are there words that you would like to speak?"

The man averted his eyes and mumbled into his chest.

"Speak up, you savage!" Muttlers shouted. "'Tis never a time I have had a harder task of hearing the accused than on this blasted island. Does the heat do things to the power of a man's speech?" he asked, looking about to the crowd as if one of them might provide an answer. He glowered for a long, silent moment. "Slave! Speak louder! I will not grovel to hear your miserable voice."

The slave looked back at Muttlers with cold, fierce eyes, burning with malevolence. "I be sayin' that I want t' he free "

The magistrate looked nonplussed. "And is not that the request of every jailed man? Why should your request be better than the dozens I have heard before you?"

The slave squinted his eyes, and his lips tightened before he replied. The silent pause was deafening. "It be that man," he said, trying to lift his arms and point into the crowd. "It be that man who be tellin' me I needs t' be free."

Muttlers pushed himself up so that his head and part of his shoulders appeared over the edge of the massive desk. His eyes darted from the slave's hand to the crowd, and then back again, in an effort to determine at which man he was pointing.

"Which man do you seek? Which man, still standing free among us, has spoken such incitement? Which man called for you to rise up and take arms against your masters?"

"Dat man," the slave said, twisting and lifting and pointing his battered arms. "Dat man in de black cloth. De one wit' no hair."

All eyes and heads pivoted about, scanning the crowd, looking for the man in black. There was only one man who fit that short description. Only one man that day was dressed in black, and only one man in black had a balding scalp.

That man was Vicar Thomas Mayhew.

And from the far side of the crowd, from a distance of fifty paces, from a face buried in the gallery that rested in the shade of the north wall, came a piercing cry. All turned to see the source of the bellowing.

It was Vicar Giles Petley, pointing at Vicar Thomas Mayhew and shouting, "Traitor! I knew it was you who has caused this! Traitor! You are a demon! You are no man of God! I call this treason to the king!"

38

The crowd immediately parted from Thomas, as if he were Moses and it was the Red Sea. He was left to stand there, alone and defenseless, to be fixed by the powerful visage of the magistrate, who had pulled himself forward on his desk, so his shoulders hung over the forward edge. He sputtered out commands to the bailiff and the barristers, and in less than a moment, Thomas was swept before a livid Bernard Muttlers.

"You are a vicar?" Muttlers hissed.

Thomas nodded. "I am Vicar Thomas Mayhew. My church meets within the walls of this fort."

Muttlers looked about him, as if he were seeing it for the first time. "Behind these walls? In this fort?"

Thomas nodded again.

"Vicar Mayhew," Muttlers continued, his voice icy, "this prisoner has accused you of a most serious crime—fostering a treasonous act. 'Tis as serious as taking up arms yourself."

Thomas nodded.

"And as such accusations are issued, they must be investigated. You will have to take to the witness bar as well. Are you prepared to defend yourself this day?"

Thomas felt no fear nor worry, and replied as such. "I have done nothing as this man has said. I have nothing to fear before God. If you call me to offer witness, then so I shall."

By this time, Vicar Petley had elbowed through the crowds and was standing only a few steps from the conversation. His face was red, and he was sweating, and it looked as if he was straining to prevent a grin from slipping across his features.

"If I had been asked," Vicar Petley whispered loudly, "I might have told them that this man is dangerous and cannot be trusted. First it is his consort with harlots, and now his descent is complete—fermenting seditious and murderous acts." As he spoke his words grew louder with each breath. "I demand that the court place this man under arrest and charge him with the same crimes!" Vicar Petley near shouted. "He should face hanging as well!"

Magistrate Muttlers looked over to Petley, annoyed at his interference, and waved his words away with a swat of his hand through the air. "Vicar Mayhew," he said in a loud voice, "I shall call upon you to stand by the witness bar. I shall need ask you questions regarding your role in this."

Thomas nodded and stepped about the bar. The slave was pulled a dozen paces away by the bailiff.

As the players in this drama were set, the crowd, now excited and abuzz, nestled in closer and closer, their bodies drawing nearer and nearer, the aroma of so many unwashed becoming a most volatile and potent mix.

Before any of the barristers could react and before a single question was phrased, a stinging insect scuttled its way under Muttlers' wig. With a yelp, he began to beat at his head and then tore the wig from his scalp and proceeded to whack at his wet and matted hair with an open palm. After a dozen or so most violent strikes to the back of his head, as the audience and barristers stood transfixed by the image of the magistrate beating on his own person, he fell back into his chair and tossed his wig across the desk, where it fell with a wet thump to the grass.

"'Tis an island bedeviled by most vicious bugs as well as men," Muttlers muttered. Then he stood, itching at the spot he had just beaten on his head. "This trial will commence tomorrow at the ninth bell," he shouted, then stomped from behind his desk in a most incorrect dismissal of a day at court.

It was a full moment, perhaps two, until anyone moved—their stillness from shock coupled with the disappointment that the high drama of a vicar to be put on trial for treason was delayed another day.

■ ■ ■ ■ ■

No one had approached Thomas the rest of that day, save William, and eventually a handful of the regular attendees of his church. They spoke in low tones, unknowing as to what manner they might show their support.

After the few left his side, Thomas went back to the slave's cell who had accused him of setting his mind to freedom. But despite his pleas, the prisoner would not share a single word or utterance with the vicar. Thomas closed his efforts with a short, unfelt prayer, then walked alone to the sea, where he spent the next many hours until returning to his home and to Eileen at dusk.

"You no doubt have heard what has occurred?" Thomas asked his wife.

Eileen nodded. Even in their small house, the voices and calls of the trial could be heard as easily as if she had been next to them.

"You know that I am accused of complicity in these acts?"

She nodded again.

"And you have no questions for me?" he asked, his voice edging to the chilled.

She shook her head no, then looked deep into his eyes. "You are my husband now, and I trust your actions," she said in a small, almost uncertain voice.

"You trust me regardless of what I have done?" he snapped.

She avoided his eyes. "I trust you completely."

"And this without asking of me what transpired?" His voice was harder now. His afternoon was spent in growing at first angry, then angrier still at such accusations. He knew, without spending more than a moment's thought on the matter, that Vicar Petley now had all the information that he needed to successfully have him either excommunicated or removed from the list of vicars approved of by the church. Regardless of the outcome, his name and his reputation was doubly tainted and forever marked. There could no longer be a church in his future. He could no longer have a flock to pastor—regardless of the low standing of its members.

"You could not know what I have said," he spoke sharply, "yet you say you trust me." His words were cut with a bitterness that had never before been evident in Thomas's manner.

"I love you, Thomas," she repeated, her words barely audible.

And as his lips formed the next words he spoke, he knew in his heart that they were words that should never have been uttered—but utter them he did. "And how many times in the past have you said those words to a man? How many other men have you loved?" he asked, rancor thick in his voice.

It was as if she had been struck with an angry, open palm. Her eyes widened in pain, and the tears formed in a heartbeat. Thomas stood above her and watched as her face drained of color and seemingly of love. She shrank before him, retreating to a smaller and smaller place within herself. It was that tiny hidden place where no man, no person, could touch her heart.

He realized that unless he spoke she would never return to him. He had promised that her past was forgotten, but now he was proving that it was not. He had promised that her life previous was as far as the east is from the west, but his promises now rang hollow and empty. Thomas remembered the pain of watching William walk away from his life so many years ago and realized that that pain was a trifling compared to the pain that now burst upon his heart.

He dropped to his knees before her, his arms about her legs, as a small child embraces his mother or father. "Dearest Eileen," he gasped, "you must forgive my words! I . . . I . . . I do not know why they escaped my lips. You must forgive me!"

She did not reply, and her tears continued to roll down her cheeks.

"Please, I am most humbly sorry. I did not mean what I said. I have been wronged, and I have taken my pain out on you. Oh, dearest, darling—you must allow me to be forgiven!"

Still, she made no motion, nor uttered a single word.

"My heart is breaking, dear wife. I have wronged you so." He looked up into her eyes and knew that he had pierced her soul in a most grievous manner.

"No, Eileen," he said softly after several moments, "I will not ask for forgiveness. For that forgiveness may excuse my words, and there would be no such excuse for such a failing. I am angry at what is happening. I am fraught with fear that this is the day that I must leave the church—this church—forever. I am saddened to the bone over my ill-spoken words of the past."

Like a wounded bird, her hand trembled in her lap, and slowly, ever so slowly, she reached up and touched the side of his face. Her tears still fell, but she had reached out to him. He placed his hand over hers and pulled her palm to his lips.

"Do not forgive me, Eileen, for what I have done is betray my promise to you."

He heard her soft, whispered words. "But you are my husband."

Her statement was simple and pure and clean. A husband, a godly husband, is a man that a wife could trust. And that trust would not depend on his mere words, but on his soul.

"But I am your husband that failed you just now," he said, holding her hand with both of his. "Let me earn my honor back," he asked. "Let me prove that my word is true."

"But there is no need," she whispered. "You are my husband."

"But I must," he replied. "I must."

She looked down into his eyes, then nodded. "You are my husband now, and forever, and I am your wife now and forever."

He kissed her palms again.

"And I trust you, and I love you," she said, the tears slowing and drying on her cheeks. "I always shall."

Word had spread like a cannon shot fills the air and echoes across a still harbor.

"It be true—Vicar Mayhew be the man behind it all."

"I coulda told you so. For them dumb gits haven't got the brains to arrange such matters as they did. Had to have had a smart one in their mix."

"Since marryin' that harlot, I not be dumbstruck at any lows Mayhew be sinkin' to."

"Mayhew planned to split the gold with 'em. Ain't no pleasure bein' a poor vicar."

"I hear say his little tart gots most pricey tastes. A vicar can't be satisfyin' a wench like that on a farthin' or two."

"And 'ave you takin' a look upon Vicar Petley? Why, he be most like a young man on 'is weddin' day. Never seen th' man so 'appy and excited."

31 December 1645

Fort Charles was as jammed as it had been the first day of the trial. Public houses were closed. Fishermen stayed in from their nets. Two ships in harbor delayed their sailing date so their captains and officers could watch the activities. Even Governor Spenser and his bride, Lady Emily, were in attendance that day.

The court preliminaries were dispatched with alacrity. Barristers conferred and spoke in low, confidential tones to the magistrate. Muttlers looked much improved over the previous day, a new wig on his head—or perhaps the old wig had been retrieved from the grass and now recombed and powdered afresh. And he had decided to question the vicar himself.

Thomas stood near the front of the crowd. There was a gap between him and the nearest person of at least three paces all round—as if too close an association might prove detrimental. A few paces to one side was Vicar Petley, who had dressed in his finest Sunday frock and whose boots looked newly shined.

In no more than the passage of a quarter of an hour, Thomas stood once again behind the witness bar. He rested his two hands on the railing and offered a most heartfelt prayer for peace and wisdom this day as he spoke. He looked out and knew he would not find his wife's face among the crowd, for she was in their small house, on her knees.

"Thomas Mayhew," Muttlers called out, "you have the calling of a vicar?"

Thomas nodded. "I have been in God's service for more years than I care to count."

"And you have served in which parishes?"

Thomas listed them out: London, Hadenthorne, the tiny churches on the northern islands and near the Scottish border, and all the rest of his callings and assignments. He concluded his listing. "And for the past months I have pastored within this fort, at a church made up of sailors, slaves and ex-slaves, and other, less-civilized persons."

Muttlers appeared to be enjoying his work. He looked down at a single sheet of paper before him.

"And was this posting on this island approved by the church offices in London?"

Thomas was about to answer, then recognized the hand of Vicar Petley in phrasing the question.

"Sir, it was not officially sanctioned," he explained. "When arriving here there was no official posting for me . . . and rather than do nothing, this small church was most in need of assistance and I—"

Muttlers cut him off. "But was it sanctioned by the bishopric?"

Thomas stared first at the magistrate, then his eyes found the grinning face of Giles Petley, who was rocking on his heels nearby.

Thomas swallowed once. "It was not, sir. I took this assignment on my own volition. And after discussion with Vicar Petley."

Muttlers nodded and pointed to the man in charge of the prosecution of all the condemned men. Carson Sawkes, a barrister fresh from the central court in London, adjusted his robe, pulled his wig tighter, then strode forward, away from his bench.

"And, Thomas Mayhew," Sawkes called out, "have you been in contact with that slave?" Sawkes pointed to the black man in chains.

Thomas nodded.

"And in the course of your 'ministering' to this man, did you not speak of freedom?"

"I did say those words," Thomas explained, "but I did not incite him to take arms against any man."

"'Tis not the question I phrased," Sawkes replied. "'Tis only a matter of establishing your contact with the man."

Magistrate Muttlers barked out, "Get to the point, Sawkes. The sun is growing hotter every moment we sit."

Sawkes nodded and gathered his hands together at his waist, as if he had no other place to hold them.

"And you spoke of freedom, did you not?"

"I spoke of the freedom of Christ. I spoke of how Christ wishes to see every man free of sin's slavery. I spoke of the freedom in giving Christ one's life. I spoke of the rights we all possess to seek Christ and to seek his freedom."

Sawkes listened as he heard the crowd buzz and hum in reaction to the vicar's words. He then asked, "Did your words include the truth that this man is a slave, and as such has none of these rights of which you speak?"

Thomas looked to the judge, then to the black man sitting in the dust behind him, then back to the crowd. "But he is a man like the rest of us. Surely you cannot believe that he has no soul?"

Sawkes snickered. "He is a heathen from the jungle. Is our God like a heathen black man from the jungle? I think not, Thomas Mayhew. I think this man was deliberately misled. By you." He pointed his finger at the vicar.

Thomas leaned forward. "I did no such misleading. I offered the man comfort, and I shared with him the truth of God's words as they are."

"You called for him to be free."

"Free in Christ."

"Free nonetheless," Sawkes barked out. "And a slave is not a being to be seeking any sort of freedom at all."

"But Christ offers his freedom to every man," Thomas replied.

Sawkes arched his eyebrows and tilted his head to the side. His wig slipped an inch, and he slapped his hand to the side of his head to steady it in place.

"Thomas Mayhew, do you think that slave that stands before us is an intelligent being?"

Thomas looked puzzled.

"Does he possess the intelligence and knowledge that you do?"

"I do not think that he does."

"Do you think he possesses the same intelligence and knowledge of any white person in the gallery who has the abilities of reading and writing?"

"I do not think he does."

Sawkes turned his back to Thomas for a long moment, then spun about. "And yet you tell him of theological matters, of freedom from temptation and Christ's freedom. And you thought that he would understand all your words and all your meanings?"

Thomas closed his eyes for a moment. "I did not think that."

"So you told him fanciful words that do not apply to him and told him fanciful words that he could not understand?"

Thomas looked about and felt most trapped. He nodded after a long moment.

"And you tell him of freedom that he cannot gain? And now he seeks to be free by slitting the throats of innocent noblemen? Is that right, Thomas Mayhew? Is it not under your advice and counsel that he was led to commit such treason and murder?"

Thomas whispered, "No."

Sawkes turned away and returned to his barrister's bench. He turned and pointed at Thomas with a stubby finger.

"You are a liar, Thomas Mayhew. You have led him astray. You have led him, with your silvery words and fancy terms, to the path of his destruction. You are as guilty as he!" Sawkes sat down with a flourish. "Perhaps even more culpable than he, Thomas Mayhew. Even more than he." He paused. "For you know better than he."

▪▫▪▫▪

Thomas knocked at the door of the vicarage, loud and hard. He heard a scuttling sound, then a scratching at the lock, and the door parted no more than an inch open. Thomas saw the whites of a dark eye peering out at him from the black.

"Vicar Coates, it is Thomas Mayhew. I have urgent need to speak with Giles."

The door did not swing open.

"He wishes to see no one, Thomas," Alfred Coates replied, his voice deliberately hushed.

Thomas had no time for the proper politics of begging for an audience that night. He raised his arm and pushed as hard as he could against the door, its weathered paint chipping from the pressure of his palm.

Vicar Coates was bowled into the small entry hall, sputtering and calling out, "You cannot simply force your way into here, Thomas! This is a house of God!"

Thomas nodded and walked past him, pushing him out of his way with a firm right arm. In a few steps he was at the closed door to the study. He tried the handle, and it was locked. But Thomas was not a man to be deterred that evening. He placed his hand on the handle and leaned away from the door for a moment, then crashed his shoulder into the door, pushing hard with all his weight. The door hesitated only a moment, then gave way with a splintery crack.

Thomas found himself standing before a most disheveled Giles Petley, his hair and clothing a storm of hurried disarray. The long window to the study was wide open, the curtains fluttering about in the wind, slipping into the night air. There was the unmistakable aroma of lavender and lilac. Thomas looked about and saw on the floor a thin pink sheath of silk and lace. Giles's face was a mask of controlled panic.

Thomas looked about and said nothing for a long moment. Giles moved about in a flurry of smoothing and pulling and tying and buttoning. Silence filled the room. Thomas could feel Vicar Coates behind him, waiting in the dark.

"Giles, am I speaking the truth to say that you would have me leave the church?"

Giles was taken most by surprise, but leaned forward in his chair. "It is not I who think that. It is your wanton and crazed actions that demand it."

"No matter what you claim the cause, Giles, would you be best suited if I were to renounce my posting as vicar?"

Giles eyed him with a lizardlike stare. "I would," he finally replied.

"Then you shall have my resignation from the office of vicar. I will draft such a letter tonight."

Giles said nothing.

Thomas stared at him for a long moment. "I have one request, however."

Giles snorted a laugh in response. "You have no right to request any favor, Thomas. You are faced with a most serious crime, and here you come, offering resignations and demanding requests. You have no such power."

Thomas showed no sign of worry or care. "All I ask, for my leaving, is that the men and women who have attended the church at Fort Charles be allowed to worship at your church."

Giles was about to laugh again, but there was something in Thomas's words. Or perhaps his stare, the way that he looked at Giles's unbuttoned cassock and tousled hair that spoke of a true knowing. Perhaps that is what caused Giles to hold his laughter and his words. After a long pause, he nodded. "Agreed. They may attend this church."

Thomas turned to leave. Just before leaving the room, he turned back and said in an even, knife-edged voice, "Giles, remember that I know what has happened here this night. And I fully see the irony in our respective actions and fates. But no one shall hear of this from me. It is a matter between you and your God."

39

1 January 1646

Magistrate Muttlers looked out over the grinning, pushing, shoving, eager, joyous crowd of people that stood before him that day, waiting with prickly excitement over the reading of the verdict. The jury, as was the case with most juries, was most easily swayed by a judge with strong opinions. Muttlers knew before he banged the gavel down on his desk at the end of the trial that each man would be found guilty. There was no other option. They would all hang.

Muttlers stood, and every man and woman on the parade grounds that day stood as silent as a stone. He read out the name of every man charged with crimes that day, and following each name, his voice echoed out across the fort, "Guilty of said crimes, sentenced to be hung by the neck until dead." The crowd did not utter a word until the judge called out at the end, "May God have mercy on your wretched souls." Then, what first sounded as a nervous coughing spread across the crowd would have erupted into cheering, for certain, had not Muttlers called out again for silence.

When calm had been restored, he called for Thomas Mayhew to stand before him.

"Thomas Mayhew, you have not been officially charged with any crime against the Crown, but I must admonish you. Your actions with these heathens show a most callous disregard for the civil conventions of the king and the Church of England. I admonish you to cease all further such actions. A vicar in the church should know better than to participate in such foolishness."

Thomas nodded.

"And to prevent this from occurring in the future, I have been informed by church officials on this island . . ."

All eyes spun quickly to Vicar Petley, who stood by himself, almost hidden in the cool shadows of the stone walls.

". . . that you have taken your leave of the church and have removed yourself from the office of vicar of the Church of England."

A ripple of hushed and hurried words flowed through the crowd like fire. Thomas stood still and made no move to speak or nod or even acknowledge the words.

William, who had been standing on the far side of the gathering, was shocked. He felt waves of pain, loss, and sympathy wash over him. As the words were spoken, William instinctively began to elbow his way through the crowd, moving to the forward edge.

"Is not that correct, Thomas Mayhew?" Muttlers called out, a haughtiness in his words.

"That is correct," Thomas said firmly, yet without emotion.

"And do you wish to dispute this action in any way?"

"I do not," Thomas said, his words precise and strong.

"Because you have disgraced the church and are now suffering the consequences of your own actions, it is the findings of this court that you suffer no further recriminations or punishment. This trial is over. And it is my decision that the execution be carried out forthwith. On January 7, in the year of our Lord 1646, all said convicted men shall be hung from the Crown's gallows until dead."

Muttlers banged his gavel down, as the babble of shouts from the crowd began.

Some claimed an outrage; some claimed too light a sentence. Some called for the hangings to begin at once; others called for delay to afford them time to stake out a better position for viewing the executions. Merchants cried out, selling oranges and limes. The pleasure-minded laborers and sailors and a goodly portion of the Royal Marines began to jostle and shoulder their way through the crowd and back to the public houses of Bridgetown.

Vicar Petley remained in the shadows and simply smiled, rocking back and forth on his heels, his hands grasped tightly together just below the shining metal cross that hung from his neck.

■ ▪ ▬ ▪ ▬

Fort Charles was a swirl of shouts and murmurs and colors and scents. Vendors mingled among the excited gathering, selling fruits and roasted meats. At a far corner of Fort Charles near the gate, a juggler appeared, almost out of thin air, and was entertaining a large knot of curious bystanders. Crowds still milled about the grounds, some out as if on a Sunday walk, some inspecting the gallows, some shouting comments at the prisoners in their cells. A small detachment of marines kept the citizens a dozen feet from the cell windows to prevent any harm coming to the condemned men before it was scheduled to take place.

"Thomas!" William cried as he made his way to his old friend, placing his hand on his shoulder, touching the thick black fabric for perhaps the final time. "Why have you allowed this to happen? Why have you not taken this battle back to the bishopric in London? Surely there are rational men who would see your side of this matter!"

"Such an outcome would have occurred, regardless of my doing battle or not," Thomas explained as he placed his hand over his friend's.

"But, Thomas," Will insisted over the noise and confusion, "you have done nothing wrong. You spoke the truth."

"But they were truths that were heard as lies. And they were lies I failed to redress."

Will was at once excited and angry and impatient and hurt. "But if on occasion you spoke to a nobleman, and that nobleman foolishly misinterpreted your words and committed a crime—would you have also been held responsible? Is not the individual responsible for his own actions and his own destiny, regardless of his station in life?"

Thomas draped his arm about William's shoulder and began to walk him to his quarters across the grounds. "Would that what you have said was true. The nobleman would be responsible in God's eyes, but he would not be held responsible by men. But the poor man would be, Will. That is the way of the world."

"But, my friend," Will cried out, "this is wrong! You cannot stop being a servant of God! You cannot stop serving!"

Thomas pulled up short, turned to William, and put his hands on Will's shoulders. He looked for a long moment into Will's deep blue eyes—eyes that reflected his hurt and confusion. "William, at times there is little justice in this world. You know that better than most. You speak the truth when you ask could not this decision be appealed? It could be, but I am afraid."

"Afraid? Thomas, you are not yourself. You, of all men, should fear nothing! You have feared nothing in as long as I have known you! You have always stood tall for what is right!"

Thomas's face showed no emotion. The two men remained still as the crowds rolled past them in a colorful, chatty stream. "I am not afraid for myself, William. 'Tis a trifling of my safety. But if a battle is to be waged, who then wins? Do I, if I regain my standing as a vicar?"

William looked confused. "But should that not be the goal? Would that not be proper?"

"Perhaps so. But in any battle, are there not casualties? If I win this skirmish, does not the church then lose something as well?"

Thomas looked to the ground and let his hands drop from Will's shoulders to his side. "I do not believe that Vicar Petley is an honorable man, nor a compassionate servant. But he is the choice of the church to serve here. If I stand up to him, then he must lose, if I am to win."

"And you could, Thomas! You could."

"But, William, do not you see? My choice is not to battle at all. If I withdraw, I am still alive and able to serve God. I am not excommunicated nor locked in a cell, accused of heresy or treason. This choice is better for all concerned." Thomas turned, and they continued their walk.

"But, Thomas, what will you do?"

Thomas smiled, the first smile he had issued in many weeks. "William, we have just learned of the dangers of giving men only part of the truth, to speak of God's love without speaking of his demand for holiness."

Will nodded.

"I have been guilty of that. I have been on other islands and have presented only a portion of the truth to the natives who inhabited them."

A puzzled expression filled Will's face.

"I would like to remedy that. I would like to go back and give them all the truth. Or train others—natives and slave alike—to do so as well."

Will's face brightened. "As a teacher, then? As a missionary teacher of sorts, who teaches those to witness elsewhere?"

Thomas nodded, then drew closer to Will. "There is only one small problem with such a grand plan."

Will leaned even closer.

"I am a poor man, William. I will need resources of a modest level." He paused for a moment. "Do you know any men of means that might be softened to provide a few pounds for my work?"

Will looked up and saw Thomas's smile. And that is when the light of understanding seemed to fill William's being.

"I am a simple man, William," Thomas said, smiling, "and have very few needs."

CHAPTER

40

7 January 1646

The crowds had returned to the parade grounds, despite that earliness of the hour and the thickness of the mist that slickened every surface and wet every face. Dawn broke gray, hushed, and somber, as if befitting the terrible ceremony that was about to begin.

One by one the prisoners were led to the gallows. Each man's face and neck were covered with a black hood. Death might be public, but the face of death remained a private affair.

Vicar Coates came to the gaols and made his way along the cells, offering confession and communion to every white man held for death. He offered up a prayer for each man, and as he said, "Amen," he hurried to the next cell. The eyes of those men, seeing a gray sky for the last time, would haunt the vicar's sleep for weeks.

Kathryne Hawkes had not eaten the entire week before, so upset was she over the men's fate. She knew that each was guilty, but to take their lives in such a calculated manner seemed so harsh, so barbaric. That Will was forced to supervise the executioners' duties made it more unsettling for her.

Eileen had not stepped outside during the daylight hours for an entire week, either. The gallows were too close, too intimate, to be viewed during daylight. She knew that not many years prior to this date, a woman of ill-repute could have been hanged for any number of trivial offenses.

William was silent much of the time as well. It was his duty to follow the commands and instructions of the Crown, but an executioner's lot was not an easy one. He was gladdened, to some small degree, that an executioner arrived from the island of Tortuga. There would be no man on this island who could boast at future dates of his joy at pulling the release on a man's life.

Thomas sat, silent and still, on the small porch of his quarters, his eyes often closed for hours at a time. He spent those hours in prayer for each man, and for their souls, hoping and trusting God that those who would come to knowledge of salvation would do so before it was too late. He knew that as a vicar he had tried, as best he could, to share the truth with them, and that now, because he was no longer a man of the cloth, he could have no further contact with the condemned.

Governor Spenser was far removed from the process and would not attend the hangings. Much too barbaric and bloodthirsty, he claimed. Lady Emily did not speak of the spectacle, either, but her sleep was troubled. Such horrible images filled her head at night, and she struggled to stay awake and be free from them.

John Delacroix built the gallows. He had inspected them for proper workmanship and functionality. But once built and installed, he vowed never to return, unless it was to dismantle them. He claimed that he had watched too many men breathe their last. He wanted to watch no more. And though Missy had no desire to attend, he would have forbidden her to had she wanted to observe such a macabre staging.

Vicar Petley, however, seemed genuinely happy that week. The thorn in his side, Vicar Thomas Mayhew, was removed, and no longer would he have to hear the snickered and muttered comments over whose preaching was more meaningful and understandable. And the deaths of the condemned men brought many back to church. Death had a way of doing that, for many men were never totally sure of their entrance into God's heaven. If life was indeed so tenuous, then perhaps the unsure had best make haste to be assured. Attendance at St. Michael's was increased, and Giles was most content.

The crowd did not cheer or shout as the gallows door dropped the first time, spilling its human cargo into the air, rope snapping tightly and quickly about the neck, legs flailing under the weight of the sandbag tied to the man's ankle. A man, hung by the neck, could live for several long moments, suspended there in the air, flapping and kicking and slowly dying from strangulation. The weight was supposed to pull the man to his death quickly, snapping the neck as the body bounced in the darkness under the gallows.

There were few sounds in the fort that day. A hissing of rope as it coiled about the man's neck, cradled tight to the chin. The mechanical snap of metal and wood as the release was pulled, and the *swoosh* of the door as it swung away. The collective gasp of the crowd as the jolt of the weight and rope jolted the condemned man, releasing him to eternity in that snapping instant.

A dozen swooshing releases, a dozen thumping snaps, a dozen muted gasps, and it was over. Each lifeless conspirator, now a weighty, limp body, was dragged from the gallows to a waiting wagon. From there the traitors began their last journey, to a pauper's grave south of Bridgetown, overlooking the freedom of the sea.

Following the excitement of the trials, life on Barbados resumed its normal rhythm. The island colony continued to thrive and grow. The Caribbean presented so many avenues to making a quick fortune. Aside from buccaneering and treasure hunting, there was dyewood lumbering, turtle fishing, cattle ranching, and the cultivation of indigo, cacao, cotton, ginger, limes, pimento, and tobacco. But in all the English islands, the cultivation of sugar continued to eclipse everything else. The Barbados landscape was gradually transformed into a sea of plantations.

As the island's sugar came on the London market, it fetched a far higher and steadier profit than any other New World commodity. With a workforce of one hundred laborers, a plantation owner could plant eighty acres of cane and expect to produce eighty tons of sugar per year.

The cultivation of sugarcane was a slow and laborious business. The planter laid a new field by inserting cuttings of old cane stalk. These cuttings soon sprouted at each joint into new plants. Thirty slaves with hoes could work two acres in a day. Rats were a greater menace to the young canes than blight or insects, and some planters employed rat-catching gangs, armed with clubs and machetes.

Windmills dotted the landscape and squeezed the sweet juice from the cut cane. They captured both land and sea breezes, working night and day. The juice was trundled to boiling houses and transferred to huge copper kettles hung over the glowing flames. Once boiled, it became golden brown muscovado, which was further refined to different sugars. One of cane's most pleasing and intoxicating by-products was rum—a potent and wildly popular drink, its sweetly burnished taste attracting new devotees by the barrel. As the exports grew, the planters grew rich. And their riches were fueled by indentured servants and black slaves who toiled at these monotonous and degrading tasks in the hot tropical sun day after day.

It was clear, over the next several years, that the uprising did little to

affect the island's relentless push to become a bona fide plantation
society.

Four thousand miles away in England, other significant events were
taking place. Startling news from home came with every ship arriving
in Bridgetown.

In May 1646 King Charles surrendered to the Scots army, and the
following month Oxford capitulated. Charles became a prisoner of
Parliament, which clearly did not know what to do with him. For two
years negotiations between rival factions labored on. In 1648 the king
made his escape from London to Carisbrooke Castle on the Isle of
Wight. From that isolated island, he tried his best to restart the war. But
his uprising was handily crushed by Cromwell's well-knit army.

Cromwell believed that as long as Charles lived there would be no
peace in the land. He arrested the king, and the "man of blood" was
tried for treason. A high court convened at Westminster Hall, and King
Charles, despite his great nobility and dignity, was sentenced to death.
On a bitter and gray day in January 1649, Charles took his last
steps—to the chopping block. An extra shirt was under his doublet,
helping prevent him from shivering and appearing afraid to die. He
uttered only a few words, then laid his head on the block. The crowd
could only manage to call out in a loud groan as the executioner's ax
came down.

With that stroke of metal, England, and all her far-reaching colonies,
became a republic, called the Commonwealth.

She would be ruled first by Cromwell and Parliament, then by
Cromwell alone, who, backed by the army, dismissed the MPs and
ruled as Lord Protector alone.

Life under the Commonwealth was shaped by the Puritans, who
believed in a simple life and hard work. Laws were passed against
swearing, dancing, card playing, football, and even Christmas dinner.
Theaters and inns were closed. No one was allowed to work on
Sundays. Many people hated these laws and longed for a return to
things as they used to be.

But for the people of Barbados, far removed from the strict dictates
of home, island life "beyond the line" was as good as ever.

41

17 January 1650

The children's giggling slowly hushed. They loved to listen to the stories told by Uncle Thomas. Thomas Mayhew pulled the small, smiling Hannah close to him and looked at the face of her brother, urging them each to be hushed, and began on this day's installment of drama.

"On a faraway island, surrounded by rings of bloodred coral in a sea as red as crimson, lives a mighty chief. The chief on Isla del Guajiro was a mighty man, round and black, full with great gusts of laughter. He wore around his throat a necklace made from the great teeth of sharks, some as big as the palm of your hand and as sharp as the keenest knight's dagger. On his head he wore the feathers and plumes of parrots and seabirds, and he carried a great, knobby club to use against his enemies."

"But sir," called out Samuel, now a towheaded boy of five years, lean and inquisitive, "what of the gold you and Chief Tahonen discovered? You promised to tell of the gold treasure. What did the pirates do when they discovered the loss?"

Thomas smiled. *Such a memory with this child,* he thought, staring at the boy's great green eyes. *In him rests the fair future of this island.*

"Indeed, Samuel, I did speak of gold, jewels, and hidden doubloons the last time I told of this tale."

He cleared his throat and crouched lower to their faces, lit with wonder. "It was the dead of night as Chief Tahonen and I crept through the dense jungle, brushing away from our faces spiders and long, bloodred snakes that hung from the trees and branches. The great chest was left at the edge of the water and was filled with jewels and golden coins and great gold bars."

"And then you simply made off with the lot?" Samuel asked, leaning forward.

"I had no use for such treasure, and the chief just wanted bright, shiny objects for his crown. But I knew that with this gold his tribe could be freed from worry and want."

"So then you took it and fought with the pirates?" Samuel asked again, eager to progress the story.

"No, fighting is not part of this tale. The chief and I grabbed at the great, thick brass handle and dragged the chest through the sand into the warm waters of the cove. We knew the trunk would float for many moments, until the sea filled it and dragged it down. So we grasped it, pulling and paddling, and made our way to a far reef. There was a hidden cave there, and by the mouth of that cave was a deep hole under the sea. We took it there and let it sink to the bottom, into the dark depths, so that only the chief and I would know of its location—to be retrieved when the pirates tired of us and left."

"And the gold is there still?" Hannah asked, her blue eyes ablaze.

"Indeed," Thomas replied, "for no man knows its location, save myself and the chief."

Samuel's eyes lit up. "And a man could sail there and have it for the taking?"

Thomas nodded. "That be if the man knew where he was to look."

From the room next to the children's nursery came a rustle and a click as the door snapped shut. The nanny, Jezalee, slipped into the hall, peering both ways, her eyes darting and narrowed.

Softly and hesitantly she whispered to herself, "I doan believe all dat Massa Mayhew be sayin', but he been a man of God. He should be tellin' da truth. If it be true, den dere be treasure waitin' for a man to take. An' if it be dere, I believes I know who might be ready to do dat takin'."

■□■□■

As Thomas spun his wondrous tale for his young charges that day, the rest of the people of Barbados went about their lives as usual. The sun rose and fell, and the good citizens of the island carried on business, farmed, planted, drank, dreamed, ate, journeyed, became sickened, were made well, lived, or died as they attempted to follow their daily meeting with destiny.

At the far side of the docks, John Delacroix bid farewell to Missy and kissed not only his wife good-bye for the day but his sons as well—William, a rambunctious and loud two-year-old, and Andrew, now six months grown and healthy in all respects. At times it was most pleasant, John thought but never spoke aloud, to go to work amidst the hammering and sawing and leave the childhood squalls to Missy. At times he felt more at peace with the sounds of a hammer and saw than with a child's tantrum and tears.

Ship work was the arena in which John felt most comfortable. The chandlery was growing, almost on a monthly basis, and had now spread from the original tidy wooden structure to a sprawl of a half-dozen interconnected buildings and linhays. John was poised to add yet one more structure to his successful establishment—a true dry dock for repairing the hulls of ships. Setting a ship to the beach and careening her was awkward, time consuming, and more than a bit dangerous. If not done correctly, the twisting and tilting of a ship on sand could further damage a weakened hull.

More than three dozen men were now in his employ—shipwrights, joiners, canvas workers, and outfitters. Barbados had grown much in the last several years, becoming a most important Caribbean port for export of sugar, salt, tobacco, other various goods, and for the import of slaves, and every ship in port required the services of a chandlery. Competitors for his services had arrived, yet John was at ease, for they had neither the resources nor experience that he possessed. Already he had accumulated more wealth than he had ever dreamed of, and he now had the luxury of a more relaxed pace and could sit back and instruct others to do the backbreaking labors that he personally undertook during much of the early years of Delacroix Chandlery and Shipyard.

Missy had grown rounder and softer following the birth of the children, and John's love for her had grown and deepened as well. The family no longer occupied the residence at the chandlery but now lived in a modestly elegant new house that had been erected nearby, just up the lane from Hawkes Haven. With the help of her friend Kathryne Hawkes, Missy had transformed the place into a pleasant and comfortable home for John and their two sons.

North of the harbor, away from the smells and confusion of the bustling port, stood the governor's mansion, Shelworthy. Its gardens and lawns now grew with a profusion of plants, and every day seemed to generate another splash of color among the growing palms—bougainvillea, frangipani, orchid, ginger, tulip, and hibiscus—and they all intermingled to produce a heady, intoxicating scent, more tropical and more lush with each day. Lady Emily had spent much of her time

crafting and designing the gardens of the house, once she had completed the interiors. Her stepdaughter, Kathryne, had laid a grand and
most logical groundwork for both, and under Emily's guidance
Shelworthy grew to be a showplace of royal dimensions.

Aidan, over these years, had grayed some—from age, of course, but
also from the efforts of governing such a young island. It seemed to him
that he fought battles on a daily basis concerning smuggling, noblemen
avoiding import and export taxes, property disputes, arbitration
among landowners, interpretation of the Crown's rules, and a thousand
other details that the governor was forced to settle. Only recently, with
the execution of King Charles and the establishment of the Commonwealth, had Aidan been able to end his worrisome balance between
allegiance to Charles and the awareness of Cromwell's power. Barbados
lay far to the west, and while the income from her sugar mills was the
prized jewel of the Caribbean, the new government intervened little in
his administration of the island.

For Lord and Lady Spenser, though in the center of Barbados society,
the brightest place in both their lives was their marriage. Aidan told her
often that he had never been so happy and content. There had been a
short time of adjustment for him, but within a month of their nuptials
he wondered how he had survived for so long as a lonely, isolated
widower. For Emily, having the comfort of a man's arms was such a
delicious treat that every morning she woke with a smile upon her face.

Thomas and Eileen Mayhew, their union born in a swirl of contro-
versy and scorn, grew firm and deep-rock solid. For Eileen, the first
months had been a dark struggle that she admitted only to Kathryne,
and only after swearing her friend to the secrecy of the grave. Eileen
was plagued by doubt, and her dark personal history rose up at every
chance, blinding her to the happiness she had before her. Every time
Thomas spoke the words "I love you," Eileen heard "I love you, but
. . . ," and visions of him leaving and hating her for her lurid past would
emanate from deep in her heart. Yet every time he spoke those words,
meaning them so deeply, it would be less and less a surprise, and she
began to believe him as he spoke. She would lie with him at night,
hearing the waves break on the beach, hearing him breathe with his
body's studied rhythm, and fearfully wait for him to wake, for she was
certain that he would rise in the night and leave her, cold and alone,
like so many men had done before. But each day she saw new evidences
of Thomas's devotion for her. Whether it was a bouquet of flowers, or
a beautiful, weathered, and curled shell from the shore, or a sweet poem

to her beauty—each action, each word was like a solid stone on which Thomas was building a love that she could trust.

Thomas struggled as well those first months after the trials. He knew that stepping down from his position of vicar was the correct thing to do. He sought no battle to the death with the Church of England nor with Vicar Petley, and as he left his position, ecclesiastical peace settled on the island. If Thomas had been a younger man, he may have felt differently. But as he grew older, he had learned to select his battles with great care. And on this hill, at this time, Thomas saw the valor in laying down his arms. And Thomas also had to admit one other truth—a truth that he never thought he would even consider for a fleeting moment. No matter what one thought of Vicar Petley, Thomas mentioned more than once, the man was a skilled administrator.

Without a vicar's duties, Thomas had felt alone and lost. William began almost immediately building, at the far eastern edge of his acreage, a small residence for Thomas and Eileen, and next to it, a schoolhouse. For as the twins grew, Thomas had agreed to be their tutor and teacher, and now Thomas instructed other children of the island's nobility as well. The vicar in Thomas may have retreated, but he was not vanquished.

On those days when he did not teach Hannah and Samuel along with the passel of other children at the school, Thomas gathered about him a handful of sailors, ex-slaves, natives, tradesmen, and adventurers and began to help make them disciples of Christ. It was not a church, but a school of sorts for individuals who sought to take the truth of the gospel to the rest of the islands of the Lesser Antilles. These men would have never been allowed to learn at the official seminaries and colleges of the church, but with them Thomas could penetrate remote parts of this sea with God's truth and enter societies that would never accept a man in a vicar's cassock or a priest's robes. Through these men, Thomas knew, his calling widened, and his love of the Scriptures and of God could be spread, in ever-widening circles, all along the warm shores of the Caribbean.

Vicar Petley, after winning Thomas's dismissal from the church, had spent several weeks gloating—mostly to himself. But soon after Thomas stepped down from the ranks of being a vicar to that of being a mere layman, Giles began to feel a most curious sensation. He realized several months later that he was without an enemy to oppose, without a dark to his light, without a sunset to his sunrise. It was setting him off balance. And though he never spoke of it to anyone, he missed Thomas more than he would have ever considered possible.

Giles's presence in the pulpit remained much as it had been. He was educated but confusing, enlightened but obtuse. His messages were filled with odd turns and twists and often so dense and layered that frequently those in the congregation came away with puzzled looks. Yet, as Thomas Mayhew claimed, Giles was skilled at administration matters. His small parish school flourished, attendance at the church was strong, and Giles did make it his practice to visit all his parishioners on a regular basis. Yet, it was often said with a smile, he always came to visit within only moments prior to the dinner hour. And despite his sometimes clumsiness with tact and his tendency to drift into an angry harangue quickly, he had pursued a call to everyone on the island to come away from "living beyond the line" and return to the morality and the civility that marked proper English society.

William Hawkes was also a happy man. It greatly pleased him to watch as Thomas taught his children and discipled that small band of men. And William, who always attempted to honor God in all manner of activity, found his life to be filled with a wondrous array of blessings. Kathryne was the most perfect mother and wife he could have envisioned. In his eyes she grew more beautiful with every passing day, and his desire for her grew even stronger as the years went by. In his thoughts, she became a more capable and loving mother. It was true that they now employed a large complement of servants, for William knew that without such help both he and Kathryne would drown under the workload. But Kathryne remained absolutely invested in the daily life of her children, absolutely unwilling to hand all their rearing over to hired staff. She read to them, played with them, helped feed and bathe them, and was with them many hours of most days. She and Eileen spent much time in preparation for additions to Hawkes Haven, meeting with draftsmen and building masters, carpenters and joinery men, masons and plasterers. Hawkes Haven grew from a simple bachelor's cottage to a sprawling and comfortable warren of beautifully appointed annexes, wings, and outbuildings.

For William, life was good. He had a beautiful wife, wonderful children, and a growing influence on the island. His official duties at Fort Charles were minimal now that the fort was fully rebuilt and staffed. Will spent some time in management of his investments, both on the island as well as back in England. His treasures continued to grow, and his total worth, though he would never admit the fact to anyone, was now greater by a full third than that of his father-in-law, Aidan Spenser. What business dealings he made prospered, what land he purchased either doubled in value or proved fertile and produced well. What ships he invested in sailed well and full.

It was a time of peace and plenty, of security and blessing, of joy and happiness.

■■■■

Kathryne bustled into the nursery carrying a full basket of mixed flowers cut only moments before from the gardens of Hawkes Haven.

"Thomas," she scolded with a glint in her eyes, "are you again filling the children's heads with your tall tales and stories? They will come to believe all this if you persist."

Thomas drew his hand to his heart in a mock, theatrical gesture. "Kathryne, you wound me greatly. To say that I, Thomas, a man of the truth, would stoop to tell these dear children falsehoods. . . . I am aghast."

Kathryne smiled and held back a giggle. "Aghast you may be, good Thomas, but such tales are the stuff of nightmares."

Thomas hoisted Hannah off his lap, stood to help Kathryne place the new flowers about the room, and answered, "Yet the tales are indeed the truth, Kathryne."

She looked hard at him, holding back her smile, and not being successful.

"But they are indeed," he insisted.

She arched her eyebrows.

He caught the gesture and seemed to wither a few inches. "Well," he admitted, a note of sheepishness entering his voice, "perhaps I have colored a few details with a gaudier paint than what transpired—but the bones of the tale have been honestly retold."

Kathryne stepped back and folded her arms. Her gown rustled as she did, the moss green and ochre material a drab counterpoint to the bright flowers she carried.

"You mean to say there is treasure still on those islands?" she asked.

Thomas nodded. Samuel and Hannah stood nearby, watching their mother and teacher with wide eyes.

"I would say there is, Kathryne. The natives themselves, with their simple lives and primitive ways, would have no use for it. Nor would they have a means to spend it, even could they recover it, for without a safe harbor no ships arrive and seek to trade with them. Indeed, save pirate vessels in search of a place to hide, none land there, for it is known that they produce nothing of value. And it would take more than they possess to retrieve the treasure chest I spoke of, even if they desired it. I mean, with block and tackle and all that manner of machinery . . ."

Kathryne appeared puzzled. "Then why have not you journeyed back to assist them? Would not the gold help eliminate some of the brutish nature of their lives, if one could recover the treasure and use it to go and purchase the things they need?"

It was Thomas's turn to look perplexed. "Well . . . ," he said, and let his reply fade away, for he had no true answer to her query.

She turned from him and set to remove a vase full of withered buds, replacing them with a great handful of fresh hibiscus blossoms.

"I would think that with such a treasure—and I would assume the treasure belongs to those natives—they could build proper homes and pay for a schoolteacher for their children, even purchase cloth for better apparel, and needles and other metal implements for fishing, or farming. . . ."

Thomas began to nod and stroke his chin, a sure sign that his thoughts were in a heady whirl. Kathryne grabbed the last of the dried flowers and stacked them in her basket, a few crisp petals drifting softly to the floor.

"I have heard this tale a hundred times, and each time I thought to ask why the gold is not put to use. Gold under the sea, or buried, is of no use to anyone," she said.

She reached the door and, before she slipped out, turned and added, "I shall take my leave. But I remain curious as to the future of this treasure. Does not the Bible instruct us to make use of our gifts? Did the master not chastise the servant who buried his talents in the ground?"

And with that, she closed the door with a firm click and left Thomas standing there, the children about him, staring at his face lined with deep thoughts, waiting for him to finally break the silence.

42

19 January 1650

The embers hissed and popped in the great fireplace of Hawkes Haven. The dining table, bathed in the soft light of tallow candles and moonlight, was laden with a dozen platters, steaming the night air with the appetizing aromas of roasted pork, smoked fish, glazed turnips, and candied yams.

Will sat at the head of the table and bowed, offering a short prayer of thanks for the meal. Kathryne had noted that when guests were in their home, Will always offered to pray before meals, never allowing others—especially Thomas—to ask the blessing on the food, for Thomas was much more long-winded in his prayers. Will's prayers were short and to the point and were finished before any of the meal grew cold.

Thomas and Eileen were in attendance for dinner that evening, and Martha, the cook, was incapable of cooking small portions when she knew that guests were to be expected. There could be no expectation that all the food would be consumed, and what was left would be distributed to the servants of the house.

Will rubbed his hands together in a most telling manner just prior to reaching for the first platter, filled with thin strips of boucan, his favorite dish. Kathryne smiled as he did, appreciating the boyish enthusiasm with which he approached meals. Conversation around the table dimmed during the next long moments as Thomas and Will focused on the food. Eileen and Kathryne, always taking smaller portions, continued to speak as they ate, cutting and eating small, precise amounts. They both realized that while Thomas and Will had made remarkable steps in their practice of polished and sophisticated manners, there were still certain traits that were hard to modify. And to this, the women would simply smile and nod, choosing to ignore the behaviors of their husbands. Some matters of style and social practices were simply not worth continual exhortations.

After finishing a second portion of pork, Will sat back in his chair and smiled. "'Twas a most grand meal, Martha," he called out. "You continue to provide such tasty fare. I should prohibit all entertainment of guests in this house, for I scarce can move from the table when we invite others to dine."

Thomas selected some fruit and cheese and leaned back in his chair as well. He looked deep in thought.

Kathryne stood up. "I need to look in on the children," she said. "Would you like to accompany me, Eileen? We can leave the men to recuperate. I can see they shall offer no conversation of value for a long while."

Eileen giggled, and the two women rose and made their way to the children's bedchambers.

"Thomas, you have said few words this evening," Will noted. "Is there a matter troubling you? Are Samuel and Hannah misbehaving? Are there troubles with their lessons?"

Thomas shook his head, as if waking from a daydream. "No, Will," he replied, after a moment of consideration. "Their lessons progress well. The only report I may give you is that Hannah is most diligent in her learning. She hones in on the lesson like a bee to a flower and will not leave until all matters are understood and explored fully."

"And Samuel?" Will asked, almost fearing what he might be told.

Thomas grinned. "Samuel," he began hesitantly, "is much like his father."

Will leaned forward, waiting for a more complete report. "Thomas, that cannot be all of what you desire to say. There is more, I am sure."

Thomas nodded again. "Samuel is a most bright child. He grasps complicated matters quickly—just like his father did so many years ago in Hadenthorne."

"And . . . ?"

"And . . . well, because of his quickness, he tends to want to move on to other matters just as rapidly. Once he understands what the import of the lesson is to be, he simply turns to the window and stares out to sea or up into the clouds. And he is most eager to move forward—to the next lesson at times, but more often to the next locale

on this island that he can explore. He is always most anxious to leave
the room at the end of the lesson."

"And that is bad?"

Thomas shook his head. "Not *bad,* William. It merely *is.* He learns
in a rush, then acts. Yet, I have fear that his quickness could turn to
impetuousness if left unchecked."

"Impetuousness?"

"It would be like him to assess a most complex matter, grasping what
are the basic components of the problem, and then rush off pell-mell in
order to solve it."

"And that is wrong?"

"Not wrong, William," Thomas explained, "but a matter of concern.
Such brashness can often lead to most perilous predicaments."

"But the boy is young, Thomas," Will explained in his defense. "He
shall learn as he grows that such may not be the way of the world and
that he will need take his time."

"Perhaps he shall mature as his years increase," Thomas admitted,
"yet as they say—as the twig grows, there grows the tree."

William nodded as if he agreed, but he knew that such boldness
would often be required in a man—a man who faced the challenges of
bringing order to a wild and uncivilized world.

"Thomas, have no qualms. I shall talk to the lad. I shall endeavor to
set him on the proper course. He will listen to my admonitions."

Thomas nodded again, then grew silent and pensive. After a dozen
long still moments, Thomas coughed to interrupt the peace. "William,
a moment ago I spoke of brashness and boldness as things that need
concern. And in a child, perhaps that is most true."

Leaning forward, leaning his elbows on the table, Will listened. He
looked for an instant at his position, then was thankful that Kathryne
was not near, for elbows on a dining table was a matter she would have
playfully scolded him for.

"I am sure you have told your children some tales of your past, on
the high seas and in battles and all."

Will's face remained still. He had shared very little of his past with
anyone, for in the most part, he felt a lingering sense of shame and guilt
over his actions as a privateer and pirate. There was too much death
that followed in his wake, too much destruction. His path had been so
opposite of the ways of God's Scriptures that to speak of them in fond
terms would do great disservice, Will thought, to his witness now.

"I have shared a very small portion," he finally admitted. "They know I spent many years at sea. They know some of the bones of the story of how their mother and I first met."

With those words, Thomas knew that a most sensitive subject had been broached, and he quickly strove to speak past it. "I have told them," he said, "on occasion of the island where I spent so many months as a captive of San Martel. I tell them of my witness to the heathen tribe and how the Word of God was powerful and how some of the heathen came to know the truth of the Bible."

Will smiled broadly. "Thomas, I have heard your tales. That is a part of your tale, but only a part. You spend most of your words dealing with the hidden treasure and the flight through the jungle and your escape from the wild pirates and brigands."

A reddening flush draped down Thomas's face and neck. He could offer no more than a resigned laugh. "You do know me too well, William," he said, slicing off a thin wedge of sharp, yellow cheese. He had overcome his dislike of the food since he had stopped serving it to himself on a daily basis. "Perhaps I have a tendency to . . . embellish a mite, especially when in front of such a rapt and attentive audience."

He then grew silent again, and William watched his face line and furrow, as it always did when he was lost in thoughts.

William sipped from a goblet of rich, Portuguese port. "Thomas," he said, "you are a most deliberate man. You do not tell me of a story that I know, perhaps better than you by now, as a jester would after a banquet. Why do you speak of this now?"

Thomas looked up. "Why?" he began. "Because of your wife, that is why."

Now William was most confused. "Kathryne? And how does she fit into your yarn?"

Thomas folded his hands on the table before him, as if preparing for a lecture. Will sipped at the port again and leaned back, the chair groaning happily under his weight.

"I was in the midst of such a retelling—"

"And embellishing."

Thomas grinned. "And embellishing of the tale two days prior, when Kathryne entered the room with a bouquet of flowers. She had fresh blossoms to replace the old and, without being deliberate, overheard my . . . embellishments to the tale. And as she left, she asked a question of such obviousness that I have done nothing else since that day but to consider why I had not posed the very same question to myself."

Looking more interested, Will asked, "And what grand question was that? Why do we not sail back and retrieve their gold for them?"

Thomas looked crestfallen, as if struck by an avalanche. "You mean to say," he cried, "that you have considered it? In all these years I had never once let the option enter my mind."

William stood from the table and walked to the slowly dying fire and poked at it with the toe of his boot. "I have thought if it on occasion. 'Twas a fair amount of treasure left on both islands."

Thomas stood and hurried to his side, placing a hand to his friend's shoulder. "Then why not did you act on such an impulse?" he asked, his voice growing more excited. "I cannot fathom why it did not occur to me. And now to find that, in fact, it had occurred to you—well, I am most properly and thoroughly befuddled."

William stepped around to a more comfortable padded bench and sat with his feet near the flickering flames. Even on a tropical island evening grew cool at times, and Will had often stated that the heat had thinned his blood to such a degree that the chilly rains and winds of a nasty English winter would do him in. Will looked up and stared at his friend for a long moment.

"I considered undertaking such a trip on several occasions. Most often, life on this island simply came between that thought and its fruition—Radcliffe's attack, the birth of the twins, the requirements of my position at the fort."

"And that is all?" Thomas replied, aghast. "To let everyday life stand in the way of aiding poor heathens?"

William narrowed his stare and resolved not to become upset. "No, Thomas, that is not it. Had I thought they were in most dire need, I would have traveled back in a moment. But there is more to my reason."

"Such as?"

"Such as, do I have the right to send these simple people into our time? They live simple lives and, for the most part, live out their days happy and uncomplicated. If they have gold enough for all, what happens then? Do they battle over who has rights? Do they fight with barristers over who is to have which share? Do they begin to purchase all manner of modern convenience and thus complicate their small Eden?"

William lifted his hands behind his neck and slipped further into a relaxed, prone position. "I have purposely chosen to let them live as they want. The gold would be a complication. And the last report I heard of the natives at my former hideout was that all was well and that they continue to live out their simple existence."

"And when was this report, Will?"

Tightening his features, William attempted to fix the date. "A year previous? Perhaps a half year more."

"And have you heard of the people on Isla del Guajiro as well? And why have you not shared these reports with me?"

"It has been longer for that island, but no more than two years ago I heard a sailor speak of the place and he brought no ill reports." Will blinked his eyes. "I have not mentioned these facts, for I had no reason to think that you were so concerned."

"But I am, William," Thomas said as he slid to the bench next to him. "I have scarce thought of anything else these past days."

Will turned his head and asked, "And in what manner have you thought?"

Thomas leaned forward, excited and animated now, in direct opposition to Will's condition, perhaps only a dozen moments from sleep overtaking his eyes.

"These poor souls have resources that can enable them to live better lives, to purchase medicines, tools, proper clothing—and the Scriptures. Above all they could have the Scriptures!"

Will was struggling to keep his eyes open now, the food and the fire conspiring against his attention to Thomas's words. "Thomas," Will said softly, "it would do no good. Besides one child or two on my island, none of them can read. A Bible would do no good."

"And that is all part of my excitement, my friend," Thomas said as he grabbed at Will's arm. "The men I have been training in the Word—they seek a field in which to witness. These two islands would be so well suited! The natives have heard our version of God's truth. Now they shall require more solid sustenance. These men can be as vicars to them until the church has the resources to send properly equipped clergymen."

"Like Vicar Petley?" Will mumbled, a smile on his face.

"Well . . . no, not like him. But these people need the truth, Will. And with their gold, they can afford to hear it and at the same instant improve their manner of existence."

Will nodded, his words now softer in the dark. "Thomas, what you say makes sense. 'Tis a good idea. We will need speak of such plans on the morrow."

The fire made a muted crackle in the silence. Will opened his eyes slightly, then spoke out softly, "Thomas, do you miss being a vicar?"

Thomas reacted as if struck in the stomach with a full blow. "I miss it so that I ache, William. Every day I miss it. But I am just as certain that the decision I made was correct—for this island, for the church, for Eileen. It was right what I did. It was the nobler course of action. But I miss it, Will. I do so miss it."

And when Thomas finished speaking, Will nodded and his eyelids fluttered closed, like a bird seeking landing on a tree branch, and his head tilted to one side, his breath coming slow and constant.

Thomas smiled and nodded to himself. *We will speak of such plans on the morrow.* And for Thomas, that was not soon enough.

21 January 1650

The slate board was wiped clean of Thomas's flowered script. The books were stacked in order on the shelf by his small desk. The quill lay to the side of the capped inkwell. The small stack of papers was tidied into a neat stack. Thomas sat back and surveyed his small domain.

'Tis a grand thing I do, to educate these young minds. There is no greater calling than to fill them with a love of learning and with a love of God's Word and wonder at his creation.

He walked to the small window and looked out. He could see the sea, stretching away before him like an endless, rolling blanket of changing hues. This day it was slate gray and smooth, broken only by a thin surf at the shore. He looked to the north, and there lay Fort Charles, massive and ominous, overlooking the eastern edge of the island. Further north lay the harbor and Bridgetown. He could see the smoke of dozens of cook fires filling the bowl of land, scenting the air, clouding the image, waiting for a breeze to wipe the slate of sky clean.

He pulled on his doublet, straightening and smoothing it. It had been years, but he still had not fully become accustomed to not wearing a full vicar's cassock. Leaving the schoolhouse, he made his way to the cozy home he and Eileen shared. She must have seen him from the window, for she was out on the porch, drying her hands on a linen apron, waving to him as he approached. His heart lifted in his chest at the sight of her. Regardless of any disappointment in his life, any loss that he had felt as a result of the choices he made, Eileen was always there to buoy his spirits back to joyful. Every morning and evening, as he spent his time in prayer, he thanked his Lord for providing her in his life. He had often preached on love, and yet for most of the years of his life knew little of what love truly meant. To be sure, raising William Hawkes had filled his heart, but even those emotions paled in comparison to the love he felt for this woman who had become his wife.

As he made his way along the worn path to their home, her image growing larger with each step, he marveled at the gifts that she brought him. She of course offered him herself, unselfish and loving. She listened to his talks, offering encouragement and advice when she was asked. She had ready arms to hold him when doubts crept in. And if he awoke in the blackness of the night, she would be there beside him, her steady breathing vanquishing any fear that existed outside the walls of their home.

In fact, the wagging tongues and mean-spirited gossip that dogged their relationship and marriage had become muted as the years passed. But he was certain, as they walked the streets of Bridgetown, that some heads would still turn, and a few low whispers still followed them.

"She was a woman of loose morals," he had heard.

"He gave up his God to wed her," she had heard.

But the panic he felt at first had now vanished, and whatever anyone could say, he had already imagined worse and had walked beyond it.

Thomas reached the steps and embraced Eileen in a tight hug that lasted longer than was usual. He brushed back her hair to one side and gently kissed her neck.

"Thomas," she finally whispered in his ear, "I daresay that you should let loose of me, for heads will turn if we stay on this porch for much longer in this manner."

Thomas laughed, admiring her all the more for her ability to make light of such things. "Eileen, no one will say a word—at least nothing that has not been said before. And where is it written that a man cannot embrace and kiss his lovely wife with abandon?"

She pushed away from him, though he still had his arms about her waist. "No law that I am aware of, sweet husband," she laughed, "but I would think they might object to me setting my kitchen ablaze from not tending to your evening meal."

He swept her around and followed her quickly into the house. "Then let us both hurry, for I shall be no accomplice to arson."

It was later that evening, after the explosion of sunset had filled their home then drew away in more somber tones, that she set aside her needlework and looked up at him, her face troubled. "Thomas, may I ask you a question?"

He looked up from his book. "You know you need not ask permission, my dear."

She looked down at her hands for a moment. "I spoke to Kathryne this morn, and she mentioned that William and you had discussed sailing to some island in the near future."

He did not respond, for she had not yet phrased a question.

"Is that true?" she finally asked.

"We have spoken of such matters in a most general manner," he replied. "There has been nothing further decided."

He looked closer at her and realized that she was fighting back tears.

Through trembling lips, she replied, "When were you to tell me of this, Thomas? Did you not think I should hear of such a thing?"

As he made his way to her side, and just before he apologized for his careless oversight, he thought, in a flash of self-awareness, *Indeed, I still have much to learn of love and of caring for a wife. As much as I think I know the proper manner in which to treat my dear wife, I am oft befuddled by the intricacies of being a caring husband. What I think important, she does not. And what I think trivial, she considers most significant. Will there be a time when our thoughts are truly meshed with one another?*

25 January 1650

The map filled the surface of William's desk, the curled edges drooping over the sides. The far reaches of the Caribbean—Florida and the coast of the southern continent, as well as Trinidad and the Grenadines—were lost from view. But Will and Thomas's focus lay to the waters to the north and west of Barbados. Will traced, with a practiced hand, the route—first to his old hidden base, a small, unimportant, and most often uncharted island. From that point, his finger slipped north and further west to Isla del Guajiro.

"Those two locales be our goal, Thomas," he said, a hint of growing excitement coloring his voice. "And with the season's winds picking up, a sailing would be easy and swift."

To Thomas, the span of the sea between the little bits of land looked far and intimidating, the waters great and threatening. He knew that the warm waters of this ocean were small in comparison to the cold reaches of the Atlantic, but still the distance gave him pause.

"Even on this paper," Thomas said, "the journey looks more vast than I had first realized."

William laughed. "'Tis a common complaint of the man who is not a sailor. These empty stretches," he said, indicating the waters with a sweep of his hand, "seem so vast as to give any sane man reason to stay on solid ground for the rest of his life."

"Indeed," Thomas replied. "For a ship is nought but insignificant when it rests upon the mightiness of the ocean."

Kathryne looked up from her needlework. "'Tis like a single man, when he navigates the great ocean of the life God lays out before him," she called out.

Thomas nodded. "It is a most appropriate metaphor," he said. "I shall be sure to remember the illustration the next time we gather to study the Word."

Kathryne smiled and returned to her work. Beside her sat Eileen, now most content that she was included in these plans and dreams.

"Just be sure that it is properly attributed, dear Thomas," Eileen said with a smile.

Thomas nodded and went back to studying the map before him. It was marked with hundreds of Will's notations and navigational marks, indicating depths of waters, reefs and shoals, safe and deep channels through the islands, and access to harbors. This was but one of the charts he had carried with him as privateer, for running the length of the sea were small red X's, each marking the location of a successful hunt. The name of each ship was noted, as well as plunder taken. As Will explained routes, he made no mention of these markings.

"And is there a ship that can be secured for the voyage, Will?" Thomas asked.

"Is not the *Dorset Lady* in harbor?" Kathryne asked, looking up again. "I believe I saw her enter last week as I visited Papa and Emily."

"She is, indeed," Will answered, "and 'tis the ship I would perchance suggest us to use. If she be available is the question."

Kathryne and Eileen put their heads together, whispering, then both came apart in giggles and smiles.

"And what brings such mirth?" Will asked.

Kathryne held her laughter in check for a moment. "William, you speak as if use of the *Dorset Lady* might be in question. You own the ship, William. Why would it not be available?"

Will looked sheepish for a moment. "Well, I thought perhaps she may be chartered in advance. . . ."

Thomas was surprised. He truly had no idea of the vastness of Will's holdings, and this was the first mention to him that he owned that particular ship, let alone any ship at all.

"Is she sturdy enough to make the voyage, Will? Would she be large enough to carry us the distance?" he asked.

Will smiled. "Thomas, you do not remember, do you?"

Thomas shook his head.

"The *Dorset Lady* be the vessel that provided us our rescue following the incident with Radcliffe. It be the ship that my sweet and innocent wife commandeered and forced the captain to sail for us—at great personal peril, I might add."

"If not me, who else would have?" Kathryne laughed out.

"But, sweet wife, I have yet not been reimbursed for those triple wages you offered the crew."

Eileen raised her hand to her mouth to stifle a laugh, and Kathryne, laughing, threw a pillow at William. Her mark was wide, and the pillow bounced off Thomas's back and skittered across the floor.

"You dare to interrupt such high-level planning," Will called out in his best mock angry tone, but unable to hold the pose, he began to laugh as well.

"Kathryne, I have one suggestion to make," Will finally said.

"And that is?" she asked.

"That since you have traveled these waters before, that you accompany us as well."

For an instant her eyes looked as if they might accept the challenge, to visit new and exotic places. But in another instant she smiled and replied, "No, William, one seafarer per family is sufficient. I believe that Samuel and Hannah would not appreciate their mother taking such a voyage."

Will knew as well that she was indeed most correct.

"Well then, Thomas, let us draw up our sailing plans."

Thomas smiled, saluted, then bent back to the map. "And on what date would such a sailing begin?" he asked.

Stroking his chin for a moment, looking back at the map, Will replied, "In four months' time. The *Dorset Lady* needs refitting, and her hull no doubt needs scraping and coppering. And we need to order supplies and obtain copies of the Scriptures. And no doubt the men you are training, Thomas, shall need complete all the learning possible for this undertaking."

Thomas nodded. "Then four months we shall have," he said. "I shall endeavor to make each lesson most pointed."

As they spoke, Jezalee crept into the room and removed a spool of thread from Kathryne's sewing tray.

Four months, dey say, she thought. *I best be tellin' Cotton. He be wantin' to know dat fo' sure.*

CHAPTER

45

26 January 1650

She looked over her shoulder, her eyes nervous and darting. She stopped dead still by the side of the road and listened. There were no hoofbeats, voices, nor footsteps. She could hear only her fast breathing, the gentle drone of insects, and the jarring cry of a parrot or popinjay.

Jezalee, satisfied that she was alone and not being followed, picked up her small bundle and continued to walk inland. The bundle, wrapped in a thin and frayed linen cloth, contained thick slices of roasted pork, cheese, biscuits, bottles of ale, and a topping of sweet cakes. It was all food that Jezalee had liberated from last night's dinner at Hawkes Haven.

Dat Martha, she be cookin' too much all de time, Jezalee thought, *and it ain't right dat my man be goin' hungry when be all dis food be about.*

No more than three miles east of Bridgetown, the primeval jungles of Barbados still existed. They covered less of the island with each passing day the planters cleared the land for crops, but their green fingers still crawled along steep hillsides, filled up ravines and pitched valleys, and provided a hiding place to all manner of exotic creatures.

Not the least of which was a handful of men, still in hiding from the aborted uprising of a few years previous. A few had scratched out an existence by fishing, hunting, and gathering fruits and berries that grew wild in the area. Others did likewise, but augmented their difficult lives with the occasional doublet and breeches liberated as they dried upon a line and with filching other bits of civilized culture whenever and wherever they could. And some, like Cotton, did all that plus depended on the silent assistance of women such as Jezalee. From the two dozen who had escaped into the hills that very first night of the uprising, no more than eight men still lived in the dim greenness. Some had died of illness and injury, a half dozen had been caught in their petty thievery, some had slipped into town and caught a ship sailing to anywhere with a captain who asked no questions nor demanded a résumé. Neither Will nor any other government official deemed it worth the risk to offer chase to these men. They had no weapons other than a machete or dagger and posed little risk. Besides, a clever man could hide in the folds of a jungle forest and allow a pursuer to pass within feet of him.

And Cotton was a clever man; he had hung on to his freedom. "Livin' in dis dark and wet place be most better dan bein' a slave or bein' dead," he explained once. He had constructed a small thatched hut no more than a hundred paces into the overgrown jungle, just off the main road from the harbor to Shelworthy.

Jezalee now stood at the spot she had memorized from many trips before. She stopped, waited, then whistled, trying her best to sound like the parrots that had just cried out.

In a moment, she heard a rustle from the dark greenery. An arm extended from the foliage, and she reached out and took the offered hand and was drawn into the darkness.

She hated the next few minutes as they made their way through thick leaf and limb. Thinking that spiders and crawling things were lying in wait to drop on her head or crawl down her back as she walked under them, she tried her best to hurry along the path, strewn with tripping roots and moss-covered rocks.

In a moment, she was at Cotton's small hut in the middle of a small, well-hidden clearing of perhaps a quarter acre in size. At noon, the sun would stream down through the hole in the canopy of dense trees, but the rest of the day the hut was bathed in thin filtered sunlight.

After grabbing the parcel Jezalee had brought, Cotton sat at a woven mat and gnawed at the pork, the juices dripping down his chin and onto his bare chest. Jezalee liked to watch him eat. His ravenous appetite for food was indicative of other hungers and appetites that he exhibited when she came to visit. She touched his dark arm gingerly and softly, feeling the muscles coiled tight beneath the skin.

"Massa Will and dat old vicar Mayhew be talkin' 'bout dat treasure agin," she said as he broke off a thick handful of yellow cheese. "Dey be makin' plans to go visit."

He stopped chewing and turned to her, his eyes sparkling even in the dim light.

"Miz Kathryne be sayin' dat gold should be bein' used, and dey be goin' to get dat gold for dem island folk."

He smiled, his mouth full of pork and cheese. He wiped at his lips with his forearm. He chewed quickly and swallowed. "Dey be sayin' when dey be takin' dis trip?" he asked.

Jezalee scrunched her eyes together. She vowed that she would remember such details, though the number swam before her in her thoughts.

"Dey be sayin' . . . ," she said as she grimaced, ". . . dey be sayin' . . . dey be sayin' . . ."

Cotton leaned over and grabbed at her arm tight and hard. "Dey be sayin' what?" he cried out, holding her harder than needed, speaking louder than warranted.

She looked panicked for a long moment, then brightened into a grin. "Dey be sayin' dey be leavin' in fo' month time. Dey say fo' month. I be sure o' dat now."

Cotton grinned back, and his grip on her arm loosened. He began to slowly and tenderly smooth the flesh on her forearm, then slid his hand up her arm to her shoulder.

"Fo' month be givin' me 'nough time to do what I gots to do." He spoke softly and evenly. "It be givin' me time to be settin' up for revenge for all dis," he said as he looked about. "And for my dead brother, too."

Jezalee blinked her eyes, almost in fear. Cotton sometimes got angry and most intense when he spoke of his brother, who had swung to his death on the king's gallows in Fort Charles. Sometimes his anger was focused on her. Yet this day, his hand was still gentle and smooth on her, and his eyes had a dreamy, faraway look in them.

"Be most sweet, dat gold, and dat revenge. Be most sweet, indeed," he said, then turned to look at Jezalee. "Be most sweet—next to you, dat is."

And with that, his hand continued its journey.

■ ■ ■ ■ ■

Cotton stood in the dim afternoon light and peered about his green and vined home. After all this time, after all these days with so seldom feeling the sun on his face, he began to hate the narrow confines of his life.

He turned and looked at the sleeping Jezalee, her head resting on a mat of palm leaves. *Dat girl be good for Cotton—dat fo' sure. How else I be knowin' of dat gold?*

Cotton had his plan formulated weeks ago, from the very first hint of hidden treasure. It would be easy for him to slip into the harbor as darkness covered the island. There was a fisherman there, an ex-slave who had taken part in the uprising but was never caught. All Cotton would need do is speak a few words with the hint of a threat, and he would have passage to any port he could name. Until now, Cotton had no port to journey to that would not have placed a high price on his head. But now, with this information, he could sail to Tortuga and barter with what he knew for a ship or a convoy of ships—and even get a slice of the plunder.

He smiled down at the sleeping woman. *You done be makin' me a rich man, Jezalee,* he thought, then smiled and held his laughter tight in his throat. *You done be makin' me a rich man fo' sure.*

His thoughts stopped for a brief moment, then he smiled again. *I be hopin' dat Captain Bliss be round dat island. And I hope he still be lookin' fo' dat gold an' all.*

46

31 January 1650

The *Dorset Lady* lay tied to her mooring, stripped of her canvas and rigging, her helm stand in pieces on the deck, her rudder pulled to the pier. Will stood with his toe nudging at the cracked rudder. Next to him, John bent to inspect the damp wood, prodding at it with a small carving tool.

"She's been sailed hard, John," Will said with a note of sadness. "She needs a great deal of repair."

John nodded. "The rudder be fine; that can be repaired. The canvas needs replacin'. Her hull looks strong; maybe a small patch near her bow is a bit spotty. Her helm stand needs . . . well, it need be replaced, Will. The cables and all be too worn and frayed to be repaired."

Will stepped away, walking the length of the pier, taking a slow survey of the ship's condition. He called out from the far end, "Can it be done in four months?"

John stood up and pocketed the blade in his leather apron. "Four months? I thought you said four weeks."

Will talked as he walked back. "No, she'll not be needed for sail until the next season."

John looked greatly relieved. "Will, I could build you a new ship in four months. She be needin' only a month or two at most to get back to sailin' shape."

As the old friends made their way back to the chandlery office, John asked, "Why you be takin' such an interest in this ship, Will? You be generally lettin' the repairs to those who be charterin' her."

"John, that still be the case."

John looked most puzzled.

"John," Will explained, "it be I who am taking the next charter on the vessel. Thomas has it in his head that we need to be revisiting our old base—and Isla del Guajiro—and be about retrieving a few of the things we left there."

"Retrieving?"

Will turned to John. "On both islands, certain . . . objects were hidden away. Thomas wants to retrieve them, to use some of that material to pay for Scriptures and other conveniences for the natives."

Suddenly John's face lit up with comprehension. "Ah, another adventure. And you haven't asked your old second-in-command if he'd like to take the little jaunt with you?"

"First off, John, there shall be no adventure here. A simple sailing, a little digging . . . or swimming . . . and then back we come. No adventure—just a voyage of . . . merchants is all it is."

"And what be second?"

"The second is that I didn't ask you for fear that you would not come. That I should sail one last time without you at my side is a most fearful thing."

John brushed some dirt from his hands. "William, you need be confronting your fears if you want to be considered a brave man."

Will arched his eyebrows in surprise. "Then you might be coming with us?"

"Are you askin', Will?"

"I am."

"Then I be comin' with you. A last sailin'. A grand adventure. Sounds most wondrous."

"'Tis no adventure, John. I tell you that again. 'Tis no adventure."

47

25 February 1650

The small desk groaned under the weight of the piles of books, order forms, letters, and charts. Thomas stood, rummaging through the stacks, sliding the masses from one side to another, lifting one pile and placing it down on another, peering under books, looking about to determine if any errant papers had rustled from the desk and were hiding on the floor.

Eileen walked in from the kitchen, wiping her hands. She stood and watched as her husband rooted through the papers, and she smiled, knowing he was becoming more frustrated with each passing moment.

"Thomas," she called out softly.

So lost in thought was he that he offered no response.

"Thomas," she called out, louder this time. Eileen caught his attention, startling him, and he dropped an armful of papers onto the floor. They fluttered and skittered about in a rainstorm of words. He uttered a string of Latin in response.

Eileen smiled and came to his side. She knew that his use of Latin covered his anger, thinking that no one could then determine his true sentiments. While Eileen spoke none of the old language, she knew very well what he meant by the tone with which the words were spoken.

"Thomas," she said, placing her hand on his arm, "perhaps I may help you in this. What document are you searching for?"

Thomas stood, as near to fuming as he ever got, then slowly relaxed and scratched at his head. "I am searching for the document that prescribes the number of copies of the Scriptures we have ordered from London. The letter was sent the day we decided to travel, and I must be sure that the quantity is sufficient for our needs."

She bent to the floor and began to sort and stack the papers Thomas had dropped.

"Good husband, I understand your fears, but if the quantity was insufficient, there's no recourse at this date to change your requirements. You will need be satisfied with what arrives, no doubt."

He scowled for a long moment, then relaxed again. "Hmm . . . that would be correct. But there are a thousand other details that I am most fearful of overlooking. Will states the vessel will be prepared on time. Mr. Delacroix has agreed to sail with us, a most generous offer on his part. And a crew has been selected as well."

"And?" she gently prodded.

"And I am fearful that it is I who will be the weakest link in this journey. Owing to the fact that it was my desire that started us on the undertaking, I do not wish to be the one who creates its most major obstacles."

She stood, holding the papers neatly stacked in her hand. "Then, perhaps, I may make a suggestion?"

Thomas looked surprised. Eileen was sure of what he was about to say.

"But this is no matter that a woman should be concerned with, nor would I feel proper if I allowed you to worry concerning these details."

Placing the papers on the one clean corner of the desk, she stepped back and folded her arms. "Thomas, who was the person who assisted Kathryne in the building of Hawkes Haven?"

Thomas's eyes darted about the room.

"Thomas? Who was that person?"

He stuttered, then answered. "I believe it was you."

"And who scheduled tradesmen and deliveries and took care of invoicing and bills of lading throughout that time of building?"

"I . . . I believe it was you as well."

"Then who might be able to assist you in these matters?"

"I . . . I believe it might be you?"

She smiled broadly. "It is not a question, Thomas. I could offer my assistance. Yet as a good wife, I was waiting for your request. And until now I held my tongue."

Thomas's face reddened. "Perhaps I have overlooked a matter or two, and . . . perhaps, Eileen, would you be offended if I were to ask you now for such assistance?"

She smiled again. "No Thomas, I would not be offended."

He stepped back and, with a wave of his arm, indicated that the piles of paper and books and all were open to her.

"Then, Eileen, I bid you help."

She sat before the desk, shooing him away. Before he left the room, he added one last request. "I also ask you, Eileen, if you might provide me your forgiveness, for once again I have proceeded to be blinded to the obvious."

She looked back over her shoulder, the sun catching her beauty in a shaft of golden afternoon night. "Thomas, you are forgiven. You have always been forgiven." And before she turned about, she added, "You are my husband, and it is my wish to serve you."

CHAPTER

48

27 March 1650

In an unused corner of the chandlery stood a jumble of crates and barrels and wooden chests piled to the height of a man. Thomas had climbed to the very top of one of the stacks and now teetered there for a long moment, peering down and counting aloud.

"One, two, three. . . . That is all I see of the shipment from the Exeter Foundry. I believe we have been shorted again."

Eileen stood by and looked down the list she held in her hand. "Thomas, you have only ordered three. The shipment is correct."

He looked down at Eileen, surprised. "I ordered three?"

She nodded.

"Then all is here and accounted for."

And with that he scrambled down from his perch, feeling most satisfied that the numbers were correct.

"And we still await the copies of the Scriptures from London?" Thomas asked as he dusted off his breeches.

"We do, Thomas," Eileen replied, "but be of good cheer. There are two full months until you sail."

"But what shall happen if those Bibles do not arrive in two months? Can you imagine our dismay?"

Eileen smiled, a habit she was much in practice for. "Thomas, please do not fret. If the Bibles become delayed, then you shall wait for them to arrive to begin your journey."

He furrowed his brow, as if he had not considered waiting as an alternative. "Oh," he said. "Well, yes . . . I suppose that is possible. . . ."

29 April 1650

Will was worried.

When the voyage was planned, he had urged all concerned to speak to no one of their goals and their plans. Certainly, a sailing of this type could not be hidden, but the less others knew of the possibility of rescuing the treasure, the safer William felt. Each buried gold sovereign becomes a hundred pounds by the time the tenth person in a public house hears a tale of riches.

As their supplies arrived, William furnished the funds to pay for each. If the gold was found, Will could take his share from that and be reimbursed for all the supplies. If the treasure remained in that watery cavern—and of that Will had his doubts—Will would not miss the few hundred pounds that the supplies had cost.

Thomas was worried.

His odd assortment of pupils were most intrigued and excited about a posting, as it were, on an uncharted island, teaching the truth of God to those who needed to hear it. But Thomas was concerned that his pupils did not have enough knowledge for the task, and he endeavored to fill them with as much learning as he could in these few short weeks remaining. Thomas knew which four men would accompany him on the voyage, two on each island. One per island would have been less costly, but one would also be most lonely in so alien a place and so far from his culture.

The men he had selected to serve were worried.

They did not want to prove unworthy of their calling. There was Gaen Darton, a short, stocky fisherman from the Irish coast; Robert McCardle, a skilled joiner from Scotland, with a full gray beard and a hearty laugh; Hovie Lister, a slave who had received his manumission from a planter on St. Kitts; and Urias Lister, Hovie's son. Each man so desired to prove himself to Thomas. Loneliness, isolation, and even death did not worry them as much as did the possibility that they would fail in passing on the truth to those who so greatly needed it.

John was worried.

The *Dorset Lady* was a fair ship, and all the repairs that he saw as needed had been accomplished. But the vessel was old, having traversed the Atlantic so many times that the sailors aboard had stopped carving the gashes in her bowsprit after the number reached thirty.

"'Tis a long time to ride the waves," John told Will. "I fear that her luck may have sailed thin as well."

Will laughed at his friend's lingering superstitions, but John knew that these ships had a soul and a life to them. And to John, this vessel looked tired and weary.

And John was troubled that, despite the weariness of the vessel, he was looking forward to the voyage with too great an enthusiasm. He daydreamed often of the quiet seas, of the wind in the sails, and of the lap of the waves against the bow. There would be no crying babies in the black of the night, no squabbling brothers at the evening meal. But as soon as those feelings arose, John pushed them, as best he could, from his thoughts. He had no right, he told himself, to think that a sea voyage would be in any manner a pleasant, quiet escape for a few weeks. He had no right, he told himself, but there it was, always at the edge of his thoughts.

CHAPTER

50

Island of Tortuga
13 May 1650

The room stank of sweat, ale, tobacco, and the odor of desperate, lonely men. Cotton stepped in and blinked his eyes, trying to find any light in the darkness. A few candles and lanterns flickered in the gloom. He bent slightly at the waist, bringing his eyes lower into the gloom. It was then he saw him in the far corner of the room, sitting with his back to the wall, a red sash draped across his chest with a dagger and a brace of pistols tucked into the felt banding. Across his face Cotton could see his most identifying feature—a black eye patch tied against his right eye.

Cotton had arrived on Tortuga only three days prior, with a bundle of ragged clothing and a full gold sovereign nestled in a small leather pouch worn about his waist. The small boat he was on, piloted by the blackmailed Barbados fisherman, had sailed quickly into the harbor and had slowed just enough to allow Cotton to jump to a far, deserted pier, then had sailed off just as quickly, heading back to Barbados, unwilling to tarry even a single moment longer on the island that carried such a vile reputation in every port of the Antilles.

After spending his first night sleeping on that deserted pier, Cotton spent the next two days shuffling about the tangle of rickety shanties and public houses in the harbor. There were dozens of ships bobbing in the water and hundreds of sailors milling about, each hoping for a new sailing, each waiting for a new captain to take to the waters again in their hunt for gold and plunder. There were dozens of alehouses as well as houses of ill repute. Only a few threadbare shops offered any human necessities other than those two basic needs.

On the third day, Cotton Wilson found the promise of revenge he was seeking. Little did he know then what fate awaited him as a result.

In the dark corner of the seedy public house sat Captain Forge Bliss. He had what Cotton wanted—a ship. A ship that was ready to sail.

"You be Cap'n Bliss?" Cotton asked as he shuffled up to the pirate in the dim light.

He had heard Bliss's name mentioned several times during the futile slave and servant rebellion on Barbados. Cotton was too far from the planning to know how important a role Bliss was to have played in the battle. He knew nothing of the reasons Bliss did not deliver his promised support. All he knew was that this man was the man to petition if one was after golden treasure.

The captain looked up with his one good eye. Both above and below the patch over the right side of his face was a jagged, angry scar that began at his forehead and snaked down to his chin. He did not speak for a long moment, but his hand slowly rose to the nicked handle of his pistol.

"And who might be askin'?"

Cotton felt the fear rise to his chest. The man's voice was cold and malevolent. Cotton would later think it was the low, guttural voice of a demon who spoke. "I be Cotton, . . . from de island of Barbados."

"Means less than a barrel of offal to me," the captain hissed as his hand tightened about the pistol grip.

Cotton almost held his hands up in surrender, but fought the urge. "I gots information dat you might be makin' use of. It be 'bout buried treasure. I heard yer name and 'bout how you be comin' when we be fightin'."

There was silence, a cold and evil silence. Cotton gulped, trying to hide his fear as he continued, "And how you never be comin' when men be dyin' on dat place."

Bliss simply narrowed his one good eye to a slit, and Cotton took a step back.

"But dat not be why I be here. It be 'bout buried gold."

Bliss's eye opened wider, and he leaned forward. Cotton suddenly felt much relieved.

Bliss looked up. "Buried gold?"

Cotton nodded, forcing his voice to remain calm.

"Well . . . then maybe I won't kill ye . . . just yet," Bliss replied, and his lips parted into a sneering smile. "Sit down and tell me of this treasure."

Cotton blinked his eyes and forced himself to step forward and sit on the bench opposite this grinning man. Even though his heart and soul were crying for him to run, the flame of revenge burned a few degrees

hotter in him. He sat and leaned forward. "I knows when and where
Cap'n Hawkes be diggin' up dis treasure. I be wantin' to follow him,
bein' on your ship, dat is."

Bliss slowly, a finger at a time, released his grip on his pistol and
leaned forward on the table, his elbows on the worn wood, his chin
resting in his roughened palms.

"Do tell me more, Cotton. Do tell me more."

CHAPTER

51

Island of Barbados
25 May 1650

Preparations for the journey were nearly complete. Only a smattering of small details remained undone. The Bibles had arrived ahead of schedule, owing to favorable, early season winds, and Thomas breathed a great sigh of relief. The only important item that had not yet been secured was a shipment of iron hoes and cultivators from an ironmonger in Plymouth. But Will decided that the sailing would occur on schedule, regardless of their delivery.

The *Dorset Lady* rested tight to the pier, and William climbed aboard for a last once-over inspection. In days past he would have leapt from pier to deck, but making the transition with a cane and a crippled leg was much more complicated than before. More deliberate in his moves, Will made his way on board and walked the newly scrubbed and oiled decks, pulling at rigging lines, lifting canvas, and inspecting the new helm stand on all fours.

He was about to go belowdecks to inspect the rudder reassembly when Thomas, from the end of the dock, called out. "William, may I come aboard?"

Will stopped at the top of the gangway and called back, "Only if you carry with you proof of your paid passage on this voyage."

Thomas patted at his pockets and searched about with a smile. "I am afraid I will be forced to become a stowaway, Captain Hawkes, for I have no gold to purchase passage."

Will laughed, "But you have an honest face. Perhaps we can arrange to take you halfway to your destination, then."

Thomas was aboard now, and even in the light swells of the harbor, he looked most ill at ease being aboard ship, searching for his sea legs.

"William," he said, "I am most amazed. You, with one leg gone bad, have more balance and agility on this vessel than I do with two. Why is that?"

"Practice, Thomas. Practice. I have spent years on these decks, and it feels most natural to be back on a ship again—even with only one good limb."

The two made their way down the narrow passageway. The ship had been cleaned and the bilge pumped and refitted, yet the air belowdecks still grew thick and heavy with the smells of fouled water, sweat, and a curious rancid, wooden smell that seemed to exude from the very pores of the ship in the tropical heat.

Thomas sniffed loudly. "Will this . . . this thickness be lessened as we get under sail?"

Will shook his head. "This smells sweet in comparison to some vessels on which I have sailed. Though it is fortunate that we will be gone such a short time, so the smells will most likely not worsen."

"I am thankful then for small blessings, Will."

Will pointed out the cabins and berths that were appointed to each man. Most of the crew would sleep on the third deck, just at the waterline. Most of the cargo—the implements and supplies, the Bibles, the seed—was stored on the bottommost deck, tied to the sides to prevent rolling in rough seas. Will looked down into the darkness. There was room for a only a few more crates.

The two men made their way back to the main deck, Thomas breathing in great gulps of air as they stood in the early morning breeze.

"Perhaps I shall bed down on the open deck, William," Thomas said, "for this air is much more suited to my constitution."

"We shall see if you will keep that arrangement on the first night it rains, Thomas," Will said with a laugh. He then looked up and down the ship and said, "I would say that all preparations have been completed. The ship is ready. The supplies are on board. Now all we must do is wait for the moon and the tide. And a good wind from the south would be a great benefit as well."

Thomas looked about the ship, and as he saw the empty mast in the shape of the cross, he was reminded of the one thing that remained undone.

"William," he said, "we need accomplish one more task. And that is to ask the Lord to bless this journey."

"Indeed, Thomas, most wise counsel. Would now be the time, or should we make a more formal ceremony?"

"The Lord says to make use of the time that is at hand, and where two or three are gathered together, he is in their midst. And there are two of us gathered here. Now would be a wonderful time."

Thomas clasped Will's hands in his and knelt on the deck and began to pray. "Dearest almighty God, we ask that thou wilt be with us on this voyage. We petition thy blessings for our journey. We covet thy constant watchcare of those we love whom we shall leave at home. We endeavor to spread thy Word and thy blessed truth, and we humbly acknowledge that it is only through thy mighty power that these things shall be done. We seek thy protection and ask for the safety of every man who sails with us. We yearn for thy guidance on our steps and earnestly pray that thou wilt bless this journey to the glory and honor of thy kingdom. Amen."

Island of Tortuga

As Thomas offered his prayer of blessings on their journey, another crew on another island was making its last preparations before setting ships to sail. But these preparations were of a darker, colder nature. More than one hundred men had clamored to sign up for the rewards a voyage with Captain Forge Bliss promised.

In the small harbor of the island of Tortuga, Captain Bliss's vessel, the *Sea Demon,* was being readied for her sail north. A swarm of sweating and cursing stevedores hauled aboard supplies of gunpowder and shot. Bliss purchased a dozen shovels, various lengths of the thickest rope, and five dozen iron-tipped pikes. Besides the *Sea Demon,* two small pinnaces would accompany the old, graying, and worn galleon to her voyage to Barbados and beyond. The pinnaces, in reality not much more than fishing boats, would be needed if there were shallow waters to be navigated. Each could hold fifty men and sail over the sharpest and shallowest reef with ease.

Cotton sat on the foredeck of the *Sea Demon* watching the loading. He was told that Barbados was only three days away and that no captain in his right senses would leave before the season changed and the moon was full with a good strong tide. But by leaving this day, and allowing for weaker winds and the necessity of tacking into the northeast, Bliss assured Cotton that they would arrive in the waters of Barbados at least two full days before Captain Hawkes would set sail.

"I know this man Hawkes," Bliss crowed. "He be the captain who sank a ship I once traveled on. He be a most honorable man, for he stopped and transported us who be swimmin' in the sea to a safe harbor. Had it been me, I woulda sailed off and let 'em drown."

Cotton smiled and nodded, feeling ever more uncomfortable in Bliss's presence. There was an evil about the man that eclipsed even Cotton's hardness.

"And I likes that he be an honorable cap'n, for I then can know what he be tryin' to do and when. You can predict the way an honorable man be thinkin', me friend. You can be tellin' what moves he be makin' ahead o' him makin' 'em."

Cotton nodded again, hoping Bliss would walk away and tend to some detail of their sailing.

"And that be makin' it all the easier to peg the dullard when he need peggin'. This be like shootin' a baby in a barrel."

He draped his arm around Cotton's shoulder. Cotton winced at the fetid breath and the vileness that surrounded the man.

"Me and you, Cotton, we be splittin' this good treasure. Ye for knowin' where it lie, and me for knowin' how to take it. And then ye and me be forgettin' all 'bout old Bliss not deliverin' when he say he be deliverin'. Ain't that most right, me friend?"

Bliss began to laugh and cough at the same time, and was soon doubled over in a coughing spell. Cotton edged away a step.

"We be on our way by afternoon," Bliss said between his coughing. "And in a few days at most, ye can be back with your hot Jezalee for a night or two. Won't that be sweet and tasty?"

The fact that he told Bliss about how he had come on this information was no great regret to Cotton. But the fact that he knew of Jezalee, of her beauty and charms, began, in a most subtle way, to sully her image in Cotton's thoughts.

And as Bliss walked away, the crew cowering and sniveling to scramble from his path, Cotton could hear him say in a singsong voice, "Sweet and tasty, that what it be, sweet and tasty for ye and me."

CHAPTER

52

*Island of Barbados
30 May 1650*

Kathryne wrapped her arms about Will and pulled him tightly to her. She would not let tears come this night, for she knew that such a memory would not be a comfort to William on his voyage. She knew that she needed to be strong for him, for she was so very proud of what he and the rest were attempting to do. Taking the Word to these poor natives was a most noble act and one that could have no less than her fullest and deepest respect.

But she would miss him so, even if the voyage would take no more than a month to six weeks at the longest. To wake and not have him next to her . . . for so many seemingly endless days. His absence would hurt, but she would not let him know how deeply.

They had eaten their dinner, had said good night to the children, had watched them as they fell asleep, and had returned to their own bedchamber and readied for bed.

Kathryne turned to him just before sleep overtook him. "I will pray for you," she said softly.

"And I for you as well," he whispered back.

"Every morning, as well as every evening?"

"Both, to be sure."

"I am proud of you William, for what you are doing. It is most generous and wonderful."

William nodded. "And it will be good to sail one more time. I look forward to the voyage." He saw that a ripple of hurt flashed into Kathryne's eyes, and he quickly amended, "But only because I know the trip is of such a short duration. I could never leave you for longer than this voyage will take. My heart longs for you when you are not beside me."

She smiled and snuggled into the folds of his arms.

Eileen slipped out from the small bedchamber, wrapping a thick robe about her. She awoke, several moments before the midnight bell, to an empty bed. There was a flickering candle on Thomas's desk, nearly burned to a nub. Thomas, quill still clutched in his right hand, had his head cradled in his left arm and was fast asleep. The paper before him, she read as the candle sputtered out, was a listing of the most important Scriptures that would need to be taught first. It was a listing for the men he would leave on the islands.

She gently touched her hand to his shoulder and tried to rouse him. But even though her touch became more insistent, he would not leave his position, nor would he wake. Taking a woven shawl from the chest by the door, she draped it over his shoulders. She bent to his face and gently kissed his cheek. A small smile flickered across his features as she drew back.

"Good night, sweet Thomas. I love you so. May God bless you as you leave me."

Eileen then returned to bed, falling into a deep and most dreamless sleep.

Missy had Andrew in her arms and was walking across the floor by the bed, cooing and whispering into his ear, trying her best to stop his cries and then lull him to sleep. She had tried every technique that had worked so well with William, but Andrew would have none of them.

John looked up, his head propped near level with a pillow. "Perhaps he is hungry?"

Missy shook her head. "He has taken all the milk he cared to. Hunger is not his problem."

"Perhaps an illness has set in?" John said as he raised himself up on his elbows.

Missy shook her head again. "His head is cool, his eyes clear. Perhaps there may be some malady that has not been made manifest, but if so, I am most unaware of its treatment—or symptoms."

"Would he be best served to simply be allowed to cry?"

"And then William would awake as well. One baby in tears is quite enough."

Missy edged the rocking chair to the center of the room, the chair John had made for her when she first carried William. She sat down and began to rock. Slowly, with each movement to and fro, Andrew's cries became slight and distant, then after a final whimper he was still. And as he cried his last, Missy too drifted off to sleep, cradling the baby in her arms.

John smiled as peace and stillness settled over his house. That was until William, from the small room next to their own bedchamber, began at first to whimper, then cry out. John looked up at Missy, now more asleep than before. He sighed once, then slipped out of bed and made his way in the dark to his firstborn's bedside. In the moonlight, the tiny eyes looked dark and piercing. John bent to his knees, then lay down beside the cradle, placing his hand on the rocker. He began to gently rock, back and forth, humming an old sailing song.

In the space of a dozen moments, both William and John were fast asleep.

It was after the moon had settled to the far horizon and the pale yellow light gently washed the landscape that Cotton jumped from the small longboat to the rocky shore just south of Fort Charles.

"You be here when I get back?" he asked, his voice edgy and fearful.

One of the sailors, a little man with orange hair, nodded. "We'll tie her up by those rocks. We wait till dawn and no more. Best be back before first light."

Cotton made his way along the rocky shore and pushed up the sandy dune to the far side of Hawkes Haven. The house lay a half mile distant, and Cotton circled it from behind, staying at the distant edge of the land, running between the cane field and the meadow. He was out of breath and panting by the time he slipped into the stables behind the house. He edged along the walls, attempting to be silent for fear of startling the horses locked in their stalls.

At the inside corner was a narrow stairway that led to the second-floor servants' quarters. Jezalee had the room on the outside, adjacent to where the twins slept. On cat's feet he was up the stairs and slipped in the unbolted door, and within the span of a few moments he was in Jezalee's room. He spun to her bed and covered her mouth with his hand.

"Don' be screamin', Jezalee. It be me, Cotton."

Her eyes snapped open wide and in terror, which gave way in an instant to relief.

He pulled his hand away.

"I jes knowed you be back. I knowed it." She placed her hand over his and held it tight to her. "You be back now, Cotton? You be back for Jezalee?"

He shook his head. "We be followin' Cap'n Hawkes. When he gets to dat gold, we take it and we come back to you." Cotton looked about in the darkened room, listening for any movement in the house. "He still be goin', ain't he?"

Jezalee nodded. "By first light."

"Den I can't stay more dan a bit."

Jezalee nodded again and wrapped her arms around him, pulling him tight to her. He held her in return.

"It be a long time till first light, true?"

Jezalee nodded again.

"Den we gots time."

Jezalee had not released him from her embrace. "Lots of time," she answered.

A one-eyed sailor was not that unusual of a sight in the Cross and Arms. Sailing was a dangerous business. A limb missing, an eye gone—it was all part of the reality of life at sea.

Late that night Forge Bliss had slipped into Bridgetown as Cotton was making his way to Hawkes Haven. He sat at the bar and downed two tankards of proper English rum in the span of a few moments. To his right sat a ragged old man, nursing sips from a tankard of warm ale. Bliss had been a frequent customer of several taverns in port but had never entered this particular establishment. It was wise, he thought, not to stretch his luck any further than need be. Odds were that someone at his more favorite haunts might recall his face, but the same odds held that no man be foolish enough to be reintroducing himself.

"Be wantin' a drink, old-timer?" Bliss asked, doing his best to make his voice cheerful. The result was not all that convincing, but in the small hours of the morning, there was no one there to criticize his effort.

The whiskered old man nodded, and within the hour, after Bliss plied him with a half-dozen brandies, he discovered all the information he needed. In fact, the old man mentioned Captain Hawkes's initial destination—a small, deserted island, two days' sail due north of Barbados—as well as his second stop, Isla del Guajiro. Bliss had discovered early in his career as a pirate that the rum- and brandy-soaked patrons of these public houses often possessed a wealth of information—most of it garnered from sitting about looking too drunk to be a threat or too drunk to actually remember anything of substance. This particular old rummy had overheard Thomas and William discuss their sailing charts over a lunch of Irish stew. The old man, a sailor in his better days, remembered passing the island that was Will's base and thinking it deserted.

As he paid his bill at the Cross and Arms, Bliss leaned close to the barman and whispered, "If a man be wantin' a little bit of pleasure for the evenin', where would he look?"

The barman nodded and replied, "The houses at either end of this block be fine places. The one to the north be cheaper by a quid."

Bliss tossed the barman a small coin, pocketed his change, and smiled. "Thanks for the advice. Ye be savin' me a quid then."

53

31 May 1650

"Why does our leaving have to be at dawn?" Thomas asked, flexing his back, working out the kinks that had developed by sleeping at his desk, his joints popping loudly.

"Doesn't have to be," John called out, laughing. "The tide be right till evenin'. Noon would have been as proper as now."

"Well then," Thomas grumped as he pulled his bundle of papers aboard the *Dorset Lady,* "why do we not wait till noon? I could venture back to my own bed and sleep until then."

Will smiled and replied, "If we wait until noon, then there are even more good-byes that need be suffered through. It was hard enough leaving Kathryne as she was still half asleep. I do not wish to imagine the difficulty I would encounter when she becomes fully awake. Dawn is not the best time, but it is the easiest time for farewells."

"William, I would have accused sailors of being an unfeeling and unromantic lot, but what you have just said so poetically changes my evaluation of the profession."

Will called out for the sails to be unfurled and the lines cast off, and he turned the helm to the right, aiming the sturdy little vessel to the west and out of the harbor. Will had no words to describe how difficult it was to leave Kathryne that morning. It was not a dawn departure that made it easier for her, but for Will. Had he tarried, had his children been awake and laughing, had Kathryne been there to stand beside him, he would have found leaving nearly impossible.

It is good to be under sail, Will thought. *I will have the ship to keep my mind occupied and my heart from hurting overmuch.*

As the ship plowed through the light chop and set the waves to dancing in the wind, the men grew silent and thoughtful. The last sailing that they had undertaken together had nearly ended in great tragedy, with Thomas abducted and Will's ship nearly destroyed. And now, each of them had so much more to lose if such calamity befell them again. The thought of such a disaster, of such a horrible possibility, brought all three to silence.

Thomas sat at the stern, hoping the rolling would not unsettle his tender stomach. He prayed throughout the morning that the sailing would find God's blessings. John busied himself, checking rigging, examining the pulleys and weights of the rudder, making sure his work was done properly. William guided the ship, took readings from the sun, and watched the sky for signs of changes in weather.

It feels good to be at sea again, Will thought. It filled him with a sense of peace. But even in this peace, a few cracks appeared. Will struggled and could not prevent his thoughts from returning to Kathryne. He tried not to think of his wife, lying in bed, gentling rustling under the down covers, her hair cascaded about her face like a halo, her voice deep and throaty in the first light. He tried not to think of that final kiss, deep and warm, and how her arm lazed about his neck and pulled him closer.

Suddenly Will was torn from his daydream by a shout from the yardarm: "Sails to the stern!"

The *Sea Demon* plowed through the water like a slow, lumbering cow. She was not speedy nor agile, a fact that her captain overcame with brute force and bloodthirsty cruelty. The two pinnaces to her port and starboard would set a loose picket line, traveling a few leagues to either side of Bliss and further ahead. If Hawkes slipped to the east or west, he wanted those ships to know it.

Bliss stood at the quarterdeck looking smug and happy. He looked to the side, where Cotton stood to port, looking most unhealthy. The rolling of the ship was not severe, but to a man not accustomed to such voyages the combination of rolling, pitching, and yawing often proved the most vexing of maladies.

In an instant Bliss jumped to the bow, grabbing his telescope and snapping it open. He stared to the north, cursing a vile string of epithets.

He turned and screamed, "Furl the forward sail, ye cretins and louts! I see their blasted sails! If I be seein' him, he can be seein' me!"

A heartbeat later, dozens of men scrambled up the rigging and

furiously pulled at heavy canvas, tying it to the yardarm in great
bundles.

Bliss screeched at his second-in-command, "Signal the two pinnaces
to drop back! The blithering buffoons!"

Within the span of half an hour, Bliss's small convoy let several
leagues of sea come between them and the *Dorset Lady*.

"If Hawkes was worried," Bliss said, "he would sail at his best speed
to lose us. I'll let him think that he did. It's not like I don't know where
he be headin'."

"Be there any more sails to the stern?" William called up to the sentry
at the top of the mainmast.

"None since noon," came the shouted reply.

Will had taken the ship to run broad reach with the wind, her best
speed, hoping to avoid any manner of confrontation at sea.

"Then it be what I claimed," John said. "A fishing vessel or a
merchant ship is all. A little off the usual path, but no pirate, that's for
certain."

Thomas looked up, startled, at hearing the word *pirate* again. "And
why might that be?"

William sat next to John on the quarterdeck steps. "If the sail be a
pirate sail, she'd be on us by now. This ship is solid, but not the fastest
I've ever sailed. We haven't seen a trace of a sail since noon, and that is
not the actions of any pirate I've ever known. I would say our sailing
be as safe as it can be at this point."

As evening approached, the sails were reduced, and the ship continued to journey slowly north throughout the night. The crew pulled the
foresail, the jib sail, and the top mainsail, leaving only the mainsail
unfurled to gather the evening breeze. It grew quiet, the crew settling
to the evening meal belowdeck. John, Will, and Thomas, as well as the
sentries and the helmsman, were the only few that stayed atop. The
three old friends sat on the quarterdeck and shared a loaf of fresh bread,
cheese, and thick slabs of cold roast beef. The food was passed hand to
hand, and each man tore off a large portion, juggling all three in their
hands and laps. Several bottles of ale were opened and passed about as
well.

For many moments all three men concentrated fully on chewing and
swallowing.

Will was the first to break the silence. "'Tis most unlike our manners
at home," he laughed.

John nodded, coughing on his last swallow. "If I be eatin' like this at

Missy's table, well, I wouldn't be eatin' again for a long month of Sundays."

Thomas, in his most serious tone, as if he were wearing a vicar's robes again, announced, "But wherein lies the problem? This is the manner in which Eileen and myself sup every evening." His face bore no mark of amusement for a long series of moments, leaving John and William stunned into silence. But then his solid visage cracked and he began to laugh, and soon all three were rolling in laughter.

It was several moments till John spoke. "I love bein' on the sea . . . and I thought I did not miss it until this moment."

Will nodded. "It does have a language all its own. The scent, the light, the power of the wind and wave. I miss it as well."

"Then why do you not sail more often?" Thomas asked. "You both have the means."

"True," Will said, "I have the means, but sailing entails leaving Kathryne and the twins. If there be a contest between the sea and those three, well, I think I do not need tell you the winner."

John nodded. "That be the truth, William. It has not been a night, and already I miss little Andrew's cries." He thought a moment, then added, "Yet none of you need repeat that to anyone. I do not wish to be thought of as unmanly."

"'Tis not unmanly to desire to hold your children or to see them grow," William said, his voice low and soft. "'Tis no greater gift that God has given than the gift of a child."

And it was this soft talk among friends, in the quiet of a darkened ocean, that continued well past the twelfth bell of the night.

■ ■ ■ ■ ■

The curtains ruffled silently in the faint evening breeze. The candles on the table flickered and wavered, shadows dancing across the table. There was a scent of hibiscus in the winds, filling Hawkes Haven with a subtle fragrance.

Kathryne had but nibbled at her food, as did her two guests, Missy Delacroix and Eileen Mayhew. She had sent word that the three might dine together that first evening alone. She hoped that their company would lift this oppressive feeling from her heart and ease her unnamed fears. She knew that the journey was not without some danger, for any voyage on the sea carried with it a threat of mishap, and there was woven into any voyage a thread that may unravel. Yet William had assured her, had assured each wife, that they would seek out the safest and most expeditious routing, always endeavoring to place themselves

as far from peril as possible. But when William kissed her this morning, in the first golden light of the dawn, she felt a shudder creep into
her soul. She wanted so desperately to hold him to her, to keep him
from this journey. Yet she dismissed her fears and trepidation as
merely false urgings. He would be in no danger, she told herself as his
lips met hers, only hours ago. Through sleep-fogged eyes, she had
watched him as he took his worn and creased leather satchel and
hoisted it to his shoulder and slipped from the room and from her
sight. Her heart hurt for that brief instant, more than it had ever hurt
before.

A thought had run into her awareness. *What if this be the last time
I gaze upon my William? What would happen to my life if he never
returned?* She had shaken her head to chase the image away, and was
nearly successful.

Yet all during the day, as she had cared for Samuel and Hannah, as
she had made arrangements for this dinner, as she had gone about the
house touching and picking up objects and books that William cherished, the thoughts of being forever alone had stood just at her mind's
reach, just around some dark corner, lurking there, waiting to prick at
her soul, waiting to urge the tears to flow.

Early in the evening, when the sun was but a half-round of hot
orange where the sky met the sea, she had picked up a well-worn
volume that lay open on Will's desk. The pages lay open to a poem that
she had often heard Will recite, "The Good-Morrow" by John Donne.
She had sat down at the desk and had begun to read aloud softly,

> *I wonder by my troth, what thou and I*
> *Did, till we lov'd? Were we not wean'd till then,*
> *But suck'd on country pleasures, childishly?*
> *Or snorted we in the seven sleepers' den?*
> *'Twas so; but this, all pleasures fancies be.*
> *If ever any beauty I did see,*
> *Which I desir'd, and got, 'twas but a dream of thee.*
>
> *And now good-morrow to our waking souls,*
> *Which watch not one another out of fear;*
> *For love, all love of other sights controls,*
> *And makes one little room, an everywhere.*
> *Let sea-discoverers to new worlds have gone,*
> *Let maps to other, worlds on worlds have shown,*
> *Let us possess one world, each hath one, and is one.*

My face in thine eye, thine in mine appears,
And true plain hearts do in the faces rest;
Where can we find two better hemispheres,
Without sharp north, without declining west?
Whatever dies was not mix'd equally;
If our two loves be one, or, thou and I
Love so alike, that none do slacken, none can die.

Kathryne had then closed the book. And finally, in the dimming Caribbean light, she had allowed the tears to come.

And now that the three had gathered, a quietness—a somber, reflective quietness—marked the meal. All three women, all three now without benefit of husbands, acted much the same as Kathryne. They entered Hawkes Haven with smiles and hugs, though as the meal progressed, each slipped further and further into reflective silence.

As Martha cleared the table and brought out a steaming pot of Ceylon tea and sweet cakes, Kathryne looked at their faces. *I must be the strong one here this night,* she thought, almost commanding herself. *It would be what William would have me do.*

And as she thought his name, a catch formed in her throat, and she struggled to prevent that first tear from falling. "A most wonderful dinner, Martha," she spoke, breaking the stillness.

"Indeed, it was most tasty," Eileen echoed, as Missy concurred with a nod.

Then silence slipped back to fill the room.

Kathryne took her teacup, spooned in a large measure of sticky brown sugar, and stirred it, much longer than needed. "And how are the children, Missy?" she asked.

"Willy is fine, growing strong, but the baby is still most restless at night," she admitted, "and there seems to be no reason, other than a defiant personality. And the twins?" she asked in reply.

Kathryne smiled, in earnest, for perhaps the first time all evening. "They are doing so well. Hannah is a joy, and Samuel . . . well, Samuel is a handful."

Missy nodded knowingly. "It is hard to believe that such a small person can consume so much of one's attention."

Kathryne looked over to Eileen, who had been so very quiet most of the meal. "'Twas your husband who called Samuel impetuous, and I am afraid that his assessment is most accurate, Eileen. Samuel often fails to think before he acts, and most often with little regard to the consequences," she said with a smile.

Eileen tried to smile back, but it was thin and without feeling. Kathryne and Missy spoke for another dozen moments on their techniques for dealing with a variety of childhood ailments and behaviors, both finding a common ground on which to stand and on which to break the stillness of the night.

It was after a pause in the conversation that Eileen abruptly stood, her hand flew to her mouth, and she ran from the dining chamber into the darkness of the great room, her cries following her in the darkness. Missy and Kathryne looked to each other in surprise, as if to ask each other what could have caused such an outburst. Kathryne quickly stood, took a candle, cupped her hand about the flame, and made her way to follow Eileen. She found her curled on one end of the large padded bench that faced the empty and cold fireplace. Kathryne set the candle down, sat next to her, and stroked her arm, whispering, "Whatever is the matter? Did we mention something so upsetting? Why such tears?"

Eileen turned and embraced Kathryne in a fierce hug, all but startling her with its intensity.

"Eileen," whispered Kathryne again, "are you missing Thomas? Is that what has brought you to tears? 'Tis no shame, for we all feel much the same as you. I have struggled all day to not weep, and finally, prior to your arrival, I indulged myself in a good cry at Will's desk."

Eileen clutched at Kathryne, her face buried in the deep velvet of her friend's gown, and wept, her tears harder and stronger than before.

Missy came into the room and sat beside them both. "It shall be fine, Eileen. I know it shall," she said. "William and John are the two most able seamen that have ever sailed these waters. And 'tis not I who have made that judgment, 'tis all the men who have ever served with them. They shall bring Thomas back. He shall return to you."

Eileen wailed afresh, as Kathryne stroked her hair and held her tight.

After a long dozen moments, Eileen sniffed and pulled back, wiping at her tears with the palm of her hand.

"'Tis hard to be without the man you love," Kathryne said, hoping that misery shared is misery halved in severity.

"We feel as you do," Missy added. "We truly do,"

"And he shall be back after so little time away, you shall scarce have known that he was away," Kathryne said with a weak smile. "And while he is gone, you shall have the entire bed in which to sleep—no more nighttime struggles with blankets and snoring and all the rest."

Eileen looked at Kathryne, and her lips began to tremble, and her eyes clouded again with tears.

"Eileen," Kathryne asked, "what is the matter? Is it something more than just loneliness? Perhaps you are ill? Shall I fetch the doctor for a potion to aid your sleep?"

Eileen put her hand to her mouth, as if physically holding back the tears. "'Tis none of that," she said, her voice quivering. "'Tis that . . . 'tis that . . ."

"What?" Kathryne asked, taking hold of Eileen's free hand. "What is it that troubles you so?"

Eileen sniffed loudly once again and wiped at the tears now rolling down her cheeks. "'Tis that I am . . . I am with child," she wailed and dove into Kathryne's arms again.

Kathryne and Missy looked at each other with amazement, tinted with wonder. That instant, the three of them had all been made members of a most exclusive grouping—that of motherhood.

After a long moment of loud cries, Kathryne leaned back and spoke. "Have you told Thomas?"

Eileen shook her head no. "I was not certain, and if I had told him prior, he would not have gone on this journey, and to stay would have broken his heart. And now I am sure . . . and he is . . . and he is gone."

Kathryne pulled her close again and stroked her arm. "It shall be fine, Eileen. We are here. And Thomas shall be back."

Eileen leaned back and her face was lined with fear. "But the dream I had . . . a most horrible dream . . . of ships sinking and men dying on the sand. I am so afraid that Thomas shall never return to see his child born."

Missy spoke up. "'Twas merely the dream of a mother-to-be. We all have had such frights. I have."

Eileen looked up again, her face a mask of worry and fright. "That be the truth?"

They both nodded.

"And he will return?"

They nodded again.

"And the dream has no import?"

They both nodded.

As Kathryne hugged her friend once more, she hoped that the truth would not show in her eyes, for she too had had the same dream.

CHAPTER

54

Unnamed Island,
Caribbean Sea
2 June 1650

"Land ho!" came the cry from the mainmast sentry. "Off to port!"

John came running from belowdecks, buttoning his worn doublet in the fierce winds. The ship canted at a most steep angle; Will had fought for the last full day to hold her on course.

"Be nice to set in the harbor and out of this gale," John said.

"Your feet have grown too attached to the land, my friend," Will called out. "This would have been a pleasant Sunday sail only a few years prior."

John smiled back. "Perhaps, Will, though I am glad my memory had dimmed. For had I remembered well, I may have thought otherwise of this journey."

Only a few hours out of Bridgetown, the waters had turned turtle green and the winds had begun to whistle, sharp and edgy, from the south. The air was not chilled, but was not warm, either. A chilled wind meant trouble brewing, and as it stood between both extremes, the seas simply churned and roiled in response to the incessant winds. The *Dorset Lady* was a good vessel, but as it pitched and yawed and lifted and set in the swells, even the heartiest of sailors often fought the rising of their stomachs in response. Thomas had taken to his cabin as the conditions roughened and had not appeared since. John's repairs to the ship held tight, and the cargo, lashed securely to the hull and ribs, stayed dry and safe.

Will shouted out to the crew, "Furl the foresail and hold the jib at half!" He turned to John and added, "These waters are tricky enough in light winds. I choose not to run aground just yet with a full range of canvas pushing me further onto some spiky reef."

The ship pitched again as it slipped down a deep trough, and the spray came over the bowsprit in a furious shower of salty rain. Will wiped the water from his face. His doublet was soaked through and clung to him like moss on a rock. His light blond hair was matted about his face and clung in tendrils to his neck.

The vessel climbed the top of the trough and crashed through the peak of the wave with another shower pouring over the foredeck.

"Are the battens secured by the front hatches?" Will called out.

"Aye, sir," a crewman called back.

The waters ran rougher here, as the surge of the ocean lifted itself over the shallow reef and shoal of the island. The entry into their old base was a simple matter in calmer weather, but Will had no choice but to aim her bow straight at the heart of the island and let the wind try its best to push him off course. There was a jagged ridge of coral reef to his port and sandbars guarding his starboard flank. The open passageway in was no wider than a half league, and Will prayed that the conditions had not changed since his last visit so many years ago.

"To the starboard, Cap'n Will. Looks to be sand at the surface!"

Three crewmen ran to the starboard side with long stout poles in case they struck a submerged obstacle.

Blast! Will thought, his mind racing. *The entrance has shifted. That bar was not there when I sailed this water last.*

He spun the helm, and the ship began to list to port as she caught more and more of the wind. She darted from the sand on the starboard and Will breathed easy until he heard another shout: "Rocks off to port!"

And blast again! Will's thoughts shouted. *It be worse than threading a needle! And I pray this needle still has an eye about it.*

He spun back to starboard and saw a jagged jaw of bleached white coral scratching to the surface of the sea.

"John! This be a time of praying! Every man who be Christian on this ship set their hearts to God. We need to find the opening."

Will had no room to turn and try again. He could have done so years ago, but not this day. The channel boundaries had shifted and narrowed. He had to find safe harbor, or his ship would be grounded until high tide or dashed to the rocks and reef to his port side.

Let there be a way, dear God. Let this ship enter.

Will spun back and forth, tacking in sharp rides from port then starboard. He felt the vessel graze the sand three times, a raspy hesitancy in the helm and a shudder in the sails. He heard no scraping on the starboard side, but damage could have occurred and no one would know until the hull burst.

Will shouted to a crewman at his side, "Hold the helm steady for a moment." And then he ran to the bow and scanned the waters for a deeper green streak—a deeper channel in the sea.

Perhaps there. Perhaps if I follow that line to the west and then cut back to the north . . .

He ran back to the helm and pulled it with all his strength. The ship canted again and sliced westward. Will counted to himself. When he reached sixty, he cut the helm again, and the ship turned north, with the wind full at her back. Like a dolphin, she lifted up over the last swell and crashed into the trough near the shore. Will could now make out the individual palms that ringed the narrow opening. If that had not silted up, he was safe. Another swell lifted the ship, and as she crashed down then lifted up, the *Dorset Lady* was at the point where she needed to be. With many gasps and prayers, the small craft crashed through the greenness guarding the open jaws of the harbor and slipped into the still waters.

"Furl all sails!" Will shouted. "Let the anchor!"

The anchor splashed into the water, its entrance echoing about the harbor. And after that, other than the whistling of the wind, there was only silence.

████████

No more than five leagues to the south lay the three ships of Captain Forge Bliss. Buffeted and tossed by the same waves, Bliss struggled to stay on course and upright. His old galleon rode low in the seas, and the waves sloshed easily over her decks. Nearly half the crew sweated and strained over the bilge pumps, the brackish water filling the lowest deck to the depth of a man's knee.

Cotton clung to a rail on the quarterdeck, hoping to die. He had never felt as miserable and viciously sick as he had been for the past three days. He could not eat nor drink, and even the slightest movement made him want to retch.

Bliss clung to the helm with an evil fierceness, bellowing out orders and cursing the skies and the wind. He turned to the rear and saw Cotton fastened to the rail, useless. He cursed again. Anyone not pulling his share of the work was of no use to him.

████████

The ship groaned against the push of the wind as the anchor took purchase on the seabed. The *Dorset Lady* would spin around to face the wind, holding firm to the anchor weight. Will ran to the rear deck and scanned the shores. There was no cook fire smoke; the huts in which he and his crew had once lived were now a tangle of vine and brush, their frames all but lost as the jungle reclaimed its own. He peered into the direction of the small village and saw nothing. The dense green was a shield to his vision.

"Hallo!" he called out as loudly as he could. "Hallo!"

There was no response. Will felt a coldness in his heart. "Make ready a longboat!" he shouted.

Within a half-dozen moments, he boarded a longboat and approached the shore. He jumped into the surf and waded onto the white sand, his the only footprints for as far as he could see. He pushed hard with his cane, the water threatening to tip his balance. John stood beside him, a musket in his hand.

"Will, something be wrong here. Where are the villagers? Where are our friends?"

Will shrugged and shook his head sadly. "It does not appear that all is as well as we thought."

Only a few of their former huts stood. Will could see only the cane framing of his, the thatching long gone. He walked over to the ruin and stood there, silent. He closed his eyes and at once could see the image of Kathryne, standing before him, beautiful and defiant, eyes blazing. He looked up and could just see the blackness of the volcano's peak looming in the distance. The vision of Kathryne, a waterfall, and a kiss flooded his thoughts. His heart constricted from missing her. He bent to the ground and lifted what was once the bed on which she had slept. The canvas had rotted, and it fell to pieces as he tried to move it.

Will stood up, leaning heavy against his cane. "My heart hurts for the thoughts I have, John," he said somberly.

John nodded. "Perhaps they are in hiding in the jungle, and they have merely been frightened, for they think we are intruders."

"Perhaps," Will replied and began to make his way down the wide, curving beach toward the cluster of huts and fires.

In a few moments, Will's worst fears were realized.

The village was desolate and abandoned. No one had lived in these huts for at least a year, he thought, perhaps longer. Roofs were gone, the thatching lost to the winds. All about them was strewn a disarray of pots, barrels, wooden tools, crates, and bits of cloth and weaving.

"Captain Will!" shouted one of the crew from further into the cluster of huts, "You best come here."

Will and John hurried to the crewman's side. They stood in front of a single hut, a bit better preserved than most. The crewman pointed inside.

Will looked into the dim interior. There, sprawled across the floor, was a tangle of human bones, the white skull grinning at the sky. A small wooden chest was next to the bones. Will recognized it as one that he had given to Chief Sapua so many years ago. He felt his heart constrict again.

John saw Will's pain and quietly stepped inside and retrieved the small box and brought it back into the sunlight. He opened the lid, and inside were the molding remains of a book, or perhaps two, and several sheets of paper, rolled tight together and bound with a short length of twine.

John reached in and extracted the roll and handed it to William. "You be better at reading than I. Perhaps it might be a letter."

Will placed his cane under his arm and untied the twine, carefully unrolling the paper, its edges cracked and brittle, a light green tint of mold seeping onto the words.

Be knowing I am last here. Sailors hunt giant fish come, leave. Mother die, father, brother, and then many more. I am alone. I wait for God of Captain Will and Lady Kat. I not fear. No one fear. God of Captain Will and Lady Kat waits for all. God of Captain Will and Lady Kat is good God. Bon soir. Albert.

Suddenly Will could not see the words, his vision clouded with emotions.

Albert was one of the small children William met when he first arrived. He had been a smart boy and quickly learned the letters of the English alphabet. He remembered how the boy had written his name in the sand for Kathryne. Will had taught the children some of the Scriptures. It was now most apparent that Kathryne had taught them much more than just the rudiments. She passed on her faith, as she could, and they took her faith and let the seed grow in their lives.

And now they were all dead, lost to an illness born of some evil wind.

Will looked up to the sky. "Dear Father," he said in a whisper, his voice just louder than the wind, "accept these poor souls unto thyself. They believed as much as Kathryne told them of thee. I pray that thou wilt accept their simple faith. I pray that they now rest in thy arms."

And with that, Will could stand no longer and fell to his knees in prayer and in tears.

"You must eat something, Thomas," John urged. "The seas may be rough on our journey to Isla del Guajiro as well. You know what the old salts would tell you—one eats when the water is calm."

Thomas managed only a weak smile. His face was white and wan, and he felt as weak as he looked. But what doubled his pain was the story Will told of the death of an entire village.

William said that he knew that ships had come upon the island before he ventured there and that other sailors would follow after him. But he never had dreamed that an illness would sweep over them and lead them all to face their Maker.

Thomas was saddened, for this was a chance denied—a chance to witness and to teach. The words that were written were of slight comfort, for they believed as much as they could. And perhaps that would be enough.

Will stepped back into the cramped cabin carrying a full flagon of wine. He poured a generous amount into the three tankards and took a long, gulping swallow of his.

"William," John said, "be cautious of the wine. Such drink never paints over a hurt so that it does not bleed through later."

Will scowled for a moment, then his face softened. "I know, John, and I do not really seek to escape into it. I . . . would simply like this bitter taste to leave my mouth and throat."

John leaned back in his chair, his back resting against the curving hull. "'Tis indeed a sad day, William, but there was no more you could have done. Until the illness came, they had fared well. You supplied them with much. They lived well."

Will looked most glum, but nodded. "Yet the chance to do more has been lost. I find that such bitter fruit."

Thomas reached out and took a hard biscuit and attempted to nibble it. He managed to consume the entire amount and, in so doing, felt bold enough to add a small wedge of cheese and a sip of wine.

"Will not their gold be useful then to add to the treasure for the people of Isla del Guajiro?" Thomas asked.

William looked perplexed for a moment, then brightened. "I had forgotten of that. Yes, indeed, their treasure can be used for such things. Such money can keep their memory alive."

John leaned forward. "William, I never needed to know prior to this date, but how much gold did you leave buried here?"

"A full ten bars, at least," Will said after a long moment of consideration.

John whistled. "Then it best we keep knowledge of such an amount hidden from the rest. Ten bars be more than enough to tempt any man—or any hundred men, for that matter. You and I and the helmsman can retrieve it come dawn. Then no one will be the wiser."

Will nodded in agreement.

"Then we best be getting to that on the morrow," John said. "It feels like the winds have dropped a bit, and I would suggest we be on our way as soon as we may. 'Tis a long stretch of open sea between us and Isla del Guajiro. And all that gold makes me a wee bit nervous. I know what such a temptation can do."

Will nodded.

"And you, Thomas, are the only person who knows of the other gold's location. You should seek some rest for an early start at the dawn," John added.

The group broke up, and Will rose and stepped from the room to his own berth. He settled into the narrow hammock and knew that sleep would long elude him. He missed Kathryne lying warm and soft beside him. And his heart felt saddened by the death of so many people he had held dear, here on this beautiful island.

"Life is too brief for missed chances," he spoke aloud to himself. "From this day forward, I shall strive to never have such regrets again."

And with that he closed his eyes, listened to the night sounds of the jungle, and waited for the dawn.

CHAPTER

55

Caribbean Sea
5 June 1650

Looking still most pale, Thomas guided himself along, hand over hand, clinging to the railing, as he navigated his way from the bow to the helm. He hoped the sea spray and the wind would help keep his stomach from rebelling, but it did not. After gasping as the ship dove into the deep trench of a wave, he was left with a mouthful of seawater and a thoroughly drenched doublet. The taste of the sea, once a pleasure, had now turned to a trial. He wondered why as a boy he could sail his small boat on the English Sea for hours on end, and now as a man he struggled simply to hold a biscuit in his stomach.

"William," he gasped as he arrived at the helm, "could you not find smoother water? This journey will no doubt put me off sea voyages forever."

"Would that I could, Thomas," Will replied, his muscles tensing as he fought against the swells with the helm and rudder. "I seek a calmer ride as well, but the winds have precluded me from doing so."

Thomas clutched at the rail again as the ship slid sideways down another wave, all the while pitching up and down.

"Yet there is a pleasant result to such a wind-tossed ocean," Will called out.

"Please tell me," Thomas gasped. "I would greatly appreciate some good report."

"The wind is keeping our speed quick. I have never sailed this stretch of water in as little time. With luck, we will be at Isla del Guajiro on the morrow's dawn."

Thomas fell to his knees and held his hand aloft. "My prayers have been answered, William," Thomas called out theatrically. "God knew I would die here if another full day was spent on these waters."

Another wave crashed over the rail, drenching Thomas once again.

"But, Thomas," Will called out, laughing, "that is predicated on my finding the island. There is chance I may have sailed too far, and then we would need spend days tacking back and forth to find the harbor."

Thomas sputtered and wiped the water from his face. "Not if you value your life, William," Thomas warned. "I will make no guarantees as to my disposition and your safety if we do not reach land by the morrow."

And as he spoke, as if counterpointed by an angry, capricious sea, a second wave crashed over them from the opposite side, soaking them both yet again.

56

6 *June 1650*

"Land ho!" cried the sentry from the mainmast. "Off to starboard, Captain Will!"

Will craned his neck to the right and saw the faintest patch of green at the horizon. "So spotted, sailor!" he called back and turned the helm, the ship creaking further to the west.

The winds had slackened some overnight, and even Thomas was above deck this morning for the dawn meal, though he ate very little. But now with the promise of terra firma beneath his feet at last, his spirits brightened, and a smile found his face.

"Well done, William," he called out from the stern. "You have spared me from committing harm to you."

Will waved without turning, concentrating instead on finding the harbor on the eastern edge of Isla del Guajiro.

The dawning sun poured its warm, red light across the calm seas and washed the eastern edge of the island in a most curious crimson color. Perhaps it was the specific foliage on this island, for the hillsides above the small cove trembled in a reddish wave, almost as if they were catching the crimson from the dawn and reflecting it, amplifying, back into the early morning mists. The red color continued as it poured against the shallow passages about the island. The coral and rocks took on a burnished hue, perhaps from the violet seaweed and moss, perhaps from the color of the red coral itself. For a long dozen moments, it appeared as if the sea, as well as the island itself, was carved from a ruby and set upon the waves. Even hardened and unsentimental sailors, well traveled and accustomed to a thousand glorious sunsets and a thousand splendid views, began to gather at the bow rails, silent and almost reverent, as the sun brought forth a most wondrous visage.

Will could not help from being overwhelmed, for two or three sailors dropped to their knees in the presence of such a sight and bowed their heads in prayer to the God that created it.

If merely the vision of such a wonder could bend a man's knee, Will thought, *how much more powerful will be God's actual words on this little island.*

Will stood silent for a long moment as the island came closer into view. While his eyes were filled with shimmering images of reds and golds, his heart remained troubled. His thoughts went back, not so many years prior, to the desperate battle he and Radcliffe Spenser had waged on this sand and in these waters. The geography was stained with the blood of both English and Spanish. He closed his eyes and said a silent prayer, for on this island lay the remains of friends—Bryne Tambor and others—and the memories of the bloody past simmered over the green hills and jungles.

He shook his head to clear the bitter and angry images. He offered a prayer that this island would now know peace.

By noon, the *Dorset Lady* sat in the calm waters off a spacious cove on the eastern edge of Isla del Guajiro. By the time the anchor struck the floor of the ocean, a dozen native canoes were in the surf, the occupants paddling furiously to meet the ship. The appearance of any vessel was such a rare occurrence that whether she carried merchants, pirates, or sailors of any country's navy, the natives sought to trade with them all. They had little to offer, but would exchange fish, fruit, necklaces woven of shell and feather, carved bits of wood, and fresh water—anything that they had—for anything the sailors might possess.

Will called out in his boldest voice and in their native tongue, as the first canoe approached. "Is Chief Tahonen still alive? I am William Hawkes, and I bring an old friend of the chief to visit."

A native standing in the prow of the lead canoe shouted back, "He be an old man, but he lives. Who be this friend?"

"Vicar Thomas Mayhew," Will shouted back.

The sound of the name so surprised the man that he nearly toppled out of the canoe into the calm waters. "Thomas Mayhew lives? Thomas Mayhew? The God-man?"

Thomas then appeared at the rail and waved a greeting, calling out, "I am alive, Kanelo. I am alive."

Kanelo's face blanched, his jaw dropped open, and he stood there for a long quiet moment. Then gathering his wits about him, he dove headfirst into the sea and began to paddle furiously toward the ship. "Thomas!" he cried. "Thomas!"

It took a long few hours to get Thomas ashore and get to Chief Tahonen's side, such was the press of the villagers about him. Not a man nor woman would let him pass without an elaborate and heartfelt greeting. Even the children gathered about him, clutching at his legs as he passed them. Will stood behind Thomas as he walked, trying to keep up with the quick and animated chatter. He possessed only a rudimentary grasp of the language, but he did not need that skill to know how loved Thomas was among these people. Each thanked him for returning to tell them more stories of this God of his.

It was later that night—well past midnight as Will figured—before the furious celebration of Thomas's return had begun to break up. The entire village feasted, and after toasting a hundred toasts with the vile-tasting but potent native drink, after gorging on roasted fowl and pig, a certain stillness had settled back upon the village. Thomas, Will, and John sat by the front of Chief Tahonen's large hut. The chief had slipped into a glazed sleep, and his wives giggled and pulled him onto his sleeping mat. There remained a dozen or so men in a wide circle about the low fire, watching Thomas, Will, and John with a fuzzy focus. One by one, they too dropped to sleep.

Will had matched the toasts sip to gulp, as Thomas and John had attempted to do as well, but he felt lightheaded even at that small consumption. He hiked himself up on his elbows and shook his head to clear the cobwebs from his thoughts. It had been a most strenuous voyage, albeit swift, and he felt a tiredness in his bones—more tired than he had ever felt on past voyages.

It be the signs of age, he told himself, feeling a certain wistfulness about the passage of time.

Will looked over at Thomas, who was staring into the vast canopy of darkness sprinkled with the lights of a million stars. "Thomas," he called out, "are you still alert?"

"More so than I have ever been in my life," he replied.

"May I ask you a question?"

"William, you need not seek permission to do so. Ask what you will."

Will cleared his throat. "I have so often heard your tale of the hidden treasure and always in the company of children. You've admitted that some details have been . . . illuminated by a stronger light. Would you tell me the truth of the matter? There is indeed treasure here, is there not?"

Thomas laughed. "I do not blame you, William, for your question. I am only surprised that you waited till this moment and after all these miles and horrible seas to ask it."

"But, Thomas, I trust you," he replied.

"To a point, that is," Thomas said, laughing. "But, by all means, I will tell you what I can of the truth." He sat up straight and took another sip of his drink, wincing with every swallow. "This is the story as it occurred:

"I was at this village, left here by San Martel. I was no longer a worry or concern to him. If I witnessed to these heathen, it was of no concern to him. I spent so many months here—at first no more use than a dumb mute, for their language is difficult. But I learned, and gradually I began to tell them, in their own tongue, of the one true God. People believed, and I was heartened.

"Then San Martel and Radcliffe Spenser returned to this island. We knew of their return. We could smell their fires and their vile odors from here.

"It was the second night of their return. Two young men and myself made our way across the ridge to the other side of the island, to the far cove."

"And Chief Tahonen accompanied you?" Will asked.

Thomas laughed. "No, that was a bit of my embellishment. The chief would never climb that mountain. But to a child, his journey is much more exciting."

"Indeed," Will agreed.

"And we arrived at dusk, to be witness of their debauchery. They had brought women with them, and a few of the native men had made their way there as well, and I pity their souls for their behaviors. By the time the moon appeared, most were blind with drink, stumbling about, even falling into their bonfires and rushing into the sea to extinguish their flaming clothes.

"We watched from the jungle path. On shore were several sea chests. One was opened, the gold bars in plain sight. On occasion, a drunken sailor would come over and heft a bar, as if testing its worth.

"By the moon's light, a strange bravery overtook us, and we simply walked to the shore. Those of the revelers who saw us must have considered us one of their own, for no one challenged us nor called for us to halt. The tide was coming in, and the waters began to lap at one very large chest, still closed and locked tight. I motioned to one of the men with me, and he looked at the chest and nodded, as if he understood the import of my gesture. We walked to it, and he bent down and shoved it into the water. To our amazement, it was so secure and watertight that it floated, despite its cargo. It did not sit high in the water, but neither did it sink. And to compound our amazement, no one noticed our action. We waded in and pushed the chest further into the water. One of my companions motioned to the north, and that is where we headed.

"I do not think I had planned this, as much as it merely just happened. Or perhaps God's Spirit was leading us somehow. In no more than a dozen minutes we were over by the far side of the cove, by a series of caves and deep, clear pools. The chest was barely afloat now, and one of the natives took his knife and stabbed at it, and in an instant, it sank to the bottom of the farthest pool—a depth of perhaps thirty feet.

"And without another word, we waded back, slipped ashore, and made our way back to the village. The following morning Radcliffe had his men seize me, as assurance that if followed he could use me as a pawn."

Thomas paused again and took another sip. "And the rest of the story is known to you."

William nodded. "I like better the story you tell the children—much more exciting. But I am glad that it occurred as you said. I have always been amazed at your bravery in this matter."

"'Twas not bravery, William," Thomas said, "but truly, as I think back, it was the Spirit guiding us, for he knew that the treasure would draw us back one day—back with the Scriptures and teachers for these poor people. If the gold was not here, I would say that we would not be here either."

John added, sleepiness evident in his voice, "God truly moves in most curious ways."

"Indeed he does," William said. "And now, perhaps in an even more curious manner, he is using us to further his kingdom."

And to that, Thomas added a final "Amen."

57

7 June 1650
Barbados

Hannah would not cry out. She struggled in silence, her thin arms pushing and resisting with all her strength. Her brother, Samuel, older by only a few moments, was taller, stronger, and more solid than she. Yet she possessed the iron will of her mother. Samuel had his arm wrapped tightly about her neck, and he was using his other hand to rub his knuckles back and forth over her head. The disagreement had begun innocently enough as a trivial matter of ownership of a small telescope. Hannah had been using it to scan the ocean for her father's ship as she perched in the window seat of the nursery. Samuel had caught sight of her using the instrument, a tool he considered his. Words at first gentle escalated into a full-scale struggle. She now realized that she had no chance of overpowering him, so as her last resort she opened her mouth and chomped down on his upper arm as a dog might gnaw on a pork bone from the table. Samuel, who was much less inclined to suffer in silence, let loose a bloodcurdling yowl. Hannah did not release her bite and tasted the smallest trickle of blood on her lips.

Samuel's scream brought results. The nursery door banged opened and Jezalee rushed in, her eyes wide with fright and alarm.

"Be stoppin'!" she screamed, "You be killin' the po' chile." She rushed to the combatants and attempted to separate them, pulling on one and pushing the other.

"Stop de bitin', Hannah!" she cried. "Let de girl loose, Samuel!"

Kathryne arrived at the door, her gown flowing behind her as she ran into the nursery. It took only a heartbeat for her to analyze the situation. She saw the telescope lying on the floor, her two children locked in each others arms, and Jezalee wrapped about them both.

"Children!" Kathryne bellowed in her sternest and most chilling voice. In an instant, everyone loosened their grips on each other and fell apart, panting and pushing and straightening.

"Samuel! Hannah!" Kathryne shouted. "This behavior is intolerable! Your father leaves, and you turn into savages!"

Three sets of eyes turned to her, realizing the severity of the situation. Kathryne so seldom raised her voice that her shouts this day were an indication of the gravity of what she observed.

It took her more than a dozen moments to sort out everyone's role in the altercation. As she glared in disapproval, both her children seemed to shrink in size as well, hurting over how greatly they had displeased their mother.

After their tears stopped flowing, Kathryne gathered them in her arms and began to talk to them in a calm, soothing tone. "What you have done is wrong, and I am hurt over your disobedience."

Both children nodded glumly, their eyes downcast.

"You must apologize to each other this instant," she demanded.

Hannah was the first to object. "Mama, it was Samuel who started it. All I did was use the telescope for a moment to look for Papa."

Samuel rose to his own defense in a heartbeat. "But the telescope is mine! Papa gave it to me!"

Kathryne's eyes flared, and they retreated into silence again. She took a deep breath and spoke again, calm and even. "It matters not who was wronged first. It matters that you were both wrong and must offer each other apologies."

She looked in their small faces and realized that what she asked was so foreign to their emotions. *How do I tell them of the need for forgiveness?*

She took a deep breath and then spoke. "You must forgive, for that is what God wants us to do. For he has forgiven us of so much."

They hear the words, she thought, *but do not understand.*

"You must forgive. For if one cannot forgive, then life is so hard."

They looked up at her, still not showing understanding.

I must tell them. "For if I had not forgiven your father, then none of us would be here this day."

She saw the questions in their eyes.

"Your father did many things before we married that men would view as wrong."

"But he was a sailor," Samuel whispered. "Being a sailor is not wrong."

"No, Son," Kathryne said, "but he was more than a sailor. When I first met your father, he was . . . he was not just a sailor, but a pirate."

Samuel's eyes widened. "A pirate?" he whispered, his voice edged with excitement, "with cannons and the black flag and swords?"

Kathryne merely nodded. "He did things that he is not proud of having done. But he saw the error of his ways and turned from them. He asked God to forgive him of those sins—and God forgave him. He asked me to forgive him of his past—and it took me longer to do so than it did God."

She hugged each child closer. "For if I couldn't forgive him, he would not be your father. He would not be on this island. I forgave him as God forgave him."

Hannah looked up and asked in a small voice, "Would he have gone to hell if he hadn't asked for forgiveness?"

Kathryne swallowed. *How she thinks of such things so quickly.*

"He would have," Kathryne admitted. "We need to see our sin, then ask God to forgive that. Do you understand?"

They both looked at each other for a long moment, then nodded.

"And what do you ask each other?"

And in a rush of words spoken at the same time, both children asked each other, and their mother, to forgive them of the fighting.

The three sat there, hugging for a long moment. What broke the silence was the sound of sobbing in the far corner of the room. Jezalee sat there, tears streaming down her face. She wiped her cheek with the back of her hand and looked to Kathryne.

"Miz Hawkes," she sniffed between her tears, "I best be askin' for you forgivin' me dis day. I been doin' somethin' most powerful wrong."

And in the next dozen moments Jezalee laid out the entire story of Cotton and the hidden gold and the pirates following William and the *Dorset Lady.*

She concluded her tale with a moaning, crying plea for forgiveness from both God and Kathryne, saying, "I wants to gets to heaven. I doan wants to be in dat other place."

Kathryne could say nothing, Jezalee's words chilling her heart to ice.

7 June 1650
Isla del Guajiro

The early dawning was enough to wake Will, the sunlight filling the village with its crimson glow. Will walked to the edge of the sea and threw himself into the chilling water, attempting to rouse himself to alertness. He splashed there, alone for a long time, paddling about in the water, which was still as the ice on a frozen English river in January.

By the time he made his way back to shore a dozen others had done much the same. As he waded ashore, he laughed, his eyes hurting. "If this is what it takes to get a sailor to bathe, I would have provided such direction on my voyages years before."

The sailors responded with a chorus of groans and mutters. By the true first light, the women of the village were busying themselves preparing a breakfast of fruits, fish, and bird eggs pickled red by a most tangy spice.

Will called out a series of commands, and crews began to ferry the supplies from the *Dorset Lady* to the shore, the longboats filled with the crates and barrels. When the Scriptures were unloaded, Thomas insisted, in a most shrill voice, that the boat would carry only that single crate and no more.

"I have not come all this way to have the Bibles tossed into the sea in sight of the shore!" he shouted.

The crew grumbled but did his bidding, knowing that the Word of God was a most precious cargo.

By midafternoon the villagers stood around the jumble of cargo, pawing through the open boxes, marveling at the hoes and nets and needles.

The chief came out when the last crates were being dragged through the sand. In his native tongue, he called out angrily to Thomas, "What manner of gifts do you bring without asking any from us? You insult us by doing this and refusing to allow us to offer gifts in return."

"Chief Tahonen, 'tis not true. You have treasure to pay for this," Thomas explained.

"We have fish and fruit and water. That is not treasure enough for all this," he said, stepping closer to Thomas, shaking his fist.

Thomas recognized that the chief thought that Thomas was slighting his power to provide, making light of his ability to lead and care for his people.

"Chief Tahonen, you have treasure," Thomas said again. "The treasure is hidden on the far side of this island. It is hidden in your waters. The men who were here before left much treasure, and that treasure is now yours. You will pay us with that."

"And where is this treasure? Why have I not seen it before this day?"

Thomas then struggled to tell him of the story of the sunken gold, and how two men of his village spirited the gold away and hid it deep in the waters of the far harbor. Chief Tahonen listened intently, then called for those two men to come forward. Though fearful of their chief's reaction, they both agreed with Thomas's tale.

"And why did you not talk of this treasure before?" he barked out.

"We believed the treasure belongs to God-man Thomas. It was his to return for, not ours."

"Thomas!" the chief shouted. "Is this true?"

"No, Chief Tahonen," he replied. "I never intended to keep the treasure. I was taking it for you, and until now I could not return to show you where it is and to give it to you."

The chief scowled, and the two native men shrank from his view. He turned to the crates and lifted up an open lid. Inside lay rows of gleaming machetes, well suited to building huts and clearing the jungle for planting. He poked into a second crate. A row of hoes, with handles of strong English oak, lay in neat rows. And finally, he stepped to a small box, separate from the rest, and lifted up the cover. Inside were twelve books, nestled in a cradling of wool scraps.

"That be the Word of God I spoke of," Thomas said. "That be the book that tells men how to live."

The chief stepped back as if in fear. The Word of God was a most powerful image—an image of the awesome might of the Creator captured in a single book.

"Do not be fearful, Chief Tahonen. There are men on this ship who want to live in your village and tell you of God's Word. They will tell the stories from this book. They will tell you of God and his ways."

The chief stepped to Thomas, looking him deeply in the eyes. Then he turned to Will, who stood to his right. "This story be the truth, William Hawkes? That Chief Tahonen purchase this with gold he possessed?"

Will looked to Thomas. He had been having trouble following the conversation, but he thought he had picked up enough to understand the nature of the chief's concern. Praying that he would answer with the proper words, Will responded, "Yes, Chief Tahonen, it is all true."

The chief broke into a wide smile, then laughed for a long moment. "Then I declare tonight shall be a celebration. We have knives and tools and the Word of God. We must celebrate!" he shouted, and thrust his fist into the air, then wrapped Will in a fierce embrace. "We will celebrate the goodness of this God."

The celebration of the night prior paled into insignificance by the outpouring of happiness and joy that swirled around Will, Thomas, John, and the rest of the crew. Hovie Lister and his son, Urias, each holding a copy of the Scriptures, read from them aloud. True, not one man on this island could understand the English being read, yet they all knew it was God speaking to them. A crowd of thirty or perhaps forty natives gathered around each man as they read, their heads nodding at the sound of the words, smiles marking their faces.

Will watched them, knowing that in time the words would be translated or understood. But for now the simple power of the Bible was enough to warm his heart and to calm his doubts over the wisdom of this voyage.

They have the Word of the Lord now, he thought, *and the Word will move them in most powerful and mysterious ways. I am privileged to be part of this moving of God's Spirit.*

Food and drink flowed in abundance, even greater than at a nobleman's table on Barbados. Casks of the potent native drink were tapped, and while Will frowned upon such activity, he knew there would be a proper time to address it, time enough to suggest changes in the manner that the villagers behaved.

It is one step at a time, he thought. *As the saying goes, the walls of Rome were not constructed in a single day. This too will take its time.*

When the moon lit the harbor, many of the natives had eaten and drunk themselves to sleep. Will had eaten more than he drank, for he knew that a full day of labor lay ahead, if the gold was to be recovered. The moon bode well, for a low tide was in the offing, and if so, they would need to traverse the island at the dawning.

Will would have preferred to be able to sail into the harbor, and would have done so had the one on the island been safe. But the currents of the waters here continually silted the harbor mouth closed, and the strong westerly winds made an anchorage on the side of the island where the treasure was buried most unsafe.

William gathered John and his half-dozen most able men and laid out his scheme. They would carry block and tackle from the ship, with ropes and hatchets as well. Felling trees at the water's edge, they would construct a pulley and crane and send native divers to attach the ropes to the chest. Then using a simple winch, the gold could be raised from the seabed and the bars brought back overland to Will's waiting ship.

Will did not share the next part of the plan with anyone yet. He would take the gold back to Barbados and invest it. The proceeds he would employ to continue sending these people supplies, more teachers, and books. In this manner, they would have no reason to risk the gold to thievery, yet could enjoy all the benefits of its worth. Will knew that he had no need for the money, nor did he truly need reimbursement for the supplies already purchased and delivered. It was a comfort to know that his treasures could be so wisely used to further God's kingdom on such a remote and forgotten place as Isla del Guajiro.

■■■■

Aboard the *Sea Demon,* Forge Bliss was happy and drunk. His crewmen in longboats had cruised past the harbor of Guajiro in the darkness and saw the torchlights and heard the laughter and song of the celebration. This they reported back to him near midnight.

The pirate captain sat in his stuffy cabin, Cotton only an arm's length away, as he heard the news. "Cotton," he said as his men left, "what side of the island ye be sayin' the gold is buried upon?"

Both nervous and sick at heart, Cotton mumbled an answer. Bliss reached over and slapped his face with a swift backhand.

"Speak up, ye stupid darkie!" he cursed.

Cotton tried to stand in the cramped cabin, only to be pulled back to the bench by Bliss. He pushed his face close to Cotton's so his whiskers roughed against the black skin. "You best be tellin' Bliss the truth. Or I be slittin' your throat."

"I-I only knows what I be t-told. De vicar man, he be sayin' he at d-de pirate place when he be buryin' da gold." His words came in a frightened stutter.

Bliss pushed him back to the curved hull with a bang. "And that be the westerly harbor, which be closed by sand from what the longboats saw. Meaning that Hawkes be workin' overland."

Cotton sat in a heap, a blackening frown on his face. He sullenly nodded.

"Have I offended you?" Bliss oozed. "Be yer feelin's hurt?"

Cotton glared up at him.

With an astonishingly quick move, Bliss slipped his polished and razor-sharp dagger from his breast ribbon, grabbed Cotton, and spun him around, holding his back to his chest. With a single, fluid slash he drew his dagger across the man's throat, cutting nearly to the bone of the neck. Bliss kicked at the cabin window and pushed the still flailing body to the waiting sea below. He smiled as he heard the splash.

Bliss dusted himself off, looked about the cabin, smug that not a single drop of blood had marked the small room. "Be one less man to share the gold with," he growled into the dark silence.

He looked out the window and saw nothing. The currents ran deep here, and a man could be drawn under in a whisper. "And good-bye to ye, ol' Cotton. I thank ye a hundred times for everythin'."

He pulled the window shut and, taking out a bottle of fresh brandy, uncorked it, took a long swallow, then sat back down with a smile to await the dawn.

58

8 June 1650
Barbados

Kathryne slept little that night, tossing and turning as all sorts of vivid and terrible visions plagued her rest. She arose well before dawn, wrapped a thick robe about her, and stood in the star-drenched darkness. She looked up into the heavens, holding her tears back. There was no proof that any pirate followed William, she told herself. And William was a most cautious sailor and would be alert to such matters. There was no English navy to send and offer protection; there were no armed ships ready to sail off on the strength of a poor black woman's hysterical tale.

But Kathryne was troubled to the very core of her soul. She would tell no one else of this, for it would only cause heartache and uncontrolled worry in others. She would bear it alone for now.

But not truly alone, for as she stood, she began to pray, bathing William, Thomas, John, and every man on his vessel with heartfelt and urgent prayers of protection and guidance and wisdom. With every ounce of her being, Kathryne cried out to God to bring the man she loved, the father of her children, home safely.

Her prayers continued, unabated, until dawn broke over the island and she at last lowered her head and said, "Amen." Her heart was still troubled, yet she knew God had every man and every mile at sea in his great hands. And she knew that it would be sufficient.

Isla del Guajiro

Will rose early and began to gather the needed supplies. By the time he had assembled the rope, shovels, block and tackle, and other tools on the beach, his selected crewmen had begun to stumble together in the cool morning air. Within less than a half hour, they made themselves ready. Two dozen native men stood ready to join them, in the event the gold proved hard to retrieve.

Will looked up, surprised. Chief Tahonen was making his unsteady way to the beach. Will bowed and greeted him warmly. The chief returned the greeting, only when he bowed, he stumbled forward and pitched headfirst into the sand. He rolled over laughing and slapping at his most ample belly.

"Go with God, Will Hawkes," he said as he raised his hand in a manner of blessing.

"Thank you," Will replied. "We will return in two days."

"Two days?" the chief asked, surprised.

"It will take much effort to lift the gold from the sea. It will take two days."

The chief nodded and smiled. "Then in two days we prepare a great feast. In two days, we will celebrate."

Will tried not to groan. He knew that neither his stomach nor his head would be ready so soon for another bout of eating and drinking. And with a final wave, Will called out for his men to follow their native guides, and in only a single moment the green of the jungle swallowed them all from view.

▪ ▪ ▪ ▪

By the time they reached the cove on the other side, it was a few hours past noon.

The journey took fewer hours than Will had remembered, for the villagers had kept the path clear of vines and undergrowth. They had made it a regular route to the fishing pools on the other side of the island.

The men hurried to the small cove, nestled by the sea caves to the north of the harbor. Will was first in line to peer into the crystal blue waters—waters so clear that it looked as if there was no water in the cove at all, just shimmering air. He cupped his hands to his face and looked down. In the very deepest part of the pool was a square, dark object. It could only be the pirates' lost treasure. He stripped to his undergarments, much to the giggling and pointing of the natives, who dressed in simple wraps about the waist. Taking a deep breath, Will dove in, hands breaking the water in a most graceful arc. He stroked deeper and deeper and managed to get a hand on one end of the chest and gave it a pull. He was most amazed to feel the chest move under his one single attempt. Letting go, he dove back for the surface. By this time, every native had stripped bare, and each was carrying a coil of rope in his hands.

"Will," Thomas called, "they say that pulleys on trees won't be needed. They'll just tie the chest to ropes and it can be lifted out."

Sputtering from the water, Will answered, "I was expecting it to be much more hidden, according to your stories. I thought we might have to move a boulder or two to unearth it. You never mentioned it would be sitting in plain view such as it is."

Thomas shrugged and laughed.

John called out, "I hope Thomas be telling the truth that there be gold in the chest, and it not be filled with seashells or the like." For a single moment, Thomas's heart jumped. He had never looked into that chest. He had assumed that this chest, among the others with gold and jewels, would contain a valuable treasure as well.

By that time the natives had entered the water, and the ropes coiled out behind them as they swam further and further down. In a dozen moments, six thick ropes were tied about the sea chest and its handles. All gathered to pull it to the surface. Within a matter of minutes the barnacle-encrusted chest was resting in the sands of the shallow water.

Will waded over to the chest, followed by several men, and a dozen hands lifted it to the shore.

John knelt to the chest with a small ax in his hands. He drew back and swung at the lock. He struck it once, then twice, and on the third attempt the rusted metal shattered and he undid it from the metal clasp. He hesitated only a moment before swinging the lid open.

Under the gaze of everyone's eyes, there sat more than a dozen gold bars in the salty water, each glistening, pure and clean, under the noontime tropical sun.

John could only utter a low, long whistle. "Be you relieved, Thomas," he said, looking to his friend, "that there be gold here and not rocks?"

■ ▢ ■ ▢ ■

Captain Bliss staggered to the *Sea Demon*'s quarterdeck and shouted out to raise anchors. If the crewmen wondered where the tall black man was, they carefully avoided asking and went about their tasks in silent order. The sails were unfurled, and the ships began to slip to the east, around the far shore.

"Prime the cannons!" he shouted as he stood by the helm.

Men began to winch the heavy cannon into their gun ports, packing in powder and fuse. Some were loaded with cannonballs, round and deadly. Others were packed with great lengths of chain. The latter weapons carried a much shorter range, but were most efficient at slicing through the assembled flesh of men.

By the time the sun neared its zenith, Bliss and his three ships were just to the east of the village and the harbor. Bliss pulled out his telescope and focused in on the *Dorset Lady* lying at peace in the calm waters, holding gently to her anchor chain. He scanned the village and saw only a half-dozen Englishmen and perhaps a hundred black villagers.

"He be gone to get the gold," Bliss called, enjoying the sound of his voice, laughing that his plans had found purchase. Bliss knew that Hawkes would need go overland to the cove to recover the gold and that he was still there. If he had returned, more sailors would have been evident and there would have been a celebration.

"Now we go in nice and quiet," Bliss called out. "We kill no more than need be. And then we sit and wait for Hawkes to bring us our gold."

As Bliss sailed into the harbor that afternoon, most of the natives ran to the shore, thinking the ships may have been part of William's convoy. As the *Sea Demon* came to the shallower waters, she turned and faced the shore to broadside, the wind slowing her progress.

Bliss danced to the quarterdeck, feeling more gay than he had in years, and shouted, "To your cannons, men, one good broadside into the rabble."

The cannons roared, and the metal and chain sliced through flesh like a giant scythe. As the smoke cleared from the first volley, more than two dozen people lay dead or dying on the white sand of the shore. Pickets on the masts took aim at Will's men, and within a few minutes killed another dozen with their musket shot. As the shots rang out, the rest of Bliss's crew took to longboats and seized control of the entire village. Only a few of Will's crew carried weapons; the majority still rested on board the *Dorset Lady*. Those who attempted to offer further resistance were quickly and cruelly dispatched to meet their Maker.

The crewmen who remained were roughly placed in leg irons and chains and secured to trees and logs. Bliss himself left the ship and wandered through the village, pawing through the supplies that Will had brought, looking about for other valuables. He came upon Chief Tahonen, now bound with ropes to a large ceremonial pole. Bliss said not a word, but as if with a simple passing fancy, lashed out with the back of his hand, and struck the chief across the chin. Tahonen's head lolled on his shoulder from the power of the blow.

Bliss looked into a darkened hut, guarded by a leering soldier, grinning through yellowed and gapped teeth.

"They be his wives?" Bliss asked.

"Don' know, sir, but they be makin' a fancy squalor when we be ropin' the fat man to the pole."

Bliss bent down and stared at their faces with a blazing combination of lust and hate. He went to his knees and grabbed at the closest woman's arms and pulled her closer to him. He placed his fingers, greasy and black with dirt, on her cheek and traced slowly down her neck.

"Such sweet and tasty meat on this island," Bliss said as he rose. "They slept well last night, but tonight—" Bliss spun about and shouted loudly. "No man touches any man or woman on this island unless I say it be so. No man! And if he does, I will have his head on a pike before the dawn." He spun about again. "Have you all heard!" he screamed. "Your head on a pike!"

A weak chorus of "Aye, sir" and "We be hearin' fine, sir" rippled across the village.

Bliss looked back at the cowering women in the hut, then glanced over at several of the native men, chained in rows. He smiled, long and slow and evil. "I be wantin' to have first pick among the choicest," he whispered to himself. "And I'll have no man walk the path before me."

After raising the treasure and pulling and tugging the rotted chest to the edge of the path, the assembly of men collapsed under its weight. John called out for a midday meal, and several of the natives walked into the shallow waters and speared a dozen fish for their lunch as Will began a fire.

It was an hour or more past noon when they began to cut down small trees. Each length of tree would be held on the shoulders of two men, and the sling between them would be filled with two bars of gold. By the time the chest was empty, every two men, save Will due to his leg and cane, carried a pole and two gold bars between them.

"This be a true king's treasure," John said. "The gold we carry will be sufficient for Chief Tahonen to purchase proper English ale, rather than that nasty drink we have been plied with."

Will laughed in agreement. "I would prefer they do without drink completely," he said, "but if drink is needed, then ale would be my choice as well."

They entered the jungle in a long, snaking line, following the same path that led them to the cove, back up the steep ridge, along the flat interior of the island, skirting some dense, snagging thickets of brambles, and by the time the light began to fail, they reached the far ridge, just above the village.

As they stepped quietly along the well-worn path, the sound of booming cannon echoed through the thick foliage, almost setting the leaves to tremble, such was its power. Will's heart jumped as the sound reached his ears. Following the cannon fire, the crack and whine of muskets could be discerned.

Will motioned for quiet and commanded all but himself and John to stay where they stood, just removed into the dark jungle off the side of the path.

Hearts pounding in apprehension, the two raced down the path. A point no more than a mile from the village opened up onto a vista that took in the entire harbor.

Will crouched, keeping well hidden, and peered out. "Three ships, John," he said coldly. "We have been followed."

John looked up and stared. "I have seen that galleon before," he whispered. "She's run by a one-eyed pirate out of the port of Tortuga. By the name of Blass . . . no, he be named Bliss. Captain Bliss."

They remained silent for a while longer, trying to catch a glimpse of what was transpiring below them. No more cannons fired, nor were there the sounds of musket volley.

"This Bliss," Will asked, "is he an honorable pirate, such as one can be?"

John laughed in derision. "The man be a cutthroat of the first order, from the tales I hear told. A vicious, cold killer. We stand no chance to offer him negotiations. In truth, I have heard his name mentioned on more than one occasion as having taken part in our slaves' rebellion— either by stirring the ferment or by supplying arms."

Will turned about and looked back to his small gathering of men, waiting hidden on the path. He had one musket, his small cutlass, and a handful of daggers and small knives. With three ships, Bliss had more than a hundred armed men, plus cannon.

"John, we must go back. I do not want them to know we are here," Will whispered.

"Do you have a plan?" John asked. "For on the surface, our situation appears most desperate."

Will wanted to offer John comfort and say that he had devised some manner of attack in his mind, but he could not. The odds this time were too greatly placed on the other side of the table, and William felt a coldness creeping into his heart.

John and Will returned to the hidden men, their faces filled with worry and fear. Will quickly told them what appeared to have happened. The natives, upon understanding the plight of their family and friends, to a man rose to rush to the village and defend their people. Will's men forcibly restrained them from doing so.

"You'll be slaughtered as soon as you leave the jungle," Will hissed at them. "And that will help no one."

His face white from shock, Thomas sputtered, "What do they want? Why have they come?"

The last rays of the sun were filtering through the leaves, and the birds and insects began their nightly serenade, filling the growing darkness with their odd calls and chirps. Will looked to Thomas, then John, and then scanned the faces of the men who gathered about him.

In the past, as he gathered on ship deck or forest or jungle, his heart beat strong and sure, and as if catching inspiration from the winds, he would offer out plans and schemes of great boldness and daring. But this eve was different. His heart beat not boldly, but troubled. Each face he saw that dusk looked to him for guidance and leadership—and Will felt at this instant to be devoid of such skills. He brushed at his doublet, stained with sweat, pulled at the sleeves, dusted off the lapels and collar, and looked back into their faces. The same plea was there again; they wanted so desperately for Will to be their savior, to offer them hope and a way out.

Will closed his eyes for a moment and let the song of the jungle fill his ears. *Dear God,* he prayed, *I beg for thy guidance.*

"They want the gold, Thomas," he finally said. "Someone told someone else, who told these men of our plans. And now they intend on taking the gold as their own."

John, resting on his knees, looked up. "Can we not give them the gold? I know it would be a loss for you, Will, but I could offer to make up any shortfall in funds."

Thomas nodded in agreement. "That's it, Will. We give them this gold, and they simply sail away. It is only treasure."

William stood, the muscles in his legs cramping and tight. *Another sign of age,* he thought as he kneaded his crippled calf muscles.

"No, John, that would serve no purpose. They would gladly receive the gold as our gift—and then slaughter every last one of us. You yourself said Bliss was a bloodthirsty man."

"But why would they do such horrible things when all they seek is gold?" Thomas asked.

"Because I am captain of Fort Charles. They know I will hunt them down if able. And why risk such a pursuit? Easier to kill me and all who witness their acts."

John nodded reluctantly. "'Tis true what Will says. If I were Bliss, that is what course I would follow. He has already killed more than he can count. Of what more consequence to his soul would be the lives of another hundred men?"

"And no doubt he would take the women for his pleasure," Will added.

"Then what shall we do?" Thomas asked. "There must be a plan."

Will looked about. "I have thirty men and one musket against one hundred men with cannons and swords and muskets and pistols. What chance of success do we have?"

Silence descended on the small band, no one willing to speak, no one knowing what course of action to suggest.

Will assessed that they were locked in a narrow pen with no means of escape. Yet after long moments of silence, he gently said, "Perhaps, Thomas, there is something you can do. Perhaps you can pray for us."

Thomas bent to his knees, as did every other man. He bowed his head and searched his heart for the right words.

If I had not suggested such a trip, he thought before beginning, *then we would face none of this danger. The blood of innocent people is on my hands.*

"Dearest almighty God," he began, "we are thy servants and seek to do thy will. We are lost this day and seek to find thy guidance through this darkness. We beseech thee, O Lord. . . ."

And he prayed on for perhaps a quarter of an hour, then gradually drew his thoughts to a close. "And so, Lord, we ask thee for help. We are adrift on deep waters. We seek to float to the safety of thy arms. Carry us over the shoals and dangers. We beseech, thee, O God Almighty, Creator of heaven and earth—"

Will lifted his head with a start and shouted, "That's it!"

Thomas mumbled a few more words, then opened his eyes as well, looking most surprised at Will's sudden and most uncivil interruption of a devout prayer.

"Thomas! Your prayer!" Will said, excited. "Your prayer gave me the answer. It is a most precarious, thin plotting, but if God favors us, it may succeed!"

Thomas opened his mouth, then closed it, for he knew not of what Will was speaking.

"As you prayed, Thomas, I was praying as well. I sought a plan to extricate ourselves from this most precarious place. And you have provided me that escape."

"And what then, pray tell, is this means of escape?" John insisted.

Will turned to John and placed his hand on his shoulder. "What is the easiest spot on a ship's hull to breach?" he asked.

"With shot or tool?" John asked.

"With tool."

"Two places that I have seen most quickly rot and need replaced are by the drain cocks and by the rudder. More rubbin' perhaps causes the wood to be thinner there."

"And which lays deeper below the water?"

"The drain cock, for certain."

"Could a man take an auger into that wood, and cause a leak to start?

John nodded. "That would be a simple matter. It be easy on a well-cared-for vessel—easier still on a rottin' tub like Bliss's galleon."

Will turned to one of the natives and spoke in their tongue. "The shallow reefs to the south of the harbor, do they remain?"

The villager nodded.

"How deep, when the sea is low, do they lie beneath the surface?"

The native turned to several of his men and began to discuss the question. The area was prime fishing waters, so they knew it well. After a moment, the native stood and held his hand to his neck. "The sea be to this deep. Water here," he said moving his hand, "and rocks here," he said, lifting his foot.

"That be five feet," Will said, excited. "John, how much water does the *Dorset Lady* draw with full ballast?"

John thought for a moment. "Perhaps ten feet?"

"And with no ballast?"

"Well, she'd be tippin' over in the slightest breeze with no ballast," John replied.

"But how many feet would she draw?"

John tightened his face into a scowl, then replied, "Five feet, I would reckon."

"And the pinnaces in the harbor, how deep do they draw?"

"I would guess five feet as well—with ballast," John replied.

Will nodded. "That would be my guess as well. How much water could be let into a ship's hull, over the course of two hours, in a breach the size of an auger bit?"

"That question be beyond my expertise, Will," John replied.

"John, this be concerning our lives. I need you to make the best estimation you are able to draw," Will insisted.

John narrowed his face in thought. After a long moment, he replied, "Perhaps three feet, maybe five, if the hull be narrow."

"And that answer be as I had hoped."

Thomas listened to the questions, his head going back and forth between Will and John, and still could not discern any plan being drawn or formed. "William, tell me what you intend, please," he finally asked.

Will sat on the soft grass and moss and massaged his bad leg, the cramps becoming more and more pronounced as the hours wore on.

"Bliss will not leave this island without the gold. And whether he gets it or not, I believe every man and woman in the village is doomed by his hand. We have no weapons nor men to do battle. That much is most clear to us all. So this is what your prayer inspired me to do."

Thomas and John leaned in closer.

"Listen carefully, for we have only a few hours between full sunset and moonrise. And remember—we will not have a second chance to succeed."

■ ■ ■ ■

While the brigands on the *Sea Demon* under command of Captain Bliss drank and ate that night, waiting for Will's return on the following day, Will and his small band of men were silently padding through the jungle, reaching the far side of the harbor as darkness fell across the island. The men were hot, sweaty, thirsty, and tired, but knew that no rest was in the offing. Each man carried a single gold bar in his hands, and Will was the first into the water, slipping in quickly and quietly. His goal, the *Dorset Lady,* was a long swim from where he stood, but to enter the water closer to the village would risk discovery. Four men were unable to swim and remained at the edge of the jungle, Thomas among them.

"I will pray for you all," Thomas whispered as they stepped into the moonless night.

"And that be the best plan of all," Will whispered back.

As a clock would have ticked off a full half hour, Will paddled his way to the anchor line of his vessel. He handed his gold bar to the sailor behind him and pulled his way to the deck, hand over hand. He landed on the deck with a wet thump, and quickly scanned the vessel for signs of a posted guard. It was most like pirates to leave such matters ignored, and Bliss was no exception.

Will slowly and quietly lowered a rope-and-wood ladder over the far side of the ship, and within minutes, every man was aboard.

"Stack the gold in the rope box on the foredeck. I want to quickly have access to it."

John scurried belowdeck, making his way by feel, for no candle or torch could be lit. He found the carpenter's tools and thanked God that he had insisted a full complement of augers and borers be brought on this voyage. There were four such tools, and he returned to the deck, cradling them in his arms. Will was fashioning piping, each the length and thickness of a man's arm, from bamboo poles.

Two men carrying augers descended the rope ladder and slipped back into the sea. Two more followed carrying the lengths of bamboo piping. The two borers were split between the two smaller pinnaces, and two men swam to each vessel.

Will had instructed each team carefully. "Drill next to the drain cock if you can. No doubt, you'll need make several dives to cut through. If you have opportunity, drill a second by the rudder. After the hull is breached, slip this piping through the hole and let it extend as far below the hole, deeper into the water, as is possible. With the piping in place, you will need wait at the ship's hull until you see the first hint of moonrise. Then plug the breach and return at once. Is that understood?"

"Why the piping, Cap'n Will?" asked another. "Would not a hole and plug work the same?"

"If I knew the exact depth of the shoals I would say as much. But what happens if our calculations prove short by a foot or more? With these pipes, perhaps if the clearance is that close, they will strike the reef and reopen the breach again. But if we sink them further now, I am sure they would notice at once and foil our plan."

The sailors nodded at the cleverness of Will's mind.

"Why not just sink the vessels, Captain Hawkes?" one sailor asked. "Wouldn't such action cripple them?"

Will nodded, but replied, "If Bliss awoke to see his vessels at the bottom of the harbor and us sailing off into the dawn, what do you think he would do to the village?"

After a moment of thought, the sailor nodded, agreeing that all would face the sword.

"We want them low in the water—not sunk," Will stated. "Mark their waterlines as they are. If they reach five feet before the moonrise, return to the *Dorset Lady* at once."

■ ■ □ □ ■

With his feet resting in the sand at the edge of a crackling fire, Bliss was a most happy man. He had consumed a great amount of roasted fowl and had drunk tankards of the natives' drink without wincing or gasping. He patted his stomach and looked over at the chief, still roped to the pole, no more than a dozen steps away.

Bliss smiled again and called out to him, knowing that he understood no words in the English tongue.

"Fat man," he shouted, his words slurred and twisted, "would you like to watch as I take your women in turn? My heart will be gladdened to have your royalty as my audience. And whence I be done with your wenches, I'll be havin' my way with the others as well. And all my dancin' be done before you, you fat, dumb lout."

He laughed and raised his glass and took another long swallow of his drink. He heard a splash, but was too drunk with drink and victory to care from where it came.

As Will's crew made their way to Bliss's ships, Will and the remaining men—a full dozen—had even a more difficult and essential task. In complete darkness they felt their way to the bottommost deck of their ship, opened the great hatches there, and jumped into the fetid, fouled waters of the ballast hold. They bent down into this evil-smelling stew and retrieved, one by one, the great ballast rocks that lay there. Will knew that his vessel rode too low in the water to clear the shoals to the south, and his only chance was to lighten the ballast she carried. They formed a human chain—two men in the ballast hold handed rocks as fast as they could be retrieved, and passed them to the next man, who passed them to the next. The rocks snaked their way to the orlop deck, where the first open porthole was located. Will and another man carefully lowered each rock in rope slings to the harbor below so no splash could be heard.

As the darkness thickened and Will was lowering what he gauged to be the two hundredth rock into the waiting sea, his muscles, trembling and tired, slipped just an instant, and the rock tumbled into the water with a great resounding splash. Everyone held their breath, fearful for hearing a cry of alarm sound from the shore. After a long moment and hearing no alarm, the work resumed.

By moonrise, the crewmen returned from sabotaging Bliss's ships and quickly joined the chain of men removing the ballast rocks. A second and third hour passed, then a low call rang out from outside the hull. "Captain Will!" came the urgent whispered call. "We be up a full five feet. And she look most wobbly indeed."

Will passed the word that all could stand down. To the men in the murky ballast water, no more welcome order had ever been given.

As Will made his way back to the quarterdeck, he could feel the danger. The vessel normally rode sure and level in the sea, but even at anchor in a calm harbor, the slightest wave brought a longer tilt, a more pronounced canting of the decks. He knew that in order to keep her from capsizing, he would need keep the wind square at her stern. Any tack from that direction would tip her sails into the surf, and all would be lost.

Will knew that it would take all the skills he possessed to complete his plan—and possibly even more than he possessed. He paused for a long moment to thank God for allowing them to have accomplished as much as they had thus far and to pray for continued protection. As he knelt, every sailor under his flag, as well as most of the natives, gathered about him and silently offered their petitions to the Almighty.

CHAPTER

59

9 June 1650

Until the first hints of dawn, Will and his men gathered in the lee of the small quarterdeck, well out of sight from anyone on shore. Before slipping into the darkness there, Will peered at the three ships that rode at anchor next to him. At first glance, no hint of difficulty was apparent. The ships would sail as usual, the rudders would perform, the sails would fill with wind. But if one looked long enough, one would detect that the water was much too close to the bottommost ports and hatches. Will was praying that Bliss and his men would not notice, and he was certain that even if they did, they would have no time to pump the bilges clean of the extra water.

Dawn comes slowly to a man who anxiously waits, Will decided. He spent much of the time kneading the muscles in his leg. He had walked too far, and had swam too long, and had worked too furiously. But his greatest challenge lay ahead, and he would force himself to ignore the pain.

The harbor was filling with a thin, red light of a violet. The winds began to freshen and slip in from the east. With God's help, Will could hold her sails at quarter turn, push the helm to starboard hard, and keep the vessel from tipping.

Only with good fortune, he thought, *and a greater measure of God's provision than I have ever required in the past.*

He awakened each man, shaking his shoulder and whispering that it was time. Each man knew his assignment. One man carried a huge ax to sever the anchor roping, for there would be no time to haul it up. Four men would run the rigging on the mainsail and unfurl as much canvas as they could on Will's order. Three men would be set to the jib sail. Once unfurled, they would head to the foresail. John and the natives were assigned the most dangerous task. Using long poles, they would reach from the main deck and push against the harbor bottom, turning the *Dorset Lady* into the wind. They would be silhouetted against the morning sun and would make a most inviting target for any man with a musket.

Before sending everyone scuttling to positions, Will offered one last prayer. "Dear God," he began, "I ask for thy protection on my men. I know our future is in thy hands, and I seek to do thy will. If it be thy will to take us home this day, we each ask that thou wilt provide special comforts to the families who wait for our return. Give their hearts peace and assure them of our love for them—as well as for thee. Let us do what must be done, and guard our hearts from anger."

He looked up for a moment and saw the tears streaming down the cheeks of several sailors. He knew that he would wait a moment before ending the prayer so as to prevent them from embarrassment. "In your most holy and glorious name, we ask these things. Amen."

And with that, he took a deep breath and stepped with a holy boldness into the thin morning light.

"Captain Bliss!" Will shouted. "I need to speak to the plundering sea dog who calls himself Captain Bliss!"

Will knew that most of Bliss's men would still be drunk and groggy. His shouts were met at first with only silence and the caw of gulls.

"I need to see the ugly, scarred face of the one-eyed Captain Bliss! I have something he might be wanting!"

As he finished screaming, several men stumbled from under foul blankets and out of huts into the dawn and onto the sand.

"Which be Captain Bliss? Which be ugly enough to call that name his?"

Will tried to taunt as best he could, for he knew an angry man often thought less clearly. There were now more than a dozen men at the edge of the surf, staring out at what they thought was an empty ship. Will looked about. Everyone was ready to scramble at his order.

"Bliss! You son of evil! You foul, dog-eating heathen! Show your face!"

In a moment, Bliss appeared, stumbling and running as he belted his breeches and pulled on his doublet. His eye patch was gone, revealing a deep, jagged gouge where an eye should have been. Even from where Will stood, the scar looking ominous and menacing.

"Bliss!" Will shouted. "We have something you might be wanting."

Will bent to the rope box and lifted two gold bars above his head. "This is the gold of Isla del Guajiro. We have it—and you do not!"

Will almost recoiled from the power of Bliss's hideous howl. He had never heard such evil before—save the last words of Radcliffe Spenser. *This man be cut of the same cloth as Radcliffe. I can hear the malevolence in his voice,* Will thought.

He waited a full dozen heartbeats while no one moved. Then he dropped the bars and shouted, "Now! Now! Now!" and ran to the helm.

John and the natives began to pole furiously. Men scrambled up the rigging, and the sails began to catch the morning breeze. With one stroke the ax severed the anchor rope.

And the *Dorset Lady* was underway.

"God, grant us fair winds," Will prayed aloud.

A rattling of weapon fire popped from the beach as the pirates retrieved muskets and pistols. The first volley splintered all about the deck, and two villagers fell, sprawling to the wooden planking. One clutched at an angry redness on his thigh, the other lay still, blood spreading like a blanket beneath him.

"Poles, stand down!" Will shouted.

He prayed he had the space to make the turn. A musket shot splattered into the helm where Will stood, and he ducked. A second and third shot caught the deck beside him and the rail to his side. He crouched low, knowing they were firing at him. A handful of pirates were sprinting down the beach, keeping abreast with the *Dorset Lady*, standing and firing their muskets into her. Another native fell, and a sailor plummeted from the yardarm with a heart-stopping *thump*.

But Will caught the wind, and while the *Dorset Lady* leaned and canted at a most rakish angle, she held upright. Will pulled the helm back to port, and she began to right herself and pick up speed.

"Unfurl the foresail! We need all the wind we can carry!" Will shouted.

Will looked back and saw Bliss's men rise to the bait. In droves they splashed into the water and swam to their ships, clamoring up anchor lines and ropes and ladders. It would be no more than a half hour until even the slowest of the pirate ships would catch them broadside.

I pray that the time will allow us to enter the shallows, Will thought.

The *Dorset Lady* cleared the breakwaters as Bliss's three ships lowered their sails and caught their first winds. Will needed a graceful hand to turn the ship and made a wide looping arc to put the wind at her stern. The winds were strong and consistent that morning, and Will moved further and faster along the coast.

"How far to the shoals?" he called out to one of the native men.

The man looked about, and it was obvious that from this vantage point he was not certain of his location. He was used to seeing the waters from a low, dugout canoe, not from the deck of a ship some two dozen feet in the air. He shrugged once and then pointed to the starboard and shrugged again.

"Well, your guess be better than mine," Will shouted and turned to place the ship at close reach with the wind.

His crew had pulled the muskets from the armory chest and were kneeling at the stern, waiting for the distance to narrow. As the leagues passed by, the pirate ships, though heavy in the water, gained on the slower *Dorset Lady*.

"Captain Will!" a sailor shouted. "Where are the shallows? They'll be on us in less than a league."

Will did not reply. John was at the bow, searching frantically for the telltale colors of thinner, shallower water. In the shallows, colors lightened and glistened more, and as of this moment, John saw only the dark foreboding colors of a deep sea beneath them.

"Captain Will," another shouted, "we have but a moment to find 'em! They be priming their cannons!"

Will tacked ever so briefly to the starboard toward the shore. No one had said he should, no colors were seen, no shoals sighted. It was but a feeling that came to him, much like the feeling of old, as he navigated and sailed the Atlantic. He could offer no rationale for his actions, save that it was what he knew he must do.

The ship caught the wind more solidly than Will wanted, and his ship began to slow and tip to the side. Sailors accustomed to unstable decks knew that this was not the simple riding of a swell. They grabbed onto rails or rigging and held on as she canted further and further.

"Stand back!" Will shouted at the vessel as he wrestled the helm. "Stand back upright!"

The muscles in his arms trembled as he pulled at the helm tighter and harder. Another degree of incline was noted, then another, and another. He had to pull it back, for she was near to catching a sail in the surf. If that happened, they all would be dead within the day.

The *Dorset Lady* slipped down into a small trough, and the helm caught a swirl of fast water and pulled her back, a degree at first, then another and another, until she stood nearly upright, with the wind still at her stern.

Yet as she struggled, the smaller of Bliss's pinnaces drew nearer and nearer. She carried four small fourteen-pound cannons. Not as lethal as some, but full of sting nonetheless. She turned to Will's stern and fired her port cannons. Both shots flew high, tearing into Will's canvas with a flapping, empty, deadly hiss.

It was a sound that Will hated and had hoped never to have heard again. Bliss's pinnace spun again, and her starboard cannons fired. One met only canvas; the other was more deadly. It crashed into the corner of the rear deck in a howling splintery roar, sending shards of wood and hot metal in a deadly storm. Four of the sailors to the rear fell, and Will felt a shard of something catch his shoulder and spin him about. He clutched hard at the helm and stopped his fall.

"Blast it!" Will screamed. "Where are those shallows?"

In front of them, no more than an eighth of a league distant, was the sight of faster, chopping surf marked with a lighter shade of blue.

"We be headed for the midst of it!" John screamed. "Keep her steady as she goes!"

Will closed his eyes one more time and prayed that in their greed Bliss's men would not cease in their close chase or slow down. They needed to hold a full sail in their canvas to push their hulls hard into the rocks and yield the greatest damage.

The second pinnace was closing in to broadside Will's port hull. He could see them at their cannon stations; he could see the burning rope held close to the weapons' flashpans. He knew that their shots would be deadly, tearing into flesh and deck at near point-blank range.

"Where are the shallows?" Will pleaded. "We have only a heartbeat remaining."

As the cannon master on the pinnace gave the order to fire, the ship took a small swell with a jump, and he hesitated. Then as he lowered the burning rope to the flashpan, the pinnace rammed full speed into a reef waiting only seven feet below the surface. The cannon fired as the ship began to spin about in a wooden, crackling crash. The shot tore into the water no more than a dozen yards from where it had been fired, and the splash cascaded back over the ship. The pinnace spun about again, and the hull, now torn nearly in two, split open, spilling everyone into the sea.

Off to the starboard side, the second pinnace nosed down into the surf, and its stern rose. Spinning about on its bow, the ship began to list, and then the canvas caught a heavy wave, and the ship began to capsize.

The third ship, Bliss's own *Sea Demon,* did not hesitate, but kept the chase, speeding past the floundering, drowning men in his other two vessels.

"I'll not be denied my gold!" Bliss shouted into the wind. "I want my gold!"

Will jogged and tacked with small, gentle tugs on the helm, looking for the slightest shallow. He held his breath as a horrible ripping squeal shrieked from belowdecks as his own hull jarred at the edge of a shoal.

"If the waters be this shallow, then why is not the pirate torn asunder?" Will shouted. Bliss was tacking furiously, desperate to avoid the rock.

And finally it happened.

Will's vessel cleared a last underwater ridge, scraping bottom, rattling the rudder. As the *Sea Demon* closed in, she met that same ridge full force, with all her sails unfurled. The bow beam caught the reef first and shattered in two, ripping away a section of hull bigger than a team of horses. The vessel then spun, the port side of the hull battered again. Cracks and fissures spidered their way from bow to stern. The drain cock, already loose, popped open with a gush. The rudder pulleys snapped in the tension. The eight cannon at the starboard rail snapped from their moorings and tumbled, snout over breech, to the opposite deck, pulling some men to their watery graves, crushing others in an instant.

Bliss held on to the helm, still screaming for his gold as it sailed away, unscathed, on the *Dorset Lady*. He held on as what was left of the *Sea Demon* turned and presented its hull, like the belly of a cowering beast.

His last curses and screams were muffled as the ship rolled and splintered against the reef, his body caught between the bottom yardarm and the helm in a crushing, deadly embrace.

Will called out for the sails to be furled and the men to stand down and ready to rescue what survivors they might find. He then ordered the drain cock opened to let the bottom deck fill with blessed, heavy seawater.

As he made that first slow turn in the shallow waters, Will knelt where he stood and offered his prayers for the souls of the men who had died and thanksgiving for the protection God had bestowed on himself and his men.

As the *Dorset Lady* came about, she furled her sails into the wind, keeping her jib up, and the vessel stood steady in the constant breeze. The *Sea Demon* had begun to split apart as the swells first lifted it higher onto the shoals then lowered the hull back against the sharp, jagged edges with a liquid shriek. Survivors flailed in the water, crying out for help.

Will limped to the starboard rail, shouting out orders to his men. They tossed ropes out into the surf, and more than three dozen men were quickly hauled aboard. The stern section of the pirate ship had settled against an edge of coral hidden just below the waterline, and it rocked there, swaying to the beat of the waves.

Will looked over to the bloodstained deck and with no true pleasure saw the lifeless form of Captain Bliss, impaled on a stave of the helm, the wooden, splintered tip protruding through his chest like a giant nail. His eyes were open, staring into the brilliant sun, locked upon its light.

Several men scrambled out from the cocked and twisted gangway leading belowdecks. They clamored up to the sunshine, some bearing deep slashes and cuts from the rocks and the imploding timbers during the battle. After ten men had been pulled free from the wreckage, the hatch flipped open one last time. Into the sun came a tall, bony black man, squinting his eyes, his feet scrabbling at the wet deck for safe purchase.

Will stopped dead in his tracks. *This is simply an apparition,* he thought. *It could never be. . . . It simply could not.*

The black man found his steps and slipped carefully down to the rail, no more than a few feet above the surface of the sea. He looked up, his eyes straight upon Will. "Massa Will?" he called out, his voice trembling. "Is dat you, Massa Will?"

Without a heartbeat's hesitation, Will leaped over the rail and into the sea. Within a dozen strokes he was at the pirate ship. He lifted himself out of the water in one fluid motion and embraced his lost friend Luke, who was now found again.

Even hardened sailors stopped for a moment, as if hearing an angelic song for the first time, as Will's joyous cries drifted over the calming waters.

60

10 June 1650

Will stood at the shore and bowed deeply to Chief Tahonen.

"I once again offer my sorrows for the pain of these days," Will said, his words strong and earnest.

The chief bowed in return. "Hawkes, it is not the fault of you that evil follows good. You have done good thing—you have brought much to this village, and I thank you."

He turned to Thomas and embraced him in a tight hug. "And you, God-man Thomas. I thank you more. You have brought Word of God to us. And these teacher-men. We can offer no thanks worthy of such a gift."

Thomas reddened slightly at the praise. "It is our service to you and to our Lord. No more than twelve moons will pass until we return. I trust that all will go well in our absence."

Tahonen hugged Thomas again, and then, in a most nontraditional island greeting, he extended his hand to him.

"Let us seal our friendship as do English," the chief said, shaking his hand with a vigorous grin. "And, Hawkes," he added, "you have that gold on your ship?"

Will nodded.

"And you will keep gold on your island?"

Will nodded again and smiled. "And that gold will still be Chief Tahonen's gold—to purchase what things are needed for his village."

Tahonen smiled. "It be good that the gold is gone. Makes men do evil. Better on your island than mine."

Will smiled again, then turned and stepped into the longboat after Thomas, to return to the *Dorset Lady* and to his home of Barbados.

CHAPTER

Island of Barbados
17 June 1650

The sentry in the tower of Fort Charles was the first to see the ship. Kathryne, somewhat overstepping her legal rights as the wife of William Hawkes, captain of the harbor defenses, ordered a watch to be held day and night. She left explicit commands with the master sergeant that she be called the moment the *Dorset Lady* appeared on the horizon. And she gave him use of Will's favorite, and most costly, telescope. She would have paid for the watch to be held from her own funds if necessary, so great was her anxiety.

The sentry shouted down to the master sergeant, who called to his aide, who shouted to the fort's runner, who took off at a gallop for Hawkes Haven. After notifying Kathryne, he stopped at the home of Thomas Mayhew and then sprinted toward the chandlery.

By the time Will's vessel slipped into harbor, Kathryne, Eileen, and Missy were gathered at the dock. As the ship neared, they saw the holes in her canvas and splintered deck at the ship's stern. Each, no doubt, added one more prayer to the thousands already prayed that each man be returning whole and healthy.

At the distance of a hundred yards, both Missy and Eileen screamed, for both John and Thomas stood at the bow. Kathryne knew then that Will was safe. Had he been injured or worse, John would have been at the helm. She smiled, knowing that her world was now again safe and that she once more could offer breath without that small voice of worry in her heart.

As Thomas jumped from the ship, he stopped a dozen feet from Eileen. Her face had never left his thoughts for more than a heartbeat these past days—but there was now something most different about her features. The changes were subtle, yet overwhelming.

Not a fullness . . . but some sort of glow, perhaps? Thomas's face grew puzzled. *Have I been gone so long that she has so changed?* he thought.

It was when she smiled that the world dawned upon him. It was the smile of a woman with life growing inside her. No, he had no true experience with such matters, but in that instant he knew with absolute certainty that she was carrying his child. He could not move for the longest moment, nor could he utter a single word. He was all but oblivious to the torrent of emotions that swirled around him. He finally willed his feet to move and embraced her in a most tender and sweet hug.

"Are you . . . with child?" he asked, his voice tangled with emotions.

Eileen could no longer form words either, but simply nodded against his shoulder. And it was not more than a heartbeat later that she felt the first tears fall from his face, wetting her shoulder, baptizing her with his love.

■■■■■

Will did not remember how he had arrived at Hawkes Haven or even whom he had spoken with. To be with his family again, to smell Kathryne's wonderful fragrance and to hold her close, to embrace his children—such was the hurricane of happiness that swirled him home. And now, with the children asleep and Kathryne nodding by the fire, he took his cane and walked slowly to Fort Charles.

The door creaked as he slipped in. The moon was full and white and filled the eastern sky. He walked across the parade grounds to the narrow tower on the western wall. From the top, the highest spot along the western coast of Barbados, a man could take in almost the whole of the island in one view.

By the time he reached the top, his bad leg throbbed. "'Tis the sureness of age upon me," he said aloud to himself. "Perhaps my seafaring days are at a true end."

He listened to the soft tones of his words, reveling in the silence that surrounded him. He looked up into the heavens.

"Lord, thou hast blessed me in so many ways—Kathryne, my life, my children. . . . And now to have protected Luke all this time and to have brought him back into my life, that is simply a gift that I can offer no payment for. I praise thee for all these things, my Lord and my God."

Will thought of poor Mrs. Cole, to have come so far and lived such a short time. Yet he was gladdened that her last days had been filled with the thrill of seeing Kathryne's newborn babies. He had pledged to her, before she slipped from the world, that they would do their utmost to bring up Hannah and Samuel to serve the Lord as well as she had done with Kathryne. She had managed a thin smile when he had said that, the last he had ever seen mark her face.

Will looked to the chandlery and thought of John and Missy and their children. How far John had come in faith as well as in life. He knew no other man save himself that was so blessed in marriage.

He looked toward Shelworthy and thanked God for Aidan and Emily. Two more God-fearing and moral people could not have been chosen to lead this small band of English men and women so far from home.

He looked to the east and south, toward the school and the Mayhew home, and saw again in an instant the look of wondrous amazement on Thomas's face as he realized that he was to be a father. It was nearly the first time he had seen his old friend speechless for so long. It was a miracle to have seen the transformation in one such as Eileen. *God rescues and uses the most unlikely,* Will thought, and he was gladdened to know that he had blessed them so abundantly.

And then his gaze settled on his own sprawling home. Never in his wildest, most fanciful dreams as a child could he have seen himself in the life he now lived. To have a loving wife, children, wealth, to have seen the world—why, it was all so unexpected. And all so wonderful. And above it all was his faith in God, born out of pain and doubt, now filling his life with a most overwhelming sense of joy and peace and love. Such a feeling was almost more than he could bear.

And he looked down on the parade grounds of the fort and saw a form making its graceful way toward the western wall. The form disappeared, and in a moment he heard footsteps echo up the narrow, winding staircase.

It was Kathryne, who broke into the moonlight with a smile as bright as the sun.

"I saw you leave, and I knew where you would go. I allowed you a moment of solitude, then I simply could not bear to be apart from you," she whispered. "I pray that I have not upset you with my presence."

Will hugged her tightly. "Nonsense, sweet Kathryne. I would be upset only *without* your presence this night."

He bent to kiss her for the thousandth time this day. Their lips met, full and warm, and she melted into his being. As they were so joined, all time ceased to be. All care and worry vanished into the darkness.

Will looked once more at Kathryne, noticing for the first time tiny lines of joy etched about the corners of her eyes. Hers was a face that he would gladly watch age, for only laughter and smiles authored such noble lines, and only love smoothed out their harshness.

"'I wonder by my troth, what thou and I did, till we lov'd,'" he whispered. Then he pulled her close to him and felt again the wonderful and strong beating of her heart, her heart only inches from his. He held her until their individual rhythms began to sound as one, and the sounds of their love echoed over the still darkness of the sea.